Peachtree Dreams

Love Sweeter Than a Georgia Peach

Debby Mayne

BARBOUR
PUBLISHING

Published by Barbour Publishing, Inc., P.O. Box 719, Uhrichsville, Ohio 44683, www.barbourbooks.com

Our mission is to publish and distribute inspirational products offering exceptional value and biblical encouragement to the masses.

Member of the
Evangelical Christian
Publishers Association

Printed in the United States of America.

Dear Readers,

You are about to go on an emotional journey as you read these stories of three strong and determined Georgia women and the interesting men they meet in *Peachtree Dreams*. I immersed myself in their fictional worlds while writing these characters' stories, and I found that only God's truth could give them the resolution they deserved.

As I wrote these stories, several things came to mind. First, it's easy to lose sight of what's really important in life, and God has ways of letting us know when we travel down a path that's not spiritually good for us. Second, I often feel restless when I reject what the Lord calls me to do. And third, I know how difficult it is to forgive someone, even if whatever they did wasn't intended to be hurtful. However, once a person comes to Christ, they are a new person. You'll see all of these points brought out in the stories of Shannon, Judd, Jill, Ed, Cindi, and Jeremy.

I hope you enjoy *Love's Image*, *Double Blessing*, and *If the Dress Fits*. Not only do I want to entertain you but my desire is that you'll also come away with a strengthened conviction that our Heavenly Father loves us more than we can ever imagine—His love is the truest of all.

I love to hear from my readers, so please contact me through Barbour Publishing or visit my Web site at www.debbymayne.com.

Debby Mayne

Love's Image

Dedication

To my husband, Wally, and my daughters, Alison and Lauren. I love y'all very much.

Thanks to Ned, Angela, Samantha, Nikki, Joel, Jill, Meghann, Kevin, Jessica, Lisa, Kathy, Dan, Erica, Erik, Toni, Alison, and Joydine for such great suggestions and comments. And thanks to St. Petersburg College for providing a wonderful learning experience and the opportunity to fine-tune my craft. I'd also like to thank Susan Downs and Andrea Boeshaar for all their help in making this the best manuscript it can be.

Chapter 1

Shannon kept her gaze focused on Armand as the nurse eased the bandage away from Shannon's cheek. Armand's eyes betrayed his attempt to hide his disappointment.

"Will that. . ." He pointed to her face and quickly turned away. "Will that scar always be there?"

Shannon's throat tightened. *Scar?* Her eyes misted as she swallowed hard. The pain in her heart was worse than the pain from the accident. She couldn't speak.

"Maybe," the nurse replied, her expression stoic. Professional. "Probably."

"That's terrible," Armand said. He looked everywhere but at Shannon. His chiseled features had taken on a sallow cast, and a shadow covered his eyes as he tilted his head forward.

Reaching for his hand, Shannon found her voice and did her best to sound cheerful. "I'm sure I'll recover. My body heals fast." She couldn't let him know her fear. Fear of losing everything she'd worked so hard to accomplish. Fear of not being in control of her life. Fear of losing him.

Armand forced a smile but never looked Shannon directly in the eye again. Her heart sank, and her veins throbbed. She knew, deep down, that this was the end for them. No matter how much he'd professed his undying love, she was now certain that her beautiful face and ability to get any modeling job she wanted were not only what had attracted Armand, they had been what kept him. Now she had scars. Ugly scars. And he couldn't see past the surface.

Shannon's modeling career had taken off so fast, she wasn't sure if she'd gone down that path because she really wanted it or because it had been handed to her on a silver platter. Whatever the case, here she was, twenty-seven, and faced with an uncertain future because she had scars. If Armand didn't stick around, at least she'd know why. Right before the accident, he'd told her he loved her and started dropping hints about the future.

Marriage, she suddenly remembered. He'd even come right out and mentioned the word *marriage*.

Nothing had changed between them since then, except two mangled cars and a four-week stay in the hospital. And a scar.

She glanced over toward the window to avoid staring at Armand. Even the weather remained the same—a disgustingly gorgeous, sunshiny day with a few puffy white clouds hovering overhead. Why couldn't it rain? Shannon didn't have any excuse except self-pity for the sick feeling in her gut. She was alive, she had plenty of financial reserves, and her family had offered their emotional support. But Armand continued sitting there, looking past her, letting her know, without words, that he couldn't face her the way she looked now.

෨ఌ

Just as Shannon feared, three days after she returned home, a flower-delivery boy stopped by with a bouquet of two dozen red roses and a card that said Armand would regrettably be out of the country for the next month or two. Shannon blinked back the tears. She knew this was a kiss-off from the man she'd been with since their photo shoot in Nassau this time last year.

A sob threatened to escape her throat, but she sniffled and swallowed deep. There had to be a solution to this problem. There was always a solution.

Shannon would never forget the first time she'd seen Armand. While most male models spent all their time studying their reflections in the mirror or any piece of glass they passed, Armand had grinned at her and given her his undivided attention. He'd told her he loved who she was in her heart and that her looks weren't important to him. For the first time in her life, Shannon had felt like someone truly valued her for the person she was deep down. Now she knew that was a farce; they were only words spoken by a man who made a living being beautiful himself.

When she heard the knock on the door, Shannon mechanically got up and answered it. "Oh, hi, Mom."

Her mother smiled back at her, a twenty-year-older version of herself. Perfect teeth, smooth complexion, flawlessly cut, colored, and styled hair. Too bad she'd gotten pregnant and quit the performing arts program at the community college to get married.

"Don't worry, Shannon, honey," her mother told her when she opened the refrigerator and set the soup bowl on the top shelf. She turned around, glanced at Shannon, then looked everywhere but directly at her daughter. "Those cuts will heal, and you'll be back in front of the camera in no time." She'd grabbed a dishrag and started wiping down counters—a move, Shannon knew, meant to avoid looking at her.

"I don't think so, Mom," Shannon said. "These aren't just cuts. They're scars that'll be with me forever."

With a shrug and a slight grimace as they locked gazes for a split second, her mom replied, patting her on the hand, "Well, there's always plastic surgery." The lilt in her voice was a little too rehearsed. "You do what you have to do to please your fans."

Please her fans? Hardly. More like give her mother what she'd always wanted for herself—a career centered on the spotlight and superficial beauty.

Bitter feelings left over from Shannon's youth were starting to surface, and she didn't like it, so she turned to her mother and did what she'd always done. She offered a megawatt smile and got one in return.

As soon as her mother left her apartment, Shannon stood in front of her mirror, the light shining brightly on her face. For the first time since the car wreck, she took a good look at reality, really studied the damage. The windshield had gashed her when the oncoming SUV had come within inches of her face. A bright red scar started at the top of her left cheekbone and continued to the bottom of her chin. She knew if the impact had been the slightest bit stronger, she wouldn't be alive today. So why did she feel so miserable instead of grateful?

The phone rang, jolting her from the mirror and her self-pity.

"In the mood for company?"

It was Janie, the one person in her life Shannon felt certain didn't care about her looks.

"Not really."

"You don't sound so good."

"I'm fine."

"No, you're not. You shouldn't be alone right now. I'm coming over."

"You don't have to," Shannon said.

"I know I don't have to, silly. But I want to. What are friends for?"

Shannon felt a little better as she replaced the phone in the cradle. Janie had been her closest buddy back in high school, back before Shannon McNab had become a household name among the fashion conscious, TV producers, and magazine executives. Janie couldn't have cared less what Shannon did for a living or how many times her picture had been on the covers of magazines. In fact, she hated the spotlight, which worked well in their relationship, because Shannon was always the one who had it, not her.

The only thing about Janie that bothered Shannon was the fact that she liked to talk about God and her relationship with Jesus. Sometimes she spoke as if she wanted to convert Shannon. It wasn't that Shannon didn't believe in God or anything. She just didn't need religion right now. Maybe later, when she was a little older.

"Hey, Scarface."

Shannon opened the door to a grinning Janie.

With a groan, Shannon said, "I thought you wanted to make me feel better."

"Sorry. I was trying to lighten things up."

"I know. Want some soup?"

Janie chuckled. "Did Sara cook her famous chicken noodle soup? She's such a *mom*."

"Of course. Isn't that what she does every time someone gets sick?"

Janie took a step back and glared at Shannon—without the flinch or grimace Shannon was starting to expect. "You're not sick."

Okay, so Janie wasn't going to feel sorry for her. "You didn't answer me. Want some soup?"

"Sounds good." Without hesitating, Janie headed toward the kitchen and opened the refrigerator where the big glass bowl of soup sat on the top shelf. "This it?"

Shannon nodded and sank down on the vinyl kitchen chair as Janie dumped the contents of the bowl into a saucepan and set it on the front burner. She joined Shannon while the soup heated.

"Are you totally bummed about Armand?" Janie asked. She'd never minced words.

Shannon nodded then shrugged. "I guess, sort of."

"If he leaves you just because of a stupid scar, he's not worth having."

"I'm sure he had other reasons," Shannon argued. "Armand's not that shallow."

"Other reasons?" Sarcasm laced her words as Janie held up her hand and counted off on her fingers. "Let's see. You're still strikingly beautiful, even though you have that red line on your face that will probably, given time, fade to practically nothing. You're one of the sweetest people I've ever known in my life," she said as she pointed to her second finger. "Then there's the fact that you were class salutatorian, and you're smart as a whip. I guess your love of animals doesn't count since he's allergic to them." She shrugged. "Perfect woman in my book."

In spite of the pain in her heart, Shannon smiled. Janie always did have a way of putting things into perspective and bringing the positive to light. "You forgot to mention that I make a mean German chocolate cake," Shannon added, trying to get into the spirit of things and pretend none of this really mattered.

"Yeah, but you never ate any of it," Janie reminded her. "Always trying to keep those pounds off your skinny hips."

"My hips are not skinny," Shannon argued.

"Oh, come on. They are, too."

"The camera adds—"

"I know, I know," Janie interrupted. "The camera adds ten pounds. But who cares?"

"I do," Shannon said. "Well, at least I did until now."

Janie reached over and covered Shannon's hand in hers. "Maybe now you can do something you really want to do, Shannon. You never really liked modeling."

"I liked it."

Janie didn't reply to that comment, but a pensive look washed over her face as she stood. The soup had started bubbling on the stove, so she went to scoop some for both of them.

As the two of them ate the chicken noodle soup in silence, Shannon felt the comfort of sitting here with her die-hard best friend, knowing that her life was about to go in a completely different direction. She wished she could predict where it was headed, but she knew she couldn't. Nothing had prepared her for this.

"I've got a friend who just started vet assistant training," Janie blurted, interrupting Shannon's thoughts.

"What?"

"Vet assistant training," Janie repeated. "You know. Learning how to work in a veterinary office."

"Interesting."

"You might think about it, Shannon. Seriously. You love animals." She paused. "Or you can do something else."

"I don't have to do anything for a while. I have plenty of money."

"No surprise," Janie said. "But somehow I can't see you sitting back, doing nothing."

"I can read books."

"Then what?"

"Who knows? Maybe Armand will send for me."

Janie licked the soup off her lips and put down her spoon. She looked down at the table before she glanced up and locked gazes with Shannon.

"Look, sweetie, I know how hard this is for you to face, but you can't wait around for some guy to come crawling back when it's not even likely in the first place."

Shannon didn't feel like arguing. She knew how Janie felt about the whole modeling industry. At first she'd been happy for her, but after the first year, she'd told Shannon she didn't like the changes she'd seen in her.

"I haven't changed," Shannon had told her.

"You have but you just don't see it," Janie had said sadly. The whole conversation popped into Shannon's mind, and she remembered it word for word, as she often did when things became too quiet.

Shannon put down her soup spoon and leaned back. "Do you still think I've changed?" she asked.

Janie inhaled deeply as if she needed time to gather her thoughts. "Do you want the truth?"

Shannon nodded.

"You've changed in so many ways, I'm not sure where to start."

"Do you not like me anymore?"

Even if the truth hurt, Shannon needed to hear it. This was the time when she had to know what people were thinking.

"I like you, Shannon. But you used to be so much fun. You loved hiking, talking on the phone for hours on end, and acting silly with the girls. Now all you do is worry about what people think."

Shannon thought for a moment. "That's important in my business."

"But in the big scheme of things, how important is it, really?"

Janie had a point.

"I guess not very."

"My sentiments exactly."

"So what now?"

"You have to decide. Maybe you can kick back for a few weeks and read. Armand might even surprise us and call for you; I don't know. But is that what you really want, Shannon?"

"I thought it was."

"Do you want the constant threat of losing Armand just because he can't deal with the slightest imperfection? Think about it some more," Janie said as she pushed her chair back and stood. "In the meantime, I have to get back to the nursing home. Mrs. Willis needs therapy this afternoon."

They said their good-byes before Janie left. Shannon sank back on the sofa and picked up the remote control, flipping through the channels. Nothing good was on, so she turned it off. Fear clutched her chest.

What if Janie was right, and Armand didn't call?

❦

After a week went by and she still hadn't heard from Armand, Shannon knew. How could she have been fooled so easily by someone she thought loved her for her heart? He'd told her all that, hadn't he? Why would a little scar change that?

Shannon could understand why even the slightest scar would affect her modeling career. After all, she was promoting the impossible—perfect beauty, something almost every woman aspired to. But true love was blind—at least that's what she'd always thought.

"Want me to come over?" Janie asked during one of her daily phone calls. "You don't need to be alone right now."

"No, I'm fine," Shannon tried to assure her friend. "Really, I am."

"You're still in denial. What are you doing now?"

"Watching television." Which was what she'd been doing all day every day since she'd been home from the hospital.

"That's not good, Shannon. You hate TV."

Janie remembered. All her life, Shannon had been active. She played sports, hung out with friends, and stayed busy. She never had time or the inclination to sit around and watch TV. Until now.

"Look, Shannon, I'll be there in a few minutes. We'll figure something out."

"Okay."

She couldn't keep putting Janie off just because she made her face reality. Shannon's voice had suddenly become squeaky and meek. For the first time in her life, Shannon had no idea what tomorrow would bring, and she let fear take over.

Janie was at her door less than half an hour later.

"I don't like this a single bit."

"Well, hello to you, too," Shannon said with a smirk.

"You've gotta get outta here. This place will close in on you if you don't."

"I'm fine."

"Stop saying that. No, you're not." Janie took her by the arm and gently shoved her toward the front door. "Where's your purse? I'm taking you out."

Instinctively, Shannon ran her fingertips along her cheek. Her insides lurched at the thought of people seeing her like this.

"I can't go out."

"Oh, get over it, Shannon. The sooner you face people the better. Staying inside, cooped up, hiding, won't solve any problems."

Shannon numbly let Janie guide her toward her car. Fear clutched her once again as she thought of riding in a car. "I can't."

"You can and you will." Janie held the door and nodded for Shannon to get in.

They were both buckled in the front seat of Janie's car when Shannon spoke again. "This is so silly. I'm really not in the mood."

"At the rate you're going, you'll never be in the mood."

Shannon looked out the window before turning back to face Janie, who seemed determined not to listen. "Where are we going?"

"Church." Janie put the car in reverse and carefully backed out of the parking space. "I'll be super careful. I know how hard it is to get back in a car after an accident."

Shannon remembered when Janie had hit a car head-on seven years ago. It took three strong friends to get her to ride in a car after that.

"Church?" she asked. "It's Monday. What church is open on Monday?"

"It's my singles' group."

Shannon tilted her head back and chuckled. "You go to a singles' club at a church? Now I've heard everything."

"I didn't say singles' *club*. That's for desperate people. This is my church singles' group."

"What's the difference?"

They were stopped at a red light, which gave Janie a chance to turn and face Shannon while she explained. "We discuss issues in the Bible that relate to things single people have to face today."

"Hmm."

"Yeah, hmm." Janie grinned. "This is what normal, Christ-loving people do in Atlanta. I know it sounds strange after your jet-set modeling career, but it's really nice. I think once you get into it, you might actually enjoy it."

"How long have you been doing this singles' thing at your church?" Shannon asked. This was the first she'd heard of it, although she did remember something Janie had said a couple years ago about how her life had turned completely around now that she'd let the Lord into her life. Not being one who needed that sort of thing, Shannon had glossed over it and changed the subject as quickly as she could. Now that she was being held captive, she was curious about what she was about to face.

"The singles' group started up about a year ago, and I'm one of the founding members."

Shannon shook her head. "Did you tell them about some of your shenanigans back in high school?"

"They know I'm not perfect."

Janie turned into the parking lot of a small building that looked like a converted house. Shannon looked from left to right then back at Janie.

"Where's the church?"

"We're there."

Pointing to the building, Shannon said, "This is a church? Sure doesn't look like one."

"A lot of things aren't what they look like. You should know that." She put the car in park, turned off the ignition, and opened her car door. "Let's go. Everyone will be here soon, and we start in a few minutes."

Shannon followed her friend into the building, trailing close behind. She'd always been the one eager for new experiences, but this was different. This was scary. This was church. A foreign place to Shannon.

"Hey, Janie," said a deep, masculine voice from a dark corner.

"Paul, I'm glad you're here. I have someone I want you to meet."

Suddenly, the man materialized from out of nowhere. In the semidarkness, Shannon saw him reach over and flip a switch on the wall. Light filled the space and illuminated chairs, positioned in a full circle around the room.

"Paul, this is my friend Shannon," Janie said softly.

When Shannon looked him in the eye, she saw his gaze dart to her scar. She started to lift her hand to her cheek, but he reached for her arm. "Don't," he said. "Janie told us what happened."

Shannon pulled away and looked down, letting her long, straight blond hair fall in front of her face. She'd never hidden behind her hair before, but then she'd never been scarred before either.

Instead of making a big deal of her reaction, Paul turned his attention to Janie. "Did you talk to Jason or Dana?"

"They'll be here, but Dana said she might be late."

"That's okay. I just finished making the coffee. It's her turn to bring cookies."

Janie turned to Shannon and explained how they took turns bringing treats for the group. Shannon only half listened. Her shame was blocking her senses.

Within a couple minutes, people began to arrive, some alone and others in pairs. Fifteen minutes later, the room was filled with twenty- and thirtysomething people, all of them laughing and greeting each other as if they'd known everyone all their lives. Shannon felt ill at ease. She was perfectly comfortable at black-tie affairs where she was able to show off the latest elaborate gown some designer had created for the occasion. But this was real. She wasn't in costume. These people could see her for who she really was.

"Hey," Janie said as she walked up behind Shannon. "Lighten up. I've never seen you so shy before. You were always the life of every party."

"That was before—" She cut herself off as she reached up to touch her face again.

Janie leveled her with a stern look. "Look, Shannon, no one here cares about your scar, other than the pain you must be feeling. They don't see the scar when they look at you."

"Hey, you're that model in the corn chip ads, aren't you?"

She heard Janie groan.

Shannon whipped around and saw the man as he walked up, grinning ear-to-ear, like he'd just discovered gold. He was nice-looking but not devastatingly handsome. What she liked about him right away, though, was the way his eyes seemed to twinkle when he smiled. Like stars.

"Yeah, so she sells corn chips," Janie said before Shannon had a chance to speak. "Don't hold it against her."

The man chuckled, showing teeth with character—not perfectly straight like Armand's. But still, there was something that compelled her to continue studying him. He was interesting-looking, the corners of his lips slightly upturned, and he gazed right at her, not past her.

"What brings a famous model to our church in downtown Atlanta?" he asked.

"My friend Janie brought me," Shannon said, taking his comment at face value.

"Janie has always been full of surprises. C'mon, let's go grab some coffee before the rest of the vultures arrive."

She glanced at Janie, who'd already turned to grab a stack of Bibles from the table behind them. Shannon realized she was on her own.

Shannon followed the man to the long row of tables lined up against the wall. "I'm terribly sorry, but I didn't catch your name."

The man stopped and pivoted to face her, thrusting his right hand toward her. "Sorry. My name's Judd Manning. I'm the pastor's nephew, so I didn't exactly have a choice but to join this singles' group when I came to stay with him a few months ago." He laughed as if he knew a joke he wasn't telling. "These goons seem to think I might know something. Don't tell them my secret, but I'm just as lost as the rest of them." He made a face before adding, "Maybe even more so."

Shannon instantly felt at ease by this very nice man who became handsomer the longer they chatted. Taking his hand in hers, she tilted her head toward him. "I'm Shannon McNab."

"Yes," he said quickly. "I know."

"You know my name?"

"Uh, yeah. It's not like your picture isn't plastered all over the place."

"I guess being a model has a few drawbacks."

"You don't like it?" he asked, pulling his hand back and once again edging toward the tables.

Shannon shrugged. "Oh, I like it all right. It's just that. . ." Her hand went up to touch her face. Janie shot her a warning look, so she jerked it back down to her side.

Judd studied her face, his eyes resting on her scar, the smile fading from his lips. "What happened?"

"I thought Janie told everyone," Shannon replied.

He shrugged. "I wasn't here when Janie announced the details. I had to go out of town."

Although Shannon hated talking about it, Judd's openness made it easy for her to reply. "Car accident."

"Man, that's rough. How are you otherwise?"

"Fine, I guess."

"You're fortunate, then. It could have been much worse."

Obviously, Judd Manning didn't know what he was talking about. How could it have been any worse than it was? Did he realize she was scarred for life and would never be able to earn a living doing the only thing she knew how to do?

Chapter 2

"Who wants to lead the prayer tonight?" Paul asked as he scanned the room. "Janie?"

"Sure," she replied.

Shannon listened to her best friend as she thanked the Lord for the many blessings, asked for guidance in the Bible study, and begged forgiveness for sin. The prayer wasn't long, but Shannon could tell it was heartfelt.

When everyone opened their eyes, Shannon noticed several of them looking at her, smiling. She started to reach up and cover her face, but she remembered what Janie had said. She resisted the urge and shyly grinned back.

"Janie, why don't you introduce your guest?" Paul said.

"Everyone, this is Shannon McNab. She and I have been best friends practically since we could talk," Janie began.

Judd interrupted. "And you haven't stopped talking since."

Janie shot him a glare, then continued. "Several weeks ago, Shannon had the misfortune to be in a really bad car crash. The man driving the other vehicle wasn't as fortunate, and he didn't make it. We need to pray for his family."

Shannon gulped. It hadn't crossed her mind to pray for that man's family until now. After all, the accident had been his fault. If he hadn't been drinking, she wouldn't be sitting here right now feeling like the world was staring at her scar.

"How long will you be in Atlanta, Shannon?" Paul asked.

"I, uh. . .I'm really not sure," Shannon said. She hated being put on the spot. "Probably until my—"

Janie cut in. "She's got to figure out what to do with the rest of her life now that she won't be modeling anymore."

Shannon had never told Janie she wasn't going to model anymore. That was just an assumption she had based on her own ideas of what she thought Shannon should decide.

Hoping to end the conversation as quickly as possible, Shannon just smiled and nodded, fully intending to talk to her friend about this later—to set her straight. At some point, she needed to start speaking for herself, something she always did whenever Janie wasn't around.

As the group settled into their discussion of the scripture topic of the evening, Shannon felt the warmth of Judd's stares. She'd gotten used to people looking at her, but this was different. He never looked away when her gaze met his. He only smiled and occasionally winked. She felt her cheeks grow hot each time.

When Paul called a break, everyone stood and made a beeline for the snack table, including Janie. Out of habit, Shannon hung back. She'd learned early on that munching on snacks wasn't conducive to keeping her model figure.

"Not hungry?" Judd asked as he joined her.

She shrugged. "Not really. I don't generally eat anything after dinner."

"Which consists of a salad without dressing and water to drink, right?" He leaned away from her, studying her face, making her squirm.

She held her breath. Was he testing her?

"Whatever gave you that idea?"

"Well, isn't that what models eat? Rabbit food?"

Shannon started to argue with him, but she stopped short. What was the point? He obviously understood her as well as he possibly could, considering they'd just met. Besides, she didn't owe him anything—certainly not an explanation as to why she wasn't gorging at the snack table.

"Not exactly," she said. "But close enough."

"Yeah, I try to stay away from the desserts myself. I have to watch my figure, too." He quirked his eyebrows as she snapped around to look at him.

A retort started to form in her mind, until she realized he was having fun and kidding around with her. *Okay, time to lighten up.* She tilted her head back and forced a hearty laugh.

"You're too much, Judd."

"Too much of a good thing, I hope." He suddenly looked serious, and his voice was laced with hope.

She felt a quick flash of satisfaction.

"Oh, I'm sure," she said with a little flirty hair toss. This felt really odd for Shannon. She hadn't flirted since before she'd met Armand. Who was this guy, other than some man with nothing better to do than hang out at a church on a Monday night?

"Good," he said with a self-satisfied smirk. "I'm glad you agree. I like you, too, Shannon McNab. You're not half bad for a beauty queen."

"Wait a minute." Shannon felt her defenses rise. "What, exactly, do you mean by that?"

"What I mean is," he said very slowly, drawing closer to her and lowering his voice to where no one else could hear him but her, "you're a very sweet woman. Unpretentious. Smart. Not what I'd expect from a world-class model."

His backdoor compliment caught her off guard. Her face heated once again, and her senses were out of balance. She couldn't think of a quick comeback, so she flashed one of her famous smiles. "Wow," he said. "Now I know what it's like to experience my own personal sunshine."

Most people had the wrong idea about models. They had no idea who she was deep down. Nearly everyone thought that with her looks, she could have everything she wanted with a snap of her fingers, but that simply wasn't true. Sure, Shannon was satisfied with her life for the most part, but the reality of losing it all just as quickly—as her accident had proven—was stressful.

"I have a feeling—" he began.

"C'mon, everyone," Paul said to the group, interrupting Judd. "We have a lot to cover tonight, so let's get going. Bring your coffee and cookies with you, and we'll get back to our topic."

"You have a feeling. . . ?" Shannon prompted Judd as they turned back toward the circle of chairs.

"We'll talk later," he said as he turned his attention to the speaker.

Throughout the remainder of the evening, Shannon was fully aware of the effect Judd was having on her. Each time he looked at her and smiled, she felt a tingle coursing through her. Sometimes she smiled back, but other times she tried to pretend not to notice.

After an hour, Paul requested another prayer. "Why don't you say the closing prayer, Judd?"

"You sure you want me to do this?" Judd asked.

"Yeah, but try to keep it sane, okay?"

A few snickers could be heard through the room, but Judd began his prayer. As Shannon listened to his simple words, she realized they were open, honest, and sincere.

She liked Judd Manning. He was a different kind of guy from anyone she'd ever met, but he made her feel good on the inside. She had a feeling he might be attracted to her because of who she was or how she once looked, but that wouldn't be what determined their friendship. There was nothing pretentious about him. His face wasn't perfectly chiseled like Armand's, but he was handsome enough—in a sort of scholarly way. He wore glasses and dressed in khaki slacks and a polo shirt. Nothing out of the ordinary. But he'd struck a chord in her that made her want to know more about him. The warmth of his brown eyes offered her a sense of peace and understanding.

Shannon wasn't surprised when Judd cornered her immediately after everyone stood to leave. "How long will you be in town?" he asked.

"I'm not really sure yet. Everything's still up in the air at the moment."

He studied her scar. "Tough break on the car crash, but you're still just as beautiful as ever. More beautiful, if that's possible."

Shannon chuckled. "You're too kind." She wasn't able to keep the sarcasm out of her voice.

"Really," he said as he folded his arms. "The scar gives you character."

"Character?"

"Yeah." A slow grin crept across his lips. "Perfection isn't nearly as interesting as a little flaw here and there. It shows something—"

Shannon was waiting to hear what it showed, but Janie came up and grabbed her arm. "We gotta go, Shannon. I need to drop you off and get home."

Judd tipped an imaginary hat. "Nice meeting you, Shannon McNab. Maybe I'll see you again."

"Here's her number," Janie said as she thrust a small slip of paper toward him. "Call her later."

On their way out the door, Shannon crinkled her forehead and glared at Janie. "Why'd you do that?"

"What?"

"Give him my number. I don't generally make a habit of giving my phone number out to strangers."

Janie tilted her head forward and glared at Shannon from beneath her thick eyebrows. "Judd Manning isn't exactly a stranger, although I have to admit he can get strange at times."

"You're avoiding the point," Shannon said.

"Look, Shannon. This group is tight. If you want them to accept you as an individual and not a celebrity, you have to act like the rest of us. We exchange phone numbers." She paused before adding, "That's just something we do."

"Oh."

Once again, Shannon was given something else to think about. She'd never considered herself a celebrity, although she'd stopped giving out her number several years ago for personal reasons. Stalkers had begun invading her modeling friends' personal space, and her name was becoming known to the extent that she needed to guard a piece of her personal life. Only after getting to know someone well would Shannon give out her phone number, and even then she was nervous about it.

"Besides," Janie continued, "these people couldn't care less about what you do for a living. They're there to study the Bible."

"Is that why Judd's there? He didn't seem all that well versed—at least not as much as the rest of you."

Janie laughed. "Judd's a different subject entirely. His uncle's the pastor, so he's sort of been pushed into the group."

"He's not a Christian?"

"Oh, he's a Christian, but he admits he doesn't know scripture. We're working on him."

Shannon smiled. "He acted like he enjoyed being there."

"Judd Manning loves an audience, in case you haven't noticed. He's a clown. Everything's a joke to him."

The more Shannon heard, the more she wanted to know Judd Manning. What an interesting man.

"I like jokes," Shannon said.

With a snicker, Janie shook her head. "Yeah, but it gets old after a while." She hesitated before saying, "We still love him, though. Deep down, he's a terrific guy."

They rode in silence to Shannon's apartment. After a quick good-bye, Janie drove off, and Shannon let herself into her apartment, flipping on lights as she headed back to her bedroom.

She'd just slipped out of her shoes and into some slippers when the phone rang. She recognized the voice as Judd's even before he identified himself.

"Look, I know this is quick, but I don't believe in wasting time," he said. "Wanna get together for coffee soon?"

"Sure."

Shannon couldn't help but compare him to other guys she knew. Armand had watched her from a distance for nearly a month before he'd called the first time. She'd been aware of his gaze, so she hadn't been surprised when she'd finally heard from him. This call from Judd, on the other hand, had been completely unexpected—and very quick.

"What?"

"I'd like that."

"Cool. I wasn't sure I heard right."

"Well, you did."

"Good. How about tomorrow?"

"Okay."

"Want me to pick you up, or should we meet somewhere?"

Shannon swallowed hard. She'd always been so careful not to give out her address to people she didn't know well, but she still hadn't summoned the courage to drive, although her bright and shiny new sports car was sitting in the apartment complex parking lot, waiting for her.

"Shannon?" he said. "You still there?"

"Oh, yes, of course. Would you mind picking me up? I'm still a little skittish from the accident."

Janie knew Judd, and the worst thing she'd heard about him was that he was a clown. Where was the harm in that? Besides, he was the pastor's nephew, so he was accountable to someone respectable.

"No problem. I was thinking we could do a little catching up on the Bible study. In case you haven't noticed, I'm pretty lost in there. Those people are way ahead of me."

Shannon laughed. "I know what you mean. I feel so inadequate among all those Bible scholars."

"I don't think they'd want you to feel that way. They're a great group of people, and they'd never want to make anyone feel inadequate."

Shannon felt like she needed to backpedal. "No, that's not what I meant. I should have simply said that I felt lost and let it go."

"I know what you mean. That's why I wanted to get together with you. We can try to catch up."

Shannon's heart did a quick thud. She was surprised at her reaction of disappointment that Judd only wanted to get together with her to study and not because he was attracted to her.

"Okay, give me your address, and I'll pick you up at eight in the morning," he said, taking control.

"Eight?" She sniffled. "In the morning?"

"Yeah, unless that's too early for you. If you want to sleep in, I can make it later."

"No, no, that's okay. Eight'll be fine."

Shannon hadn't awakened before noon in years unless she had an early-morning shoot on an outdoor set. She'd have to set her alarm and do whatever it took to go to sleep at a decent time.

Strangely, she'd been very attracted to Judd and became even more so by the minute. She closed her eyes to bring his image to mind. His constantly changing expressions made him interesting to watch. One minute his forehead and the corners of his eyes crinkled with humor, and the next minute he had a pensive look on his face as the subject changed. She'd watched him throughout the Bible study, and she was intrigued by what she saw. Talking to him over the phone enhanced her desire to see him again.

❧

Judd couldn't believe he actually had a coffee date with Shannon McNab. What was he thinking? This woman was definitely out of his league.

To top it off, she'd accepted without hesitation. He swelled his chest. Maybe he wasn't such a nerd, after all.

Being the son of a military officer, Judd had moved every couple of years. Just when he'd gotten used to a place and started making friends, he'd been uprooted again. Eventually, he quit trying so hard to fit in and worked on being funny. People around him enjoyed his antics, and he didn't miss many party invitations—but he used humor to distance himself. Holding people at arm's length was his only defense in relationships.

Judd had started working for the Department of Defense, teaching in military dependent schools right after college, and he'd transferred to wherever he was needed. He had a heart for military dependents because he knew what it was like to constantly be uprooted, and he could relate to the kids. However, after teaching three years in Japan and two years in Germany, with various other short-term assignments in between, he decided to pick a spot to settle.

He'd spent quite a bit of time with his aunt and uncle in Atlanta. He loved the soft vibrancy of the southern city, so he applied for a job in a Christian school near Atlanta to finish out a vacancy left by a teacher on maternity leave. To his surprise and delight, they'd called him in right away. After the teacher's baby had arrived, she'd decided not to return, so the permanent position had been offered to Judd. Naturally, he'd accepted. As soon as summer break was over, he'd have next year's batch of lively seventh graders, some eager and others squirming over the idea of having to learn another year of language arts.

Since Uncle Garrett and Aunt LaRita had a spare bedroom after their own children had grown up and moved out, they'd offered him a place to stay until he had enough saved to buy his own house. However, there was one condition to hanging out with his favorite uncle, who happened to be a pastor—Judd had to attend weekly services and get involved in church activities. That was okay, though. Judd needed to meet and get to know people his age. Besides, he was a Christian, even though his own parents hadn't made their faith as much a part of their lives as Uncle Garrett had.

His excitement about seeing Shannon had rendered him sleepless. He went to bed early, after making plans with Shannon, so he'd be refreshed and bright in the morning.

Tossing and twisting in the sheets, trying to get comfortable, Judd couldn't still his heart. Finally, he gave up trying. He flipped on the light switch and picked up his Bible. Might as well make use of the time rather than flop around like a fish.

He reread Ephesians chapter 2, verses 8 and 9, the verses they'd discussed in the Bible study. "By grace are ye saved through faith; and that not of yourselves: it is the gift of God: not of works, lest any man should boast."

Faith. What a simple word. But it meant so much when he thought about it. For years, he hadn't given his faith much thought. The extent of Judd's churchgoing had been on Christmas and Easter, and even then his mind had been on the celebration afterward and not on the message.

Staying with Uncle Garrett had been an eye-opener for Judd. Uncle Garrett and Aunt LaRita started each day with a prayer, never began a meal without a blessing, and literally stopped in their tracks to close their eyes and say a prayer throughout the day. At night, before he padded to his own room, he could hear more whispered prayers coming from behind the closed door of his aunt and uncle's room. Those two were truly steeped in their faith.

When he'd asked Uncle Garrett if he was always happy, he'd been surprised when his question was returned with a solemn stare, then the words he hadn't expected.

"No, Judd, I can't honestly say I'm always happy. But happiness isn't my goal in life. If you think about it, happiness is a very fleeting thing. When LaRita puts a good meal down in front of me, I'm happy. But when she's away or I have to fend for myself, I'm rarely happy with what I have to eat. Last year, when I bought a new car, I was very happy, but before that, when I got the bill from the mechanic to fix my old car, I was not happy at all."

Judd had thought about what his uncle was saying and nodded. "Yeah, I see what you mean. But you always *seem* happy."

Uncle Garrett smiled. "You might be getting contentedness confused with happiness. I'm quite contented with my life because I know I'm walking close with Jesus."

That simple statement was enough to arouse Judd's curiosity. He listened more attentively to sermons now, and he did his best to understand scripture. There were times when he got lost, and he was afraid to ask others in the Bible study group. Maybe with a study partner, he'd be able to find some of the answers he'd been seeking.

Or maybe her beauty would divert his attention.

Judd sensed a restlessness in Shannon, and he couldn't put his finger on the cause. She paid close attention as everyone spoke about the lesson they'd read. Although he'd read it, he was still slightly confused, so he fell back to his clown nature.

There were times when he wondered if he had anyone fooled. The only one in the group who didn't always laugh was Shannon's friend Janie, and he sometimes thought she might actually pity him. He hoped that wasn't the case. Judd Manning wasn't to be pitied, even if he was taking baby steps in his Christian walk. He was a proud man, and the thought of anyone feeling sorry for him was annoying.

Okay, so he'd admit, pride was one of his flaws. If he could get past worrying about what people thought about him, he might be able to ask some questions and get the answers that continued to gnaw at him.

He read the same scripture lesson over and over, going back and forth between his Bible and the workbook the group was using. He underlined text and pondered it, worrying that he might be missing something.

Finally, his eyelids grew heavy. After closing both books, he said a brief prayer and turned off the light.

꙳

Shannon must have tried on three different outfits before she found the right one. This was so not like her.

The first thing she'd put on was a black dress, but she realized that wasn't the right outfit for a morning coffee date. Did she dare call this a date? She hadn't been on a date with anyone but Armand in more than a year. And before that, she rarely went out because she was never sure why men wanted to be with her. She hated to be any man's arm decoration, and quite a bit of emphasis had been put on her looks, so she'd become jaded and cynical when it came to men's motives with her.

Although Judd had complimented her beauty, she had the feeling he would have asked her out regardless of her looks. Something about him seemed real. Vulnerable, even. Shannon liked that. It made her feel less on display and more equal in the relationship. One of the things she'd liked about Armand was his vulnerability—although now that she was apart from him, she saw that his weakness was from worrying too much about image. Had she been the same way?

Shannon shoved that question to the back of her mind. She hated to think she'd been as shallow as so many other people she'd known in her industry.

She settled on black cotton slacks and a soft pink knit pullover. It was a simple outfit that wouldn't demand attention. Her makeup had to be kept to a minimum, although she followed her urge to cover the bright red line streaking down the left side of her face. Even the thick cover stick didn't completely conceal the reminder that her professional modeling career was most likely over.

As usual, Shannon was ready a half hour early. Her nerves had awakened her before the sun came up, so she'd gone ahead and taken her shower. Now all she had to do was wait.

To her delight, the knock came at her door at precisely seven fifty-five. Judd was early, too.

"Wow." His face lit up the second she opened the door.

"Hi, Judd. Come on in."

"Last night, I thought you were a mirage. I can't believe you're actually going out for coffee with me. You look beautiful."

Shannon's stomach knotted. She stood there staring at Judd Manning as he cast an appreciative gaze over her. Maybe she'd been wrong about him.

Chapter 3

Judd felt an instant barrier form between them as soon as he spoke to her. Her eyes had glazed over, and her smile wasn't nearly as bright as it had been last night.

"Do you like little diners, or are you the designer coffeehouse type?" he asked.

She shrugged. "It really doesn't matter."

Yep, something had changed. Her emotional distance was so obvious, it was slamming.

"Tell you what. We can go to the Dunk 'n' Dine this morning, and I'll treat you to the best two-ninety-nine breakfast you've ever tasted." He held the door for her as she slid into his car, then he leaned forward, hoping for some sort of reaction.

"That's fine," she said as she buckled her seat belt. No smile, nothing.

Judd ran around to the other side of the car, wishing he could start over. He must have said something, but what? That brightness was in her eyes when she opened her door to him, but she quickly put up her guard.

Once in his car, Judd started to crack a joke about the cat getting her tongue, but he decided to use a more direct approach instead. "What's wrong, Shannon? Did I say something?"

Not looking him in the eye, Shannon shook her head. "It's nothing."

He knew that wasn't the case. "Look, if I said something stupid, you need to tell me so I won't do it again. I've always been pretty bad about saying the wrong thing because I talk too much."

A smile tweaked the corners of her lips, but she still didn't meet his gaze. "Don't worry about it, okay?"

Now he was worried more than ever. Based on his experience, when women said not to worry, that was when a man needed to start groveling.

"I see you brought your Bible," he said, gesturing to what she was holding with a death grip.

"This is a Bible study, right?" Now that they were at the stop sign, she'd finally looked at him, but not with the cheerful expression he'd looked forward to all night.

"Yes, it is." He felt dejected and more than a little frustrated.

There had to be some way to bring back the woman he'd met last night.

He didn't like the thought that something he'd said had cast a gloomy shadow over her, and he was certain she was pulling away from him because of something he'd said or done. Not being one to let things go, Judd decided to address the issue as soon as they arrived at their destination—before they went inside.

Once in the parking lot of the Dunk 'n' Dine, Judd turned off the ignition and turned to face Shannon.

"Okay, spill it, Shannon. I'm sure I said something that's making you wish you'd stayed home, and I want to know what it is."

"No." Once again, she didn't look directly at him.

"C'mon, Shannon, I'm not into playing games."

Suddenly, as if he'd flipped a switch, she turned, daggers shooting from her eyes. "I don't play games," she hissed.

Frustration flooded Judd as he carefully pondered how to put his thoughts into words. "You can't expect a guy like me to know what's going on in your head unless you tell me what you're thinking."

Shannon pursed her lips and studied his face before turning to look away. He could tell she was contemplating something, hopefully an explanation that would let him know where he stood with her.

❧

This is silly, she told herself. *Just because he made a comment about my looks doesn't mean that's all he's thinking about.*

"Judd, you really didn't do anything wrong," she said slowly. "It's just that I've been ultrasensitive since the accident." Instinctively, her hand rose to her cheek.

He reached out and caught her wrist, freezing her movement. His touch sent an electric current up her arm, and time seemed to come to a screeching halt. She wondered if he could hear her heart pounding.

"Shannon, I understand your feelings. If I looked like you, something like this would probably bother me, too. But you have so much more going for you, that even if you didn't have a pretty face, you've got the world at your disposal."

Her doubts about his motives had just been squelched, at least for the moment. She turned to face him, allowing the warmth to flow between them once again.

"Thank you, Judd. You're a good guy."

He snickered. "That's what I keep trying to tell you. I'm glad you finally believe me."

Once inside, Judd ordered a short stack of pancakes and encouraged Shannon to do the same. She started to tell the waitress she only wanted coffee then decided she might as well splurge. What did it matter if she put on a pound or two now that she couldn't model?

"I'll have what he's having." Shannon stuck the plastic menu back between the napkin holder and ketchup bottle.

"You're full of surprises, Shannon McNab," Judd said. "So you *do* eat normal food."

"Yeah. What did you think I ate?" She remembered what he'd said earlier. "Rabbit food is in my past."

"Are you gonna be okay?" he asked.

"What are you talking about, Judd? Of course I'm gonna be okay. Why does everyone keep looking at me like they're afraid I'm about to shatter?"

"Maybe it's because you have a lost look on your face," he said softly.

"Lost?" Shannon cleared her throat as she slammed her Bible on the table. "I think we need to change the subject. I don't like where this is headed."

"I'm with you," Judd agreed. He began flipping the pages of his workbook. "Now where were we?"

Pointing to the workbook, Shannon asked, "Where can I get one of those? Do I have to order it?"

"I think my uncle might have some in the storage room behind his office. I'll ask this afternoon when he comes home." Judd met her gaze and turned the workbook around where they could both see it. "In the meantime, I'll share."

Once they got into the lesson, Shannon was surprised at how many answers Judd had left blank. "I thought you were the pastor's nephew. You should know these things."

Judd tilted his head back and laughed out loud. "A lot of people are disappointed to find out how little I actually know."

"I didn't say that, did I?"

"In a roundabout way, yes, you did."

"You probably know more about a lot of stuff than most people."

Leaning forward on his elbows, Judd looked her in the eye for a long moment, giving her a rush that flustered her. "From what I've heard about you, Shannon, you're a pretty smart woman yourself."

"What have you heard?"

"Oh, things like you graduated at the top of your class. And you were considering going to medical school after you graduated from high school, but some modeling agency snatched you up and made you sign a contract."

"That's not exactly how it happened, but close enough," she said.

"Wanna tell me the details?"

Shannon narrowed her eyes. "Why would you care?"

"That's a good question. I don't know why I care, but I do."

"Let's see," Shannon said. "I wasn't at the very top of my class. I was second."

"Big whoop."

Shannon chuckled. "I had one fleeting conversation with Janie about majoring in premed in college, but I wasn't serious about it." She paused and sniffled. "Janie's the only person I had this talk with, so now I know who's got a big mouth."

"Cut her some slack, McNab. I called her and pounded the answers out of her. She didn't want to talk, but I threatened bamboo torture."

Once again, Judd made her laugh. "Janie's tough. She's not afraid of anything. She must have wanted you to know, or she wouldn't have told you. I'll have to have a talk with her. I don't want her blabbing my personal life all over town."

"Janie's concerned about you. She's not blabbing anything."

"I know it," Shannon admitted. "But she does need to be careful."

"Does it bother you for me to know things about you?" he asked as he studied her face, making her squirm.

"Well, sort of," she admitted. "I'm not used to letting people see into my life—at least not people I don't know very well."

"I can certainly understand that. I'm kind of the same way."

"You are?" Shannon hadn't seen Judd Manning as a particularly guarded person, so the thought intrigued her.

"Yes, my father was a career military man. He moved the family at the whim of a government that didn't care much about my social life."

"That must have been difficult," Shannon conceded. "Is your father in Atlanta?"

"No, he and my mom live in Arizona, where they retired. I moved here because I always enjoyed staying with my uncle and aunt."

"I've heard some good things about them from Janie," Shannon said. "Janie also told me you're teaching at a Christian school."

"Your friend Janie *is* a big mouth," Judd said.

Shannon laughed as she saw Judd crack a smile. The waitress arrived with two plates stacked with half a dozen pancakes each.

"Whoa!" Shannon said. "I've never eaten that many pancakes at one sitting in my life."

"You haven't lived." He turned to the waitress. "Do you have any of that fabulous blueberry syrup?"

"Coming right up," the waitress said.

"Well?" Judd asked as Shannon chewed her first bite of buttermilk pancakes laden with blueberry syrup. "Like it?"

"Mmm." She stabbed another bite of pancake, stuck it in her mouth, and chewed very slowly. "This is the best thing I've ever tasted."

"Told you."

"We can't come back here, or I'll have to get a whole new wardrobe."

Judd's eyes lit up as he grinned. "Okay, we'll go somewhere else."

Her simple statement gave him hope. She'd said, "We can't come back here," as if she might be considering spending more time with him. If she'd told him, "*I* can't come back here," or "*I* don't want to go out with you," he wouldn't have the hope that had quickened his heart. She'd said, "We—"

"Why are you looking at me like that?" She put her fork down and studied him.

"Oh, nothing. How do you like fondue?"

"Love it."

"Wanna try a new fondue place that just opened on Peachtree Street?"

"Are you trying to make me fat?"

He shrugged. "Quite honestly, I don't really care. You'll still be beautiful."

Her expression suddenly became guarded again as she raised her hand to her cheek. He wanted to kick himself for reminding her of her accident.

"I am so sorry, Shannon," he said softly as he slapped his forehead with the palm of his hand. "I've been such an idiot."

"What?" She regarded him with a curious expression, like she thought he was nuts.

He shook his head and looked at her, then took a sip of his coffee so he could gather his thoughts before saying something stupid again. When he finally did speak, he hoped she'd listen and not shut him out.

"I keep opening my mouth and saying all the wrong things."

"What are you talking about, Judd? Make sense, okay?"

"Let me start over." He paused, borrowing time to run several thoughts through his mind. "Just hear me out, okay?"

Judd started to explain how he'd spent most of his free time taking education classes while working on his master's degree. He told her he'd dated a little, but it wasn't easy for a middle-school English teacher to meet women, and he didn't want to hang out in nightclubs.

"I don't like that either." She gave a quick shudder. "That environment is creepy."

"My sentiments exactly," he agreed and paused to give her a chance to process her thoughts before slamming her with a little-known tidbit about himself. "What I'm trying to tell you, Shannon, is that I don't have much experience with women in a one-on-one relationship."

"Have you ever had a girlfriend?" she asked.

He shrugged. "Once, in eighth grade. But she jilted me when she found out Billy Bateman liked her. I haven't been the same since."

To his delight, Shannon tilted her head back and belted out a laugh. "Poor Judd. But I'm surprised."

"Surprised?" he asked.

"You're a very sweet guy," she began. "And nice-looking and fun to be with, and—"

"Whoa!" He held his hands up. "You're starting to embarrass me. I can't handle all this flattery at once."

"Well, it's the truth."

"Of course it is, but let's not tell all of our secrets, okay? I don't want my head to swell so big that I can't get through the door."

Shannon nodded. He loved her smile, which had returned, and he wasn't about to take any chances with another of his stupid comments.

"I need to run a few errands this morning. We've made quite a dent in the lesson. Maybe we can do this again sometime."

"Yes, I'd like that," she said.

As hard as it was to take her back to her apartment, Judd managed to be stronger than his desire to spend the entire morning with Shannon. He was truthful about the errands. Uncle Garrett had asked him to take the choir robes to the cleaners, and then he needed to go to the school and meet with the parents of one of his students from last year. Shannon could have gone along with him, but too much of a good thing might wind up making her sick of him. He needed to take this nice and slow.

❧

Shannon jumped every time the phone rang, hoping it would be Judd. The afternoon after they'd had breakfast together, she'd opened her apartment door and practically tripped over the Bible study workbook he'd left on the stoop, with a brief note attached that it was hers to keep.

Maybe if she spent a little time working on the lesson on her own, time would pass more quickly. But it didn't. In fact, it dragged even slower than before.

The days literally crawled by. Janie was working late all week, so she couldn't call her. Mom made too much of a fuss over the accident and her scar, so she wasn't in the mood to go to her parents' house.

Why wasn't Judd calling?

Shannon tried to reason with herself, thinking he didn't owe her anything. They'd finished the lesson, so there really wasn't any reason for him to call other than to chat.

Being honest with herself, Shannon knew what she really wanted was to see Judd again. He was fun, interesting, and intelligent, which made her forget her problems.

Maybe seeing the scar bothered him more than he let on, she thought as she studied her reflection in the mirror. Without makeup on, it was still dark pink with tiny dots on each side of the line from the stitches. With makeup, the line was still evident, but it wasn't so bright. Since it itched like crazy from healing, she didn't wear makeup around the apartment. The numbing ointment the doctor had given her was the only thing that soothed the itch. Cold compresses worked in the beginning when there was swelling, but now that seemed pointless.

Finally, after four days had passed, Janie called. "Wanna go to the Bible study Monday night?"

"Of course I want to go," Shannon blurted.

"I don't want to put pressure on you, because I know how you hate that."

"I said I want to go," Shannon repeated.

"It's just that—" Janie stopped before she squealed. "You what? Did I hear you say you wanted to go? This is so great, Shannon. Totally cool."

"I enjoyed it."

"Oh, good." Then Janie grew quiet before adding, "Uh, we need to get you caught up on the lesson. I wouldn't want you to feel lost just because you haven't had a chance to prepare. Maybe Pastor Manning has some extra workbooks. I'll call him right now and ask."

Shannon laughed. "That's all taken care of, Janie. I have the workbook, and I'm up-to-date on the lesson."

"You are?"

"It's about time you stopped yammering and listened." Shannon chuckled. "Judd dropped off a workbook last Tuesday afternoon. And since I'm still not going out much, I've had nothing but time to catch up."

"You have?"

This was the first time Shannon had ever heard her friend at a loss for words. "Yes, I have. I'll be able to sound halfway intelligent in the discussion Monday night."

"How about church tomorrow morning?" Janie asked. "Or is that pushing it?"

"No, I'm fine with church," Shannon replied. "Maybe I can wear a big, floppy hat so people won't be able to see my face."

"Oh, no one wears hats to church anymore."

"I was just kidding, Janie. Lighten up, okay?"

"Uh, okay, that's fine." Silence fell between them for a few seconds before Janie asked, "Since church starts at ten, want me to pick you up at nine thirty?"

"Fine."

"Okay, see you then."

"Janie, you haven't told me what to wear."

"I didn't think you'd need to be told."

Shannon was embarrassed to admit she hadn't been to church in a very long time—not since she'd gone with her parents several years ago. But now she had to.

"It's been a long time, Janie."

Again, silence.

"Janie?"

"Why don't you just wear slacks and a nice top? We're pretty casual, since we're so small and most of the people are pretty young."

After she hung up, Shannon sank further down in the overstuffed chair, allowing the upholstery to envelop her. She was now reaching far out of her comfort zone, with all this church and Bible study business. But it felt right.

Shannon still hadn't heard from Judd since they'd gotten together for breakfast. He had mentioned going out again, so why hadn't she heard from him?

As much as Shannon hated to admit it, she was terribly attracted to Judd, in an odd sort of way. Although he was pleasant to look at, there were plenty of guys around who were better-looking. What she was experiencing went way beyond the physical; it was more of a spiritual and emotional connection.

Judd had admitted to not being a whiz at the Bible, but he was eager to learn more, just as she was, which also surprised her. For the first time in Shannon's life, she was actually thinking about eternal life and what would happen to her soul when her earthly body wore out.

Perhaps the accident had changed her, or maybe she was going through a phase. At any rate, she found herself thinking quite a bit more than usual. For the past eight years, she had been too busy to stop long enough to worry about anything beyond her next photo shoot or Armand's whims.

Shannon picked out something to wear to church and then took a long, relaxing, lavender-scented bubble bath to relax. She needed to get some sleep, or she'd have dark circles to go with her scar.

Her normal nightly routine of flipping through the latest beauty magazines didn't hold her interest, so she picked up her Bible study workbook and began reading ahead. She felt the Holy Spirit working in her heart after she finished the next chapter, and her eyelids fell shut. She awoke as the sun rose, and she felt more rested than she had in a very long time. A smile crept over her face as she remembered she'd see Judd in a few hours.

Janie picked her up at precisely nine thirty. "Anything I need to know before we get there?" Shannon asked as soon as she was safely buckled in her friend's car.

With a shrug, Janie replied, "Only that Judd won't be there this morning. He took some boys on a weekend camping trip, and he won't be back until late tonight."

Disappointment fell over Shannon, but she tried to hide her thoughts and feelings. "That's not what I mean. Is there anything different about church that I need to prepare myself for?"

With a chuckle, Janie shook her head. "No, God's pretty much the same as He was last time you were in church. We have a few songs that are different, and it's a lot more casual, but the message hasn't changed at all."

Shannon finally got to meet Pastor Garrett Manning, a tall, middle-aged man with graying temples and a quick smile. His wife, LaRita, radiated a glow of warmth that drew people close to her. She spoke softly and with sincerity.

"It's so nice to meet you, Shannon," LaRita said as they shook hands. "Janie has said so many nice things about you."

Pastor Manning came up from behind her. "Judd told us you're thinking about staying in Atlanta."

Shannon shrugged. "I'm not sure yet. It all depends. . ."

Her voice trailed off as she saw his gaze drop down and focus on her scar. Automatically, she reached up to touch it.

"Sorry to hear about the accident," Pastor Manning said. "But you were very fortunate, according to what I hear."

"Yes, I suppose I was." What was with these people, noticing her scar and telling her how fortunate she was?

Janie took Shannon by the arm and tugged. "We need to go find a seat now. See ya later, Pastor. LaRita."

Once they'd gotten away from the pastor and his wife, Janie leaned over and whispered, "You looked like a deer caught in headlights. I had to get you away from there." She patted Shannon on the hand and smiled. "Take a couple deep breaths, sweetie. I don't want to have to scrape you off the floor."

The sermon dealt with compassion and reaching out to those who were less fortunate. Rather than talking about pitying the poor, Pastor Manning spoke of believers sharing their faith with the lost. His words gave Shannon plenty to think about later. She took notes in the margins of her church bulletin.

After the services, Shannon turned down an invitation to join Janie and some of the other singles who had plans to get together at a buffet restaurant. She wanted to get home so she could look up a few things in her Bible. Although it didn't appear she'd have a modeling career anymore, so many years of watching every bite that went into her mouth had become habit and instilled guilt. That would take some time to change, if she ever did.

"I hope you don't mind taking me home first," Shannon said.

Janie shook her head. "Of course I don't mind."

૭ન્ટ

"Did she ask about me?" Judd said when he called Janie right after he got home from the camping trip.

Janie laughed. "She didn't have to. I told her where you were before we got to the church."

"Did she sound disappointed?"

"Look, Judd, you're a grown man. Why don't you call her and find out for yourself?"

"I wanted to give her space."

"Okay, so give her space. You'll see her tomorrow night at the Bible study."

"Yeah," he agreed, "you're right. It's just that. . ."

"You really like her, don't you?"

"Yes, I do."

"Good. I think she likes you, too. But go slowly. Shannon had a double whammy, between the scar and Armand dumping her."

"I remember you telling me about that guy. What a jerk."

"He's not really a jerk," Janie argued. "Armand is actually a very nice man. He's just a little shallow and can't see beyond the scars."

"Janie, you and I both know we all have scars. I'm sure this Armand guy has plenty of his own."

"Yeah, but he does a great job of covering them."

"And Shannon can't see that?" Judd asked.

"I think she does now. You still need to give her time."

"I have all the time in the world."

After they got off the phone, Judd thought about Shannon and how difficult it must have been to have someone she loved turn his back and run when she needed him most. That had to be the most painful part of the whole ordeal.

Judd had been accused of not allowing himself to get close to women, but he couldn't help himself. Moving so often while growing up had done something to him. Getting close to people was scary, he admitted only to himself. However, he felt different around Shannon. She needed him more than he needed her, and he liked the feeling.

The only thing he wondered was how he'd handle a relationship if the opportunity ever did arise for him to get close to her. It wouldn't be easy for either of them, considering their pasts.

He went over the lesson in the workbook and reread the Bible verses they were supposed to study. For the first time since he'd joined the group, he was prepared to participate without having to resort to clown tactics.

He held back the urge to call Shannon and offer her a ride to the Bible study. He knew it would be best if she went with Janie. He sensed that crowding her would cause her to turn and run from him, and that was the last thing he wanted now.

Paul was the only one at the church when Judd arrived half an hour early. "I see you're eager this evening," Paul chided. "Anything I need to know?"

"Not really," Judd replied with as much nonchalance as he could muster.

With a look of understanding, Paul motioned for Judd to assist with arranging the chairs. "Janie's bringing the food. Why don't you get the coffee started?"

Paul had just left the room, and Judd was about to flip the switch on the coffeepot when he heard the door open behind him. His hand stilled. He glanced over his shoulder in time to see Shannon and Janie enter the room.

As soon as she spotted him, her lips widened into a glimmering smile, making his heart thud with the anticipation of being near her for a couple of hours. He grinned back, feeling like a foolish adolescent.

"That coffee won't make itself," Janie said as she reached his side. "Ya gotta turn it on."

People began filing into the room, so Judd was forced to broaden his attention. He was still aware of Shannon's presence, something he suspected would always unnerve him.

Once everyone had arrived, they all sat down. Paul started the prayer. Suddenly, the sound of a car backfiring, then squealing tires on the pavement right outside the church filled the room. Judd turned to Shannon to make a wisecrack, but he stopped cold. Shannon's face turned white. Her eyes widened as she jumped up and ran from the room. Judd stood to follow her, but Janie motioned for him to sit back down. "Don't. I'll handle this."

The room grew very quiet as Janie jumped up and flew down the hall after Shannon. Judd's throat constricted as he did what Janie ordered. His ears rang with the hush that fell over the group.

Chapter 4

Shannon fell against the wall and squeezed her eyes shut. Her heart continued to hammer.

When would the fears go away? Or would they ever?

"Shannon?"

She blinked as she looked up and spotted Janie tentatively approaching, appearing almost afraid to get too close.

"Are you okay?"

Shannon opened her mouth, but no words came out.

"Of course you're not okay. What was I thinking? Want me to take you home?"

Janie continued to step closer, her arms extended, and when she got within reach, she gently placed her arm around Shannon's shoulder.

"You're shaking. Why don't we get you to a place where you can sit down, and I'll pull the car to the door?"

Still numb with fear and shock, Shannon allowed herself to be led to a chair at the end of the long hallway. She sat erect, her hands folded in her lap, staring straight ahead. When Janie came back, she didn't move.

Although she could see, she was numb. Her ears rang, and her mouth was dry.

"Shannon." Janie tugged on her hand, but Shannon couldn't move. Her legs felt like they were filled with lead. "Your hand's icy cold. Let me see if someone can help us, okay? Wait here."

The car's backfire had long since passed, but the memory of the sharp sound echoed in Shannon's head. The only thing she felt was a numbing fear as it held her in its clutches.

&

Judd held his breath as he paced and waited to hear how Shannon was. When Janie appeared at the door, he shot over toward her.

Crooking a finger, Janie motioned for Gretta, a woman Judd knew was a nurse in the local hospital emergency room. "I think she's in shock. Can you come take a look at her?"

Now there was nothing that could hold Judd back. He might not know much about medicine, but he did know how he felt about Shannon.

When Janie looked at him, he tightened his jaw. She wouldn't dare tell him he couldn't go to Shannon. Janie didn't say a word when he followed her and Gretta to where Shannon sat staring blankly ahead.

Judd stood back a few feet while Gretta checked Shannon's vital signs. He closed his eyes and said a brief prayer for healing for her and guidance for himself. Shannon's car crash had caused more trauma than he'd realized—and much more devastation than a scar on the face.

"How's she doing?" Paul asked from behind. He kept his voice low, almost to a whisper.

Judd quickly turned around and took a step back so Shannon wouldn't overhear. "I'm not sure yet. She looks pretty shaken."

"I can imagine. What she went through was serious."

"Yeah, I know."

Janie took a step back and joined them. "I've never seen her like this, and I've known her since we were little."

"Any idea what we can do?" Paul asked.

"Just be there for her. Let her know you care."

"I do care," Judd said.

Janie looked at him for a moment before turning back to her friend.

"Why don't you stay close by and be there when she comes out of this trance?" Janie's expression was one of concern and deep affection. Judd could tell her and Shannon's friendship was strong.

"I'll do whatever it takes," he replied.

He didn't want to interfere. However, when Gretta turned and said she thought Shannon would be fine in a few minutes, he didn't waste a single second. He was beside Shannon before anyone could stop him.

He took her hand in his and felt the clamminess. At least she didn't pull away.

"Want me to take you home?" he asked.

Shannon blinked at him before slowly turning toward Janie, who tilted her head and held her hands out to her side.

"Your decision, Shannon," she said. "I just want you to be comfortable."

All eyes turned back to Shannon to see what she'd say. She finally nodded. She tried to stand on her own, but her wobbly legs gave out, and she fell back onto the chair.

"Put your arm around my neck, and I'll walk you to my car," Judd said softly, hoping to offer comfort to this broken woman. He stuck his hand in his pocket and pulled out a set of keys. "Janie, would you mind running out to my car and pulling it closer to the exit?"

"Sure thing."

Janie grabbed the keys and took off running. Judd positioned Shannon to make it easier for her to walk.

He loved the way her body felt next to his. Although she was still shaky, she was firm and athletic—nothing like a frail woman who nibbled rabbit food to keep her weight down.

As they hobbled down the hallway toward the exit, he inhaled the spicy fragrance from her hair whenever it brushed across his face. He wanted to lean over and bury his face in her hair, but he wouldn't dare do anything so bold and presumptuous.

Once they got to the door, she stopped and shifted, pulling away a little. He hated that he had to let go of her in order to get the door.

Janie pulled up at the exact moment that they reached the edge of the sidewalk. "You sure you wanna do this?" Janie asked.

"Positive. Go on back inside and finish the Bible study. I'll take her back to her place and make sure she's okay before I leave."

"Thanks, Judd." Janie smiled at him in appreciation. "You're a good guy. No, make that a *great* guy." She leaned over and snapped Shannon's seat belt into place, then slammed the car door shut.

Judd cringed at the harsh sound, until he glanced over and saw that it hadn't fazed Shannon.

Once Judd was buckled in, he turned back to Shannon. He was surprised to see her staring at him, a half-smile on her lips.

"Feeling better?" he asked.

She nodded. "A little."

He offered a few minutes of silence to let her recover and regroup. Her ordeal had taken its toll on her in a big way. Although he knew he couldn't be beside her every minute of every day, he wanted to help her as much as possible right now.

"Wanna hear some music?" he asked. Maybe that would drown out outside noises and help her relax.

"Sure. That's fine."

Judd turned on the radio and pushed the button he had tuned to the contemporary Christian music station. The sounds of a heavy metal band blasted through the car.

Shannon flinched. He quickly hit the POWER button and silenced it. "Sorry."

She managed a weak smile. "You didn't know. What kind of music is that?"

"Christian rock, believe it or not."

"Amazing."

When Judd pulled up to a stop sign, he took the opportunity to study her in the light of the streetlamp. Good. Her hands weren't shaking anymore, and her eyes didn't have that glazed look.

When they reached her apartment complex, he pulled into a parking spot and instructed her to stay put so he could walk her to her door. This time she was much steadier on her feet, but he didn't let go, just in case.

She had the presence of mind to dig in her purse and have her key ready before getting out of the car. He stood, feeling rather awkward, while she unlocked her door. What should he do now? Leave her alone and risk something happening to her, or ask if he could come in?

Holding the door open, Shannon turned around and touched him on the arm. "Would you like to come inside?"

"I, uh. . ."

"Please?"

Her one simple plea turned him inside-out. "Are you sure?"

"I insist. Come on in, and I'll fix you a cup of chamomile tea."

"Okay, I'll come in, but let me fix the tea. You lie down on the couch."

Shannon snickered. "Such a caregiver. Not many guys are like that."

"Well, I am a teacher, and I'm used to watching after children."

The instant he said that, he knew it was a mistake. Her eyebrows shot up.

"I'm not a child," she said firmly.

"No," he said, trying to think of the best way to backpedal. "I didn't mean it like it sounded. What I meant was. . ."

"No, don't explain. I understand."

"You do?"

"Yes. I'm always sticking my foot in my mouth, so I know how things can come out completely wrong."

Judd couldn't believe she was being so nice about his stupid comment. "At the risk of sounding insensitive, let me get the tea started."

Shannon tilted her head back and belted out a hearty laugh. He felt a joyous sensation coursing through him at the sound of her happiness. She was doing much better than she had been back at the church.

"That's not insensitive at all," she said. "In fact, I find you to be a very sensitive man."

"Sensitive, but strong," he said, playfully flexing a muscle.

"Oh, yes, of course. Very strong. Macho, in fact."

"Let's not get too carried away. We don't want this to go to my head."

Judd left Shannon sitting on the couch with the remote pointed at the TV. As he rummaged through the cupboards, he once again found himself in prayer—something that was happening more often these days.

Lord, I pray for wisdom as Shannon and I get to know each other. Guide us in our relationship and help us get closer to You.

"The tea bags are on the little shelf to the left of the stove," Shannon called out. "Use the big mugs on the mug tree."

"Sure thing."

Judd made himself at home in Shannon's kitchen. He was fascinated and amused by the way everything matched with a pig motif—from the small row of tea tins on the shelf beside the stove, to the mugs and wire rack they hung from.

Once the tea had finished steeping, Judd carried both mugs into the living room, where Shannon sat with her legs curled beneath her. She accepted her tea with a smile as she patted the cushion next to her.

"I'll sit over here." He chose the chair that was angled toward her position on the couch. "I can see you better."

He wasn't about to sit next to her now. Every time he caught a whiff of her fresh, clean scent, he felt an overwhelming urge to wrap his arms around her and draw her closer.

"Mm, this is good," she said as she sipped the tea.

"There really wasn't much to it. Just heat the water and pour over the tea bag."

"Some men can't even do that."

Judd opened his mouth to make one of his typical sarcastic comments about men who couldn't boil water, but he caught himself. That might touch on something that would send her over the edge again.

"Can you cook?" she asked with interest.

"Oh, yeah," he replied. "I heat up a mean can of soup."

Her smile brought a flash of sunshine into the room. "How about real food?"

"A few things. Roast beef, baked chicken, meatloaf, chili, spaghetti. Usual stuff."

"I'm impressed."

"How about you?" he asked. "How are your culinary skills?"

"Not good, I'm afraid. My mom always shooed me out of the kitchen. She told me I didn't need to cook with my looks."

Surprisingly, she didn't sound conceited when she said that. Her statement was very matter-of-fact rather than boastful.

"So you've always wanted to be a model?"

"My mom wanted that. I wasn't sure what I wanted, so I figured I might as well go after her dream."

Her confession hit him hard. How many times had he heard about the expectations of parents forcing their children to do what they had no business doing? More than he could count, that's for sure.

"Did you like modeling?"

"Some of it, but not all. A lot of people think it's all glamour and fun."

"That's what I would've thought." Judd blew into his tea before taking another sip. "Is it really bad?"

"No, not bad. Just constraining. I had to watch everything I put in my mouth. I couldn't get sunburned when I went to the beach. Even tan lines could be a problem if I had to model clothes."

41

"Yeah, I can see where tan lines might be bad."

She took a sip of tea before adding, "Not to mention the big blemish that would pop up the day before a big shoot. It never failed."

"Oh, that had to be awful. I feel sorry for the makeup artist having to deal with that one."

Shannon's warm smile let him know his teasing wasn't painful for her. That was a huge relief. "How about you? Have you always wanted to be a teacher?"

"Not really. I never knew what I wanted, but I figured I like kids, and English is something I understand. It seemed like the most natural thing to get into."

A flash of pain shot through her expression. She glanced down into her mug as if all her thoughts centered in the hot, steamy liquid.

"I'm sorry."

Her head quickly shot up, and she looked at him quizzically. "Sorry? For what?"

"For upsetting you."

"You didn't upset me. You just made me think."

"I hate making people think. Forgive me."

"There you go again." Her laughter was rich and genuine. "I like being around you, Judd. You're such a happy person."

"I like being around you, too, Shannon," he said as he stood. "But unfortunately, I need to leave. Tomorrow morning comes awfully early, and I have to get up with the birds."

Shannon walked him to the door. He saw that she was steady on her feet. "Thanks, Judd. I don't know what I'd do without you."

He suddenly felt awkward, like one of the seventh grade boys in his classes. Should he just tell her good-bye and leave? Or should he risk a kiss?

Taking a chance and pulling up all the courage he could, he leaned toward her and dropped a quick kiss on her lips before backing away. She grinned and waved.

❧

Shannon never imagined herself in this situation, with such an intense feeling for anyone besides Armand. Judd's simple, chaste kiss had sent tingles down her spine and made her feel all wobble-kneed.

As soon as she closed the door behind him, she headed for her bedroom. It wasn't very late, but the ordeal of going into shock over some stupid car backfiring had wiped her out.

She changed into her nightgown and crawled under the covers, hoping to get plenty of rest so she could think straight in the morning. However, thoughts of Judd kept popping into her mind, preventing her from falling asleep. Her lips still tingled from the sweetest kiss she'd ever had.

She eventually gave up and flipped on the light beside her bed. Maybe reading something would make her sleepy.

At first, she reached for a fashion magazine, but it bored her to tears. She got up and wandered around the apartment, until she spotted her Bible on the kitchen table. *Maybe this'll help*, she thought.

Curling up with the Bible and a concordance she'd gotten from Janie, Shannon figured she needed to see what God had to say about her fears.

Her concordance showed a long list of scriptures that spoke of fear, so Shannon looked up each one and tried to relate to what it said. Finally, she read Matthew chapter 14, verses 22 through 36, and found comfort. Surely, if Jesus could protect Peter on the stormy sea, He'd watch over her in this turbulent time.

Although she'd never immersed herself in the Word before, Shannon never questioned the existence of Jesus—or that He was the Son of God. But until now, she hadn't given Him much thought.

She read the passage over and over, shutting her eyes occasionally to let it sink in. Just as Jesus had reached out His hand to Peter, He had offered a hand to Shannon and allowed her to survive the horrible car crash. There had to be a reason she'd gone through it, just as there was a reason she'd survived. Could it be that He'd allowed her tragedy so she'd slow down and pay attention to Him?

Finally, she closed the Bible and turned off the light. Darkness only seemed to enhance the sounds of night, causing her heart to hammer in her chest.

For several minutes, Shannon stared up at the ceiling, illuminated by the moonlight that filtered through the sheers on her window. Christ's love filled her heart as she accepted Him as her Savior. Eventually, she shut her eyes and prayed.

Lord Jesus, my life is in Your hands. I know You don't want me to be fearful like this, but I don't know what to do to make the horrors of my experience go away. Please show me what you want me to do.

She let out a deep sigh before finally whispering, "Amen."

❦

The sound of the telephone startled Shannon from her sound sleep. She lifted her head and glanced at the clock on the nightstand as she reached for the receiver. It was already after eight.

"Don't tell me you're still sleeping," Janie said.

"Afraid so," Shannon replied as she sat up and rubbed her sleepy eyes.

"You okay?"

"I guess. I had a hard time going to sleep last night."

"Judd was really worried about you. I hope you didn't mind me letting him take you home."

"Of course I didn't mind. He's very sweet."

"Do you need anything?"

"Like what?"

"I don't know," Janie said. "Like maybe someone to come over for a little while? I can take off work if you need me."

Shannon managed a chuckle. "I'm not that bad off—not yet, anyway. Don't take time off work for me."

"I'll do it, you know."

"Yes, I know you will. And I really appreciate that."

"You have my work number, right?"

"Yes," Shannon replied, "and your cell phone number."

"Don't hesitate to call me if you need me."

"Okay, okay."

"Promise?"

"Stop trying to mother me, Janie. I'm a big girl. I can be alone."

"Yeah, but—"

"Don't worry so much. I just had a little setback last night. I'll be just fine."

"Well, if you're sure. . ."

"I'm positive. Now go on and get to work. I need to get up and do a few things around here."

After they hung up, Shannon stepped into her slippers, grabbed her Bible, and trudged through her apartment. She started the coffee before sitting down to go over the Bible verses she'd read the night before. It was amazing how much peace she got from reading scripture and realizing how much Peter had to rely on God. Jesus never let him down, just as He promised He'd never let her down.

Later in the afternoon, after Shannon finished straightening the apartment, her mother dropped by.

"Have you even left the apartment at all today?" her mom asked.

"No, not yet."

"You really shouldn't be sitting around this place, Shannon. You need to get out, be around people."

Her mom had stormed through the living room to the kitchen. She put several plastic containers into the refrigerator before plunking her purse on the dining room table and rummaging through it. She whipped out a couple of brochures featuring young, perfect-looking women on the front.

"I've gotten some information about plastic surgery. I thought you might want to start looking around for someone to take care of your. . .scar."

Shannon reached up and touched her cheek. Her mother made the same face she always did and quickly looked away.

"You don't have to live with that, you know."

"I know, but I'm not ready to have plastic surgery."

"You don't want to wait too long, Shannon."

"It hasn't been that long. Let me rest for a little while and figure out what I need to do."

Her mother turned to face her, planted her fist on her hip, and shook her head. "Shannon McNab, you're smarter than you're acting. You know as well as I do that your agent won't be able to hold everyone off much longer. All your accounts will start looking for a replacement if you don't come back soon. You need to get better as quickly as possible, or your career might be over."

"Would that be so bad?" Shannon asked defiantly.

"How can you say something like that?" her mother shrieked. "You know that would be awful. You've worked too long and hard to let it come to this. You're a supermodel. That's what you do. That's who you are."

Shannon fought the urge to argue with her mother. Being a supermodel was only what she did for a living—not who she was. But arguing with Sara McNab was futile—this was something she knew from experience. Once that woman set her mind to something, she was a shark. She chomped down and never let go. Shannon pursed her lips and offered a slight nod, holding back all her thoughts and frustrations.

Her mother reached out and gently touched her undamaged cheek. "I'll leave the list of plastic surgeons for you to look at when you're feeling a little better. Don't wait too long."

"Thanks, Mom," Shannon said.

"I can tell you're still pretty down about this, Shannon. The only thing that'll snap you out of this mood is getting back to work. Trust me."

Taking the path of least resistance, Shannon let her mother talk. There was nothing she could say to change her mind. All her mom had ever wanted for Shannon was fame and fortune—mostly because that had been what she'd wanted in her own life many years ago. Instead, she'd gotten married and had Shannon six months later, which had killed her dreams of acting or modeling. Besides, enough people had told Sara that she was too short to be taken seriously as a model, and her Southern accent was too thick to make it as an actress—which was why she'd enrolled Shannon in diction classes at a very young age.

"I don't want my daughter sounding like a bumpkin," she'd told everyone who stood still long enough to listen.

As Shannon's mother chattered incessantly about all the things they'd do to get her back on her modeling career path, Shannon pretended to listen. Instead, she kept thinking about the scripture she'd read to find comfort.

When silence fell between them, Shannon turned to her mom. "We used to go to church when I was little. But I was wondering. . .well. . .have you ever read the Bible, Mom?"

"Some of it. Back when I was a little girl, my parents made me go to Sunday school. They made me memorize Bible verses." Tilting her head to one side, she offered a questioning look. "Why?"

Shannon shrugged. "I was just wondering if you ever stopped to think about all the things Jesus did for us."

Looking a little stunned, her mother let out a nervous giggle. "All that Bible stuff took place a long time ago, Shannon. This is now. I'm sure God would want you to go back to your job and not worry about such things."

"I'm not worried," Shannon said.

"Look, sweetheart, I really need to run. Some of the women at the club are expecting me. Let me know if you need something, okay?"

"Sure, Mom."

After a quick air kiss, Shannon showed her mother to the door. After closing it, she let out a breath of frustration. Obviously, her mom hadn't given much thought to her faith. Just as obviously, talking about it made her very uncomfortable. Shannon understood. She'd been the same way until her first brush with Janie's Bible study group.

Shannon went back to her room to play with her makeup when the doorbell rang again. Probably her mother. She must have forgotten something.

She went to the door and yanked it open. There stood Judd, grinning, a cake server in one hand and a plastic sack dangling from the other.

"Hi there. Thought you might be hungry."

"Not really," Shannon admitted. "My mom brought some food, but I haven't gotten into it yet."

"I'm sure it's better than what I have, but remember, it's the thought that counts." He nodded toward the kitchen, and Shannon moved out of his way. "Maybe you can eat just a little for me."

Judd's very presence brought a smile to Shannon's face. She followed him and watched as he put a big round plastic cake server on the counter. Then he stuck a couple tubs of yogurt on the top shelf of her refrigerator. He groped around the bottom of the bag and pulled out some Ramen noodles that he placed on the counter beside the cake server.

Shannon pointed to the plastic container. "What's that?"

"German chocolate cake. I hope you like it."

It had been years since she'd tasted German chocolate cake, but she remembered how it tasted.

"I love it," she said as her mouth watered. "How about the noodles? What kind?"

"I wasn't sure what flavor you liked," he said, "so I just grabbed some creamy chicken."

"Mm, my favorite."

"Want me to fix it for you?"

"No, you took care of me last night. Now it's my turn to take care of you."

"I really don't mind."

Shannon stabbed her finger toward the kitchen table. "Sit."

Chapter 5

Y es, ma'am."

Not wasting a second, Judd did as he was told.

Shannon leaned over and checked out the contents of the refrigerator. She pulled out one of the bowls her mom had brought and placed it on the counter.

"I'm not the best cook in the world, but I can heat stuff up."

"That's all that matters," Judd said as he watched her with interest.

It took Shannon less than five minutes to microwave the vegetables and turkey her mother had brought, as well as cook the noodles from Judd. She piled two plates and bowls with food, a heaping one for him and one with much smaller servings for herself.

He frowned at her plate before offering her a questioning glance.

"I'm really not that hungry," she reminded him.

"This food wasn't for me. I brought it for you to get your strength back."

"I know, but I hate eating alone."

"In that case, let's chow down. But first, I want to say a blessing."

Shannon bowed her head as he said a short prayer of thanksgiving for the food on the table. When he said, "Amen," she opened one eye and caught him staring at her, smiling.

"What?" she asked. "Were you peeking?"

"No, of course not."

"Then why are you looking at me like that?"

"I'm happy to be here," he replied. "Let's eat."

Judd scarfed his food down quickly, while Shannon nibbled at hers. She was sure he noticed she hadn't eaten much, but he didn't say anything.

With each bite she took, he seemed to relax a little. He even made a few comments, like "Atta girl" and "That'll make you feel much better."

It made her uncomfortable that he was watching, even though she liked having him there. She knew she needed to eat, but she didn't need an audience cheering her on.

Finally, she put down her fork and pushed her chair back. "I can't eat any more."

He slowly nodded. "I understand. I guess I'd better get going. I have papers to grade and stuff to do tonight. Let me know if you need anything, okay?"

"Of course."

"Oh, one more thing," he said as he reached the door. "I'd like to get together with you one more time before the next Bible study." He tilted his head forward and looked at her from beneath his heavy eyebrows. "That is, if you plan to go back to the church."

"Of course I do."

"Good."

Shannon bit her bottom lip.

"How about tomorrow night?" he said.

Maybe if she agreed, she'd have a little peace. Although it was nice having him here for a little while, being under such intense scrutiny wore her out. "Okay, tomorrow night's fine."

"Seven okay?"

"Sure, seven's fine."

For a second, it looked like Judd might kiss her again. She braced herself for the sensation, wanting it but dreading it at the same time. When he backed away instead, she felt awkward, almost like a teenage girl who didn't have a clue what to do around a guy.

She hated her vulnerable state. Her mental health and emotional state were even harder to deal with than her scar. There was no doubt in her mind that the giddiness over being around Judd was mostly the result of feeling alone and without the safety net of Armand or work.

And there was this Christianity thing. It baffled her. She'd always been happy and carefree before she'd ever gone to a single Bible study. Why did she suddenly feel this huge weight of responsibility to study scripture? Was it part of overcoming her trauma? Or was it something else?

Reading the Bible made sense while she was doing it or when she was with the group from the church talking about their faith. But now, alone and confused, she wondered if it was more of a crutch than anything—something she was using to make herself feel better.

Her mind whirred with all sorts of crazy thoughts, flip-flopping back and forth between the desire to lean on the Lord and wanting to go it alone. As she picked up her Bible and flipped through it, stopping to randomly read scripture, she became more confused than ever and worked her way into a state of exhaustion.

After changing into her gown, she sat on the edge of her bed and contemplated an appropriate prayer. What should she pray for? Healing? Her relationship with Judd? Answers to her questions about the Bible?

Finally, she bowed her head and said a general prayer, touching on everything she'd been thinking. If nothing else, it felt good to get it off her mind.

She woke up the next morning feeling more refreshed than she had since the accident. Her first thought went straight to her bedtime prayer the night before.

Feeling better made it so much easier for Shannon to function throughout the day. She managed to shower, dress, and get through her chores without dreading her next step, as she had so many times since the accident.

Her emotional state had leveled, at least for the time being—until another car backfired. Now was the time for her to prepare herself for her future and any surprises she might encounter along the way. She needed to do something to continue feeling better.

The problem was, she didn't know where to start. Should she make an appointment with a psychologist or psychiatrist? That seemed pretty drastic right now, in the light of day.

Glancing over at the brochures her mother had left on the table, Shannon thought about plastic surgery. Would that help? It certainly couldn't hurt.

She picked up the list of certified plastic surgeons, headed to the phone, and stopped in her tracks. What was she thinking? She hadn't even given the scar time to heal on its own. How would anyone know what needed to be done? Besides, what was the purpose of getting plastic surgery? She wasn't sure she wanted to go back to modeling.

Shannon let out a huge sigh. If she kept thinking like this, she knew she'd make herself crazy. So she grabbed her purse and her car keys and headed for the door.

She hadn't driven since the crash. The brand-new car her parents had delivered still sat in the parking lot, shiny and waiting.

Sucking in a deep breath, she forged ahead, moving with determination to get over this major hurdle of driving a car for the first time since she'd been hit.

As she slid in behind the wheel, she felt fear clutching at her throat. *Okay, you can do this. Just take it one step at a time.*

She stuck her key in the ignition, took a deep breath, and started the engine. So far, so good.

Knowing how susceptible she was to a panic attack, she decided to take her first spin around the block before venturing out any farther. Heart pounding in her chest, she pulled to the stop sign at the road and waited for all cars to pass before pulling out.

Shannon made her way around the block, not blinking, talking to herself, being extra cautious as cars approached from all sides. She jumped at the sound of a car honking behind her.

One quick glance at the speedometer let her know she was driving way too slow. She offered a wave to the person behind her and accelerated a little harder. But not too fast. Each mile per hour she increased seemed to speed up her heart rate.

Finally, when she took her last turn back into the parking lot, she blew out the breath she'd been holding. She'd done it. She'd gotten back behind the wheel and driven—something she wasn't certain she'd ever be able to do.

It wasn't until she got out of her car and stood up that she realized how traumatic her experience had actually been. Her knees buckled beneath her, and she had to grab on to the car to keep from falling to the asphalt.

Shannon knew she needed help. And she needed it very soon.

She spent the rest of the afternoon contemplating what kind of help she needed to seek. After being away from Atlanta so long, she had no idea who to call. Janie had always been such a together person, so she probably didn't know anyone to refer her to. Her mother's solution to the problem would be to get plastic surgery and head straight back to a modeling career, hopefully picking up where she left off.

Then she thought about Judd. She felt more comfortable around him than anyone besides Janie. Surely she could talk to him about this, and he'd understand. Maybe he'd know someone, or at least have a direction to point her toward. Now, with that settled, Shannon headed for the kitchen to whip up something healthy for dinner. She needed to get back to as normal a life as possible, and just because she didn't see herself going back to modeling didn't mean she shouldn't be careful what she put into her mouth.

The phone rang exactly half an hour after Judd was scheduled to get out of school. He'd been calling her every day at the same time, asking how she was doing.

"Whatcha been up to all day?" he asked as he always did.

She found comfort in the familiarity of his voice. "You're not going to believe this, but I drove a little."

"You're right! I don't believe it. Where'd you go?"

"Just around the block."

If she'd been talking to anyone else, Shannon wouldn't even have mentioned her short excursion, but she felt completely comfortable with him. He seemed to understand the significance of what she'd done.

"That's a great start. And not a bad idea. You can go just a little farther each day until you're back to your old self."

Good. He'd given her an opening to ask her question.

"Speaking of getting back to my old self, do you know anyone I can talk to?"

"You can talk to me, Shannon."

"I know. But I mean about some deep things. Like mental problems."

"Mental problems?" he asked. "I don't think you have mental problems. What you're dealing with is a normal fear after an immensely traumatic experience."

"Whatever you want to call it, I need to talk to someone."

"How about my uncle?"

"The pastor?"

"Yeah, he's pretty good with things like this."

"I don't know."

"Tell you what, Shannon; let me talk to him and see what he says. He might be able to help you, and if he can't, he can refer you to someone who can."

She paused for a few seconds. "Okay, that's fine."

"Now, for tonight. Since you're driving, would you like to meet somewhere?"

"I haven't worked up the courage to drive at night yet."

"Okay, I'll pick you up. How about dinner? Do you have plans?"

Shannon remembered the extra large salad she'd made and put in the refrigerator. It was plenty big enough for both of them if she added a little of the chicken her mother had brought.

"Why don't you come over here for dinner?"

"I thought you couldn't cook."

"I can't. I just tossed some romaine in a bowl with a few tomatoes and some celery. Mom brought marinated chicken breasts. I thought we could have that."

"Yum. You make healthy eating sound good. What time do you want me there?"

❧

As soon as Shannon gave him the time, they hung up. He then turned around and dialed his uncle's office number at the church.

"Hey, Judd. Whatcha need?"

Judd told him about Shannon's need to seek counseling. "I think she's got a few issues she hasn't told me about, and she needs someone to give her some guidance."

"I'll be glad to talk to her, Judd. What's her number?"

After giving his uncle Shannon's number, Judd hung up and grabbed the shopping list Aunt LaRita had given him. Although his aunt and uncle had told him he could live with them rent-free until he saved enough for his own place, he insisted on helping out wherever possible. LaRita had reluctantly given in and handed over occasional lists that freed her up to do some of the charity work she enjoyed.

Without another moment of hesitation, he ran the errands, then went home to put things away. A quick shower and shave later, Judd was on his way to Shannon's place.

She greeted him at the door, wearing a pink velour jogging suit and running shoes, with her blond hair hanging naturally over her shoulders. She was beautiful in spite of the scar she hadn't bothered trying to hide with makeup.

"Your uncle called almost right after we hung up. You don't waste time, do you?"

"No, there's no point. What'd he say?"

"I have an appointment with him tomorrow afternoon."

"Talking about not wasting time. Must be genetic."

"I just hope he doesn't think I'm shallow and self-absorbed."

Judd felt a thud in his chest at the look of helplessness on her face. "Why would he think something like that?"

"I don't know." She held her hands up as she shook her head. "It just seems that all I can think about anymore is how I feel about things. *My* fears, *my* career, *my* happiness. Somehow, it all seems so wrong to be thinking about myself so much."

"I think that's all normal stuff to think about."

"Yeah, but not to this degree."

"You've got to give yourself some time, Shannon. You've just been through one of the most harrowing experiences a person can have. Be patient with yourself."

She audibly sighed. He watched the range of emotions flit across her face. She finally nodded.

"You're probably right. But I still need to get help. I can't do this alone."

"You're not alone. You have a whole bunch of people praying for you."

She smiled. "I know, and I appreciate every prayer that's offered."

Something had changed in her. Judd noticed that, even when she gave lip service to accepting prayer, she didn't seem to believe it like she had a couple days ago.

"Come on into the kitchen. The salads are ready. All I have to do is make some tea, and we can eat."

Following her into the kitchen, Judd noticed how her strides were long and purposeful. As each day passed, she was getting stronger physically, but she obviously didn't realize it. He was beginning to see the confidence of a world-class supermodel. That was good, but he worried she'd eventually have no use for someone as normal and plain as him.

Once they were seated at the kitchen table, Shannon propped her elbows on the table and leaned toward him.

"You wanna say the blessing, or do you want me to?"

"It doesn't matter," Judd said. "Whatever you want."

"Hey, what's going on? Are you okay?"

"Sure, I'm fine," he replied with a smile. "Why don't you say the blessing?"

"Thank You, Lord, for the blessing of this food," she began, sounding unsure of herself. "We're thankful for Your kindness and mercy. Amen."

As she spoke, Judd wondered where her conviction was. She certainly didn't sound sincere. Something had happened to her since he'd last seen her.

She chatted happily as they ate. He didn't have to say much, which suited him just fine. Once they were finished, he stood to carry the dishes to the sink.

"Leave those," she told him. "Let's get started on the Bible study. I'm eager to get ahead again."

Judd didn't argue with her. He followed her into the living room and sat on the chair across from the loveseat where she'd flopped.

Throughout the evening, he felt somewhat mechanical, just going through the motions of discussion and answering questions. Finally, when they got to the end of the week's lesson, he shut his workbook.

"Well, I guess that's it for now. I need to run. I have to get up early in the morning for school. We're doing poetry this week, and I always start each day reading some of my favorite poems."

"You like poetry?" she said, sounding surprised.

"Of course. I'm an English teacher."

"What's your favorite?"

Judd shrugged. "Anything but the dark stuff. I have to admit, I tend to be a romantic when it comes to poetry."

Suddenly, her eyes glazed over. He must have said something wrong, because the bright, cheery smile she wore had suddenly disappeared.

"Good night, Shannon," Judd said as he walked out the door where she stood, holding it open. "See you soon."

"Yeah," she replied. "G'night."

Whatever had happened in her apartment was a mystery to him. While nothing physical had happened, it seemed like the night had been a major turning point—and not in a good direction. His heart sank at the memory of the look on her face as he left.

❧

Armand had loved poetry, too, Shannon remembered. But he was the opposite of Judd. His favorite poet was Poe, king of darkness.

After Judd left, she closed and locked the door before going to the kitchen to clean up the small mess from dinner. He'd offered to help, and perhaps she should have let him, but she didn't want him to see how much effort she was having to put into maintaining her equilibrium.

He kept looking at her, almost as if he was confused by something. That had made her very uncomfortable and self-conscious.

She noticed that he was quiet tonight, almost moody. He'd tried to pretend nothing was wrong, but she could tell something bothered him.

After the dishes were done, she went through her nightly routine of flipping through magazines, channel surfing, then giving up and going to bed. She grabbed her Bible off the loveseat where she'd left it and placed it on the nightstand. After she got ready for bed, she picked it up, looked at the cover, then put it back. She was tired. She didn't feel like reading or trying to find comfort in scripture at the moment. Her heart felt too heavy for something like a gospel message to be able to help.

After a long night of tossing and turning, Shannon crawled out of bed and plodded to the bathroom. Leaning over the sink, she studied her face in the mirror and took a really good, long look at her scar. It was still bad.

Then she thought about the guy who'd hit her. He was dead. Although people around her had tried to cover the details, she'd learned that he had a wife and young children. Yes, it was his fault that he'd been drinking and should never have been behind the wheel. But what about those kids? They were innocent, and just because of some stupid error in judgment on their father's part, they'd grow up without a father. Shannon couldn't imagine what life would have been like without her dad in her life.

Her parents had been complete opposites. Where her mother was always looking over her shoulder and wishing for things that never could be, her father taught her to count her blessings and enjoy life. Her mother was focused on her own desires; her father was active with Habitat for Humanity. He'd been in construction all his life, so he figured that was the best way he could give back to those less fortunate.

Maybe she could find out something about the family of the man who'd smashed into her. If his family needed something done around their house, perhaps she could talk to her father about helping out. It wasn't much, but at least it would be something. Plus, she had a nice nest egg that would more than provide a decent living for the rest of her life. It wouldn't hurt much to help them out financially.

Shannon kept a close eye on the clock. She didn't want to be late for her appointment with Pastor Manning. Although she seriously doubted he'd be able to help her, hopefully he knew someone she could go to for psychological help. Being in his profession, he must know people in all fields. In fact, she might even try enlisting his help with the family.

Pastor Manning greeted her at his office door, his hand extended, a warm smile on his face. She instantly felt comfortable and able to open up to him without holding back.

"Why don't we sit over here where we can be more comfortable?" he said, gesturing toward a conversational seating arrangement of a worn but matching sofa, loveseat, and chair.

Within minutes, she found herself babbling about every thought she'd had on her mind since the accident and even some things she'd been pondering before her trip home. He continued to nod and make brief comments to encourage her.

Finally, she flopped back on the couch. "I can't believe how much I just talked. I didn't give you a chance to get a word in edgewise." She paused for a second and smiled. "Just call me motormouth. That's what all my friends called me back in high school."

"Motormouth, huh?" He nodded and chuckled. "I guess that's a term of endearment if it comes from the right people."

"Oh, only my closest friends would dare call me that." Then, Shannon started going on and on about Janie and some of her other friends before she realized she was at it again. "Oops! Sorry."

"No, that's quite all right. I like to hear you talk. You're a delightful young woman and a great conversationalist."

She laughed. "I guess that's a nice way of putting it."

Pastor Manning's smile slowly faded as he leaned forward in his chair across from Shannon, clasped his hands, and looked at the floor for a moment before meeting her gaze. "I understand you're having a rough time dealing with some things. Would you like to talk about it?"

She started to tell him she only wanted a referral, but he was so easy to talk to, and he truly did seem to care. After a brief pause, she nodded.

"Yes, I am having a hard time."

"I'm listening."

Shannon started slowly, telling him how consuming being a supermodel was and how she was never allowed to forget about what she did for a living. There was always someone there to remind her, like cameras, crew, fans, and Armand. Although she'd once thought she loved him, she now realized he was the path of least resistance—the way she chose to go to keep up the pretense of living the perfect life.

"Do you still hear from him?" Pastor Manning asked.

"No. He left right after the bandages were removed. Sure, he sent flowers and a couple of postcards, but that's it. My relationship with him is over."

"Are you sure?"

"Positive."

"Does this upset you?"

"No, not really," Shannon replied truthfully. "After being apart from him for this long, I see how it was all just for show, not to mention convenience. We were both in the same profession, and we understood each other. Neither of us ever wondered if the other had ulterior motives."

"Sounds like you might have been mistaken about that."

"Maybe." Shannon grew silent as she thought about his comment. Perhaps she was mistaken, and they did have ulterior motives. Their motives could have been to appease those around them rather than joining together as two people who truly loved each other. That was very possible. Highly likely, in fact.

Pastor Manning studied his steepled fingers before looking back at her. "Sounds like you're also having problems dealing with the fact that the accident involved a death."

"Yes, that's really bugging me," she admitted.

"I can certainly understand that. But you should never feel guilty. It was completely out of your control."

"Yes, I know," she agreed. Then she told him what she'd overheard about the man's family.

"You have a good heart, Shannon. I'm sure the Lord would love for you to give to the man's family. That shows the forgiveness in your heart."

"Oh, it's not out of forgiveness."

"Is it from guilt?"

Slowly, she nodded, admitting her shortcoming. "Afraid so."

"That's something you need to pray about. You also need to know that there are some things you just can't fix. No matter how hard we try as humans to make everything right and just, it's impossible."

"But doesn't God want us to be good and pure in our thoughts?"

"Yes, of course He does. But it's not going to happen one hundred percent of the time, and He knows it. That's why He sent His Son. Jesus was the only perfect man ever to walk this earth, and it's our job to worship Him and share the good news that He's saved us from our sin nature."

Shannon had a lot to think about. "I still want to help that man's family."

"Yes, of course you do. So do I. Fortunately, the Lord has placed a kind nature in your heart, and He's given us the ability to know right from wrong."

Shannon suddenly felt shame because she suspected he was talking about what the Lord did for believers, those who walked in His Word and knew scripture.

"I'm not so sure it has anything to do with my faith," she managed to sputter.

"There are kind people who don't believe in Jesus," Pastor Manning assured her. "The big difference between them and us is that we want to please Jesus, and we do kind things for people to His glory."

"Wow!"

Pastor Manning snickered. "Yeah, my sentiments exactly. I never cease to be wowed by all the goodness of God."

Two hours after Shannon walked into his office, she stood at the door getting ready to leave. He took her hands in his and said a short prayer for mercy and healing.

When she opened her eyes, he smiled. "Would you like for me to find someone to work with you? If you feel like you still need some help, I know a few people."

Shannon shook her head. "No, I don't think so. Not now, anyway. You've made some things very clear to me. Now I need to go home and do some serious thinking."

"And praying," he added.

"Yes, and praying and studying my Bible."

"Oh, just a minute. Let me get the tracts I subscribe to."

He quickly moved over to his file cabinet, flipped through some papers, and came back with a pamphlet in his hands. "This one deals with understanding why bad things happen in this world and allowing the Lord to work through them."

"Thank you so much, Pastor Manning. You don't know how much you've helped."

"I can't take credit for any of it," he replied, pointing his finger heavenward.

Shannon hurried down the hall toward the exit, when suddenly a familiar figure stepped out from a darkened room. "Judd! What're you doing here?"

Chapter 6

I thought I'd stop by to see Uncle Garrett."

Shannon lifted one eyebrow. "Really?"

"Well. . ."

"Level with me, Judd."

He rolled his eyes and slapped his forehead with the palm of his hand. "You caught me."

Shannon glanced at her watch. "Shouldn't you still be in school?"

"Teacher inservice day. Kids aren't in school, so when the workshops are over, we're dismissed."

"Well, good for you."

Shannon took a step back and watched as Judd's expression changed from contrition to calculating. She loved the way he let his feelings show. He'd make a lousy actor. . .or model, which was good.

"Since I'm here, and you're here," he said slowly, "how about doing something together this afternoon?"

"Sounds good, but I can't."

"Why not?"

Disappointment shrouded Shannon. "I wish I could, but I have plans."

"Oh." He glanced down and shifted his feet. She saw how his expression changed once again. Disappointment and worry had taken over.

"With my mom," she said.

"Oh," he said again, only this time a smile covered his lips, and he looked at her. "In that case, don't let me keep you."

As they parted, Shannon felt like she was walking on air. Seeing Judd always did that to her. He wasn't nearly as handsome as Armand by most women's standards, but he looked much better to her. More real. More animated. He never minded showing his feelings. And while Armand worried about getting lines from smiling, that concept never seemed to worry Judd in the least.

Shannon was still nervous about driving, but she'd been forced to venture out more. She couldn't very well expect other people to drive her everywhere she needed to go, so she tightened her jaw and moved ahead, forcing herself to deal with life. Her inborn streak of independence had returned.

No matter how much she talked to herself about how safe the back roads she took were, by the time she got to her parents' house, her hands were shaking, her palms were sweaty, and her head ached. When would this fear ever end? Or would it?

The neighborhood hadn't changed much since she lived here, with the exception of the trees, which had grown a few feet taller. The long driveway, which led to the garage in the back of the house, was shaded by oaks with branches that overhung the concrete path, almost like long, sheltering arms protecting the people who'd arrived.

Shannon took her time, allowing the scents to fill her nostrils and the sounds to bring back memories. The back-facing garage door was open, exposing both of her parents' cars, parked side-by-side as they had been for as long as she could remember.

"I've been worried about you, Shannon," her mother said first thing. "I was afraid you wouldn't make it. You're late."

"Just by ten minutes," Shannon reminded her, defending herself.

"We can't keep Cissy waiting. You know how busy she is. When you have the best hairdresser in town, you have to be there early. She's booked into next month, you know."

"Yes, I know. You keep reminding me."

"Don't get sarcastic, Shannon."

Just then, her father rounded the corner, his arms extended, a wide smile on his face. "Shannon, baby, come give me a hug."

"Daddy. Why are you home this early?"

Shannon noticed her parents exchanging a glance before her mother ushered her out the door. "C'mon, let's go. We can't dilly-dally any longer."

"I need to talk with you about something later," Shannon told her dad. Then she turned to her mother. "Want me to drive?"

Her mother paused, then nervously flicked her wrist toward her own car. "No, I'll drive. We don't have much time."

Shannon wasn't sure if her mother was being polite or if she didn't trust her driving. Whatever the case, Shannon didn't argue. As always, she went along with her mother to keep the peace.

The woman was white-knuckled as she maneuvered the oversized luxury car through the streets of the Atlanta suburbs, her gazed fixed on the road ahead. She was on a mission. They were halfway to the hairdresser her mother had picked after interviewing a two-page list. Cissy, the hairdresser, had a clientele that impressed her, so that's who she insisted Shannon choose. Being the dutiful daughter she was—or not wanting to make waves because she couldn't stand the repercussions— Shannon had agreed to this awkward time for her hair appointment.

"I'm curious about something," Shannon said.

"If you have questions, just ask," her mother snapped. "Don't beat around the bush."

"What's going on between you and Daddy?"

"I don't know what you're talking about, Shannon."

Her expression was guarded, but her grip on the steering wheel grew even tighter. Shannon knew she'd hit a nerve.

"I saw that look you gave each other."

There was a long silence. Shannon studied her mother, who was trying to focus on her driving but was clearly distressed. Whatever the problem was, Shannon suspected her mother wasn't ready to discuss it.

"We've been married nearly thirty years. We do look at each other occasionally."

Shannon could tell it was no use to press any further, but her radar was up. She was determined to find out why her parents were acting so odd. After she'd left the hospital, she'd seen her father only once, and that was very briefly, before her mother had almost pushed him out the door.

"Here we are," her mother said as she quickly swung the car into the parking space of a strip mall. "Better hurry."

Shannon glanced at her watch. "We're not that late. I'm sure she's used to waiting a few minutes for some of her clients."

Cissy stood tapping her foot with a scowl on her face. "You're late," she said sternly.

"I'm so sorry," Shannon's mom apologized. "It won't happen again."

"I'm booked tight, you know."

"Yes, I'm fully aware of that. My daughter's still dealing with the fear of being in a car. This isn't easy for her."

Shannon watched the two women as they looked at each other with understanding. She decided right then and there that she'd find another hairdresser before the next time she needed a trim. No way would she grovel for being just a few minutes late—especially when the hairdresser had such an uppity attitude. Even as a supermodel, Shannon never spoke to anyone with the haughty attitude Cissy had.

Shannon sat in the chair while her mother gave orders to Cissy, explaining what she wanted, which wasn't what Shannon wanted at all. Finally, before Cissy's scissors were anywhere near her hair, she stood up from the chair and turned around to face her mother.

"Stop right now. I'm not five years old."

"Oh, sit down, Shannon. You've been through a lot lately. I'm just trying to help."

"Maybe so, but I don't want my hair looking all fussy. I don't have time to take care of anything elaborate." Turning to Cissy, she added, "Just take an inch off the ends. That's all."

A look of disapproval flitted across Cissy's face as she glanced at Shannon's mother, who shrugged.

"Well?" Cissy asked.

Her mother let out a heavy breath of exasperation. "Just do what she says. It's taking a little longer to get over it than I thought."

Cissy lifted the scissors with one hand and pushed Shannon back down into the chair with the other. "Whatever. But next time you come here, you need to let me tell you what you need."

There won't be a next time, Shannon thought as she stiffened with anticipation over having her hair trimmed. She watched closely to make sure Cissy did as she was told. The last bad haircut she'd had took months to grow out, and that involved wearing hats and tons of hairspray, which she hated.

When the ordeal was over, Shannon managed to beat her mother to the front desk. She pulled out a wad of bills, but her mother was even faster, shoving money into Cissy's pocket before Shannon had a chance to pay.

Shannon tried to swat at her mother's hand to keep her from paying. "I have plenty of money, Mom. You don't need to pay my way."

They glared at each other, while Cissy stood there, waiting, for the first time showing patience. Shannon won the battle as she shamed her mother into backing off.

"Don't embarrass me like that again," her mother said as they got in the car.

Shannon sat, tight-jawed, forcing herself to remain quiet. She wasn't in the mood to argue.

Her father was waiting for them when they got back to her parents' house. "You don't look any different," he said with a chuckle. "And I bet you paid a fortune to stay the same."

Shannon's mom made some unintelligible sound as she stormed past him and headed for her room. He winked at Shannon.

"Hey, Dad, what's up with you two?"

"Nothing with me, but I think your mother's been suffering from empty-nest syndrome since you've been gone."

"I've been gone a long time."

"And your mother's been acting like this the whole time."

They exchanged a look of understanding during a moment's silence. Suddenly, Shannon remembered her idea about helping the family of the man who'd hit her. When she told her dad, his face lit up.

"I'd love to help. Where do they live?"

"North Carolina," Shannon said.

"That's a long way for me to go."

"I know, but I'll rent you a hotel room if you're willing to do it."

"You don't need to pay my way, Shannon. It'll be my pleasure."

"Okay, then, I'll send money for their bills," she said. "Even if he had life insurance, I'm sure every little bit will help."

Nodding, her father agreed. "You're right."

Shannon chatted with him for a few minutes over coffee before she stood. "I really need to go home now. The stress of driving totally wears me out."

He walked her to the door, where they hugged. "You turned out to be quite a woman, Shannon," he said. "I'm very proud of you."

All the way home, she thought about her mother's mood and realized there was something else going on. Depression, maybe? Whatever it was didn't look good.

When she got home, her answering machine light was blinking. The first call was from Janie. The second was from Judd.

She called Janie first.

"You are going to the Bible study, aren't you?" Janie asked.

"I'd like to, but after what happened last time I was there, I'm not sure I should show my face."

"Don't be silly. Of course you should go."

"They're going to think I'm a complete nerd for acting like I did."

"So? We all act nerdy sometimes. Get over it."

Shannon laughed. "Well, I guess I do have to face people sooner or later."

"Yeah, and what better place than where we're all studying God's Word?"

Judd had called to ask if she wanted a ride to the Bible study. "I wasn't sure if you wanted to go alone, with Janie, or if I could take you."

"Would you like to take me?" Shannon asked.

"I'd love to."

"Okay, then it's a date."

The second she said that, she felt like kicking herself. It wasn't a date. It was just a ride to the Bible study.

"Sounds good," Judd said.

At least he hadn't made an issue of her faux pas. Shannon decided she needed to be more careful with what she said from now on.

When Judd arrived, he looked her over, but he didn't say a word about her appearance. She'd spent quite a bit of time getting ready, so she was a little disappointed.

All the way to the church, Shannon chattered about getting her hair trimmed and seeing her parents. He listened but didn't say more than an occasional "mm-hmm" and "that's nice."

A few people were scurrying around, moving chairs, and getting the refreshments ready. A few of them stopped and hugged her, saying it was good to see her.

"Good to see you back," Paul said as he came up to her. "How're you feeling?"

"Much better."

Everyone in the room approached her at some point, both before the Bible study began and during the break. They were all concerned about her, and they expressed their gratitude that their prayers had been answered.

All the studying she and Judd had done paid off. Not only did she understand everything they talked about, she participated as much as anyone else. With each comment, she felt more a part of the group. During the social time, when they talked about what was going on in their lives, Judd shared that he'd had a particularly rough day at school with some behavior problems. Shannon was relieved that she hadn't caused his bad mood.

When it was her turn, she talked about how she was overcoming her fear of driving. They all promised to continue praying for her recovery—mental, physical, and emotional.

She appreciated all they were doing. And she didn't doubt their sincere concern. The only problem was, she wasn't sure if she truly felt God's message like everyone else did. Was she just giving lip service, or did she actually "get" it?"

On the way back to her place, Judd stopped at a light and turned to her. "Something's bothering you. Wanna talk about it?"

Shannon shrugged, thinking she'd be better off not discussing her doubts. After all, what good would it do to question the very fiber of what he believed in?

"Not really."

"Okay, if you're not ready, that's fine. But I'm all ears if you change your mind."

He asked her if she wanted to stop off for coffee, but she turned him down. "I really need to get home. It's been a trying day for both of us."

That was true, but what she didn't tell him was that she'd been wrestling with her beliefs, until he'd picked her up. He let her off the hook for now.

Over the next several weeks, Shannon went through the motions of studying and bringing what she'd memorized to the Bible study. It appeared that she had everyone fooled—everyone, that is, but Judd. She knew it was only a matter of time before he said something.

"Something's going on with you," he finally told her one night after a long study session. "I'm sensing that you're not as into this whole Bible study thing as you want everyone to believe."

"Don't be silly," she replied.

He gave her one of his looks, reached out, and squeezed her hand. Then he hopped out of the car and ran around to her side to open her door. Shannon liked that about him—the fact that he was such a gentleman. Armand had been nice and polite, but it had never dawned on him to hold doors or let her go first. But then, he hadn't grown up with parents who'd taught him to be a gentleman. He came from a long line of jet-setters, which meant he'd been raised by a series of nannies.

That night, after she got home, she decided she needed to do some serious soul-searching. If she planned to continue with the Bible study, she felt like she owed it to everyone there, including herself, to believe the words that came out of her mouth.

First thing she did was call Janie. It was hard, but she confessed what had been plaguing her.

"I could tell something was wrong," Janie said sympathetically. "Why don't you venture out and find some scripture that speaks directly to you?"

"Where do I start?"

"Do you still have that concordance I brought over?"

"Yes, that's what I've been using."

"Then start with the word *faith*, and go from there."

"Okay, I'll give it a try."

"Don't forget to open and close with prayer. Ask the Lord to show you what you need. He listens."

"Thanks, Janie," Shannon said softly. She knew she could count on her best friend.

Shannon looked up all the verses listed in her concordance. She read Job chapter 19, verse 25, and silently pondered the message about how it related to faith. Then she moved on to Isaiah chapter 12, verse 2, which dealt with trusting the Lord. But it was the ninth chapter of Mark that really touched her heart, especially the twenty-fourth verse, when the demon-possessed child's father said, "I do believe; help me overcome my unbelief!"

Shannon thought about how she could relate to that situation. Until Janie had dragged her to the Bible study, she'd been caught up in worldly ways, which didn't appear evil on the surface. It was much subtler, but the gentle tugs away from God's Word had been there. The fame, the fortune, and the shallow relationship she'd had with Armand had been veiled attempts by Satan to pull her away from what was truly important in her life.

An incredible feeling of understanding washed over Shannon. Although she knew she still hadn't gone deep enough into the gospel message for a true understanding, she knew the Lord was speaking to her through His Word. Janie had been right. All she had to do was look to the only true message in this world, and the answers would be there.

The following week, she got a little behind on the Bible study lesson because she'd taken a side trip in her own studies. However, no one seemed to mind that she didn't participate. She listened attentively and made up her mind to get back on track with everyone else.

Each week that passed brought more strength of conviction to Shannon. She did her lessons and allowed herself to get sidetracked to other verses when she needed a better understanding. If something wasn't clear, she looked it up in the concordance. And then, if she couldn't find what she needed, she called Janie, even though she didn't always have answers.

"You might want to call Pastor Manning. He's a very wise man."

Judd had backed off to give her space, which she appreciated. However, she missed the warmth of his friendship and the way he made her feel inside.

He still hadn't rushed her or made an issue of her external beauty. In fact, after the first couple of comments about her looks, he hadn't said a word about them.

As much as she appreciated the space, Shannon couldn't stand it anymore. She finally picked up the phone and punched in Judd's number. His answering machine picked up after the fourth ring, so she left a message.

Two hours later he called her, panic evident in his voice. "You called?"

"Yes, I was wondering if we could get together and study. You know, like we used to."

"Is everything okay?"

"Yes, everything's fine. Why?"

He blew out an audible breath. "Oh, man, you had me worried. Your message said it was urgent and to call as soon as possible."

She hadn't thought about how her message would sound, but she had wanted to talk to him soon. "I'm really sorry, Judd. It's just that when I get my mind set on something, I don't like to waste time."

"Don't worry," he said. "Why don't we meet somewhere?"

"I thought we could study here."

"Maybe it would be better if I met you somewhere, like halfway."

"Okay," she said slowly. His tone had changed, and it worried her.

❧

Maybe being out in public with Shannon would keep his mind off his feelings toward her. All Judd had been able to think about since meeting her was how he was starting to fall head-over-heels for her. In fact, for the first time in his life, he understood what it meant when people said they'd "fallen" in love. That was exactly how he felt—like he'd fallen and couldn't get up.

They made arrangements to meet at the Dunk 'n' Dine, at her suggestion. "For old times' sake," she'd said. "We can eat pancakes until they're coming out our ears."

Judd concentrated hard on the current week's Bible study. He took turns with Shannon, looking up the answers. She smiled often, and he had to restrain himself, when all he wanted to do was reach across the table and touch her.

At the end of the lesson, they agreed to meet weekly, since they were at the same level of understanding. Shannon hesitated, looking at him with questioning eyes, but she didn't ask anything as she turned to leave. He felt like a piece of his heart left with her.

Over time, Judd was able to be around Shannon and still focus on the Bible study lesson, but there were times when their hands brushed and he got a tightening sensation in his chest. It was a feeling of anticipation, of excitement, and of wondering if the other person felt it, too.

Something else Judd had noticed was that Shannon's scar had begun to fade. In fact, he had to look hard to see it, and the only reason he could was because he knew it was there. He wasn't sure she was aware how it had almost disappeared, because she still, on occasion, touched her cheek with her fingertips. He wanted to reach out and cover her hand with his, but he didn't dare.

Judd delighted as Shannon's faith grew and she became more confident in her knowledge of scripture. She had become bolder in speaking up about her faith, and when they had new members or visitors, she was often one of the first people to greet them. She didn't hesitate to speak out about her newly discovered faith, and when they were in the question-and-answer part of their study, she spoke out as often as anyone else in the room. That also quickened Judd's heart. He loved watching the transformation. He also knew that Shannon was responsible for his own faith growing to the level where it was. She'd challenged him by asking questions, making him study harder, and proving that a person could come from rock bottom to the top by allowing Jesus to touch her heart. Jesus had worked a miracle in both of them, something Judd was grateful for.

"I have something special to discuss with you next time we get together to study," Shannon said as they walked out to the church parking lot together. "I know you like to go to the Dunk 'n' Dine, but I was wondering if we could study at my place."

Judd thought for a few seconds before nodding. "Sure. That would be fine." After all, he'd gotten used to the feelings she never ceased to awaken in him. He could manage the heart palpitations at her place as much as he could at the Dunk 'n' Dine, couldn't he?

❧

The first thing he noticed when she yanked open the door was the twinkle in her eye that showed her mischievous side. She was up to something, he could tell.

The instant he sat down, she plopped into the oversized chair across from him, tucked her legs under herself, and leaned forward. "We need to talk," she said.

Judd gulped. What had he done now?

"Okay," he said slowly, almost wishing they were at the Dunk 'n' Dine rather than her cozy living room. "What's on your mind?"

"I've got all this time on my hands, and I'm starting to get antsy. I feel like I need to do something."

"Any thoughts about what?"

She shrugged. "I've thought about getting a job, but there's not much I'm trained to do."

"You could always go back to modeling."

On cue, her hand flew up to her cheek as she shook her head. "No, I don't think so."

"Any other ideas?"

"Since I have a little money stashed away, I don't have to get a job. Not yet, anyway. I was sort of thinking I might want to volunteer. I'd like to help others."

Judd smiled. He loved how Shannon thought about other people. Janie had told him how she'd sent money to the family of the man who'd crashed his car into hers. He was amazed at her ability to forgive and show compassion for those less fortunate.

"Any idea what you'd like to do?"

She made a funny face as she shook her head. "That's the problem. I don't even know where to start. What does a former model know how to do that can help society?"

"I'm sure there are lots of things. Why don't we start with your gifts?"

"Janie told me to look in Romans chapter 12. I think my gift is serving."

"I can see that," Judd said.

He'd noticed how quickly she volunteered to help out when someone was needed to deliver food to homebound members of the church. And she didn't hesitate to visit people in the nursing home.

"I think you're also an encourager," he added.

"You think so?"

"Yes, I do."

"Funny you should say that. Janie told me the same thing. Okay, now what do I do?"

"I'm not sure."

"What do you think your gifts are, Judd?"

"Well, I am a teacher, and it seems like a good fit. The kids in my classes are all doing well, and they're pretty happy—most of the time, anyway."

Shannon nodded. "I have no doubt teaching is one of your gifts. You know, I think you might be an encourager, too."

"Hmm. I never thought about being anything other than a teacher," he said.

"Look at it this way. You encouraged me to keep going to the Bible study. You encourage people in the group to participate. And one of the reasons you're such an effective teacher, I bet, is that you encourage the kids to be the best they possibly can."

"Good point."

Shannon lifted her hands and let them fall back to her lap. "Now what?"

"I guess we should figure out where we fit best."

"We?" Shannon asked, her head tilted to one side.

"Yes, we. I'd like to volunteer, too."

"Are you just saying it because that's what I want?"

"No. I'll admit you thought of it first, but I have time and the desire to help others, too."

A slow grin took over Shannon's face. "It'll be wonderful to do something together, Judd." She jumped up, crossed over to where he sat, and threw her arms around him. "You always know the answers."

"Not always," he argued as he tried to squirm away from her warmth.

She leaned back and gave him a puzzled look.

"For me, you do. Whenever I'm stumped, you always come through for me."

She'd pulled away from him a little more, but he could still feel her closeness. The urge to reach out and touch her was too strong to resist. Tentatively at first, he touched the side of her face with his fingertips. Then, slowly and deliberately, he slid his hand to the back of her head, his fingers getting caught in her tangle of long, blond hair. Her eyes widened as he pulled her to him for a kiss.

❧

Shannon's breath suddenly felt shaky. She'd kissed Armand countless times, but he'd never had this effect on her. But then again, Judd's kiss had so much more meaning than any of Armand's kisses ever had.

"I'm sorry, Shannon," Judd said as he suddenly let go of her. "I shouldn't have done that."

She struggled to find her voice. "Don't be sorry. I liked it."

"You did?"

Nodding, she had to swallow to find her voice again. "Yes. Very much."

He grinned. "Knowing that makes me happy."

Shannon wasn't sure if he had any idea how she felt. He'd distanced himself pretty quickly after the kiss—almost as if he was afraid to stay close to her.

After Judd left, Shannon leaned against the wall. Something significant had just happened, and she wasn't sure what to do about it. That one simple kiss had changed things between them. He'd kissed her before, but the emotion behind this was incredible. She wondered if he felt it, too.

As the minutes ticked by, and then the hours, feelings of doubt began to take over the excitement of the kiss. What if he'd only meant it as a gesture of friendship? Or perhaps he didn't mean anything at all. Which would be worse? Given the fact that she thought she might be falling in love, neither appealed to her. She wanted him to care as much for her as she did him. The very thought of her love being one-sided sent her heart into a free fall and then landed in a giant thud.

Shannon wasn't sleepy, so she decided to do a little channel surfing, hoping to make her eyelids heavy. When the phone rang, she glanced up at the clock. Who could be calling at this hour?

Chapter 7

S   hannon?"

"Judd? It's late."

"Were you sleeping?"

She paused before replying, "No, I was watching TV."

"I've been thinking."

"So have I," Shannon quickly replied. "What were you thinking about?"

"You tell me first."

"No, you called me."

She heard him inhale before clearing his throat. "I was thinking about what you said."

She thought for a moment and tried to remember anything she said that would elicit a late-night phone call. "What did I say?"

"You were saying you wanted to do something constructive with your life. I've got some ideas."

"Is that what you were thinking about?"

"Yeah, how about you? It's your turn."

Shannon briefly pondered letting him know what was really on her mind, but she figured it was best left unsaid. "Nothing, really. My mind was racing about everything, and I wouldn't even know where to start."

"I'm patient. I'm also a good listener."

"Yes, I know, but we can talk about that later." Shannon sucked in a breath, then slowly blew it out. "What ideas did you have for me?"

"Well, there are a couple of things the church is involved in, plus some secular stuff in downtown Atlanta."

Shannon thought for a moment. "What all is the church involved in?"

"One thing I think you might like is the 'Room at the Inn' program."

"Room at the Inn? What's that?"

Judd explained how the homeless shelters always filled up early, which left hundreds of families on the streets during the cold winter nights. Area churches coordinated sponsoring "Room at the Inn" nights, where they let homeless individuals and families stay in sanctuaries, fellowship halls, and classrooms. People from each church provided meals, clothing, and messages about Christ's love.

"Sounds wonderful," Shannon replied. "I'd love to get involved. What do I need to do?"

"Uncle Garrett told me about it. I think our church has a turn coming up in a few weeks. I'll find out who's coordinating it."

"Let me know, okay?"

"Sure thing," Judd replied. "How're you feeling?"

"You were here just a little while ago. You saw me."

Yes, Judd saw her. That was for sure. He saw her long, blond hair flowing freely around her face, her sparkling eyes lighting up as they discussed anything and everything.

"Judd?"

Shaking himself back to the moment, Judd said, "I'm getting tired. I just wanted to call and make sure you were okay."

"Yes, I'm fine."

As they hung up, Judd thought about the real reason for his call. After he left her apartment, all he could think about was the kiss. It still lingered on his lips. He doubted he'd get any sleep, thinking about Shannon and how she affected him.

This wasn't supposed to be happening. Judd had plans, which didn't include falling for a woman—at least not yet. He'd just started to get his feet on the ground, and he wanted to do a few things for himself before meeting someone he could get serious with.

Who was he kidding? Getting serious with Shannon McNab would be like trying to grab a star with his bare hands. It would be impossible and way too much for him to handle. Women like Shannon didn't fall for men like him.

He ran his tongue over his lips and tried to force her out of his mind. He'd be much better off staying away from her, but he knew it would be impossible. All she had to do was call, and he'd be there for her.

The week went by quickly for Judd, due to the reading fair he was hosting at the school. He barely had time to do the exercises in the workbook to get ready for the Bible study.

Shannon was at the church when he first arrived, getting the coffee ready. "I tried calling you," she said as she glanced over her shoulder. "You're never home anymore, and you didn't pick up your cell phone."

"Sorry," he said, hovering a few feet away. "I've been busy."

"That's what I thought. Janie came over, and we went over the lesson."

Suddenly, Janie stuck her head in the door. "Did someone say my name?"

Shannon chuckled. "Were you eavesdropping?"

"Yes." Janie came all the way into the room, carrying a tall box that was obviously heavy.

"Let me get that," Judd said as he quickly moved to her side.

As Janie tried to hand Judd the box, she tripped over the place where the carpet met the tiled floor, and the box fell with a loud bang before Judd could get a grip on it.

Janie gasped and all eyes quickly turned to Shannon, who stood there stunned for a few seconds. Shannon's heart raced, but she was okay. She slowly allowed a shaky smile as she moved toward Janie.

"I'm so sorry," Janie said as she reached out to Shannon. "You okay?"

Shannon glanced over at Judd, who stood with his hands in his pockets, watching her, concern evident in his expression. But he wasn't making a move toward her. It was as if he wasn't sure what to do.

"I'm fine. It scared me, but nothing like before. I think I'm starting to heal on the inside."

Janie, Judd, and the couple of people who'd drifted into the room let out a collective sigh of relief.

The Bible study was brief, since everyone seemed to be in a hurry. Judd darted out of the fellowship hall before Shannon had a chance to chat with him. Janie eyed her but waited until Judd was gone to approach.

"Wanna do something, since we're out early?" she asked.

Shannon nodded. "Sounds like a good idea."

"How about a snack?"

"I'm putting on a bunch of weight."

Janie's gaze raked her from head to toe, but she didn't say anything.

"A snack sounds good," Shannon finally said after an uncomfortable silence. "Where do you want to go?"

Janie shrugged. "How about the Dunk 'n' Dine?"

Shannon paused, thinking about how she and Judd liked to go there. She'd begun to think of that as their place, but that was silly.

"I'll meet you there in fifteen minutes. I need to help clean up here first."

"You can go on," Paul said. "I can finish up here."

"No, I want to help."

Paul handed her a broom. "You're a good woman, Shannon. I hope you decide to stick around. We like having you be part of the group."

"I like it here, too," she said with a smile.

"Oh, and before you leave, there's a wet rag on the table. If you don't mind—"

"I'll wipe everything off before I leave," she said before he got the words out.

"I need to run this coffee urn to the kitchen, then I'm outta here."

"See you next week, Paul."

When Shannon finished cleaning the meeting room, she went straight to the Dunk 'n' Dine, where she saw Janie waiting at a booth toward the front. Good. At least she wasn't in the back, where Judd liked to sit.

"We need to talk," Janie said the second she sat down.

"You don't waste any time, do you?"

"No, I try not to. What's going on between you and Judd?"

Shannon pulled her bottom lip between her teeth as she thought for a moment. "I wish I knew."

"What happened? Did you have an argument?"

"No, he came over one night last week, and suddenly he acted like someone had bitten him on the foot. One minute we were talking about what I should do with the rest of my life, he kissed me, and then suddenly he couldn't wait to leave."

"Wait a minute. Slow down." Janie leaned toward her, her eyebrows pulled together in a tight line. "He kissed you?"

Shannon smiled and nodded. She felt as shy as she had in junior high when Bobby Anderson had told everyone he loved her.

"Yeah."

"You never told me."

"It was just a kiss."

"With guys like Judd, it's never just a kiss. Maybe you're used to faster men, but in our crowd, guys don't kiss women unless they mean it."

"I know," Shannon admitted. "That's what makes it so strange."

"And what's this talk about what you want to do with the rest of your life? Are you planning something I should know about?"

Leave it to Janie to know where to dig, and then get right to the point. She was smart, and she wasn't the type to leave anything alone.

"I feel like my life doesn't have meaning. Judd was trying to help me figure out where to go from here."

"Somehow I don't think Judd's the type to tell you what to do. Have you come up with any ideas?"

"I think I might like to do some volunteer work."

"Volunteering is good. Any thoughts about where?"

"Judd mentioned something about Room at the Inn."

"That's a good start," Janie said, "but it's only for one week a year. That's an excellent ministry, though, so it's a worthwhile thing to do. Gretta coordinates it. I'll tell her you're interested."

"I haven't thought about what to do besides that."

"You're a very talented woman, Shannon."

"Only when it comes to fashion. But somehow I don't know if I can figure out how to work fashion into a ministry."

"You want to do something in the ministry?"

"I'm not sure yet. I thought I might."

"Look, Shannon," Janie said as she fidgeted with her napkin, "I don't want to discourage you from doing the Lord's work. But you've only recently started studying the Bible. There are many ways you can put your talents to work that will please God. All work, if done to His glory, can be a ministry."

Shannon listened to the wisdom of Janie's words. "I just don't know where to start."

"Why don't you go back to school? Remember how you always said you'd like to work with animals?"

"That was a long time ago. I'm not sure if I'm up to going back to school."

"You don't have to go full-time until you're ready. I do think you should sign up for one class next semester. It would get you out, and you can explore options."

"I'll have to think about it."

"In the meantime, if I come up with any brilliant ideas, I'll let you know."

Shannon smiled at Janie, knowing she would have more than one brilliant idea. She always did. Janie had always been the type of friend who didn't let up. If there was a problem, she set out to solve it, and she didn't quit until she'd accomplished her mission.

After she ate her salad, Shannon went to her apartment. Judd had called and left a message, but it was too late to return his call. She knew he had to get up extra early for school because the book fair was still going on at the school. He put in long days for those kids, which endeared him to her even more. The man was so selfless that she felt small and insignificant next to him.

He called her the next day around noon. "I was worried about you last night," he said, not even bothering to identify himself.

"Janie and I went out for a snack after the Bible study."

"I'm sorry. I didn't mean for you to feel like you had to account for every minute."

"I didn't take it that way."

Shannon was actually flattered that he cared enough to worry.

"Good. I'd never want to do that to you."

"How's the book fair?"

"As much fun as it's been, and I feel bad for saying this, I'm glad it's almost over."

"You've put a lot of work into it."

"Yes," he said, "I have. At least I've documented everything that needs to be done, so next year it should be much easier."

A few seconds of silence filled the phone line before Shannon spoke.

"Would you like to come over soon?"

"To study?"

That wasn't what she had in mind, but she couldn't tell him she just wanted to look at him and hope for another kiss. "Yeah, to study."

He paused, allowing a feeling of concern to wash over Shannon. "Sure," he finally replied. "How about the day after tomorrow?"

"Sounds good."

She called Janie later because she'd promised to let her know if she talked to Judd. Why, she wasn't sure, but it seemed important to Janie.

"Remember he's not used to women like you," Janie reminded her.

"Women like me?"

"Yeah. Women who can get any man they want with the snap of her finger."

"That's silly. I've never snapped my finger at a man."

"Maybe not, but you could if you wanted to."

Shannon laughed out loud, but after hanging up, she thought about what Janie had said. It seemed odd that people would think that just because she was a model, deep down she was any different from the rest of the women in the world. Quite the contrary. Shannon had the same desire for love and acceptance anyone else had.

Her mother paid her a visit the next morning. "Shannon, honey, have you looked in the mirror recently?"

"Of course I have. I look in it every morning when I brush my teeth."

Gently nudging Shannon toward the bathroom, she said, "Go take a look at your cheek."

"What about my cheek?"

"The scar is almost gone. I can't believe it healed so well without surgery, but it looks like you were right."

As Shannon studied her cheek, she saw the reflection of her mother right behind her, an expectant look on her face. She spun around and faced her.

She opened her mouth to comment, but her mother interrupted her.

"I'm not saying you have to do anything right away, Shannon, but you might want to put in a call to your agent. Let her know it won't be too much longer before you can get back to work."

"I'm not sure if that's what I want anymore, Mom."

"That's ridiculous. Don't let a setback like this keep you from the career that was meant for you."

This was such a standard argument between them, Shannon knew it was pointless to continue. So she shrugged. "I'll think about it."

She didn't have to think too long. Her agent, Melinda, called her early the next morning.

"I spoke to your mother yesterday afternoon. She says you're almost ready to return. I'm sure all the accounts will be very happy."

Shannon listened as her agent chattered on and on about how she had big plans for Shannon's return to the business. She even planned to take advantage of the fact that Shannon had found peace through the spiritual guidance she'd gotten at her church.

"How did you know about that?" Shannon asked.

"Your mother told me you've become something of a religious zealot."

"That's a distortion," Shannon said. "I don't want you exploiting my faith."

"Whatever," Melinda said. "Just let me know when you're ready, and I'll make sure you come back with a splash."

Shannon sighed but didn't say anything.

"Oh—and congratulations on your scar healing. After talking to Armand, I didn't think it was possible."

Alarm bells sounded in her head. "You and Armand talked about me?"

"Yes, dear, he was very concerned about you. He said his biggest fear was that your modeling career was over for good. He told me the scar was very deep."

The scar on my face wasn't the only one that was deep, Shannon thought.

"It is deep, but not as deep as others."

"You have more scars?" Melinda asked, sounding distressed.

"None you can see."

"That's good. I can hardly wait until you're ready to return, Shannon. You'll come back bigger and better than before. Sometimes it's good to take a little time off from the business. It stirs public interest."

That was the last thing Shannon cared about. Public interest. What was it, really? Just perception and nothing of any significance.

Shannon's mother started coming by the apartment every afternoon. The first time, she was thrilled to have heard from Shannon's agent.

"Melinda called and asked when I thought you'd be ready to come back."

"Maybe never."

"Oh, don't be silly. You have to go back. What else will you do with your life? All you know is modeling. It's the only real job you've ever had."

Real job? Hardly. "I'm sure there's something else out there for me."

Shannon's mother stepped back, folded her arms, and shook her head. "Nothing else that can pay your bills, unless you go back to school for at least four years."

"I've got money in the bank," Shannon argued. "I don't need more than what I have."

"Then think about all the other people who depend on you. And how about the contracts you've signed? According to Melinda, you still have two years with the corn chip company, and the hair products company needs at least another year's worth of ads. And then there's. . ."

Shannon remained silent as her mother rattled off other companies and people who counted on her supermodel status. This was an angle she hadn't yet considered.

"Don't forget how Melinda has stuck her neck out for you. Remember, back when you were just getting started?"

Shannon nodded. How could she forget? Melinda had literally taken her by the hand and led her to her first audition. Then, when decision-making time came, she'd pulled all sorts of tricks to get Shannon her first television commercial. She'd taken chances—which had paid off big-time—but it could very easily have gone the other way.

"Melinda's agency is counting on you, Shannon. She's counting on you for her agency's survival."

Oh, man, her mother knew right where to hit.

"Yeah, you're right," Shannon finally agreed. "Looks like I need to do whatever I can to get back to work."

Next time Shannon saw Janie, she pointed to her face. "Do you see any trace of the scar?" she asked. "Be honest with me."

Janie narrowed her eyes. "Have I ever been anything but honest?"

"No, and that's why I'm asking you."

Taking a step closer and inspecting not only by looking but by reaching out and touching Shannon's face, Janie shook her head. "Looks to me like it's completely gone."

"Well, it's not completely gone, but it's faded enough to where I can hide it with makeup."

"That's great," Janie said. "You heal well."

Shannon managed a weak smile. "Yes, I'm very fortunate."

"So, what do you plan to do?"

With a brief lift of one shoulder, Shannon glanced away. "I haven't decided yet."

Janie groaned. "Don't tell me you're going back to modeling."

"It's a distinct possibility."

"Why would you wanna go and do that?"

"It's all I know how to do. Besides, my mother reminded me how my agent depends on me."

Janie snorted. "Don't give me that. There are plenty of things you can do."

"Name one," Shannon challenged. "And don't start talking about me going back to school."

"Okay," Janie agreed. "Since you don't need to work for money, you can do something that'll really help people. You've always cared about others. As for your agent, you know as well as I do, there are plenty of girls lined up waiting to take your place."

"I suppose you're right."

"Let's talk to the group about it after we finish the Bible study. I bet someone will come up with something."

"Good idea."

The next morning, Shannon's mother called, her voice laced with excitement. "I spoke to Melinda a few minutes ago. She's been lining up some things for you to do. We figured you could start back slowly and work your way into a full schedule."

"Don't you remember I'm not sure I'm going back?"

"I can't imagine why you wouldn't, Shannon."

"I've been thinking I might want to do something here."

"Modeling? Really, Shannon, you know New York's the best place for you. There's no way you can have a decent modeling career in Atlanta."

"No, not modeling. I was thinking about volunteering for a worthy cause. I really want to help people who aren't as fortunate as I've been."

"Let's discuss that later, okay?"

Shannon knew her mother needed time to think of an argument. "I really have to run now. I'm meeting Judd for lunch. He gets out of school early today."

"You're still seeing that schoolteacher?"

"We're friends." Shannon didn't think her mother would understand her feelings for Judd, so she didn't even try to explain them.

"Don't let this relationship get too tight," her mother warned. "I've heard Armand is coming back soon. In fact, he's been talking to Melinda, and he asked about you."

Shannon was surprised at how quickly she'd gotten over Armand. The initial shock over his departure had worn off in a matter of days, and now she realized her pain was more from injured pride than love lost.

Once she was off the phone, Shannon went into the bathroom to put on her makeup. She studied her face in the mirror. As each day passed, her scar faded a little more. It was barely visible without makeup, and once she applied her foundation, it wasn't noticeable at all. The doctors had done an excellent job of stitching up her skin. Plus, she'd eaten very healthy food, taken plenty of vitamins, and gotten more rest than she ever had in her life.

When the phone rang, a sense of dread came over her. Hopefully, it wasn't Judd having to cancel.

It wasn't.

"Hey, Shannon, this is Melinda."

"Oh, hi."

"I'll pretend you didn't sound disappointed to hear from me," Melinda said in a voice that was a little too enthusiastic. "I just spoke to your mother. She said you want to do some charity work."

"Yes, I've been thinking about it."

"That's excellent. We have a whole list of opportunities here for celebrities to make a difference. This would provide excellent exposure for you in your comeback."

"I'm not doing it for myself," Shannon informed her.

"No, of course not. You're giving your time unselfishly. But why not capitalize on your kindness?"

Shannon started to tell her she needed to run, but Melinda kept going on and on about how much good she could do for underprivileged children all over the world if she participated in one of the world adoption programs. Then she started in on women's abuse shelters and how she'd already started talking to the woman who headed up the one in New Jersey.

"We have all sorts of wonderful things planned, Shannon. I guess I don't have to tell you I'm thrilled to have you back."

"Melinda, I really need to run now. I'm meeting someone in a few minutes."

"Okay, sweetie. Just remember, if you want to help others, it's always good to have greater means. If you stay there, you won't be able to help as many people as you can if you come here. Give me a call when you have more time."

After she hung up, Shannon glanced at the clock. She had to hurry so she wouldn't be late to meet Judd.

Chapter 8

One look at Shannon, and Judd knew something was wrong. Although she was smiling, pain clouded her eyes. There was something else, too. Confusion, maybe?

"Hungry?" he asked.

A brief look of panic shot across her face, then she shook her head. "No, not really."

"Why don't we go somewhere else, then. Wanna go for a walk?"

"Yes, that might be better."

Shannon had told him she was in the habit of keeping her running shoes in her bag from being in New York and having to run from one assignment to another early in her career. He waited while she changed from her dress shoes to sneakers.

"Always prepared, aren't you?" Judd asked.

"I try to be."

"So, what's on your mind?"

Judd forced himself not to look directly at Shannon. From being around her, he knew she had a hard time putting her thoughts into words when someone was staring at her.

"I'm still hung up on what I should do with my life. It's so hard."

"That can be really tough," he agreed. "What are your thoughts so far?"

Shannon slowed her pace to a crawl. "My agent called."

"Your agent?"

"Yeah, my modeling agent. She wants me back in New York."

"But I thought. . ." He turned to face her, and they both stopped. "I thought you wanted to stay here."

"I thought so, too, but I'm not sure now."

Judd felt like his heart had been yanked out of his chest. He was speechless. Suddenly, he felt the familiar shield he'd used growing up—the one that protected his heart against getting too close to people.

"My agent, Melinda, has some things lined up for me already. I told her I was thinking about doing some charity work, and she pointed out that I could do a lot more good for people if I went back to my old career."

"How does she figure that?"

"She said I can help homeless children and abused women all over the world because of my high visibility in modeling. If I don't go back, I'm limiting the good I can do."

Anger instantly welled in Judd's chest. It was obvious to him that her agent was playing with her emotions and taking advantage of Shannon's desire to be involved in a charity and to help others with her gifts. But he couldn't point that out to her now at the risk of sounding selfish. He wanted her here in Atlanta, and he suspected she knew that.

"Which way are you leaning?" he asked, trying hard to keep his anger from showing.

She lifted her shoulders, held them up for a few seconds, and then let them drop. "I'm still confused."

"Then I guess you'd better pray about it," Judd replied before correcting himself. "*We* need to pray about it."

He took a chance and looked directly into Shannon's eyes. It took every ounce of self-restraint not to grab her hands, pull her to him, and beg her to stay. But he knew he didn't have the right to keep her from following her dream. He'd gone after his, in spite of many people advising him to go into a higher-paying profession.

"Thanks, Judd. I wish the decision were easy. Nothing's clear to me."

"Sometimes the right thing isn't clear."

Or maybe it's clear and the selfish people in your life are trying to make it muddy. Judd was dying to yell those very words at her, but he held back.

"We'll just have to keep this in prayer and trust the Lord," Judd said, feeling like he was giving lip service to something he wasn't sure he believed at the moment.

"Yes, that's what we'll do."

When she left to go home, Judd felt an emptiness in his chest. But it wasn't nearly as painful as when she announced her dilemma to the Bible study group.

"It's a difficult decision," she said, "but the opportunity is there, and I feel like I at least need to consider it."

Everyone crowded around Shannon, talking over each other, promising prayers and best wishes. Judd remained on the sidelines as he watched, feeling like the ground had been pulled out from beneath him.

Janie cornered him in the parking lot.

"How can you let her even think about doing this?" she hissed.

"In case you haven't noticed, Shannon's a grown woman," he said.

"Do you love her?"

"What?"

"You heard me. Do you love her?"

Judd didn't want to risk sounding harsh, but Janie had no right asking such a question. "I think that's between her and me. I don't care to discuss it right now."

"I thought so," she said as she backed away. "You're gonna be sorry if you don't stop her, Judd. I know how Shannon lets people jerk her around. When her mother decided she needed to go into modeling to fulfill her own dream, she pushed Shannon into it."

"I'm sure Shannon didn't mind. She's done quite well."

"By the world's standards, yes, she's done great. But I don't think she's ever been happier than she's been since she started coming to church."

"Let's give her a chance to make up her own mind, okay?" Judd said.

Janie shook her head. "Like I said, you're gonna be sorry."

❧

"Melinda's right," her mother said. "Just think of all the things you can do when you go back. If you stick around here, you're so limited."

Shannon shook her head. "I've got such a great group of friends here, though. I never had this feeling in New York."

"You have friends everywhere. All over the world, thanks to your career."

"They're nothing like my friends here in Atlanta," Shannon said.

"Is there one in particular?"

What was the point in not being honest? "Yes, you know there is."

"I know you like this boy. What's his name? Judd? Whatever. I'm sure he's nice, but he's not Armand."

No, Shannon agreed. *He's not Armand, which is a good thing.*

"There are some wonderful churches up there, too. They're all over the place."

Shannon knew there were churches everywhere, so that wasn't an arguable point. "I really missed Janie when I was in New York."

"You'll see Janie when you come to visit us."

"It's not the same."

"But you can call her whenever you feel like talking. And there's nothing stopping either of you from flying back and forth to visit. You make more than enough money to pay her way if you can't get down here."

This was another thing Shannon knew, but she also knew it wouldn't happen. When she'd first left, she and Janie planned trips and talked about it for hours. It happened a couple of times, but both of them got too busy to keep it up.

"We tried that, but it was too hard," Shannon said as she ran out of steam.

Finally, her mother drove the biggest point home. "You know all the sacrifices your father and I have made for you. This is something we've worked hard for. All parents want what's best for their children, and this is what we've worked toward all your life."

Shannon had argued in the past that modeling wasn't her life's goal, but then her mother had reminded her that all the classes, from modeling in junior high school to acting in high school, had prepared her for where she was today.

Her mother even reminded Shannon that she hadn't been able to have her own career in order to concentrate on making a good life for Shannon.

"Let me think about it some more," Shannon agreed.

"Just don't wait too long. There are hundreds, maybe even thousands, of girls waiting to take your place. You know what a dog-eat-dog world it is out there."

Yes, Shannon did know about the kind of world it was out there—which was precisely the reason she doubted she wanted to jump back into it. Her life in Atlanta had begun to feel safe, and it made sense, unlike the insanity of the life she had in New York. Even her social life there was centered on her career. She had to be seen at certain events, which took all her free time. One of the reasons she and Armand had gotten so close was that they had the same obligations. They understood each other—or at least they thought they did.

A few days passed, and Shannon began to feel numb. Her mother's words had gotten to her. With the sacrifices her parents had made, how could Shannon have considered abandoning what they worked hard to achieve? All her own desires had to take a backseat to what her mother wanted for her. Was this how the Lord chose to answer her prayers?

She'd been asking for answers—no, begging. And her mother had been very clear in her message.

One morning, right after Shannon had finished going through her apartment, dusting and tidying the place, her doorbell rang. She cast a quick glance at the wall clock and wondered who it could be at this hour. The only person who didn't have a job with regular hours was her mother, and she was supposed to be at the club with some friends.

Shannon unbolted the door and pulled it open.

"Armand!"

Shannon felt as if her life had suddenly gone into freeze frame. The man she thought she loved, once upon a time, was standing at the door of her apartment, a bouquet of flowers in his arms and a wide, perfect smile on his lips.

She went numb, but only from shock. That flutter of the heart wasn't there.

"Mind if I come in?" he asked.

"Not at all," Shannon said as she stepped to one side.

He was dressed from head to toe in designer apparel, most likely that of one of the clients who paid him handsomely to show off clothes only the best-looking, perfectly shaped, chisel-featured men could carry off.

"You look fabulous, Shannon," he said as his eyes focused on her cheek.

"Other side, Armand," she said, turning her head and tapping the side of her face with her finger.

"Oh." His smile faded as he glanced at her other side. He abruptly looked away. "You've healed. . .nicely," he stammered. He quickly regained composure as he handed her the flowers. "For the most beautiful woman on earth."

"Thanks." She took them and turned toward the kitchen. "I'll put them in water. Have a seat."

It took Shannon a few minutes to stop shaking, so she didn't hurry with filling the vase. Why hadn't he called first? It wasn't cool for him to have shown up on her doorstep without some warning, at least.

When she got back to the living room, Armand was still standing, looking very uncomfortable. "Nice place," he said. "Something like this in New York would cost thousands of dollars a month."

Leave it to him to think of money. She'd noticed that about him before, and it hadn't bothered her. But now it did.

"It's not cheap, even by Atlanta standards," she said. "I like it."

"I understand you're thinking about coming back to work."

She looked him squarely in the eye without blinking. "Yeah, and I heard you've been talking to Melinda."

Armand shrugged as he darted his gaze away from hers. He wasn't a good liar, which made this very easy. It wouldn't take long to find out what his mission was.

"What's going on, Armand? Why are you here?"

Holding his hands out, he said, "I just wanted to see you, sweetheart. We've been an item for a long time, and I missed you."

"You missed me?" *Yeah, right.* She tossed him a crooked smile of disbelief as he squirmed.

"Yes, Shannon, I can't tell you how many sleepless nights I've had since your crash."

That sounded a little too rehearsed.

"I've had a few sleepless nights, too, Armand."

He came toward her, a look of genuine concern on his face. "Because of me?"

She shrugged. She didn't want to hurt his feelings, even after what he'd done to her. "Maybe."

"It was awful for me, too." His tone was a little tight, which she knew from experience meant he wanted something.

Now she couldn't hold back. "It must have been really rough at the chalet in Europe," she said, trying to mask the sarcasm.

"Harder than you can imagine."

"Oh, I can imagine, all right," Shannon said. She was amazed at how clueless Armand could be. "So what's the deal? Melinda sent you here to make sure I come back?"

He opened his mouth, snapped it shut, then snorted. "Okay, so Melinda did ask me to talk to you. But that doesn't matter. I've missed you, you've missed me, and that's all that counts."

"Actually, that's not all that counts, Armand," Shannon informed him. "I really did miss you at first, before I realized how little I meant to you."

He gasped. "That's simply not true, Shannon. You know I had to go to Europe for that photo shoot. You mean everything to me."

"What's your excuse for not calling?"

"You know how crazy the schedule is when you're busy working."

"Oh, yeah, the schedule." Shannon sometimes worked twenty hours a day, three days in a row, just so the photographers could get the light they needed for a single picture.

"It was awful."

"Who took my place?" Shannon asked. She just now realized she didn't know, and until now, it hadn't mattered. Amazing. That should have been one of the first things she'd found out when she got out of the hospital.

"Patrice Hunt," Armand replied. "She felt terrible about what happened to you."

"I bet she did. Patrice has been watching every move I make for years, just waiting for me to mess up."

"That doesn't sound like you, Shannon."

Suddenly, she felt bad. *Catty* wasn't an adjective anyone had ever used to describe Shannon McNab. She'd been known as a playful, athletic, kindhearted girl who just happened to look gorgeous enough to be on magazine covers, television commercials, and designer runways.

"You're right, Armand," Shannon said remorsefully. "That was wrong of me. Patrice is a beautiful model who was the perfect replacement."

He reached for her. "I wouldn't say the perfect replacement. No one could ever take the place of Shannon McNab. You're the best model in the business."

Shannon pulled back and took a step away from Armand. She didn't want him touching her.

They stood and stared at each other for what seemed like forever. Armand took a tentative step toward her again, and she forced herself to stand still.

"I want you back, Shannon. I miss you something awful. Without you in my life, nothing seems real."

A shiver ran through her. His words made her want to turn and run out of her apartment, but she couldn't be rude. Armand hadn't done anything all that terrible.

"Where are you staying?" Shannon asked to avoid responding to his comment.

"The Hilton."

"Can we get together a little later in the day? I have someplace I need to be in about an hour."

"Sure, sweetheart. I just had to see you as soon as I got to town."

"Tell you what. I'll meet you in the lobby of your hotel at six. We can go somewhere for dinner and talk then."

"Sounds wonderful." Armand moved toward the door, graceful and fluid in the movement he'd learned from years of being one of the highest paid male supermodels. Shannon couldn't help but compare him to Judd, who took long, purposeful strides, his arms swinging dramatically by his side, like a man on a mission—not someone trying to sell something.

As soon as Armand left, Shannon threw on a dress, ran out to her car, and headed straight to the club where her mother played tennis and had lunch twice a week.

"Shannon!" the maitre d' shouted as she entered the main dining room. "It's been a very long time. You look lovely, dear!"

"Thanks, Maurice. Have you seen my mother?"

His smile quickly faded. "No, I just came on duty about fifteen minutes ago. Would you like for me to have one of the wait staff look for her?"

"No, that's not necessary. I can look for her, if you don't mind."

He gestured around the grand expanse of the room. "Be my guest, Shannon. You're always welcome here at my dining room."

"Thanks, Maurice. It was good seeing you."

"It's nice seeing you in person again. All these years of seeing you in magazines and TV, I feel like you never left. But you look much more beautiful in person."

As Shannon walked away, she chuckled to herself. Maurice was such a charmer, which was probably why he'd kept his job for so long. He'd been there since her parents first joined the club, back when she was in late elementary school.

There were half a dozen places where her mother could have been. Passing through the snack bar, Shannon saw that she wasn't in there. It was a small area, with booths and counter stools all in a position to offer a nice view of one of the three televisions suspended from the ceiling.

The banquet room was dark, so she didn't bother checking there. That area was reserved for special occasions, like weddings, awards banquets, or birthday parties for overprivileged children. Shannon remembered the parties her parents had thrown for her in that very room—most of them forgettable. She always preferred small gatherings in someone's living room, with Pin the Tail on the Donkey. Her mother wouldn't have dreamed of doing something so simple and unsophisticated.

She had to ask around before she found her mother in the garden terrace, a green room filled with tropical plants and flowers that took a full-time staff to maintain.

"Shannon!" her mother exclaimed when someone alerted her that her daughter was behind her. She beamed at Shannon. "What a lovely surprise!"

With a tight face, Shannon glared at her mother. "Mom, did you know Armand was in town?"

The sincere surprise that registered on her mother's face told Shannon everything she wanted to know. "Why no, but how nice for him to come!" She turned to her friends. "Remember my daughter, Shannon McNab?"

All the women grinned at her. She offered them a clipped nod then turned back to her mother, who had a beatific expression that annoyed Shannon more than she cared to admit.

"Where is he?" She craned her neck. "Did you bring him with you?"

"Sorry to disappoint you, but no. I'm meeting him later for dinner at his hotel."

"You should have brought him," her mother said. "I'm sure these ladies would have loved to meet him."

"Yes, I'm sure."

"Well, I'm glad he came to see you, Shannon. See? He does love you. He's just been very busy lately, just like you'll be once you're back in the business you know best."

"Melinda must be fully responsible for this," Shannon muttered under her breath.

Her mother talked her into hanging around for lunch with the ladies. They all gushed and cooed over how beautiful Shannon was, and she smiled, accepting their compliments as gracefully as she could. But it was more of the same old adoring-her-for-her-beauty talk, making her very uncomfortable. The only time she could relax was when her mother told them how Shannon had talked her father into helping the poor family of the man who'd crashed into her. In fact, he was up in North Carolina now, working on some roof repairs.

"A good person as well as beautiful," one of her mother's friends said, sighing.

There it was again—another comment about her physical beauty. As soon as she could, she left.

Back at home, Shannon dialed Melinda's number. "Why didn't you tell me you were sending Armand?"

"He wanted to surprise you," Melinda said in her own defense. "The man's been pining over losing you, so I rearranged his schedule for the next several days."

"Pining over me?"

"Yes. You should see how he's been moping. I was worried the clients would notice, so I figured this would be the best thing for both of you."

"Hmm. Okay, if you say so." Shannon wasn't sure what to say next.

"You are coming back with him, aren't you?" The high-pitched sound of Melinda's voice grated on Shannon's nerves.

"I'm not sure yet," Shannon admitted.

"I've got an idea. Why don't you come up here and give it a try? If you decide you don't like it anymore, fine. But at least you'll keep your place in the industry in the meantime."

"Keep my place?"

"Yes, dear. It's getting harder and harder to hold off the clients. They're all starting to wonder if something's seriously wrong with you."

"They know about the scar, right?"

"They know you were injured."

"What did you tell them?"

"I said you had some healing to do and that you'd be back as soon as you could. By the way, Armand says you look even more beautiful than before. He couldn't see even a trace of a scar on your face."

"He called you already?"

"Yes. Right after he left your apartment. You should have heard him. He was giddy with delight over seeing you. That man is completely and totally in love with you, Shannon. You're one very fortunate girl."

Shannon knew she should have been overcome with joy about the news, but she wasn't. Instead, she found herself wondering how Armand's feelings for her compared to Judd's.

As she got ready to see Armand, Shannon thought about how Armand had come all the way here to drag her back to New York. Judd, on the other hand, hadn't taken any steps to try to keep her in Atlanta. Even Janie had said she had to make the final decision herself. They'd all been praying for her, which was good. Maybe the answer to her prayer was Armand's surprise arrival.

After sorting through her jumbled thoughts, she made the decision on the way to see Armand to give modeling another try. Melinda had told her that was an option, and she didn't have to make a long-term commitment. She wouldn't sign any new contracts that would tie her down, so if she decided to go back to Atlanta, she could at any time.

As always, Armand was five minutes late. He didn't bother with an apology because punctuality wasn't in his vocabulary. This suddenly became a sore spot with Shannon, but she didn't say anything. Why had she put up with it for so long?

Throughout dinner, Armand worked on her, telling her about all the excitement in New York. Finally, she couldn't stand his sales job any longer, so she figured she might as well put him out of his misery.

"I'm going back, Armand."

"You're what?" he asked, stunned.

"I think you heard me. I'm going back to New York."

"This is wonderful news! Have you told Melinda?"

"I figured I'd call her first thing tomorrow."

Armand's eyes flickered with excitement through the rest of dinner. Neither of them ate dessert, but Shannon was dying for the chocolate cheesecake she knew the restaurant was known for. With a sigh, she resigned herself to living without desserts for as long as she remained in the modeling business.

By the time Shannon got back to her apartment, there was already a message on her machine. It was Melinda letting her know she had a test photo shoot scheduled for the following week.

Shannon knew that a test shoot meant they weren't sure she still had what it took. There was risk involved here, but she didn't feel the pressure like she once had. She'd done all this before, and it didn't matter to her any longer whether she succeeded or not.

Now all she had to do was tell her friends in Atlanta.

"Please don't go," Janie begged. "I tried my best to hold back, but I can't anymore. I think you're making a huge mistake."

"Why didn't you say something before?" Shannon asked.

"I thought you needed to make this decision without my interference."

"Since I've already committed to the photo shoot, I have to go. I'm still not sure that's what I need to do. It's only a test."

"Well, I hope you fail miserably."

Shannon laughed out loud. "Some friend you are."

"I'm the best friend you ever had," Janie said with a pout.

"You're right."

At the Bible study, when Shannon announced her big plans, Judd just sat there and stared at the wall. When the session was over, Shannon walked up to him and nudged his arm.

"You didn't say a word when I made my announcement."

He shrugged. "There wasn't much I could say."

"What do you think about me doing this?"

Judd reached down, took her hand, and held it as he looked into her eyes. Her heart stood still for a moment before he spoke.

"I think this is something you need to do, Shannon, if for no other reason but to find out if it's something you still want."

Suddenly, her heart fell with a thud. That wasn't what she wanted to hear.

Chapter 9

As Shannon left Judd, she felt empty, almost as if nothing really mattered anymore. And there was nothing to keep her in Atlanta other than her own desire to stay.

She'd expected her mother to be overjoyed, but she'd expected something completely different from Judd.

All the way to her parents' house the next morning, she braced herself for the smug satisfaction her mother was sure to show. She wasn't in the mood to deal with it, but she might as well get it over with.

"I would go with you, but I have commitments at the club," Shannon's mother said.

"Hey, don't worry about it. I'm a big girl. I lived alone in New York for years."

"I know, but this is such an important event for you, sweetheart. A turning point."

Yes, it sure was a turning point. But Shannon wasn't sure it was turning in the right direction.

"I'll be just fine. My old apartment still hasn't been leased, so I'll be able to stay there."

"I really think you should have taken Melinda up on her offer to find some roommates for you."

Shannon almost laughed at her mother this time. When she'd first moved to New York, her goal was to make enough money to move out of a crowded apartment with three other roommates. Her mother had done everything in her power to help her. And now she wanted her right back to where she'd started. No thanks. Shannon enjoyed the peace and quiet of her own place after a long day of being in front of cameras and crews who told her where to stand, what to wear, and how to look.

The time between announcing her decision and leaving went by in a blur. She stepped on the plane, hesitating for a moment as her insides lurched. Finally, she steeled herself, put one foot in front of the other, and found her seat. Why she'd bothered with booking a first-class seat was beyond her. As numb as she was, it was a total waste of money.

Melinda had a car waiting for her at LaGuardia. The driver, a stodgy middle-aged man with a frayed jacket and cap slightly resembling an old navy officer's uniform, held the door for her without uttering a single word.

He didn't wait for her to tell him where she was going before whisking her off toward Manhattan. He seemed to have a destination in mind, so she focused on the sights whizzing by.

She should have known. He pulled up in front of the mirrored building that housed the Glamour Agency, where Melinda and a few of her underlings held court. He promised to deliver her bags to her old apartment as he waited for her to go inside the building.

As she remembered, the lobby was crowded with dozens of young, fresh faces, all of them hopeful of having a career at least half as good as hers had been.

"There's Shannon McNab," she heard someone whisper.

"I don't think so," the girl next to her whispered. "I heard her face was burned beyond recognition in the car accident."

Shannon flashed her trademark smile. "Hi. I hope you girls get the contract of your dreams. Have a wonderful day."

Their eyes all widened as she breezed past them. "That *is* her," she heard as she went through the double doors without stopping at the receptionist's desk.

"Shannon!" shouted the agent in the front office. "Hey, everyone! Shannon's back!"

People came out of offices like bees out of a honeycomb, all of them hugging her and laughing with pure delight. Maybe this wasn't such a bad idea, after all. It felt good to get such a warm reception.

"Shannon!" Melinda said as she came out of her office, her arms open wide. "How wonderful to see you!"

"It's good to see you, too, Melinda." Shannon leaned over for the shorter woman to do her cheek-to-cheek greeting.

"Are you ready to get started?"

Shannon nodded. "I'm probably a little rusty, though."

Melinda flipped her hand from her wrist. "Nah. You'll do just fine. I've got several test shoots lined up."

She narrowed her eyes and studied Shannon's face.

"The scar's on this side," Shannon offered, tapping her left cheek and leaning forward.

Melinda's face lit up with delight. "I can't see it at all. Now we only need to wait and see what the camera tells us. The lighting they use will tell the whole story of your future in a second."

Shannon gulped. So that was what it all boiled down to.

Throughout the years she'd been modeling, Shannon hadn't deluded herself into thinking she'd get this much attention if she hadn't been beautiful enough to land such great modeling gigs. But she did feel like once people got to know her, they liked her for who she was deep down. However, the doubts continued to plague her—even now, seven months after Armand had walked away from her.

"Let's get moving, shall we?" Melinda had already started gesturing and motioning for her assistants to get back to their desks and get to work putting Shannon's career back in motion.

By the end of the day, Shannon was exhausted. The driver dropped her off in front of the building she'd once called home. At least she knew where everything was.

The stark white furniture and light wood floors nearly blinded her when she walked inside and flipped on the light. She walked through the apartment and saw that everything had been cleaned for her homecoming. Melinda had thought of everything, all the way down to stocking her refrigerator with Shannon's favorite yogurt and bottled water.

Someone had unpacked her suitcases, which were lined up in the back of her room-sized walk-in closet. All she had to do for herself was eat a quick snack, change into her pajamas, and turn down the covers.

Sleep came easily for Shannon, as exhausted as she was. But when the alarm clock buzzed at five thirty, she was already awake. The sounds of the city had startled her from her sleep, and she hadn't been able to turn off the thoughts that had popped into her mind.

She met Melinda at seven to get her schedule. Then she let the driver take her around to get quick snapshots and fifteen- to thirty-second takes on film. In spite of how busy she was, images of Judd flashed through her mind, and she wondered what he was doing. Was he lecturing? Or was he spending time going over an assignment with one of the seventh graders he cared about so much? She'd never known anyone like him before, and she doubted she ever would again.

Judd's suggestion about doing what she was called to do played over and over in her mind. Had the Lord sent Armand to her so she could go back to modeling? Or was this just temptation designed as a test? Whatever it was didn't feel right at the moment.

"Stop frowning, Shannon," the photographer said. "Where's that spark?"

"I'm sorry, Pete. I've sort of gotten out of the groove."

"Think happy thoughts. You and Armand strolling through Central Park."

Shannon took a deep breath and imagined herself with Armand. *That doesn't do it*, she thought as she felt her forehead growing tight. Then she remembered Judd's kiss.

"That's it, Shannon! You've got it, girlfriend!"

The quick clicking sounds of the camera were familiar to Shannon, bringing back all sorts of memories of France, Italy, and Spain. She'd spent several summers in Europe doing photo shoots and developing an international presence.

After three days of grueling photo and filming sessions, Shannon sank back on the sofa in Melinda's office. "Now what?" she asked.

Melinda shrugged. "Now we play the waiting game. We have to see how you do on film."

No matter how well known Shannon once was, in spite of how she'd recovered, her entire future modeling career hinged on lighting, cameras, and illusion. That very thought put a knot in her stomach.

Playing the waiting game didn't mean they sat back and did nothing. Melinda had arranged for Armand to escort Shannon to various functions, dropping hints in the media that he'd been by her bedside, worrying over her, being her motivation to get back to work. She even had the nerve to capitalize on Shannon's desire to help others who were less fortunate than her.

"I haven't done all this," Shannon growled at Melinda as she read the package put together for her new media campaign. "This article says I've been working with the homeless in Atlanta."

"You haven't yet," Melinda offered. "But you will. As soon as we get the results of the photos, we're setting up a homeless shelter with your name on it. It's such a brilliant move, I don't know why I didn't think of it before. In fact, I think I'll do it for all my top models in their hometowns." She leaned back in her chair and added, "Just think of what it'll do for your career."

This whole thing made Shannon sick to her stomach. Her motive hadn't been to help her career. She sincerely wanted to help people. And she wanted to do it because she felt like that was what Jesus wanted her to do.

The following week, Shannon noticed that Armand had suddenly disappeared from her itinerary. He'd been outwardly attentive to her lately, but she felt like they'd lost a deep personal connection. He smiled at all the right times, and he knew exactly when a camera was about to click. That was when he gazed lovingly into her eyes or gently placed his hand on her back to guide her as they walked to a celebrity function. It was all show and had no substance.

Life for Shannon was beginning to feel like an empty shell. Nothing had really changed. Why had she not seen this before?

"Where's Armand?" Shannon asked Melinda the morning they'd agreed to get together to go over the results all the photographers had sent by courier.

"He's getting ready to go back on the European tour," Melinda said as she stuck her letter opener in the envelope and started ripping.

"Isn't it a little early for that? They usually have the European tour during the summer, don't they?"

"You know how this business works, Shannon. We have to move schedules up all the time to get a head start on the competition."

Funny how Armand never mentioned he was leaving. If they were as close as the media said they were, surely they would have discussed his tour.

Deep down, Shannon didn't care. However, it did hurt her pride. The whole thing with Armand was forced and awkward. It didn't feel right.

Being with Judd felt right.

Shannon blew out a sigh as Melinda read the reports. When she looked up with a twitching grin, Shannon knew the results were good.

"You're back in business, Shannon. Not a single camera saw your scar."

"Great!" Shannon replied, although she didn't feel as good as she hoped she sounded.

"No doubt you'll get contract-renewal offers from all the former clients. We'll have to review them and see if they're worthwhile. I'm also putting out some feelers for some new contracts."

"But why? If the old companies want me back, don't you think you should consider them first?"

Melinda glanced at her from above her glasses perched on the tip of her nose. "Bargaining power, Shannon. This business thrives on competition. People want what someone else has. That's how you make money in the image market."

The image market. That's what Shannon was in. It was all image. Illusion. Nothing real.

She slowly nodded. "I understand."

Melinda grinned. "Yes, I know you do. That's why you've done so well. You deliver what the client wants. Every woman wants to be you, Shannon. As long as we have that, you have a career in modeling."

How sad that people wanted her life when she wasn't sure she wanted it. Shannon stood and crossed the room to the door.

"One more thing, Shannon, before you leave."

Shannon stopped and turned to face Melinda. "What's that?"

"Armand is having an intimate get-together at Pierre's. Sort of a going-away party. He'll pick you up this evening at eight thirty."

Shannon nodded. All she wanted was to hang around in her apartment and read her Bible, but she knew she had to maintain this image thing Melinda had stressed from the moment they'd met.

On the way to the party that night, Armand turned to her, lifted her hand to his lips, and looked into her eyes. "Shannon, I'll be gone for a few weeks, but I feel that what we once had is worth bringing back."

She blinked as she stared back at him. He kissed her hand again and instructed the driver to hurry a little faster.

Throughout the evening, as people hugged and patted her, Shannon felt like she was living someone else's life. None of the chatter seemed significant to her. It was all about who was doing what and where they were going. There was no discussion of any relevance to her as a Christian. She could only imagine what

Jesus would do in this room. That thought brought a smile to her lips.

"You look positively gorgeous," Armand said as he offered her a glass of sparkling water. "Everyone's thrilled you're back in town."

She smiled back at him and took a sip of her water. More than anything, she wanted the comfort of her friends who didn't care what she looked like.

"Armand?" she asked slowly.

At first, he didn't respond, but when she gently placed her hand on his shoulder, he turned to her. "Yes?"

"Do you ever think about eternity?"

He let out a nervous chuckle. "Not much. It's hard enough to worry about the here and now."

"I'm not talking about worry. I'm talking about. . ."

He winked. "I know where you're going with this. We can discuss our plans for the future when I get back."

She started to correct him and mention how her whole perspective had changed—how she now thought about her life in relation to her walk in the faith. But he'd already turned around and gotten into a conversation about the latest men's hairstyling product he was promoting. This obviously wasn't the time or place to discuss eternity with Jesus.

When Shannon began to yawn, Armand smiled. "I'm tired, too. We can leave in a few minutes if you want."

With a nod, Shannon replied, "That would be nice."

They were on their way to Shannon's building half an hour later. Armand walked her to the door, where the doorman pretended not to be listening.

"It's wonderful having you here with me, Shannon. I look forward to a long career and life together."

"But. . ."

He lifted a finger and held it to her lips to shush her. "I know, it's going to be hard being apart for the next several weeks, but it'll be good for both of us. We'll have time to think about the time ahead."

He left her with the doorman and got back into the limo before Shannon had a chance to respond. He lowered the window, blew her a kiss, and waved before the car sped off.

Once inside her apartment, she stepped out of her shoes, leaned against the wall, and rubbed her aching feet. It had been months since she'd worn high heels.

Shannon felt like talking to someone who understood. She glanced at the clock on the mantel and realized she'd have to wait until morning to call Janie, who was probably in bed, sound asleep by now.

After setting her clock and slipping into her nightclothes, Shannon reached for the Bible she'd brought to New York. Settling under the covers, she opened to the book of Matthew, where she often found comfort. She read chapter 9 over and over, taking to heart Jesus' healing power. He'd healed her physically and emotionally. Now she prayed that she'd be given the strength to do what she knew was right.

If she stayed in New York, she'd need to find a way to stay spiritually grounded. Janie would know what to do.

Shannon closed her Bible, turned off the light, and snuggled down under the covers. Light from the city filtered through her sheers, so the room wasn't completely dark. She watched the shadows dancing on the wall and listened to the sounds from the street below until her eyelids grew heavy.

The alarm woke her early, before the sun came up. She sat up, rubbed her eyes, and trudged to the kitchen, flipping lights on along the way.

When she was fairly certain Janie would be up and almost ready for the day, she reached for the phone in the kitchen and punched in Janie's number. She answered right away.

At first, Janie sounded excited to hear from her, but after Shannon asked for advice, her voice became cool and distant. "I can't tell you what to do, Shannon."

"I'm not asking you what to do. All I want is for you to pray for me."

"You didn't have to call to ask for that. I've been praying for you nearly all my life."

When Shannon hung up, she felt even worse than she had before she'd called. The rest of the day, all she could think about was Janie's attitude. It hurt.

After spending most of the day with Melinda and running a few errands, Shannon went back up to her apartment. No matter how hard she tried to resist calling Judd, she knew she had to hear his voice. He sounded thrilled to hear from her.

"Hey, how's it going?" he asked.

"Oh, pretty good. I did great on the test shoots."

"I knew you would. So, when will we see your mug on TV? Anytime soon?"

"I'm not sure. There's still a bunch of preliminary stuff that has to be done."

"You don't sound overjoyed."

"I'm not, Judd. In fact, I've been miserable since I've been here. I miss all of you so much, I'm thinking about coming back."

He let out a chuckle. "You haven't exactly given it much of a chance. It takes more time than a week or two to get back into the swing of things."

"But I loved the way things were in Atlanta. I miss the Bible study group. I miss you and Janie and Paul and. . ."

"Find a group up there. New York is a big place. I'm sure you can connect with a Christian Bible study if you ask around."

"Yeah, you're right," Shannon said as her heart fell. She didn't realize it when she first placed the call, but now she knew she'd been hoping he'd beg—or at least encourage—her to come back.

They chatted for a few minutes, until Judd said he had a parent-teacher conference in an hour and he really needed to go.

"Don't give up so quickly, Shannon," he said before they got off the phone. "And if you can't find a Bible study group, I'll ask Uncle Garrett if he knows someone. He has friends all over the world. I bet he can hook you up in no time."

"Thanks, Judd."

She dropped the phone back into the cradle and leaned back on her elbows. Everything seemed wrong to her.

Miserable, she figured she might as well find a way to entertain herself tonight and then, tomorrow, she'd look for a place to worship on Sunday. It wouldn't be easy, because none of her acquaintances in New York went to church. Sunday was their day to sleep in, when agents wouldn't bug them and clients spent time with their families and friends.

The first services Shannon attended were in a small church three blocks away from her apartment building. The preacher was an elderly gentleman whose bifocals kept falling off his nose. The man next to her kept nodding off to sleep, while the woman in the pew directly in front of her struggled to keep up with her two toddlers, who kept trying to climb over the back of the pew. Shannon had a very hard time concentrating on the message.

After church was over, she went up to the pastor and asked about singles' Bible study classes. Shaking his head, he said, "No, we haven't tried that here. I'm not sure how it would go over. Maybe. . ." He squinted as he adjusted his glasses again. "Do I know you from somewhere, missy? You look awful familiar."

"No," Shannon replied, shaking her head and backing away. "I don't think so. Thanks for the good service, Pastor." Then she turned and ran out of the church before he figured out who she was and where he'd seen her.

The following Sunday, she went to a different church—this one a little bigger and a little closer to Greenwich Village. The crowd was younger, and the services were more contemporary. Maybe they'd have something similar to what her church in Atlanta had.

When the pastor asked everyone to turn to greet those around them, she shook the woman's hand behind her and asked if they had singles' Bible studies. The woman's eyes widened, she nudged the woman next to her, and they both squealed.

"I can't believe Shannon McNab is actually here!" the second woman said. That got everyone's attention, and before Shannon realized what had happened, she was signing everyone's church bulletin.

After church, all the people who hadn't been sitting close enough to get her autograph were thrusting pieces of paper and pens in her face, scrambling to get her signature. One man even asked her to pose for a picture with his teenage daughter. Shannon did it, then ran out as fast as she could to hail a taxi.

This wasn't working out. All she wanted was quiet worship on Sunday and a group to study the Bible with. Why was she having so much trouble in New York? It couldn't be that hard, could it?

Apparently so. The following Sunday was like a repeat of what had already happened. Shannon got to her apartment feeling like she'd been beaten in a very long race.

Armand was scheduled to return later on the next week. Melinda had a welcome-back party scheduled for the day after his arrival. She had always been good about celebrating every event in the lives of her superstars.

Doing as she was told, Shannon was there, waiting. She was one of the dozen people Melinda had invited to her office to greet Armand. He gasped, acting surprised, then crossed over to where Shannon stood. Placing his arm around her shoulders, he leaned over and whispered, "We need to talk."

Shannon nodded while Melinda grabbed him by the hand and pulled him off to the side to discuss some urgent business. She didn't keep him long, but it gave Shannon enough time to catch her breath before it was time to leave.

In the car, on the way to her place, Armand turned to her. "So how were things for you while I was gone?"

Shannon shrugged. "I went to a different church every Sunday."

He tilted his head back and howled, like she'd told him a very funny joke. She didn't see the humor in the situation.

Dropping the smile, he said, "You don't need church, Shannon. Maybe you did after your accident, but things are all better now. You're modeling again."

Shannon sat there staring straight ahead as her thoughts tumbled over each other.

"Hey, what's wrong? Aren't you happy about how things are turning out? Isn't this what you wanted?"

"I'm not sure about modeling, but I do know one thing. I love the Lord, and I want to find a church where I can worship Him without feeling like I'm sitting in a fishbowl."

"That's silly," he said. "Your life was always good, long before you ever went to church. What did all those people in Atlanta tell you?"

She looked him in the eye. "Armand, I feel sorry for you. Without Jesus in your life, you're lost. Until I understood all He did to save people like us, I had no idea. But now I know, and I don't want to turn my back on my Savior."

Armand rubbed his hand over his mouth as he shook his head. Shannon sensed his discomfort, but she didn't say what she knew it would take to make

97

him smile again. She couldn't lie to him and say she didn't need the Lord now that she had modeling back in her life. One was nothing but shallow, empty promises—an illusion—while the other was eternal and solid.

"Look, Shannon, why don't you go on inside and get some sleep? I'll come over in the morning with breakfast."

Nodding, Shannon hopped out of the car and scurried in past the doorman while Armand's car sped off. She sensed that things were about to come to a head between her and Armand.

The next morning, when Shannon got up, she put on some jogging pants and a T-shirt and didn't bother with makeup. All she did was brush her teeth and wash her face before running a brush through her hair, letting it fall freely over her shoulders.

When she opened the door to Armand, he shuddered. "Go make yourself presentable, Shannon. This is so not like you."

"It is me, Armand. The real me."

"I've never seen this side of you."

"That's because you've never really looked, Armand."

"Your image—"

She cut him off. "I don't care about image—especially when I'm just hanging out around the apartment. Do you care how I look?"

He reached up and touched his perfectly styled hair and made a grimace. "I guess I do sort of care."

"Fine. Then find someone else who cares, because I don't."

Shannon was shocked at the words that had tumbled so easily from her mouth, but she felt free and relieved it was out. She really didn't care what he thought. And now he knew.

"You haven't been yourself lately. Maybe that accident was more traumatic than we realized."

"No, Armand. Now I am being myself. The way I was before the accident wasn't the real me." She gestured toward the kitchen. "I've got some tea ready. What'd you bring for breakfast?"

Shannon nibbled on the croissant and fruit Armand had brought, while he just sat there staring at the wall behind her. He clearly didn't want to look at her without makeup.

When he left, Shannon suspected she'd never see him again outside the agency, which was fine. He wasn't the right man for her anyway. This had been the second time he'd bolted when her image wasn't what he wanted. He only loved her when she was picture perfect. In other words, he loved her image and not the real Shannon McNab.

The man she truly loved was Judd. Shannon longed for things the way they were back in Atlanta. She had an urge to call Janie and talk, and if Janie acted cool and distant, she'd fuss at her until she loosened up.

"Whoa, Shannon, slow down," Janie said after Shannon rattled off all her feelings. "Let me see if I got this right. You don't like New York or modeling, and you don't ever want to see Armand again. You miss Atlanta and the church, and you're pretty sure you're in love with Judd."

"That's right," Shannon said firmly.

"Are you sure about this?"

"Positive."

"Okay, then I guess it's okay to tell you Judd's in love with you, too. He's been a wreck since you've been gone."

Shannon's heart fluttered before falling again. "Why doesn't he let me know?"

Janie laughed out loud. "You're not stupid, Shannon. It's pretty obvious. Here you are, a supermodel, bringing down more money in a year than he'll make in a lifetime. He's a school teacher in a small Atlanta suburb, and he's never even sure if his shoes match half the time."

"I don't care about all that."

"Maybe you don't, but he does."

"Judd has never cared if I wore makeup or not."

"He probably never even noticed," Janie agreed.

"And he was nice to me, even when my scar was bright red."

"We all have scars, Shannon. Judd knows that. It's just that some of us have scars on our faces, and others have them hidden inside."

"That's what I love about you, Janie."

"I know, I know. I don't beat around the bush."

"What should I do?"

"How would I know? I've never been faced with anything like this before."

"I don't know if I want to model anymore, but I do know one thing. I don't want to stay here. I want to come back and be with my friends."

"If you come back here, you sure won't get those big modeling contracts you get up there."

"Maybe I can commute."

"Now that's a thought."

"Thanks, Janie."

"For what? Confusing you?"

Melinda called three hours later. "Are you feeling okay, Shannon?"

"Sure, I'm fine. How about you, Melinda?"

"Never mind me. Armand's worried about you."

"Tell him to relax. There's nothing wrong with me."

"Good," Melinda said, her voice tight with excitement. "Because I've got some wonderful news for you."

"You do?"

"We've just been offered a two-year extension on the corn chips contract, and I think we can renew the makeup contract before the week's over. Looks like you're really back, Shannon McNab."

Shannon's insides clenched as Melinda went over all the details. Dread washed over her with each statement and contract point. How would she ever get out of this?

"Well?" Melinda finally said. "Aren't you excited?"

Chapter 10

Shannon gulped. For most people, this would be the best news ever. But not for her. Not now, anyway.

"Can I get back with you on this, Melinda?"

"What are you talking about, Shannon? This is exactly what we were hoping would happen."

"Yes, I know, but. . ." Her voice trailed off. She wasn't yet sure how to handle this.

"Tell you what, Shannon. Come to my office first thing tomorrow morning. Maybe by then you'll be over the shock of all this good news. That'll give us time to have all the paperwork in."

Panic gripped her throat.

"Shannon?" Melinda said. "Are you still there?"

"Yes, I'm here. I'll see you in the morning."

The second Shannon got off the phone with Melinda, she dialed Pastor Manning's office back in Atlanta. He answered.

She started right in, talking ninety miles an hour, explaining everything, baring her deepest thoughts and feelings, including how much she cared for his nephew.

"I can tell you've been doing quite a bit of thinking," he said when she slowed down to catch a breath.

"What do you think about me commuting?"

"I have no idea how your business works, Shannon. You'll have to decide that."

"What would Judd say?" she said, her voice softer as she asked one of the hardest questions she'd ever asked.

"I'm not sure that matters. I do know he wants you to be happy, though." He paused before asking, "Do you want to continue modeling?"

"I'm not sure."

"Maybe you'd better decide that before you take your next step. Just don't sign anything until you're positive you want to wrap years of your life around something so demanding."

"I'd like to ask one favor of you, Pastor."

"Sure, what's that?"

"Please don't discuss any of this with Judd. I'd like to be the one to bring it up."

"That goes without saying. I never reveal anyone's private conversation, even to LaRita. My family understands that about me."

"But I would like for you to tell Judd I've been thinking about him."

"He'll be glad to hear that, I'm sure."

"I don't know what I'd do without all of you," Shannon said as her eyes misted.

"You wouldn't have such a dilemma, would you?"

She laughed. "I guess not."

"Let's say a prayer, shall we?"

Shannon closed her eyes as Pastor Manning prayed for her wisdom for her in this monumental decision. He prayed for her continued healing and her witness to the people she came in contact with every day. "In Your name, Jesus, amen."

"Amen," Shannon whispered before saying good-bye to Pastor Manning.

By the next morning, Shannon knew what she was going to do. There was no way she could give 100 percent to her modeling career if she commuted from Atlanta. She had enough experience to know how grueling the assignments were, and putting herself through that would be too stressful and distracting from her faith. The Lord didn't intend for any of His followers to have more on their plates than they could handle.

There were plenty of hurdles she had to deal with now that she'd made up her mind. First of all, she needed to discuss this with Melinda, who would never understand. Shannon didn't expect to have an easy time of it, explaining how she'd chosen to walk away from a career Melinda had carefully crafted for her. Although Shannon was grateful, she had to be firm.

Armand would give a little resistance, but she knew his attention span was short. He'd argue for a little while, but he'd quickly get over her and move on to the next flavor of the month. What they had was a boatload of mutual professional respect—not love. She'd tell him that, and he might or might not understand.

The hardest person to talk to would be her mother. Not only had Sara McNab been known to be the proverbial stage mom, but her daughter was living her dream. Shannon knew she had to brace herself for some of the biggest guns her mother would pull out—quite likely the guilt speech about how she'd given up everything so Shannon could have the life she was so carelessly turning her back on.

Melinda greeted her the next morning, smiling and chipper. "Ready to sign for the next two years, Shannon? Things are looking up for you."

"Uh, Melinda, we need to talk."

Shannon gently guided Melinda back into the office, where she sat down and started explaining what she planned to do. Melinda's face turned pasty white, but she didn't utter a word until Shannon was finished.

"You're making the biggest mistake of your life, Shannon. These people were reluctant to take a chance on you. I had to twist a few arms to get these contracts."

"I know," Shannon replied. "And I appreciate what you've done, Melinda."

"You have no idea."

"You've been like a second mother to me."

Melinda stared a hole through her, making her feel like she'd committed some sort of sin.

"Do you want me to be miserable?" Shannon finally asked.

Rather than answer directly, Melinda stood from her chair, nodded toward the door, and said, "You may leave now, Shannon. And don't even try to make another comeback. I'll make sure you never get another decent contract again."

"Melinda," Shannon said. "I'm—"

"Good-bye, Shannon," Melinda said as she moved toward the door and grabbed the knob. "I'll deal with the clients. There's no need for you to contact anyone."

This was final. Shannon had never seen such a staunch expression on Melinda's face before. As she passed her agent, she turned and smiled, but Melinda didn't bother to acknowledge her. Once she'd gotten out the door, it shut so quickly, she could feel the breeze behind her.

Shannon went straight to her apartment and dialed Armand's cell phone number. He picked it up right away.

"What do you think you're doing, Shannon?" he bellowed.

"You know?"

"Yes, I know. Melinda called me right after you left her office."

"I want a life that's truly my own," Shannon replied. "I want to go back to Atlanta and have my old friends."

"You do realize we're finished, then, don't you?" he asked.

"Yes, Armand. I realized that a long time ago."

"Good-bye, Shannon."

When she hung up, she realized she could never turn back now. She'd closed some doors, walked the plank, and burned bridges. From now on, she'd have to free fall and land wherever the Lord put her. Every single cliché she'd ever heard about moving on with life entered her mind.

Suddenly, she burst into a fit of giggles. Nervous giggles. Shannon McNab was now a civilian—not the famous supermodel she once was. Sure, she still had some ads in print, and she'd see her commercials on television until they played out. But once they were over, that was it. She needed to look ahead and find a new purpose in life.

It was exhilarating but scary. She'd never done anything so drastic in her life.

Although she considered herself a strong woman, she hated the idea of hurting her mother, which she knew was inevitable. Now it was time to place the dreaded call to her parents.

She picked up the phone and started punching in the numbers, but before she pushed the last number, she hung up. No matter how much she needed to do this, she simply couldn't.

After several false starts, Shannon finally gave up and decided this was news best delivered in person. She called the airline and made reservations to Atlanta for the next day.

&

Once she arrived in Atlanta and picked up her luggage, she headed straight for the first taxi she saw. After giving the driver directions, she settled back in her seat and shut her eyes. This would be difficult at best—maybe even the most emotional experience she'd ever have to deal with once her parents realized she'd completely shut the door on modeling.

"Thanks," she said as she paid the cab driver and pulled her bags from the trunk.

Standing at the curb for several seconds, Shannon shut her eyes and said a prayer for guidance and strength. Then she trudged forward.

The front door was unlocked when she turned the knob. "Mom!" she hollered once inside the Williamsburg-style home.

Her mother suddenly appeared, her eyes wide, her face pasty white. "Shannon! What are you doing home? Has something happened?" She took Shannon by the arm and led her to the couch in the living room.

"I'm just fine, Mom. Nothing happened."

Shannon's dad came into the room and gave her a hug. "Good to see you, sweetie."

"Good to see you, too, Dad."

He let go and grinned at her. "I did all the repairs for that family in North Carolina. The man's wife was grateful, and she let me know his drinking problem had been turning their family upside down. She told me to thank you for being so understanding."

Shannon felt a lump in her throat and couldn't speak. She reached out and squeezed her father's hand.

"I thought you were back at work in New York," her mother said. "What are you doing here?"

Shannon cleared her throat and started slowly but managed to get the story out as her mother's eyes glistened with tears. She could tell she was ripping the heart out of the woman who'd sacrificed everything just so she could have the princess-style life of a supermodel.

"I just can't believe all this," her mother said. "You're throwing it all away."

"No, I'm not, Mom. I had a wonderful time modeling. Now I'm ready for something more challenging."

"What can be more challenging than what you were doing in New York?"

"I want to live the type of life that would be pleasing to Jesus."

"Don't tell me you've done all this for religion."

Shannon paused to carefully choose her words. Since her mother had never had a personal relationship with Jesus, she didn't understand what Shannon was talking about. To her mother, anything related to church was lumped into the category of "religion."

"It's not for religion," Shannon said slowly. "I just can't continue going through the motions of pretending to be something I'm not."

"But you're beautiful, and everyone wants to see your face in magazines and on TV."

"That's just an image, Mom."

Shannon watched her mother as everything sank in. They stood in silence as her mother's initial shock turned to grief then anger.

"Shannon McNab, what you've just done is as good as slapping me in the face."

"I'd never do that. I love you and Dad. I just want you to understand."

"Well, I don't understand, and I'm not sure I ever will."

Shannon's father remained silent, watching, his fingers steepled in front of him.

"Dad, do you understand?" Shannon asked. Until now, he'd never said a word about his feelings.

He started to nod before glancing at her mom. Then he took a step back before speaking. "Shannon, honey, I'm okay with whatever you want to do. If you're tired of modeling and need to be in Atlanta, for whatever reason, it doesn't matter; I'm glad to have you here. Life's too short to be unhappy."

"But—," her mother said before he silenced her with a stern look Shannon had never seen him use before.

"Shannon's a grown woman with plenty of money, Sara. She doesn't need anything from us. All she's asking for is understanding. I think we owe her that. She's been a model daughter, no pun intended, and I'm proud of her whether she's a model in New York or a churchgoing Atlanta girl."

"Thanks, Dad." Suddenly a thought occurred to Shannon. "Would you two like to go to church with me sometime?"

Her mother started shaking her head, but her father lifted both eyebrows. "We just might do that. If it's good enough to bring you all the way back to Atlanta, there must be something to it."

"That's not all that brought me back," Shannon admitted. "There's this guy. . ."

"But what about Armand?" her mom said between gasps.

"I'm not sure about Armand," Shannon told her.

"What's there not to be sure of? You and Armand were an item. Everyone knew the two of you were in love. You were the perfect couple."

"Not perfect," Shannon said. "And not in love. It was just the image of being in love."

"I don't know if you even know the meaning of love, Shannon. Armand was good to you. He looked at you with adoring eyes, and he took you to the nicest places."

"So he could be seen," Shannon explained.

"What does this other guy do for a living?" her mother asked.

"He teaches school."

"Very honorable profession," her father said. "And I see nothing wrong with our daughter dating a schoolteacher."

"But a teacher doesn't make nearly enough money to support our daughter in the style she's used to."

"Wait a minute," Shannon said, figuring it was time to interject her two cents. "Who said anything about him supporting me? All I said was that I liked him."

"You always have to think about these things," her mother told her. "Especially at your age."

"Give it up, Sara," her father told her. "Our daughter is smart. She can figure out what she wants. If she's tired of modeling and hanging out with her male-model friend, she's earned the right to come down here and be with anyone she wants."

Shannon offered her father a smile of gratitude. He didn't talk much, but when he did speak, his words meant something.

Her next surprise visit would be to church on Sunday. She hadn't let anyone know she'd be there. Hopefully, she'd find her friends to be as welcoming this time as they had been when she'd first met them.

Fortunately, she'd held on to her apartment, so she wouldn't have to stay with anyone. Her car had been at her parents' house, so she drove it home. When she got there, she pulled the curtains and blinds open, then started dusting. Since no one knew she was coming, the place hadn't been prepared. She liked the fact that she had something to do to keep her busy until Sunday.

After dusting and running the vacuum over the carpet, she took off for the grocery store to stock up on essentials, like bottled water, yogurt, veggies, fish, and chicken. And now that she didn't have to watch her figure quite as closely, she made a side trip down the ice cream aisle, grabbing her favorite flavor, creamy pistachio.

On Saturday she had to resist the urge to call Janie. As much as she knew she could trust her best friend, she didn't want to take a chance on people finding out. She wanted everyone to know at the same time that she was back to stay. That way no one's feelings would get hurt.

Shannon was a lot more conscious of how she dressed Sunday morning. She didn't want to stand out, but she knew people would stare from shock. She chose navy slacks and a tan turtleneck. She brushed her hair to a glossy shine and let it flow freely over her shoulders. One quick glimpse in the mirror let her know she looked fresh, clean, and ready to face the people who mattered most to her.

❧

"Shannon!"

LaRita Manning was the first person to spot her when she pulled into the parking lot. Pulling her husband by the hand, LaRita came running, her arms open wide and ready for a hug.

"I'm so happy to see you! I thought you were still in New York. What brings you to Atlanta? Are you on location?"

Shannon smiled back, suddenly feeling shy. "No, I'm just here because I want to be here."

"Great reason for coming." She turned and hollered, "Hey, Judd, look who's here!"

Before Shannon could catch her breath, she found herself surrounded by all her friends from the Bible study—all except Janie. She glanced over her shoulder, then back to the group.

"Looking for someone?" she heard from the side.

"Janie!" Shannon ran over to her and lifted her off her feet.

"Put me down, Amazon Woman."

They both cracked up. It had been years since Shannon had heard Janie call her Amazon Woman, a name she'd used back in junior high school when Shannon shot up in height before anyone else. She stood a head taller than any guy in their grade until a few years later in high school.

When Judd approached, she noticed how a small smile twitched at the corners of his lips, but he never said a word. He just stood there, gazing at her as if he wasn't sure this was for real.

Shannon sat between Janie and Judd during church. It felt good to be sandwiched between two people she loved. After the services ended, Janie told her she wished she'd known she was visiting, or she wouldn't have made plans.

"That's okay," Shannon tried to assure her. "I'm not visiting. I'm here for good."

Janie offered a look of disbelief. "I'll call you later this week."

"I'm sorry, too," Judd said as he stood a few feet away, his hands thrust deep in his pockets. "I'm working with some kids in my class on the school play."

"Hey, don't worry about it," Shannon said. "Will you be at the Bible study tomorrow night?"

"Of course. I'm always there."

"Good. I'll see you then."

Judd nodded, but she could tell he was guarded. It was painfully obvious that no one believed she was here to stay.

"Can we ride to the Bible study together?" Shannon asked, feeling like it was time for boldness.

After a brief hesitation, Judd nodded. "I'll pick you up at six thirty."

She'd hoped he might offer to go to dinner first, but she figured this was better than nothing. "See you then."

&

From the moment Shannon got in Judd's car to the time they arrived at the church, he talked about the kids at the school where he taught.

At first, Shannon listened with interest, but soon she realized he was using an evasion technique. He didn't want to talk about anything personal.

"Stop," she finally said when they pulled into the parking lot.

Resting his hand on top of the steering wheel, he turned to her. "This is my life, Shannon. I love what I do. Just like you love what you do." Being the perfect gentleman, he came around to her side of the car and held it as she got out, but he still hadn't warmed up to her.

"Thanks, Judd," she whispered. She hadn't corrected him or tried to explain anything. It was painfully evident words wouldn't change anything; she'd have to prove that she was here because she wanted a permanent change in her life. She wanted to live in a more Christ-centered way.

Shannon wasn't up on what they were studying, but now she knew she could sit back and listen. No one thought any worse of her for doing that, and she was comfortable with this knowledge.

She briefly reflected on her first time at the Bible study. She'd felt like a fish out of water. Now she felt the connection between these followers of Christ. A warmth flooded her as she thought about the value of what she'd learned.

Once the study session was over, each person shared events from their lives since the last meeting. They prayed for each other, friends, and families. Then everyone turned to Shannon, waiting for an explanation.

Suddenly feeling put on the spot, Shannon lifted her shoulders, grinned, and said, "It's great to be back. I'll participate more next week, after I have a chance to catch up." She looked around at all the wide-eyed people and added, "I'm here to stay. I'm not kidding."

No one said anything. They just looked at each other before breaking for the evening. Shannon got the impression they didn't believe her about coming back.

Janie gave her a perfunctory hug before taking off. Shannon stood and stared after the friend she'd known longer than anyone else. This reception wasn't what she expected. No one was mean, but there was a distance she hadn't anticipated.

As she and Judd walked to his car, she turned to him. "Can we go somewhere and talk?"

"Sure, that's fine. Where?"

"How about the Dunk 'n' Dine? I'm kind of in the mood for some of their fabulous pancakes."

"Your wish is my command," he said as he wriggled his eyebrows.

All the way to the restaurant, Judd told one anecdote after another, making her laugh. But she knew he was avoiding discussing anything with meaning. Had she caused this?

"I'll have the Monster Stack," Shannon said, pointing to the picture on the plastic menu.

"You said you were in the mood for pancakes, but I never expected this," Judd said as he leaned on his forearms. "Aren't you worried about watching your figure? I've always heard cameras add at least ten pounds."

"Haven't you been listening to me?" she countered. "I told you I'm here to stay. I'm not going back to New York. My modeling days are over. I want to stay here."

"But why?"

"Because this is real. What I had in New York was just a dream. One scar that doesn't go away, and the image is shattered."

"But your scar did go away. You can have your old life back."

Shannon groaned. "Sometimes, Judd Manning, you can be impossible."

He chuckled. "That's part of my charm."

"Yes, you're right," she agreed.

A serious look replaced his grin. "Okay, so let's say you do stick around. What then?"

"I don't know. Why don't we take it one day at a time?"

"You'll have to understand if it takes awhile for everyone to accept this as a reality," he said. "We care about you, but we don't want to have our hearts broken again."

Shannon understood. And he was right. She'd taken off at the first sign that she might be able to have her old career back. How could they ever believe she was serious about staying and this was what she really wanted after how she'd taken off so quickly?

Judd drove her home after they finished eating. As he walked her to her door, she reached out and took his hand. He didn't pull away, which was a good start. Shannon had to hold on to what little bit of hope she could find. When they reached her doorstep, Shannon hoped he might kiss her. But he didn't. He reached out, tweaked her nose, and then took a step back, almost as if he'd been burned.

"G'night, Shannon. See ya on Sunday."

With a heavy heart, she said, "Good night, Judd. Thanks for the ride."

Once inside her apartment, Shannon instantly headed for the phone. She called Janie.

"I gotta talk to you, Janie."

"It's late. Can we talk tomorrow?"

"Yeah. Come over after work. I'll cook dinner."

Janie sighed. "Okay, fine. See you then."

The next day seemed to drag, but finally Janie's knock came at the door. Shannon had dinner cooked. She opened the door and directed Janie to the kitchen.

"I hope you're hungry. I cooked all your favorites."

Janie sniffed the air. "Pot roast? Mm. You must want something."

Sticking her fist on her hip, Shannon spun to face her best friend. "You think I'm up to something?"

"Of course I do. You're always up to something."

"You're right," Shannon conceded. "I'll tell you about it while we eat."

She explained how she'd come back for good and that she knew for sure she wasn't the slightest bit interested in going back to modeling. Janie ate and listened but didn't utter a word.

Finally, Shannon couldn't take it anymore. "Well? You haven't said what's on your mind. What are you thinking?"

Janie swallowed her food. "I don't know if you really want to know."

"Yes, I do want to know. This is important to me, Janie."

"Okay, but brace yourself. It's gonna hurt."

"I can take it."

"Everyone in the group really cares about you. Especially Judd. In fact, he's been moping around since you left. And when we saw that shot in *Entertainment Tonight* with you leaving the award show with Armand at your side, I thought he'd fall over from grief."

"You watched the award show with Judd?"

"Yeah," Janie said. "The whole group got together because someone said you might be there. We were hoping to catch a glimpse of you. What we hadn't expected was seeing you hanging on Armand's arm."

A combination of dread and panic flooded Shannon. "That was all set up."

"Are you saying you didn't try to get back with Armand?"

"No, that wouldn't be true. But the old feeling I once had for Armand just wasn't there. It was all for publicity. My agent arranged for Armand and me to be seen together every chance she got."

"I don't know if Judd will believe that," Janie told her.

"He has to."

"You know, I feel sort of bad about this whole thing because I brought you to the group."

"You regret that?"

Janie put her fork down, pushed away from the table, and looked Shannon in the eye. "This is hard for me to say, Shannon, but I have to. We've known each other too long for me not to level with you."

"Just say it."

"When I saw you on TV, I felt like I'd been used. You needed someone after your accident. Then once you were all better, you ran back to New York. You didn't need us anymore."

"Used?" Shannon pointed to herself. "You think I used you?"

Shaking her head, Janie replied, "I don't know what to think. After listening to you now, I'm not sure."

That hurt more than anything Janie could have said. Shannon had never used anyone in her life. But then again, she couldn't blame Janie or any of the rest of them. At least she knew what she was up against now.

"I'll prove to you and everyone else I'm sincere," Shannon said as Janie stood at the door.

"You don't have to prove anything to us. Just remember, we have flaws, and we don't always see things for how they really are."

"How well I know." Shannon hugged Janie, then watched out the window as her friend walked to her car.

Early the next morning, after Shannon came in from her morning run, she showered, dressed, and headed for her parents' house. Maybe her mother would understand now.

"Shannon, I'm still not happy about this. You're giving up way too much to suit me."

"That's not why I came, Mom."

"I called Melinda earlier this week. I think she'll take you back if you call and tell her you had a brief spell of insanity."

"That's not what I want."

Sara leveled her with a glare. "Then you're making a huge mistake, and I'm afraid you're on your own this time. I can't keep fixing your problems, Shannon. Not when you intentionally sabotage your own career."

As Shannon left her parents' house, she felt more alone than at any other time in her life. Without her mother giving her support and Janie not completely trusting her, she felt like she had to go out on a limb without a safety net below.

Once back in her apartment, Shannon pulled the drapes, turned on a light, and pulled out her Bible. She shut her eyes and prayed for guidance and the ability to overcome all doubt from her friends. She wanted to let them know she was sincere. Now that she knew Christ, her entire perspective had changed.

Before she went to bed, she called Janie. "Please stop by in the morning."

Janie groaned. "You know I have to work in the morning."

"Then get up half an hour earlier, and I'll have coffee and a pastry for you."

"Okay, if it's that important to you."

"It is."

Chapter 11

I never thought I'd see this," Janie said as they sat sipping coffee the next morning in Shannon's apartment. "Especially after you went back to New York."

"Everything changed for me once the Lord came into my life."

"Yeah, that happened with me, too." Janie set her coffee mug down on the table. "I believe you now, Shannon, but you can't blame Judd for being guarded."

"I'll do whatever it takes."

"I guess you just have to give him time."

"That's all I can do."

After Janie left for work, Shannon straightened her apartment. All she could think about was what she and Janie had discussed. If only there were something she could do to make Judd believe her. She had a strong suspicion, verified by Janie, that he cared about her as much as she did him, but he was concerned about her commitment to the Lord, so he continued to guard his heart. She really couldn't blame him.

When the phone rang, she hoped it was Judd, but it wasn't. It was Melinda.

"I hate to bother you like this, Shannon," she said, her voice cool and emotionless, "but you still have to finish two of your contracts."

"I thought everything was complete."

"Everything except a couple of photo sessions and one commercial. As far as I can tell, that'll be it."

Shannon blew out a breath of frustration. She'd already given up her lease on the New York apartment, so she'd have to find a place to stay.

"Can you try to schedule it all together?"

"You know how hard that can be," Melinda replied. "I'll do my best."

"That's all I can ask. Thanks, Melinda."

"I'll let you know when you need to be here."

After she got off the phone, a weary feeling descended over her. Actually, it was more like dread. Just the thought of posing for magazine ads and shooting more commercials wore her out.

A couple of weeks went by, and she still hadn't heard from Melinda. Maybe she'd managed to get her out of the contract. If she didn't hear back in a few days, Shannon figured she'd call to make sure.

Her mother was still upset, but she tried not to let it affect her. She understood how much time, money, and energy her mother had put into her career, so she tried to be sensitive. Her father, on the other hand, seemed overjoyed to have her back in town. He'd pulled Shannon off to the side a few times and told her he thought she was making a wise decision.

In the meantime, she hadn't missed a single Bible study session. That was the one thing in her life in which she found total comfort. Jesus was constant—never changing. He loved her no matter what, and she never ceased to be amazed by the extent of His grace and mercy.

When Judd called and asked if she'd like to get together to prepare for the lesson, Shannon gave him a resounding "Yes!" After she hung up, she danced around her apartment, singing and praising the Lord. Maybe things were looking up between them!

The next day, Shannon got up, went shopping, and came home to get the apartment ready. She wanted it squeaky clean and neat. She even baked cookies.

He walked in and sniffed the air, his expression warm and tender. "Did you bake something?"

Shyness overcame her ability to speak. This had never happened to her before, so she wasn't sure how to react. As she nodded, a smile found its way to her lips. He grinned right back at her.

"You're amazing, Shannon."

"You're pretty amazing yourself, Judd." Her voice barely came out in a whisper, so she cleared her throat. "Would you like a cookie?"

"Of course."

She scurried to the kitchen, then brought out a plate of cookies. His eyes widened.

"You baked those?"

"All by myself with these two hands."

"Is there anything you can't do?"

Shannon let out a nervous laugh. She was used to praise from her fans, but this was different. This was coming from Judd.

He led the study session. As they went through all the questions in the workbook, Shannon felt his gaze as it lingered on her long after she responded. After they finished the lesson, he closed the book and placed it on the table.

"Shannon, I guess you've probably noticed I've been acting sort of weird lately."

"Well, yeah, I have noticed. What can I do?"

He shook his head. "It's me. I'm dealing with some issues."

"I understand," she said. He obviously didn't want to talk about it. Maybe she needed to give him a little space to make up his mind to talk to her about his feelings. And she also needed to pray about the relationship. What she wanted and what the Lord had in mind for her might be two entirely different things.

That week's group Bible study went extremely well. She and Judd contributed more than most of the others, which gave her a great feeling because they'd been so far behind in the beginning.

As they were gathering their things to leave, Janie came up to her and gave her a hug. "I'm so happy to see you deeply immersed in the Word."

Shannon hugged her back. "Thanks for leading me here."

"It wasn't me." Pointing her finger upward, Janie reminded her, "He did it all. I'm just the vehicle."

Judd watched Shannon as she animatedly chatted with Janie. Every time he looked at her, his heart rate increased. And when she looked back at him, he felt like he could jump over the moon. It wasn't just infatuation, either. He was in love.

When he'd first met Shannon McNab, his reaction was the same as any other male's. Her beauty stunned him. With the exception of the scar from her accident, she seemed perfect. If anything, her beauty was a turnoff to him. He was so far from perfect, he didn't want any part of a relationship with a woman who'd make all his flaws more obvious. Then, as he got to know her, he'd learned some of her imperfections, and that was when he started falling in love. As confident as Shannon seemed, he knew she had some insecurities. That made him love her even more, and he wanted to protect her. He'd also learned that her modeling career hadn't been her idea. She was living her mother's dream, something else that endeared her to him. She wanted her mother to be happy—even going so far as to center her whole life around it.

But the one thing that excited him most was, just as his own faith had begun to grow, he was able to witness the same thing happening to Shannon. Her love for the Lord was evident on her face and in every action. She was truly dedicated and loyal to her faith.

When she'd gone off to New York after her scar had healed, he had to face the possibility that he'd only been a temporary distraction for her while she was healing. Her return had surprised him. At first, hope welled inside him that possibly she was here to stay. But what if she left again and he had to go through the emptiness he'd felt the first time she'd gone? Could he deal with that?

Janie had tried to talk to him, saying Shannon was sick of modeling. He heard her words, but he didn't want to take them to heart.

What if she was right? Did he dare take a chance and allow the love he felt for Shannon to show?

All his life, Judd had wanted the security of a stable home and being surrounded by people who knew him and loved him no matter what. He'd resorted to being the class clown in school, which helped him as a teacher. He knew what made children tick, and he could handle those kids who acted out for attention because he'd once been one of them. His knack for working with children and his love for reading and the English language had earned him a dream position in an excellent school. His aunt and uncle had provided him with a roof over his head while he saved money for a down payment on a house. And through his uncle, he'd found a fabulous group of friends he knew had good hearts and the desire to live in a way that was pleasing to Christ. What more could a man ask for?

The only thing Judd could think of was a woman to spend the rest of his life with. To his dismay, he'd been mentally putting Shannon in that role, although he knew his chances with someone like her had to be slim.

Over the past week, Janie had encouraged him to pursue his feelings for Shannon. Did he dare?

After long hours and days of worrying about it, he decided to just go for it. What did he have to lose? It wasn't as if he hadn't been defeated before.

With a sigh, Judd resigned himself to having to face another disappointment. He could do it. He had enough practice.

Armed with prayer and the desire to follow his dream regardless of the consequences, Judd headed for church on Sunday hoping to have a chat with Shannon immediately afterward. The only problem was, she wasn't there. He craned his neck and looked over the sea of heads around him, but he couldn't find Shannon in the entire congregation. Janie smiled and waved as their gazes met. She'd know where Shannon was. He'd just ask her after church.

The sermon seemed to be directed at him, as always. Even the worship songs got to him. When his uncle dismissed the congregation, he said a silent prayer, then jumped up to find out where Shannon was.

Janie shook her head. "Sorry, Judd. She had to take off for New York yesterday afternoon. Her agent called and ordered her back."

He gulped hard, the lump in his throat nearly choking him. "She went back to New York?"

Offering a look of sympathy, Janie nodded. "Sorry, Judd." She reached out and touched his arm. "I wish my news was different."

"Hey, don't worry about it. At least we can all watch her on TV, right?"

Several people from the Bible study group joined them, and Janie quickly started chatting with one of the other women. Judd turned down an offer to go out to lunch. He'd much rather go on home. Besides, he had an appointment with his Realtor in a couple of hours. He'd been looking at houses, and he was ready to get serious about buying his first home.

❧

"I'm giving you one last chance," Melinda said as she stood in front of her desk. "If you want to sign, I think I can save the contracts."

"No, Melinda, but thanks. I really don't want to do this anymore."

"How does your mother feel about this?"

"You know how she feels. This is what she's always wanted for me."

For the first time since she'd met Melinda, something happened. Melinda came toward her, draped her arm over Shannon's shoulder, and pulled her to her side. "Ya know, Shannon, I really don't think your heart was ever into modeling. This was your mother's dream, and she was able to live it through you. If you want to live in Atlanta and do something else, I don't think anyone should stand in your way."

Tears instantly sprang to Shannon's eyes. "Thanks. I appreciate that."

"Keep in touch, okay, honey?"

Unable to speak, Shannon nodded and left. Now it was time to go to the hotel, gather her things, and get on the next plane home to Atlanta. She had a whole life ahead of her.

She got back just in time to freshen up and get to the Bible study, where she hoped to see Judd. Janie looked shocked that she was there.

"I thought you left again."

"I just had to finish out a contract."

"Uh-oh." Janie covered her mouth with her hand.

"What?" Shannon reached for Janie's hand and pulled it away. "What happened?"

"Judd—"

"Say no more."

Before anyone could stop her, Shannon ran out the door, hopped into her car, and drove straight to Pastor Manning's house. LaRita answered the door.

"Come in, Shannon," she said in her usual sweet voice. "What a nice surprise. Garrett, Shannon's here."

Pastor Manning came around the corner, his hand extended. "How's the modeling business?"

"I wouldn't know. I quit."

He frowned. "I thought you went back to New York." He paused, raised his eyebrows, and added, "Again."

"I think I have a few things to explain. Where's Judd?"

"He isn't living here anymore."

Shannon gasped. "What happened?"

LaRita led Shannon to a loveseat, then sat down next to her. Patting her on the leg, she said, "Judd found a nice house close to the school where he teaches. He moved out last weekend."

"Oh," Shannon said as relief flooded her. "I need to talk to him."

"Let me call him over," Pastor Manning said as he grabbed the phone and started punching numbers.

Shannon listened to the phone conversation and heard Pastor Manning's firm tone, insisting Judd come over right away. There was some arguing, but it wasn't too serious.

"He's as stubborn as his uncle," Pastor Manning said as he hung up. "He'll be here in about twenty minutes."

"I've got cake and coffee in the kitchen," LaRita said. "Want me to bring you some?"

"I'd like that," Shannon replied. She'd always loved the warmth of the Mannings' home. It felt inviting—like a place a person could totally relax. She now realized this was something she'd missed growing up.

Shannon explained what had happened with her modeling contract. They listened attentively and told her they understood and respected what she'd done. That meant quite a bit to her.

When Judd arrived, LaRita turned to her husband and said, "Let's leave them alone. Why don't we go on to bed now?"

Judd stood with his hands in his pockets, his jaw set in determination. Shannon rose and walked toward him, but he didn't budge.

"Please sit down, Judd. We need to talk."

"I don't have anything to say."

She expelled a sigh. "Look, I know how stubborn you can be, but I'm just as stubborn—maybe even more so. You might as well listen now, or I'll never give you any peace."

She looked at his face as it softened somewhat. Finally, he nodded and walked over to the chair where his uncle had been sitting.

"I just got back from New York this afternoon, and I went to the Bible study, hoping to see you there."

"I moved."

"Yes, I heard. That's great. Congratulations. Would you like to tell me about your house?"

He darted a glance at her, then looked away before he stood up and started pacing. "Look, Shannon, I don't know what kind of game you're playing, but I don't like it. You come and you go, back and forth, whenever the mood strikes. This isn't how I want to live my life."

"I understand," she said.

"I don't think you do. I'm going to tell you something that might rock your boat a little, but I feel like I need to be honest with you. I've tried hard not to, but I think I might have fallen in love with you. It's not something I should admit, I know, but it's the truth. If I let you continue to waltz in and out of my life like this, I'll wind up a crazy man."

As Shannon listened to his profession of love for her, she felt like her heart might explode. It took every ounce of self-restraint she had to hold back her announcement of love for him. He needed to get this off his chest.

He stopped for a few seconds, grimaced, then resumed pacing. "What's more, I bought a house, deluding myself into thinking you might consider becoming my wife. I have no idea what I was thinking. What would a woman like you want with a man like me?"

As he wound down, Shannon sat there with her hands in her lap, joy slowly rippling through her, then flooding her like a tidal wave. It took every ounce of self-restraint she had to keep from jumping up and flinging her arms around him. Finally, when he stopped, she ordered him to sit.

"Finished?" she asked.

He nodded. "Yeah."

"Okay, my turn. I'll have you know, Judd Manning, that I've been in love with you for a long time. I was wondering the same thing you were. What would a man who had his act together want with a woman like me? After all, I was never sure what I wanted to do with my life. I figured you'd want someone with her feet planted firmly on the ground."

She dared to take a look at him. He'd raised his eyebrows, and he was watching her with interest. She knew she needed to make this good, or she'd blow what could be her only chance to convince him of her love.

"All my life I dreamed of finding peace, contentment, and a little happiness," she said, carefully choosing her words. "When I met you, I found it all rolled into one masculine bundle. I love you, Judd."

"But what about your modeling?"

"I quit."

"You went back, though."

"I had to finish out a contract. Now it's all over. I'm here to stay."

Taking one of the biggest chances ever, she reached out and touched his hand. *Please, Lord, don't let me lose this man.*

Slowly, he turned his hand over and wrapped his fingers around her hand. Shannon felt the tug as he pulled her to his side. Their gazes held until their faces were inches apart.

He lifted both hands and cupped her face. "Shannon, I love you. I tried my best not to let it happen, but it was impossible."

The feeling was so overwhelming, the urge so strong, Shannon couldn't resist reaching out and pulling his face to hers. She lightly brushed his lips with her lips before backing away so she could look him in the eye.

"I've loved you since the first time you kissed me," she whispered.

"Really? Me, too."

Shannon's heart pounded as she held her breath and wondered what to do next.

Suddenly, Judd sucked in a breath, blew it out, and said, "Shannon McNab, will you mar—"

The words weren't even all the way out of his mouth when she shouted, "Yes!" Then an odd feeling overtook her. What if she'd mistaken what he was saying? "Uh, what were you about to ask, Judd?"

He chuckled. "I was about to ask if you'd be my wife."

"That's a relief." She kissed him again then pulled back. "I'd be honored to be your wife."

Applause sounded from the hallway before Garrett and LaRita appeared. "Good move, nephew."

Judd cast a warning glance toward his aunt and uncle. "Eavesdropping?"

"Of course," LaRita replied. "But only after we heard Shannon shout, 'Yes!' We wanted to make sure you didn't blow it."

"Well? How'd I do?"

"Magnificently," Pastor Manning replied. "And Shannon didn't do too badly, either."

LaRita motioned for everyone to join her in the kitchen. "Cake and coffee for all."

Shannon laughed. "You've already fed me cake. I'm gonna get fat."

Judd nudged her. "Who cares? You've caught your man."

"In that case, I'd love some cake."

On the way to the kitchen, Shannon pinched herself to make sure she wasn't dreaming. Then she said a silent prayer. *Thanks, Lord, for making my dream come true. Amen.*

Double Blessing

Chapter 1

Three things in life made Jill crazy: serious people with so many rules they couldn't relax, pantyhose, and a checkbook that wouldn't balance. And here she was, ten dollars short. She'd been staring at the same numbers all morning, scratching her head and chugging coffee so strong it could walk.

She didn't have to worry about serious people because she worked alone. Pantyhose were unnecessary in her business. That left only one thing to annoy her. With money as tight as it was, she couldn't afford to be relaxed with her finances. She chewed on the end of her pencil as she perused the numbers again—but with no success.

The bells jingled as the front door opened and closed. Jill glanced up, still in a daze from the numbers that didn't balance, but she forced a smile.

"May I help you with something?" She could barely see him since the sunshine was streaming in the front window behind him. As he came closer, she saw his outdoorsy good looks with short, streaked blond hair, light eyes—were they gray or light blue?—she couldn't quite tell in this lighting—and a natural-looking tan.

He glanced at a slip of paper. "I'm looking for Jill Hargrove." Then he turned to her. "Is she in?" She couldn't help but notice his soft Georgia accent.

Jill lifted one eyebrow. "You're looking at her." This guy sure was cute.

He nodded and extended his hand, which she took only briefly. "I'm Ed Mathis." He stepped back and looked around for a moment before turning to her again. "This is the Junktique Shoppe, right?"

"Right." This guy didn't look anything like what she'd expected. "You're Ed the handyman?"

"Yep. I'm here to fix whatever needs fixin'. Anything that's broken." His eyes crinkled as he smiled.

Jill had expected a much older man, someone with years of experience. Someone who didn't look as if he'd just stepped off the page of a men's catalog. Someone she could work alongside without thinking about how handsome he was.

He gazed around and let out a low chuckle. "Looks like you've got yourself quite a mess here."

Hmm. Jill loved her mess—her collectibles—and she didn't need anyone else calling her place a mess. Suddenly she felt defensive, something that reminded her of worse times, and an awful feeling washed over her. He obviously couldn't tell the difference between vintage collectibles and what he called "a mess." She didn't need negativism. She'd give him a quick and easy job to do and then call the service she'd planned on calling in the first place. The guy in the business next door had meant well when he recommended Ed, but she didn't need someone to judge her and plant seeds of doubt about her lifelong dream.

"Okay," Jill said, looking away. "Let's start with the shelves in the back room. They're about to collapse." That should take a competent handyman a day or two; then she could send him packing.

He nodded. "Let me take a look at 'em."

"C'mon back." She kept her voice calm, but his presence was unnerving.

Jill heard his boots clicking behind her on the hardwood floor. She felt self-conscious in the tattered jeans and ratty T-shirt she'd grabbed on the run this morning. She lifted her hand to the back of her head where her hair had fallen loose from the clip.

"There they are." Jill gestured toward the lopsided shelves she'd installed for extra storage. Ceramic and glass pieces were perched precariously on the shelves, which looked ready to come crashing to the floor at any moment.

Ed whistled and shook his head. "I can tell you now what the problem is. You put too much weight on 'em."

Jill took a step back, placed her hand on her hip, and glared at him. "Excuse me?"

He nodded toward the shelves. "I said, you put too much weight on these shelves."

"I need them for storage. Can you fix them or not?"

He stood still when his gaze met hers, then turned and stared at the wall supporting the shelves before turning back to face her. "I s'pose I could give 'em some support so they can hold all your junk, if you wanna keep piling it on."

"That's not all junk," she said. "Some of it's collectible."

Jill hadn't been sure what to do with these things she'd gotten when bidding on an entire garage filled with Depression glass that was surrounded by. . . junk. Yes, Ed was right, but she couldn't let him know she agreed. Besides, he'd caught her at a very bad time. She was in a lousy mood from the checkbook that wouldn't balance.

"Just do whatever you have to do to fix it," she said. She knew she didn't sound friendly, but this was not a good time.

Ed snorted. "You treat your customers this way?" His look of intense scrutiny caused her to reach up and fidget with her hair again. She knew she must look as if she'd tangled with a bear. "Cuz if you do, they won't keep coming back."

She paused before sniffing and looking him in the eye. "Don't worry about it, Ed. My customers and I get along just fine."

He turned and headed for the door.

"Can you do it?" she called after him.

"Yeah. I just have to go out to my truck for more tools. This job requires more than I can carry on my belt."

"This is not going to work out," Jill mumbled to herself when she was alone. She went to the showroom, straightened a few items, then went behind the checkout counter and moved several things around on the desk. She wondered why Ed was taking so long.

Jill wandered out from behind the desk and glanced out the front window. She saw him pulling an extension ladder from the back of his truck. Then she quickly scurried behind the desk.

The phone rang. "I see Ed made it there." It was Josh Anderson, the neighbor who'd recommended him.

"Yeah, he's here."

"Ed Mathis is the best handyman in the whole Atlanta area," Josh said. "He did quite a bit of renovation in Sandy Springs and Marietta. You'll like his work."

She let out a long sigh. "I'm sure I will. Thanks, Josh."

When Jill got off the phone, Ed returned. "Okay if I prop this door open?" he asked.

"Uh, sure."

Ed fidgeted with the door and figured out a way to make it stay open so he could bring things in from his truck, while Jill straightened some pieces on the shelves. Seconds later, he came walking into the store with the ladder balanced at his side.

"Better be careful with that," she said. "I have some fragile things in here, and I'll—." She stopped short of saying she'd have to charge him. She didn't want to sound mean.

"Don't worry," he said as he went into the back room and extended the ladder, leaning it against the wall. "I'll be careful. Want to help me get these things out of the way, or are you too busy?"

Without hesitation, Jill was at his side, holding out her hands, reaching for the oversized ceramic rooster he'd lifted from the top shelf. "That piece is very fragile."

Ed snickered. "If you'd left all this stuff up here much longer on the shelves the way they are now, your fragile junk would be in bits and pieces on the floor. I'm surprised it's not already. Now, are you gonna help me find another spot for it so I can fix these shelves, or shall I do it myself?"

"I'll help."

It took them the better part of an hour to get everything down. The anchors she'd tried to brace the shelves with had pulled from the wall, and the toggle bolts were fully exposed and hanging out of the holes in the drywall.

Ed laughed as he pulled the shelves away from the wall. "Whoever put up these shelves didn't know what he was doing."

"For your information, I installed these shelves myself, and I'm not in the mood for your insults."

His shoulders sagged. "Sorry. I didn't mean to come across as insulting."

The bells jingled again. "Customer," she said quickly and hurried away.

Out of the corner of her eye, she could see him watching her for a few seconds as she ran out to see about her customer. Fortunately, now there was a wall section between them, and she wouldn't be tempted to pay more attention to him than to making a sale.

⁓

Jill's breeze left behind the scent of a blend of sweet flowers and spices. Ed looked at the shelves, which were lopsided on one side and coming apart on the other. He didn't see how someone as petite as Jill had managed to maneuver the shelves enough to bolt them to the wall, even in this slipshod way. He had to hand it to her for trying.

Her defensive nature appeared to be an attempt to hide pain, so he squeezed his eyes shut in a brief prayer that he could do his job without angering her further. Something besides the shop's state of disrepair appeared to be bothering her. He hoped he'd be a good witness throughout this project. Jill was cute, and he loved the way she smelled, but he was pretty sure she had issues.

Ed tried to concentrate on what he needed to do in order to brace the shelves, but he couldn't help but overhear Jill's conversation with the woman in the front of the shop. He moved to get a better view.

Jill's auburn hair was carelessly swept up on top of her head and held with a single clip. Curly strands had fallen loose, and they hung around her face, framing her scrubbed, pale skin and nearly hiding the eyes that had bored a hole through him.

Several times she reached up and took a swipe at her hair, most likely so she could see. He noticed the big brown eyes that were free of makeup, something he suspected she hadn't bothered with because she'd probably just rolled out of bed and thrown herself together to come to work. But that wasn't all he noticed. He was impressed with the respect she showed her customer.

In spite of his resolve to do his work and mind his own business, he was intrigued by this diminutive woman with the obviously kind heart toward the elderly woman she was trying so hard to help. He could tell she had much more patience than he'd ever have with someone who would buy very little, if anything at all, and she seemed to sincerely care about helping that woman.

"I'm not sure we have what you're looking for," she told her customer. "Take a look around and see if anything interests you." She started to walk away, but she stopped when the woman reached out and touched her arm.

The customer asked another question, then chattered incessantly while Jill gave her all her attention. Ed had already grabbed his ladder and was working on steadying it, but he continued to observe. Jill told the woman to let her know if she needed help, and the woman told her she would, thanking her for being such a sweet girl.

Jill glanced over her shoulder and caught Ed staring at her. Ed grabbed his measuring tape and pretended he hadn't been watching her or eavesdropping. Pretending wasn't his strong suit; he'd always been such an up-front guy. He was relieved when the customer came back to the sales desk and put something on the counter. That distracted Jill enough to take the heat off.

"Come back and see me," Jill said as she rang up a purchase Ed couldn't see because he was now hidden on the other side of the wall. He couldn't keep gawking, so he'd actually begun prepping the wall.

"Oh, I will." Then the door opened, letting in the sounds of Atlanta's historic district.

Still distracted, Ed dropped the power drill on his foot and let out a grunt. He bit his bottom lip to absorb some of the pain. Now he was suffering for not paying enough attention to what he was supposed to be doing.

"I bet that hurts," he heard a soft voice say.

Ed glanced up and saw Jill leaning against the doorframe, her arms folded, a slight smile playing on her lips. Now he really felt bad. It had been a mistake to eavesdrop. From now on he'd concentrate on doing the work she'd hired him to do and ignore her—if that was possible.

Josh, one of his buddies from church, had told him Jill was a single woman who needed a lot of help. *That's an understatement*, Ed thought as he glanced around at the merchandise in the store. What she needed was a bulldozer and a deep landfill.

He shrugged. "Not really."

She took a step closer and looked down at his foot. "You sure?"

"Positive."

The tension in her face faded, and she offered a crooked grin. "Good. Then you'd better pick it up before it starts making a hole in my floor," she said, nodding toward the drill that still lay across his boot.

"It's not even plugged in," Ed said.

"I don't want to take any chances." She turned and walked away, leaving him to deal with his absentmindedness alone. He was pretty sure, but not positive, that she was being playful.

Ed squeezed his eyes shut and prayed silently, *Lord, please give me the strength to know when to open my mouth and when to be silent. I can't do it on my own around this woman.* He opened one eye and saw her profile before closing it again and adding, *She's the cutest boss I've ever had.*

Jill wished she'd gone with her first plan and called someone from the service. The entire time she'd been waiting on her customer she'd been thinking about the man in the back room. When she saw the drill lying on his boot, she resisted the urge to run to him, pick it up, and insist he get off his feet.

One look into his eyes, though, and she backed off. She couldn't afford to let the chemistry between them affect her. She had a career mission, and he would certainly distract her from her goal.

Ed Mathis was only there to fix things in her shop—something any number of handy types could do. She didn't need his critical eye studying her. Okay, she decided, first thing in the morning she'd give him one more thing to do; then she'd pay him, thank him, and send him on his way.

"I have to run out and get some drywall," he said, startling her from her thoughts. "Some of those holes are too big to patch. Besides, I need to add more stud reinforcements behind the drywall, so I might as well start from scratch."

Jill nodded. "Do whatever you have to do. I need those shelves."

He offered her a grin as he raked his fingers through his short-cropped hair. He certainly acted as if he knew what he was doing. Jill had sneaked peeks into the back room to see how he was coming along. He'd cut around the holes where the toggle bolts had pulled out of the wall, then looked inside them with his flashlight, shaking his head and mumbling something she couldn't hear.

After Ed left the shop it was suddenly very quiet. Too quiet. Jill had to flip the switch on her boom box to have something to keep her from thinking too much. She knew every single word of the praise song and sang along. She'd turned it off to balance her checkbook. Music was wonderful when she needed it for creative flow, but when she needed to focus her energy on anything logical, she had to have extreme quiet.

But now wasn't the time to try to balance her checkbook. Logic had taken a hike after Ed walked in. Jill knew she needed to learn plenty of things, but she wanted to do it without someone hovering over her, watching. He had already shown signs of being too much like her father—organized and meticulous to a fault. He'd measured every single angle on the wall where the shelves had fallen. Even his toolbox was organized and labeled.

A couple of regular customers came and went, each of them buying a few pieces for their collections, but not enough to make a significant improvement in her bank balance. In the short time Jill had been in business, she'd developed relationships with people who came into the shop. They'd found her shop mostly from the small ads she'd placed in the local collectors' newsletter. To stay in business, she knew it would take a lot more than the handful of collectors who'd found the Junktique Shoppe.

Jill glanced at her watch every couple of minutes, wondering what was taking Ed so long. When he finally came back, she let out a deep sigh. Okay, so she liked having him there. That was the main reason he needed to go.

"How's your foot?"

Ed shook his head. "Foot's fine."

"Good."

She glanced out the window at his loaded truck. "How much will this cost?" Jill asked.

He smiled. "I'll give you a little discount."

Now she was even more worried. "I didn't ask for a discount."

"This needs to be done right, and from the look of things you can't afford the full price." He set his jaw, widened his stance, and folded his arms. "I don't know if Josh told you, but I don't do things halfway."

Yes, Josh had told her, which was why she had chosen Ed.

"Okay," she finally said while doing a quick mental calculation of how many days in a row she could eat boxed mac and cheese. "Do whatever you have to do to get those shelves up. But that might be all I can afford." There was no point in hiding the fact that she was a struggling new business owner. He'd figure it out soon enough anyway.

The bells on the front door sounded again, so Jill left Ed and concentrated on taking care of her customers. The young couple told her they had just bought an old house in the heart of Atlanta and were looking for pieces for their new place.

"I don't want department-store, cookie-cutter kinds of things," the woman said. "I want my first house to have character."

The man behind her nodded, clearly smitten with his wife. If Jill had to guess, she'd say they were a newly married couple, perhaps right out of college.

"Take a look around," Jill told them. "If you see something you like, I'll be glad to help you. Or if you have something in mind that you don't see, I'll write it down and call you if anything like it comes in."

The woman beamed. "Thanks so much." Turning to the man, she said, "C'mon, honey. I can already tell this is my favorite antique store."

By the time they'd gone from one side of the front sales floor to the other, the woman had piled the man's arms with so many trinkets and knickknacks, he couldn't have held more if he'd wanted to. Jill came to their rescue.

"Here—let me take those things so you can shop some more. Have you been upstairs?"

The woman's face lit up. "There's more?"

Jill nodded. "I have a whole floor of nothing but ceramic and porcelain."

As soon as the couple went upstairs, Ed came out from behind the back wall. "I was wrong about this place."

Jill jumped. He'd startled her. "What?"

"I just said I was wrong. When I first walked in here, I thought this place was doomed to failure. I'd never seen so much junk under one roof in my life."

She felt an overwhelming sense of pride, not to mention the fact that she enjoyed his praise.

Before she had a chance to comment, he continued. "Apparently you've found a niche market, and because of that you'll be quite successful." The respect in his voice took some of the bite out of his first comment.

"You really think so?"

He nodded. "If you can keep your head above water for the first couple of years, I have no doubt this place will be a raging success."

Tilting her head to one side, she squinted as she studied him. "How would you know this sort of thing?"

"Business experience," he replied as he turned his back on her. "Lots of it."

❧

Ed thought she knew who he was, but apparently not. He could tell she thought he was just a neighborhood handyman.

His business, Mathis Construction, just happened to be the most successful home improvement company in north Georgia. His specialty was restoring old homes. Only recently he had decided to develop a brand-new neighborhood up in the Ackworth area, but the zoning would take months, which freed him up to do odd jobs here and there. He also welcomed a break from the long ten- and twelve-hour days spent working on a project of that magnitude. Handy work was something he actually enjoyed for a change of pace. Ed had figured he'd take a break and spend more time with his twin daughters, who were becoming a huge handful. He'd accepted this short-term job as a favor to his friend Josh, who said a very sweet, young entrepreneur needed a little help getting started. Now he found himself wondering about her spiritual side. She seemed defensive and troubled.

He wanted to run before getting involved with her, but his conscience and faith wouldn't let him. She might be good with customers, but this place was ready to be condemned.

The whole place was falling apart. The first thing he'd noticed was how the wooden planks of the porch floor were rotten—a lawsuit waiting to happen. The inside wasn't any better. He'd seen evidence of termites, but he wasn't yet sure if any live ones were in the building.

Another thing Ed needed to talk to her about was holding on to her profits. He'd overheard her offering huge discounts to people who seemed willing to buy at full price.

With the drywall and two-by-fours lined up, Ed began ripping away the existing drywall, exposing everything behind it. That was when he saw how the wiring was brittle and cracking in some places. And there they were. Live termites. If they were localized to one area, they could be spot treated. But if they were as bad as he'd seen in other houses, she'd need to have this place tented.

He took a step back and inspected what was in front of him. It was much worse than he'd thought. Most likely the whole place needed rewiring, a project he'd have to subcontract out to a licensed electrician. From the looks of things, this house hadn't been the best investment for a young businesswoman who didn't know a thing about repairs. He wondered why the bank had allowed the loan to go through with all the problems he spotted.

Ed narrowed his eyes as he considered his options. Should he repair the wall and ignore the wiring? No, he couldn't do that. Should he tell Jill what he'd noticed and duck? Her stress level was already high enough. Then there was the other option, one he'd tried to push from his mind. Plenty of people from church would help out if he asked them to, but somehow he doubted the prickly Jill would accept that offer.

"Something wrong?" she asked as she came around and caught him deep in thought.

Ed's heart twisted as he noticed the expectant look on her face. She was waiting for an answer.

Chapter 2

Her initial reaction was exactly what he'd expected. She admitted she'd put all her money into the place, and it was paid for free and clear, so she hadn't gone through the traditional bank financing. The owner had obviously sold it to her "as is" and rushed her through the process, which should have alerted her to something being wrong. But it was too late to go into that now.

Her face turned a deep shade of red. Then she offered a sheepish smile.

"I should have had this place inspected before I closed on it," she said softly. "I bet you think I'm stupid."

"No, I don't think you're stupid." He paused and held her gaze until she quickly looked away. "Just very eager to go into business for yourself."

She swallowed hard. "Thank you for understanding."

Sensing she needed her space, Ed stepped outside and called his best friend from church, an electrician he'd met on a job years ago. He explained the situation. "Any way you can come right over?" he asked.

"I'm just now leaving today's job. I'll be there in a half hour," Matt said.

"Be careful," Ed warned. "She's fragile."

"She? You mean the shop?"

"Yeah, that, too, but I was talking about the owner."

Matt chuckled. "I can handle fragile women. Trust me."

Ed hung up and said a prayer of thanks for his friend. Then he prayed for more guidance with Jill.

When Matt arrived, Ed left him to inspect the wiring while he moved on to the next area that needed repairing.

"You sure you wanna cover this?" Matt asked after a few minutes. "It'll cost you some bucks."

Ed looked at the frayed wires Matt held in both hands. Slowly he nodded.

Matt grinned. "She must be pretty special, Ed. I had no idea you were getting serious about some girl. How long has this been going on?"

"Nothing's going on, Matt. I just met her this morning."

"Whoa!" Matt said as he took a step back. "Run that one by me again."

"You heard me."

"Why are you about to plunk down some hefty change to rewire this house, then? She hired you to do work for her, which means she's supposed to pay you.

Not the other way around."

A long silence fell between the men. "Yes, I know," Ed finally replied. "Just wait until you get to know her. You'll see."

Matt chuckled. "Okay, then. First I have to pull out all the existing wires, then snake new ones through to the same locations. And most likely the breaker box will need replacing, too."

Ed knew Matt would come to the rescue.

"There isn't a breaker box. This house is old, Matt. It still has fuses."

"Fuse box has never been replaced?"

"Nope."

"Then we'll definitely have to put in a breaker box." He rocked back on his heels, then rubbed his neck. "Seeing as how you're doing this for charity, I'll donate my time and just charge you for materials."

"Donate your time for what?" a female voice said from the doorway.

Ed glanced up to see Jill staring at him, a curious look on her face. He'd thought she was upstairs, helping some customers. Obviously not.

Matt shot Ed a panic-stricken glance, then turned away, leaving Ed to do damage control. "Uh. . ."

Narrowing her gaze, Jill shook her head. "I'm not asking for charity. I pay my way. Nothing's free."

Ed held out his hands. "C'mon, Jill. It's not that big a deal. We're just tryin' to help. We do that a lot for each other."

"Yeah, but you've got a friendship for who knows how long. I just met both of you."

"How long do we have to know each other before we can say we're friends?" Ed challenged. "Just because you and I only met today doesn't make us any less friends, does it?"

Jill didn't say anything as he tried to find the right words.

Finally she sighed. "Maybe we can work something out."

"Work something out?" Ed asked.

"Yeah," she replied. "Like a two-way deal. If you and this guy"—she said, nodding toward Matt, who was pretending not to listen—"want to do some work for me, then I want to do something for you in return."

"Like what?"

"I can cook."

Matt suddenly spun around. "And I like to eat. It's a deal."

With a shrug Ed said, "Okay, sounds like a pretty good plan. We do the work around here and only charge for materials. You can cook a meal for us."

"Not just a meal," she said slowly. "Dinner for a month."

Ed thought about his daughters and his responsibility of feeding them each night. Oh, well, he'd work out something. For now he'd be agreeable.

"Fine," he said with a grunt.

"Sounds good," Matt said as he backed away, moving toward the door. "I'll see ya first thing in the mornin', Ed."

After he was gone, Jill closed her eyes and blew out a deep breath. "You okay?" Ed asked.

She nodded. "How bad is it?"

"The wiring in this house is shot, Jill, just like quite a few other things. I don't think the plumbing's in good shape, either."

She leaned against the wall and closed her eyes.

"Everything will work out," he said as he took a step closer. Her face had gone pasty white.

"I don't have any idea how I'm going to pull any of this off. My father died eight months ago and left me barely enough money to buy a small home and this old house, which I thought was the perfect location for the business I've always wanted."

Ed felt a heaviness in his chest. Now he felt more compelled than ever to do something to help her out. No wonder she was frustrated. This was her inheritance.

"I'm really sorry," he said.

"Why are you sorry?" She sniffled. "The fact that this house is falling apart isn't your fault."

Ed rubbed the back of his neck. "I'm sorry to hear about your father." He held up his hands and gestured around the room. "I'm sorry this place is such a wreck."

She shrugged as she pulled a tissue from her pocket and blew her nose. "Maybe I should just have it condemned and move on."

The sound of desperation in her voice kicked him in the gut. "Whatever you want to do, just let me know before we go any further." He took a small step back, then stopped. "I didn't mean that. This place has to be fixed. I'm not leaving until it's done." No way would he leave her in the lurch.

Jill glanced up at him with a questioning look. "What?"

"I said I'm not leaving. In fact I'm sticking around until every last thing in this place is taken care of."

What had he just committed to? Days, maybe even weeks or months, of hard work and time that would most likely go unpaid? He had plenty of money to last him until he started on the new housing and commercial development— that wasn't the point. But this was supposed to be a little hiatus for him between major remodeling jobs and the new development.

Jill had opened her mouth, but she shut it again as she hung her head. Ed knew she was scared. And she should be. All her money was tied up in a place she'd never be able to sell if someone had the sense to hire an inspector before buying it—as *she* should have done.

"We need to start with the foundation and wiring first," Ed offered when he saw that she was speechless.

"Look, Ed," Jill finally said. "I know all the dinners I can cook for you and your friends won't be enough to pay for the work this place needs." Glancing around frantically, she said, "I'll pay you a little bit each month until it's paid off."

He didn't want to take money from her, but he wasn't about to take away every last shred of her pride, either. Nodding slowly, he replied, "Okay, it's a deal, but only for the materials. We'll exchange labor for dinners."

"Keep track of everything," she said as she looked directly at him with big brown eyes that sent his heart into overdrive.

"You bet I will."

And he meant it, too. He would keep track of absolutely everything—from her soulful eyes, her creamy skin, her hair that was in desperate need of brushing, all the way to her pink-painted toenails that peeked out from her sturdy sandals.

Keeping track of the cost of the project was altogether another thing, though. He was certain that some of the material receipts might get "lost" somewhere along the way.

Jill scooted away from Ed and made her way across the room. Ed was staring down at his boots when he noticed she'd stopped by the door to the front sales floor.

He looked up and found her staring back at him. "Is there something else?" he asked.

"Yeah," she replied. "I was wondering why you're doing this."

He was stumped. How can a man describe that overwhelming urge to protect a creature he barely knew? The Lord had brought him here to help her, but he wasn't sure if she was ready to hear that. So he tried to act nonchalant. "I'm just a nice guy, I guess."

"Uh-huh," she said as she disappeared around the corner.

Ed felt awful for not jumping on the opportunity to witness. Hurrying after her, he said, "There's something you need to know, Jill."

"What?" She stopped and issued a challenging stare.

"Matt and I are in the same Bible study group from church. We have a few more friends from church who are in the building business, and I want to get them to help out, too."

She closed her eyes for a few seconds, then looked directly into his. "So you're doing this because of your faith?"

"Well, sort of. As Christians, we're supposed to help others—even people who don't believe the same way we do."

"So you think I'm not a believer?"

"Are you?"

"Yes."

Her one-word statement gave him a rush of pleasure.

"Then you understand why we want to help you," he said.

"I've already said I'm not a charity case."

Ed wanted to remind her that everyone was a charity case, and Jesus had to bail them out of their own depravity. But she didn't appear to be in a listening mood at the moment. He chose to take a more tactful approach and save the best for another time.

"We're getting meals, remember?"

"Trust me, I won't forget."

"Do you have a church home?"

She shook her head. "No, but I read my Bible daily."

"Would you like to be my guest at Good Shepherd?"

She paused for a couple of seconds. "Maybe later," she finally said before walking away to tend to a customer.

Ed managed to get the area cleaned up enough so he wouldn't face a mess in the morning. The gaping hole in the wall was still there, but he needed to leave it alone in order for Matt to have full access to what he hoped would be the worst part of the electrical problem.

Most of the old drywall had been hauled outside and the new drywall stacked when Jill came back, took a long assessing look around the room, and shook her head.

"You'll be fine," Ed said. "Matt's good at what he does, and he'll fix you right up." He glanced her way and saw those big, trusting brown eyes looking at him. Now his heart was involved. How could a man turn away from that?

પર્જ

Jill hated feeling vulnerable and helpless. Her father had been a powerful man in the military, and then he'd come home and expected her to accept the orders he barked at her. She had known that because she depended on him, she had to do things his way. But she'd promised herself that once she was grown and out on her own, she'd never put herself in a defenseless position again.

Yet here she was, depending on a man to take care of her. Ed was sweet; she still didn't like the fact that she'd owe him something, though, even if it was only meals and the money he'd have to front for the materials.

She stood and watched him clean up, not saying a word. His silence left her wondering what he was thinking, but she was glad he chose not to make idle chitchat.

Finally he stood and brushed his hands off on the front of his jeans. "What time do you get here in the morning?" he asked.

She shrugged. "The store opens at ten. Sometime around then."

He tilted his head and looked puzzled.

"Why are you looking at me like that?" she asked as the heat rose to her neck.

"Don't you come early to set up or get ready for business?" he asked.

"It's not necessary."

Jill had to step back to keep from being too heavily scrutinized by those gray blue eyes that seemed to penetrate her thoughts. She stumbled over a quilted stuffed animal she'd dropped yesterday but had forgotten to pick up and put away. That only made it worse. She wanted simply to tell him it was none of his business when she arrived at the store, but that wasn't the case. She knew he probably wanted to get an early start.

He glanced down at the stuffed animal then back at her. She tried to look away, but his gaze held hers.

"I reckon that'll be okay," he said, surprising her. "I have a few things to do down at city hall anyway."

"Okay, so I'll be here early tomorrow, but don't expect me to make a habit of it," Jill said as she turned toward the front of the store.

"I never asked you to—," he began.

"No, you didn't," she conceded, interrupting him. "But if that'll get this whole project over with faster, I'll work with you this once. What time do you want to get started?"

"Seven."

"Seven?" she shrieked. "I won't even be up at seven."

With a shrug Ed said, "Okay, what time do you want me to be here?"

Jill glanced down at her feet, thought for a moment, then looked at the wall behind him, not daring to meet his gaze again. It was too dangerous.

"I'll be here at seven."

He chuckled. "I've already told you this job will take a few weeks. If you trust me enough to give me a key, I can let myself in."

Jill gulped then nodded. "I'll have it for you in the morning."

The moment Ed left, the place seemed empty. Most of the remainder of the afternoon was slow, with the exception of a few stragglers, one of them Mrs. Crenshaw, who came in once a week and purchased every piece of milk glass Jill had been able to find. As soon as she'd wrapped the order and carried it to Mrs. Crenshaw's car, Jill glanced at one of her many clocks and decided she could go ahead and leave now. The sign on the door said she was open until six, and she still had fifteen minutes to go, but she was mentally exhausted.

She grabbed her purse and backed toward the door. Maybe tomorrow she could work on the checkbook and figure out where the ten-dollar mistake was since she'd be here before the store opened. She'd planned to call the bank today, but Ed Mathis had distracted her, and it was too late now; the bank was closed.

Oh, well. Jill started to pull the door to, then remembered her keys were on the counter. She shoved the door open, ran across the wooden plank floor, grabbed the keys, and headed for the door again. When she got to the porch, she saw a familiar male figure coming up the sidewalk.

"Closing for the day?" Ed asked as he took a glance at his watch. "A little early, isn't it?"

"It's my business, and I can leave whenever I feel like it."

"So why do you even bother posting hours on the sign?" he asked, nodding toward the wooden plaque on the door. "Instead of saying you're open from ten to six, you should have said you open whenever you get here and leave whenever you feel like it."

Jill reached up and shoved an annoying strand of hair behind her ear. "Hey, don't worry about it, Ed."

"I'm not worried," he said. "But wouldn't it be a shame to miss out on a big sale just because you didn't stick around until closing time?"

"Why?" she asked as she stopped in her tracks. "You planning on buying something big?"

He shrugged and hooked his thumbs in his belt loops. "Maybe."

She fumbled with her keys. "Want me to open back up?"

"Nah," he said as he continued looking at her in a way that made her very uncomfortable. Those eyes seemed to be all-knowing, his mouth set in a perpetual tilt of amusement, not to mention the fact that he was very handsome in an almost too-perfect sort of way. His hair was clean and freshly cut and his jeans appeared to have been ironed, maybe even starched.

Jill glanced down at her own tattered jeans. They weren't dirty, but they'd never seen an iron. And her T-shirt had been a promotional giveaway from the bank when she'd opened her account. His shirt had a collar and an emblem on the pocket. They were obviously polar opposites.

As if to drive the point home, another strand of hair fell over her eyes. Ed reached over and gently tucked it behind her ear. What was up with that? She stepped back and shook her head, letting the strand fall loose again. She tilted her head to one side and watched him grimace. Served him right for being too persnickety. Without a word, she headed toward her car.

"Don't forget to have a key made," he said as he watched her unlock her car that was parked along the side of the curb. "That is, if you trust me."

"I'll have it made sometime tomorrow," she said. "Probably during lunch."

"Sounds good." Ed remained standing on the sidewalk.

She wished he'd leave or at least turn around.

"I need to run. The nanny can't stay past six."

"Nanny?" She stopped cold in her tracks.

He nodded. "Yeah, I have twin daughters."

"You do?" She didn't know he was attached, but what should that matter? "You're married?"

He shook his head. "My wife developed complications during her pregnancy and died after she delivered them. As soon as I was able to get back to work, I had to hire a nanny."

She swallowed hard. "I'm sorry. It's none of my business. I'm really sorry. Sometimes I say stupid—"

"That's okay." Ed's smile was tender. "My girls and I are just fine."

Jill didn't know what to do, so she smiled back. Now she felt even more awkward.

It had been a very long time since Jill had been self-conscious because, quite frankly, she hardly ever cared what a man thought about her. She was what she was, and she wasn't about to change her ways.

Her perfectionist father had been such a stickler. He'd ruined any desire she might've had for ever wanting to dress up or do housework, which was why her shop and her house both looked as if someone had shaken them and left things where they'd landed. But that was the way she liked her life, and it was too bad if someone thought she was a mess.

Her small house was situated on a narrow, tree-lined residential road off Peachtree Street, about a mile from the shop. She'd decided to start out small, and as the shop grew she would reassess her life and maybe get something nicer or fix up her place. For now, though, the cottage with the overgrown yard was perfect for her. One of these days she planned to do something about the shaggy shrubs and the weeds in the flower garden. She'd already pulled up some of the kudzu, because one of the neighbors had warned her how it would take over everything else if she didn't. But that's where she stopped. She had other things to fill her time for now.

Since her driveway was covered in weeds and she didn't want to take a chance on getting a flat tire from whatever else lay in the path, she didn't bother parking in the carport in the backyard by the alley. She pulled up and parallel-parked at the curb in front of her house.

The front porch still needed a coat of paint, something she'd intended to do first thing when she moved in, but she hadn't gotten around to it yet. Even if it never got done, as far as Jill was concerned, it was no big deal.

She had no doubt all of this would annoy Ed. He was a perfectionist—just like her father, which was the biggest reason she needed to keep her emotions in check.

Jill slipped the key in the lock and turned it as she jiggled the handle to open the door. This thing always stuck. Almost everything in Jill's life stuck, creaked, or squeaked. She was used to it.

Once inside her tiny house, Jill flipped on the switch. The ceiling light cast a dull glow over the room. She hadn't bothered picking up her blanket from the sofa, where she'd fallen asleep the night before. *Oh, well, let it stay there,* she thought. She'd need it again tonight.

Ever since Jill had started her business, she'd had a hard time falling asleep in her bed. So she reclined on the sofa and watched late-night talk shows, which had become so boring and predictable she was eventually able to go to sleep. This pattern would be a tough one to break, but that didn't matter. Jill lived alone, and she could do anything she pleased.

Her father would turn over in his grave if he could see how his daughter lived amidst all this clutter. His motto had been, "Everything has its place."

Sure, at times Jill felt guilty that she'd abandoned her upbringing and his rules, but he was gone and couldn't see it anyway. So what did it matter?

Dishes were still piled in the sink from breakfast, so she opened the dishwasher and shoved them all inside to expose a little counter space. Maybe she'd run a load soon and put them away. Or maybe she'd just leave them in the dishwasher and pull them out as needed. What did it matter?

She popped a frozen dinner in the microwave and left the kitchen to find her collectibles magazine to read while she ate. By the time she returned to the kitchen the buzzer had gone off, letting her know her food was ready.

Although this wasn't the way she'd envisioned her life, Jill was perfectly content. . .well, most of the time, anyway. No unnecessary rules; no one to tell her where to be or when to be there; no restrictions on food or someone standing over her making sure she had three squares. Just her life to be lived the way she wanted.

She wasn't lonely.

Jill sighed. Who was she trying to kid? She'd give her favorite knickknack to have someone to talk to right now. Someone who understood her and cared enough to listen.

"Oh, well, it's not going to happen anytime soon," she mumbled to herself. She picked the magazine back up and forced herself to look at it.

As she flipped the pages, she noticed how neatly the items in the pictures were arranged. Once Ed finished building her shelves in the back room, she could do a much better job of organizing her merchandise and have arrangements ready to be placed on the shelves.

Suddenly she slammed the magazine shut. Once his image had popped into her head, she wasn't able to get rid of it. She so needed a break—which included not thinking about the man who reminded her way too much of her father and his neatnik ways.

Jill let out a sigh. It was still early enough that she could probably head for the mall and find someone to duplicate the key to the store. Any work Ed did before she arrived would put him that much closer to completing the job and getting him out of there. He had daughters. That one fact alone was a good enough reason to stop thinking about him. She did not need to worry, or even think, about children—too much responsibility.

❧

Ed fully expected to have to wait for Jill, but he reached the store bright and early the next morning. He'd picked up a sack of muffins on the way so he could have breakfast under the big oak tree outside the shop and enjoy the early morning hours.

Life was so busy these days that he loved taking a few minutes here and there to enjoy some of God's blessings. There was nothing better than the sounds and smells of early morning. *Animals work hard for survival,* he thought, as a squirrel scampered by, carrying a nut to the next tree. He inhaled deeply and relished the freshness of the crisp north Georgia air. Fall had arrived, but a few protected floral stragglers remained in the yard around Jill's shop. Ed loved everything about the Atlanta area—from the terrain to the variety of people who'd made it their home.

"You weren't kidding, were you?" he heard from behind.

He licked his lips and swallowed the last bite of his muffin. "I never expected to see you here this early."

She rolled her eyes and shook her head. "Then why did you come? For the thrill of making me feel guilty for making you wait?"

"Maybe," he teased.

Jill brushed past him and headed straight for the door. She shoved her key in hard and turned it. She had to lean into the door to get it to open; then it creaked.

"That probably just needs some WD-40," he said.

"Whatever." Jill reached over and flipped a light switch, then went to the counter and dropped her purse and the other bag she was carrying on the floor. She spun around and held up something shiny. "Here's your key."

Ed smiled as he reached for the key he thought he'd never have. "So you do trust me after all."

Chapter 3

Ed felt an overwhelming urge to reach out and take her hand, to assure her he was trustworthy.

He would never do anything to hurt any client, especially her. In the short time he'd known her, his protective nature had kicked into high gear.

"Is there any reason why I shouldn't trust you?" she asked, her voice low and unsure.

"No reason at all, Jill. C'mon—let me show you what we have to do." His voice cracked.

Jill's eyes grew rounder as she followed him from room to room.

"This is going to cost me a fortune, even if I'm only charged for materials," she said with a groan. "And I'm sunk."

"Not necessarily," he said. "It's not as bad as it seems. The only thing you have to remember is to let me do my job. As a builder I get construction materials at wholesale."

She finally sighed and nodded. "Okay, do what you have to do. I have to trust you."

Ed felt his chest constrict. He wanted her trust more than he'd realized.

Less than an hour later Matt showed up. "Finish it quickly," Ed quietly told him. "Keep in mind Jill's getting a little nervous about all this. Whatever you do, don't let on how much it costs. Just give me the bill, okay?"

Matt grinned. "She's your new pet project, huh?" Ed's friends had always teased him about wanting to rescue people in distress. Matt leaned back, looked at the woman with the wild curls piled on top of her head, then glanced back at Ed. "Not bad, Ed. She's really cute. You could do much worse."

Ed knew Matt couldn't possibly understand the conflicting feelings he had for Jill. Even *he* didn't fully understand them. Yes, he was attracted to her; but, no, he wasn't about to act on his feelings.

But he wasn't able to get her out of his mind, either, even when a wall stood between them. Her innocent and trusting expressions chipped away at the shield he'd placed over his heart after his wife died. He tightened his jaw. Being around Jill evoked a feeling he hadn't experienced in a very long time.

Each time he caught a whiff of her spicy fragrance, he found his mind drifting into territory he'd been avoiding since Marcy died. After all he'd gone through with losing his wife, Ed felt it was best to guard against any chance of losing his heart again.

"Ed!" he heard Jill holler from the front room. "I hate to bother you, but could you come in here a minute?"

He propped the sheet of drywall he'd been working with against a stud and rushed to see what she needed. When he got to the door, he saw her standing dangerously close to the edge of the top rung of a stepladder, reaching as high as her arms would go, but still not high enough to get the ceramic rooster off the top shelf.

"Don't you know you're not supposed to stand on the top step?" He offered her a hand.

"I really need that rooster," she said as she took his hand and cautiously stepped down.

"Okay." Ed helped her down, then moved the ladder to one side.

"Hey, what are you doing?" she asked. "Even you can't reach that without a ladder."

Ed moved quickly to the back room, grabbed the taller ladder, and hoisted it into place. "If you're gonna stick stuff up that high, I suggest you get the equipment you need."

"You're the one who put it back up there."

"Only because you wanted it there," he replied as gently as he could.

She placed her hands on her hips and watched him. Her eyes showed a combination of emotions besides frustration—anger, relief, and maybe even a little admiration—as he grabbed hold of the rooster and began to descend the ladder.

"Hey, be careful with that. That thing cost me a fortune."

Ed chuckled. "Who woulda guessed?"

As soon as Ed offered it to her, Jill reached for it. "Don't pass judgment on something you know nothing about," she said as their fingers touched.

The tight sensation in his chest should have served as a warning to keep his distance, but the look in her eyes held him captive for a few seconds—just long enough for him to lose his breath.

Jill glanced down at the floor as she took a step back, nearly falling over the basket that lay on the floor behind her. Ed caught her just in time.

"Whoa there," he said as he cupped his palms beneath her elbows.

He refrained from saying anything about the clutter on the floor. That wouldn't serve any purpose at the moment, and he knew it.

To keep her from falling, he instinctively pulled her to him. She was still hanging on to the rooster, which slammed him in the chest.

"Ouch!" he said. He let go and inhaled deeply. "That thing's lethal."

Jill tilted her head and glared at him. "You're determined to make me feel stupid, aren't you?"

"Why would you say that?"

She backed toward the counter and carefully set the rooster down. "First of all, you tell me I can't build sturdy enough shelves to hold my excess stock. Then you tell me this place is falling apart and that my investment is worthless. And now you're making fun of what I sell. I'll have you know—"

Ed held up his hands to shush her. "Stop right there, Jill. I'm just here to do a job. I didn't mean to insult you."

"But you did."

"I'm sorry."

She sniffed. That protective feeling still hadn't left Ed. He shuffled his feet and tried to redirect his thoughts.

"Apology accepted."

"You asked me to help you get something down off the top shelf. If you want me to stay away from you, just tell me right now."

She blinked a couple of times, but to his surprise she didn't say anything.

❧

Jill couldn't remember the last time she'd shown her emotions in front of a man. Her father had forbidden her to shed tears, because he said it was a sign of weakness. After practicing keeping a stiff upper lip, Jill couldn't imagine letting her fears be known to someone she'd only met yesterday.

This business was what she'd dreamed of all her life. Her grandmother had had a house filled with knickknacks and fun little figurines that delighted Jill from her earliest memory. Moving around from one military base to another had prevented her from collecting all the items she'd loved as a child. So she'd promised to surround herself with pretty and fun things when she was grown. Her own collections had inspired her desire to be in the collectibles business, where she could talk to and help people with common interests all day long.

Opening the Junktique Shoppe had been like a dream come true, until she realized she wasn't capable of doing everything that needed to be done around here. Her underestimation of the cost of a business could ruin her before she had a chance. She'd had no idea how much utilities were before she'd actually had them turned on. All she'd figured on was the price of the building and purchasing items for resale. Going into business for herself was like being doused with a bucket of ice water when reality kicked in.

Being self-employed beat working for someone else. But it wasn't nearly as much fun as she'd thought it would be because of the hard, cold, money issues.

Now her handyman—her kindhearted, great-looking handyman with the penetrating eyes that could see through her facade—was trying to save her from herself.

She'd put everything into this business. A nice, elderly woman from the Greater Atlanta Small Business Administration had given her some advice and helped her to work up a plan. She would do her best to stick to it, despite the bad news about the building.

"The biggest reason businesses fail is that the owners don't make plans and stick to them," the woman had said. "You'll have to tighten your belt, but if you can get through the first couple of years, you'll do just fine."

But what if she wasn't able to make it through the first couple of years? Everything her father had left her would go down the drain if the Junktique Shoppe failed. And if she kept throwing her profit into fixing this dilapidated house, she was certain to face bankruptcy in no time.

Maybe she should have stayed in her apartment in Dallas, kept her receptionist job with the small advertising agency, and invested her inheritance money for retirement. That would have been the safe thing to do. Much safer to her heart, at least, than facing this man every day for the next few weeks. But she would always have felt a pull to the place her mother loved and wanted to return to until the day she'd passed away.

Her mother used to tell her about Atlanta and how wonderful it was. She had talked about the people from all over who came together in the sprawling metropolis, the beautiful terrain, the shopping, and the Varsity, which at that time laid claim to being the biggest fast-food restaurant in the world. When she got to Atlanta, the first thing Jill did was go to the Varsity and order a frosted orange and some onion rings.

Fearful of having Ed look at her again, Jill turned away from him as she said, "Thanks, Ed."

"No problem."

The sound of his boots on the hardwood floor let her know he was walking away from her. Now she could relax and get on with the business of figuring out the error in her checkbook.

Jill chewed on the tip of her mechanical pencil, studying the rows of numbers in the bank book, still confused over where ten dollars could have gone. She was so deep in thought, she jumped when she heard the sound from the other side of the counter.

"Didn't mean to scare you," he said. "Having a problem?"

"Uh, yeah," she admitted. After all, it had to be obvious she wasn't having fun.

"Mechanical pencils aren't made for gnawing," he said with a half smile, one corner of his lips lifted in a make-my-day tilt.

She blew out a breath. "I just hate when my books don't balance."

A snort escaped Ed's lips. "I never would have figured you for the balanced-checkbook sort of gal."

"What?" She looked at him with a squint.

Right when she was ready to defend herself, Ed glanced down, then looked back up at her. "Sorry," he said. "That was totally uncalled for. Sometimes I stick my foot in my mouth and say stupid things."

All the fighting wind had been blown from Jill's sail. "Hey, don't worry about it. I understand." And she did. Everything else in her life was in chaos. Why wouldn't he think her checkbook would be, too?

Nodding toward the checkbook, Ed said, "Mind if I take a look at that? I'm pretty good with numbers."

She hesitated for a moment then pushed it toward him. What harm was there in letting him see what she had—or didn't have—in her business account? He wasn't blind. He could see she was struggling.

Ed hadn't been looking at her checkbook more than a couple of minutes when his friends started to arrive. One by one Jill met them, and she found herself amazed by their kindness and eagerness to get started right away.

&

At the end of a long, whirlwind day, Ed showed Jill where her checking account error was. The bank had coded one of her checks improperly. It was their error, not hers. Fortunately, catching the mistake was in her favor. "Thanks so much, Ed," she told him more than once as he gathered his tools and began stacking things while getting ready to leave for the day.

"No problem," he replied. "I need to get home soon. My daughters' nanny has to leave early today, and I can't be late."

He noticed how she visibly tensed at the mention of his daughters. She didn't appear wild about children, which was another very good reason to keep his emotional distance from her. Although he was attracted to Jill, he knew he couldn't get involved with her. He and his girls were part of a package, making it even more difficult to think about getting into a relationship. Not many women were prepared for two very lively preschoolers who could outsmart most adults.

After Ed left the shop he headed straight home. The girls had their noses pressed against the big picture window in the living room. Suddenly their little faces disappeared from the window; then the two reappeared at the front door.

"Daddy!" Stacy said as she flung open the door. She threw herself into his arms, while her twin sister, the more demure Tracy, pulled at his hand. "We're starving."

Mrs. Cooper, the nanny, already had her purse hooked over her arm. "Sorry to do this to you, Mr. Mathis, but I really must go. I thawed the ground beef as you asked me to."

"Thanks," he told her. "See you in the morning."

The second she was gone, Stacy piped up. "Daddy, we wanna go to the Varsity for chili cheese dogs."

"I thought we'd cook hamburgers on the grill tonight."

"Let's do that tomorrow," Stacy said. "I want a chili cheese dog."

"That okay with you, Tracy?" he asked as he glanced down at his other daughter. She nodded. "Okay, Varsity it is. We'll cook out tomorrow night."

"Can I have french fries?"

Ed blew out a sigh. "You can have whatever you want, Stacy."

"What'd you do today, Daddy?" Tracy asked after he fastened them both into their car seats in the backseat of the cab of his truck.

"Well," he began, "there's this really interesting shop I've been helping restore." Then he told them about the Junktique Shoppe while they listened, paying close attention to every word he said.

Finally Stacy said, "Is she pretty?"

Ed squinted. "Is who pretty?"

"The lady. Jill."

"Oh, her. Yeah, I guess she's pretty."

With a quick glance in the rearview mirror, he could see Tracy turn around and look at her sister, a smile quirking her face. "I wanna see her," Stacy said.

He should have figured as much. "Maybe later."

"When?"

"How about when I finish the job?"

Ed knew from experience he needed to change the subject quickly, or he'd have to answer more questions about Jill. They took the bait, but he knew this wasn't the last he'd hear from his daughters.

After they got home from the Varsity he helped them with their baths, read stories to them, tucked them into their beds, and said prayers with them. "Love you, girls," he said, backing toward the door.

"Love you, too, Daddy," they said in unison.

Later on that night Ed lay in his own bed, thinking about the progress he'd made at the shop. He had an odd sensation about Jill. Something besides the state of disrepair of her shop was going on with her. What had happened to cause her so much worry?

Maybe the Lord had brought Ed into Jill's life for a reason other than fixing her shop. He wasn't sure about much in his life, but he did know one thing: Whenever things didn't make sense to him, he needed to be quiet and let the Lord take over. He prayed for guidance. Being there for Jill didn't mean he needed to get romantically involved with her; he'd have to be very careful not to let that happen.

When he arrived at the shop the next morning, two of his friends were there, waiting for someone to unlock the door. "We thought you'd never get here," Matt said.

"I had to wait for the nanny." Ed unlocked the door to let them in. "Before we get started I want to tell you guys something."

They huddled in the corner while he explained his mission and how he suspected Jill needed more than handy work in her shop. They nodded their understanding and promised they'd watch for opportunities to pray for her.

"Just remember," he said, "we have to be very gentle. I suspect there's something deep going on."

By the time Jill arrived, the three men were well into their tasks. She grinned as Ed greeted her.

"Wow!" she said. "You told me you'd be fast, but I had no idea."

Ed grinned back at her but had to turn away. Her face glowed when she smiled, with the corners of her lips turned up, her eyes sparkling, reflecting the light from the sunshine that streamed in through the eastern window. Before he'd averted his gaze, he'd seen the gold flecks dancing around in those big brown eyes.

"I brought muffins," she told them. "Take a break and help yourself."

They all helped themselves, then returned to work. Jill followed Ed to the back, nibbling on the edge of a muffin, her eyebrows knit in a frown.

"You okay?" he asked.

"I guess," she said with a shrug.

Ed paused for a moment before he decided to take a leap and ask a question he knew could elicit either a cold stare or her fury—but he was willing to take a chance. "Would you like to go to our church sometime?"

She paused and stared at him for a moment. "Uh, maybe sometime."

"How about this Sunday?" he asked, looking directly at her.

Jill squirmed. "Not this Sunday."

"Why not?"

"I don't know, Ed. Maybe later, okay?"

"Sure, that's fine. I just figured you might want to visit our church. We have a lot of nice folks there, and the preacher has a great way of sharing the gospel."

"I think I'll just stick to reading my Bible for the time being. Back when my father was alive, he made me get all dressed up in stupid, stiff dresses he picked out for me. Then we had to sit quietly in hard, wooden pews while some preacher droned on and on about how bad we were. Then, when we got home, my father told me that if I didn't behave I'd burn in hell. I hated every minute of it." She paused and swallowed hard. "I know Jesus died on the cross for me, but I don't want to be miserable all the time feeling guilty."

That certainly explains a lot, Ed thought. He'd seen other Christians who worked the guilt angle on other believers, and he didn't like it, either.

"Did you ever listen to the message?" Ed asked.

A pained expression crossed her face. "Look, Ed—I'm not sure where you're going with this, but you're making me very uncomfortable. I read my Bible, and I'm a believer. You don't have to convert me."

"Yeah, I guess you're right." Time to step back.

"I'll find a church in my own time," she added. "Just don't rush me."

The bell on the front door jingled as a customer entered. "My break's over," Jill announced, jumping up to help the woman who was already perusing the shelves. "Go ahead and finish off the muffins. I'm done."

Ed sat there and stared after Jill, wondering what to do next. He didn't want to try to talk Jill into going to his church, but he did want her to come with him at least once. Even if she was getting the Lord's Word regularly through reading scripture, she still needed to worship somewhere.

❧

"Look, man. You gotta let go and let the Lord work through you," Joe advised Ed later. The three men were sitting in the small café down the street eating sandwiches for lunch. "You can't force things."

Ed nodded. "I know."

Matt turned to Joe and snickered. "I think Jill's wormed her way into Ed's heart."

Not denying it, but also not admitting anything, Ed said, "As I already told you, Jill needs help in more ways than one, and I'm not a guy who shirks responsibility."

"Let's get back to work, then," Matt said as he stood up, pulled out his wallet, and dropped a couple of dollars on the table for the tip. "The little woman's waiting for us."

The shop was crowded when they got back, so the three men went right to work. Jill was constantly surrounded by customers, and she handled them beautifully. Ed again saw that she was in her element, which reinforced his resolve to help her as much as was humanly possible.

Several hours later Jill came back to see how he was doing. "Can I get you something?" she asked.

"Nah, I'm fine." Ed finished hammering in the nail and stopped, turning to face her. "Business is good today, huh?"

"Yeah, it's fair. I can't complain." She had a questioning look in her eyes, but she didn't ask anything.

"Look—I'm sorry if I upset you earlier."

"Upset me?" She tilted her head, forcing one huge lock of curls to flop out of her clip.

"About church. I didn't mean to bring up unpleasant memories."

"Don't worry about it. I'm okay." Her voice was tight, so he knew she wasn't okay. "I'm used to people trying to drag me to church. As soon as people find out I'm a Christian without a church home"—she snapped her fingers—"they start working on me."

That comment annoyed him. "I'm not trying to drag you to church, Jill."

"You weren't? Are you saying you don't want me to come to your church?" Now she was challenging him.

"Of course I want you to come to my church."

She grinned and let out a little chuckle. "Better make up your mind."

Now he realized she was teasing. Ed was grateful she'd finally relaxed around him.

As soon as she went back to her customer, Ed squeezed his eyes shut and prayed silently. *I'm ready to do Your will, Lord. Please show me how best to serve You and act according to Your plan. I want to do everything to Your glory and in Your timing.*

When he opened his eyes, Jill was staring at him, her eyebrows raised. "Sorry if I interrupted you," she said, "but I have a question about something upstairs."

Chapter 4

After leading him upstairs, she stopped and turned to face him. "Well?" She pointed to a small shelf that lay on its side, shards of broken glass surrounding it.

"Looks like a mess."

Jill's frown deepened. "Yeah, it's a mess. We need to do something about it."

"Got a broom?" he asked.

She continued watching him. There was something in this picture he wasn't getting.

Finally he sucked in a deep breath and blew it out. "Okay, I give. Wanna clue me in?"

"You really don't know, do you? You have no idea."

"Right." Holding out his hands, he added, "I'm clueless, stupefied, and maybe downright ignorant."

"Seems to me like someone with your experience would understand what vibrations can do to glass."

"Vibrations? Glass?" He looked at the shards on the floor as it dawned on him. Pointing to the freestanding bookcase that had toppled over, he asked, "Did I do that?"

"Uh-huh. And that's not all. Look around."

He turned and scanned the room. Empty mirror and picture frames were scattered over the floor next to an interior wall. If his quick calculations were correct, that wall was directly above the one he'd been working on.

Doing a mental forehead slap, Ed offered what he hoped was a sincere look of contrition. "Look, Jill. I'm sorry. I'll replace it. All of it."

"How do you replace something that's irreplaceable?"

True. "Then I'll pay you for it. I'm truly sorry."

He saw her frustration, but there was nothing she could do or say, now that the damage was done. She lifted her hand to her face, covered her mouth, and shook her head as she glanced around the room.

"What can I do to make everything better, Jill?" he asked.

Her shoulders sagged. She had the look of a beaten-down woman with nowhere to go. Ed's heart lurched, but he refrained from wrapping his arms around her for comfort. He couldn't hold himself back completely, though. He took a step closer and gently placed his hand on her shoulder. She glanced up at him with an odd expression—one he couldn't read.

That was when he knew. "This has nothing to do with the broken glass, does it?"

She slowly shook her head and turned her back to him, placing another foot of distance between them. His heart ached for Jill. He wanted to help her, but he couldn't when she kept closing herself off from him.

"Jill? Please tell me what's troubling you."

Her body shook for a second before she spoke. "Just give me a minute, okay?"

He started to turn and head back downstairs, but he changed his mind. Bracing himself for whatever reaction she might have, he narrowed the gap between them and gently placed both hands on her shoulders. She suddenly stiffened.

"Jill," he said firmly.

She barely lifted her head an inch, but she didn't turn to face him. At least she didn't push him away.

"If you need me, I'm here. As for all this stuff I broke, I'll take care of it." Ed let go of her and backed away. "I was very careless." Then he walked away to give her some space.

He'd made it to the second step when he heard her voice. "Ed," she said softly.

He paused and counted to three. When he spun around to face her, he hadn't expected to see her so close. Somehow she'd crossed the expansive room without his hearing her footsteps.

"Yes, Jill?"

"Thanks." She sniffled. "I'm sorry I went all nutso over the stuff that fell, but with all the stress. . ." She gestured around the room. "You know."

"Yes, I do know."

"And I know this isn't your fault. You had no way of knowing I had all this breakable stuff up here. I should have told you."

"I should have asked."

Ed's chest tightened as they stood there in silence. Years of being in control of every aspect of his own life and guarding his heart hadn't prepared him for this.

One thing he knew for certain: He couldn't continue walking on eggshells around her just to keep her from skittering away from him. He needed to be bolder and stand up for what he believed. Why should he back off just because he was dealing with a flustered woman? In fact, that was all the more reason he should be more aggressive.

Ed decided to take care of the problem at hand and figure out a way to witness to this broken woman. "Now, if you have a broom I'll clean this up."

"No, that's okay. I'll take care of it."

"I want—"

She gave him a dismissive wave of the hand. "No, that's okay, but thanks."

He had to force himself not to smile. With each word from her mouth came strength. *Atta girl.*

As Ed went back to work, he thought about what made Jill tick. Was she lonely? Or had something awful happened that made her so skittish? She'd told him a little about her dad, so perhaps there was more to it than what she'd said. Everyone needed someone, so he suspected she needed friends. He had his church friends, and he wanted to share them with her.

After Marcy's death he'd been lonely, too. And angry. Her gestational diabetes was supposed to go away after the babies were born. The unfairness of it all had nearly toppled his world. But his twin babies needed him, so he'd pushed his anger aside until eventually it just faded with time. And fortunately the church had been there for him when he needed them most—the very thing that solidified his faith that had been shaken to the core when Marcy died.

He'd actually stopped going to church for a while. But one of his subcontractors had persisted, and one of the elderly women from church came over to help care for the girls. With all that Christian love, he'd finally realized his faith was the most important aspect of his life.

He nearly slammed his hand with the hammer as he heard footsteps behind him. "Must be some good thoughts goin' on over there," Matt said.

"Hey, man, what's up? You finished with the wiring?"

"Not hardly." Matt hooked his fingers in his belt loops. "We've got a couple of issues here, and I need to talk to you for a minute."

"Shoot." Ed laid his hammer on the workbench. "What do you need?"

Matt gestured toward the back door. "Step outside?"

Dread washed over Ed. Taking it outside could only mean more bad news. They'd barely stepped outside when Matt hit him with the news. "This place needs to be fumigated."

"Bugs?" Ed said with a nod. "Yeah, I did see a few."

"Yeah, there are bugs. Termites."

Ed groaned. "I saw 'em, too. Think it's bad enough to need tenting?"

"Positive. One of the walls is practically gone. Want me to talk to her?"

"No," Ed said. "Better not. Let's just handle it. I broke a few things, and that set her on edge, so I don't think she'd deal well with news of termites."

Matt nodded. "Okay, if you're sure. My wife comes home in a few days, so I need to get through this as quickly as I can and go back to my commercial job."

"Thanks, Matt."

Ed lingered in the backyard while Matt ambled back inside. Termite infestation. No doubt that would put Jill over the edge.

The door hadn't closed all the way when Ed saw Jill pushing on it. She was by his side in seconds.

"Taking a break?" she asked.

"Yeah, sort of."

He turned away, unable to face her. He wasn't going to lie to her, but he planned to wait until he figured out what to do before saying anything about the termites.

Clouds overhead floated between the earth and the sun, shading them for a few seconds. When the sun came back out, he noticed how it glistened on her hair, bringing out the copper highlights. She turned and smiled up at him.

"You're pretty when you smile," he said.

"Thank you." Her words were so soft they were barely a whisper.

❧

Jill had never wanted to kiss a man as much as she wanted to kiss Ed Mathis right this minute. His kindness radiated from his every pore. Just looking at him gave her a sense of security she hadn't had since her mother was alive.

She swallowed hard to try to get her voice back. "I really am sorry for overreacting about the broken glass. I guess I just don't deal with bad surprises very well."

"No one does, but unfortunately life has plenty of bad surprises."

"I've just had so many lately."

He smiled at her. "That's why I start and end my day with prayer."

Jill nodded and glanced away. She prayed, too, but she didn't like to discuss it. Her relationship with Jesus was very personal. When she'd talked to her father about it, he'd made her feel that her simple faith wasn't good enough, so she'd decided to keep some things to herself.

"I really appreciate all you're doing for me," she said, when she couldn't think of anything else to talk about.

"I think we've already established that. And I know you know I'm glad to do it."

She nodded. "Well, I guess I'd better get back inside, just in case I have another customer."

"Yeah, I guess you'd better."

She'd walked inside and had barely rounded the corner when Matt greeted her. "Wiring will be done soon. I have to finish connecting the upstairs; then I'll disconnect the old wires. You should be in good shape—at least, electrically speaking."

Jill chuckled at his choice of words. "Thanks, Matt."

Grinning, he slapped his tool belt. "Glad to be able to help. Gotta get back to work." Then he disappeared, leaving her alone.

Jill had barely turned toward the register area when she heard Ed hollering from the backyard. She turned to the lone customer, said, "Be right back," and ran out to see what all the fuss was about.

"I see you've met Tiger." Jill looked down at the small yellow kitten standing at Ed's feet, her back arched and her fangs showing as she hissed up at him. She was so cute!

"He looks hungry," Ed said.

"She. And you're right. She's always hungry." She moved toward Ed, bent over, and scooped up the kitten before backing away from him.

"I didn't know you had a cat."

"I don't. She's a stray."

Ed frowned. "If you feed a stray cat, it becomes yours."

Jill shrugged. "How would I know? I never had a pet before. My dad wouldn't let me."

Ed's sympathetic expression unnerved her. She nuzzled the kitten to her cheek and rubbed her as she purred.

"I guess I'd better get back to finishing that wall," Ed said. "I'll leave you and your. . .Tiger to sort things out."

Once Ed had gone back inside, Jill carefully placed Tiger on the ground in front of her food bowl. Tiger glanced toward the door Ed had slammed behind him before turning her attention to the tuna morsels. "Looks like you and I are stuck with each other," Jill said softly to the kitten.

When Jill got back inside, Ed was working steadily on the wall. Without so much as turning around, he reached out. "I took care of your customer. She bought some little glass bowls, and I stuck the money in the envelope under the cash register. Mind handing me that spackling gun?"

"Uh, sure," she said as she glanced around and tried to figure out what he wanted. "As soon as you tell me what it is."

Ed chuckled as he pointed. "That big silver tube-shaped thing."

"Oh, that."

She stood and watched as he slowly and carefully finished off that section of wall, then cleaned up what little mess he'd made.

"Why are you so persnickety?" she asked.

"I like to do things right."

"Yes," she agreed, "but there are extremes."

He glared at her, so she quickly backed off. She was relieved to hear the bells jingle on the front door. "Want me to take care of this customer?" Ed joked.

She shot him a look as she ran to offer assistance. "Thanks a lot, but I'll get this one."

The woman who'd walked into the Junktique Shoppe had only stopped to ask directions.

"You should have seized the opportunity and sold her something," Ed chided.

She shrugged but didn't bother defending herself. What was the point? He had already obviously formed an opinion of how she conducted business, and it clearly wasn't a good one.

At the end of the day Jill headed home. She'd forgotten to open the blinds that morning, so the living room was dark. She found her way to the back of the long, narrow house. Everything was where she'd left it. As they did every day about this time, her father's words haunted her. Until she'd read the Bible on her own, her father had her convinced cleanliness was next to godliness. Now she knew he'd twisted scripture and used her ignorance against her. She was thankful for learning the gospel in college, or she wouldn't have understood the truth during this difficult time.

After a quick microwaved meal, Jill grabbed her collectibles book and headed for bed. She shut her eyes and asked God for His help getting through the next few months—or years—and eventually finding her way in the world. She had a hard time with prayer. She was never sure how to put her thoughts into a message Jesus would actually want to hear.

Thumbing through her collectibles book, Jill couldn't keep her mind on what she needed to do, so she shut her eyes to try to redirect her thoughts. She fell asleep with the book facedown over her chest and awoke to incessant chirping from a bird in the tree outside her bedroom window.

After cereal and coffee, she showered and dressed. She was about to leave for the day when she caught her reflection in the hall mirror. "Ugh." She did an about-face and headed back to her bathroom to put on some lipstick and a little mascara.

When Jill arrived in front of the shop, a half-dozen work vans and trucks were parked along the curb, barely leaving enough space for her car. They were mostly parked on one side of the street that was on a steep incline.

"Good morning, sunshine," Ed said when he saw her.

She swallowed hard and looked at him, then reached up to tuck a loose curl behind her ear.

"Don't," he said as he touched her hand. "I like the way the curl falls."

"I don't."

"Sorry." He turned to face a couple of his buddies who'd come out to ask him a question. "We only have a few more minutes before opening time. Almost done?"

They both nodded, then took their turns asking him about construction issues. Jill took advantage of his diverted attention and darted past them to go inside.

❧

Ed thought Jill was gorgeous before, but today she nearly left him speechless. One look at her, and he felt as if the wind had been knocked out of him. And her obvious vulnerability left him unable to run as far from her as he could and as fast as he knew he should. No way could he take off when someone obviously needed something from him.

He watched her for a little while before turning to his own work. He had to field a couple of questions, but he managed to finish a wall.

"Hey, Ed," she said as she approached him from behind. "Who's that man crawling around under the house?"

He spun around to face her. He had to spoon-feed her in bits and pieces, or she'd freak out. "Are you talking about the exterminator?"

She frowned. "Don't tell me I have bugs, too."

"Yeah, you do have some bugs."

Tilting her head to one side, she narrowed her gaze. "What's the big deal about bugs?"

"This house needs to be treated for pests," he said, trying hard to hold back anything that might trigger an alarm in her.

"Yeah, I guess you probably don't want bugs in your food when I start cooking dinner for you and your crew." She placed her fist on her hip and studied the floor for a moment before asking, "When do you want me to start?"

"Next week okay?" Ed asked. "I'll bring the food if you'll make a few extra servings for my girls."

Her face grew red. "I don't know anything about cooking kid food."

"My girls will eat anything you cook. In fact, we're going out to dinner tonight. Want to join us?"

She quickly shook her head. "No, thanks. I have. . .plans."

"Maybe some other time?"

"Uh, sure." He watched her process her thoughts before she said, "I'll start cooking on Monday if that's okay. I can cook at home and bring it in. I'll even make enough for Matt's wife and your children. I'd cook here, but I don't have a stove or a refrigerator in the kitchen yet."

"Oh, I almost forgot," he said. "Take a look at your kitchen."

"Wha—?" she said as she backed toward the kitchen, then turned and ran. A second later he heard her squeal. "Who brought the refrigerator? And why? There's no way I can pay for this."

"It's for the guys. You don't expect everyone to do all this work and not have a place to keep their soft drinks, do you?"

"But I don't—"

He held up his hands to quiet her. "Stop it right now, Jill. It's a little gift from all of us to the new shop owner in town. It's free."

Her eyes misted over, and he had to look away.

"I'm in the building business, Jill. We get special deals on appliances all the time. Really, it's no big deal."

"Nothing's free," she said hoarsely.

He wanted to remind her of the fact that salvation through Christ was free, but he didn't. He nodded and said, "It'll give us a place to keep the food you're cooking for us until we can get it home."

Jill looked around, desperation shrouding her features, until her eyes lit up. "Then how about letting me send you home with something from my shop? I know it isn't much, but there's bound to be something you might like."

Such pride. "Okay, how about something for my girls? Their room isn't exactly a designer's paradise."

Jill nodded. "Do they like bright colors?"

"Oh, yeah. The brighter the better. Blinding, in fact."

"I just picked up a box of stuff from an estate sale," she said as she side-stepped toward the storage area. She sounded excited. "The elderly woman must have had granddaughters because she had all kinds of kid things."

He glanced down at the box she was opening. It was full of. . .junk. "Would you mind picking out a few things a couple of little girls might like?"

Finally she smiled, showing off a glowing face and beautiful, soft, kissable lips he noticed were painted a pretty shade of peach. "Don't worry. I'll fix them right up."

"Remember—just a couple of things for each of them."

She grinned but didn't say a word as she rummaged through the box.

At the end of the day Jill had a couple of boxes crammed full of picture frames, toys, character clocks, and wall hangings. With a sly grin she shrugged. "Girls need their stuff."

He reluctantly carried one box to the truck while she followed behind with the other. "Thanks in advance from the girls."

All the way home he thought about how surprised the girls would be. They greeted him at the door as they always did. He crooked his finger and motioned for them to come out and help him carry in some stuff. As soon as they saw what was in the boxes, their eyes lit up.

"Oh, Daddy, this is so cool!"

They squealed with delight as they dug in, pulling things out of the boxes, tossing items to the side as they dug some more. He noticed how spartan the living room had been before and how these boxes of junk had livened up things so quickly. Maybe Jill had a point.

"Look!" Tracy said as she held up some bright red square thing he couldn't identify.

"What is it?" Stacy asked.

Tracy shrugged. "I don't know, but it's pretty."

Ed had to hide his laughter. Jill was right.

When they reached the bottom of the boxes, Stacy turned to him. "Tell that lady. . .Jill. . .we like it."

"Hey, how about some food?" he asked.

The girls ignored him. They were back into the pile of things and were staking their claim on what they wanted. In fact, they'd both decided they wanted something he couldn't identify, other than calling it "that round thing." He had to break up their argument by saying they could take turns picking what they wanted until everything was claimed.

"Just remember you have to put all this junk away when you're finished with it," he reminded them.

"It's not junk, Daddy," Stacy said. "It's cool stuff." She turned to her sister. "C'mon, Tracy—let's go eat and get it over with. Daddy won't let us play with this until we get back."

Throughout dinner the girls grilled him with questions about Jill and her shop. He answered their questions as they came at him rapid-fire.

Tracy suddenly grew quiet as she rested her chin on her fist and stared out the window of the restaurant. Stacy was still chatty as ever, so Ed had to interrupt.

"Whatcha thinking, Tracy?" he asked.

Tracy crinkled her forehead as she leaned forward. "Can Jill be our mommy?"

Chapter 5

Okay, so maybe introducing his girls to Jill wouldn't be such a good idea. If something as simple as giving them a box of toys could get Tracy thinking like this, what would happen if they met?

"Tracy, honey. . ." He kicked his brain into high gear, trying his best to say the right thing. "Jill is just a friend. Why don't you simply enjoy her gift and leave it at that?"

She pouted. "But I want a mommy, and she's nice."

Stacy jabbed her. "How would you know if she's nice? We don't even know the lady."

Tracy turned to Ed. "Is she nice, Daddy?"

"She's very nice. But that doesn't mean she has to be your mommy. She can be our friend."

The rest of the night was spent discussing how they could do things with Jill as friends without making her their mommy. Ed had no idea what Jill would say, but that didn't matter at the moment. Besides, he didn't think she'd want to disappoint two very sweet little girls.

The next morning when he arrived at the shop he felt out of sorts. Jill had brought in some food, and she was sticking it in a microwave he hadn't seen before.

"Where'd you get that?" he asked.

Jill opened her mouth, but Matt stopped her. "I bought a new built-in for the house to surprise my wife, so I brought the freestanding one here for Jill."

"I offered to pay him," Jill said, "but he won't take it." She sighed. "So I'll just have to make breakfast, too."

Matt chuckled. "At this rate maybe you should have a café in the back of your shop."

"Now that's a thought," Jill said with a smile.

Suddenly Ed's day turned brighter—simply because Jill smiled. His heart melted at the warmth that lit up her face.

"I got a special deal on some prefab cabinets," Matt added. "One of the contractors I worked with on the last job had an extra set. They were dirt cheap, and I offered them to Jill. She's still trying to decide."

"Take them," Ed said. "You could use some cabinets."

Tension overtook Jill's face. "You said they were cheap, but you never did say how much."

"Practically free," Matt said as he glanced down.

Jill saw right through that. "I know they weren't free. Just give me a price."

"Pay me fifty dollars, and we'll be even," Matt said. "Hey, I gotta run. I have work to do. You can give me your answer later."

Ed was well aware the cabinets cost more than fifty dollars, but he wasn't about to interfere with his friend's generosity. Matt hadn't lied, but he sure had avoided Jill's question without giving a direct answer.

"Is fifty dollars too much?" Ed asked after Matt was gone.

She tilted her head and gave him a you've-got-to-be-kidding look. "I'm not stupid," she said.

"No, I realize that. But if Matt's offering you some cabinets for fifty bucks, you need to take him up on it."

"I hate being a charity case."

Ed decided to change the subject. "My girls loved their goodies. Thanks."

Jill offered a half smile. "I'm glad. You're very welcome."

"I never realized how something as simple as a box filled with trinkets would make them happy."

"I'm sure there are some things we both need to learn." The softness of her voice warmed his heart.

"Yes, I'm sure there are."

❧

The morning flew by for Jill. She had a steady stream of customers, most of them referrals from friends who'd been in before. People in Atlanta obviously loved antiques and collectibles. "This place is so charming," one woman said. "I hope you do well, dear."

Jill cut a glance over to Ed. She saw that he'd heard the woman, and that pleased her.

After the morning crowd thinned out, Ed stopped by the desk. "I'm going to lunch. Want something?"

"No, thanks. I brought a salad."

He offered a clipped nod. Once he was gone, Jill flopped into the chair beside the register desk. She was exhausted, and it wasn't just because she'd worked so hard all morning. Just being near Ed wore her out.

After giving herself a few minutes to recover, she headed back to the kitchen area that she hadn't seen since early morning. To her dismay, not only was the kitchen spotless, but a row of cabinets had been installed. She hadn't given Matt her final answer yet. Why wouldn't these guys let her make decisions for herself? Why did they assume they knew what was best for her?

She steamed and stewed until Ed returned from lunch. He took one look at her, dropped his smile, and took a step back. "Oh, no. What did I do now?"

Jill gestured around the kitchen. "Why, Ed?"

He shrugged. "I had to have someplace to put stuff, and they were right there in the back. It was easy, and I figured you couldn't pass up such a good deal."

As much as she hated to admit it, the kitchen was starting to take shape. All she needed to make it a full, serviceable kitchen was a range. But she wasn't about to mention that, or she knew one would appear.

"Okay, I s'pose you're right. But from now on please give me time, and let me decide what I want in my shop. I'm a grown woman, and in spite of what you might be thinking, I'm responsible."

As soon as those words left her mouth, she realized what she'd said. Although she'd fought tooth and nail about being tied down, she really was a responsible adult. She wasn't nearly as flighty as her father had always made her feel.

Ed's expression was unreadable. Finally he nodded. "Yeah, you're right. I apologize. From now on you call the shots. Just tell me what to do, and I'll do it."

Jill groaned. "I didn't mean it like that. What I meant was—"

"That's okay. I understand. And I totally agree. This is your place. Matt and I have no right trying to muscle our opinions through. Want me to rip out those cabinets?"

"No, of course not. I know a great deal when I see one. I'm keeping them. I'll give Matt fifty dollars when he comes back."

❧

Ed decided to tell Matt to cool it on his generosity since Jill would obviously bend over backward to repay them. They didn't need to add to her financial stress.

He went about his business while she assisted customers. Every time she entered the room where he was working, he had to fight the urge to watch her. Once, when she came back to get ceramic angels from the shelves he'd built, he found himself comparing her features to the angels'—and she won hands down.

Marcy had been softly pretty, too. But Marcy would never have ventured out on her own as Jill had. Then he remembered something important. Jill didn't exactly have a choice. Her mother had died when she was a child, and her father had died recently. She didn't have anyone, so she was stuck fending for herself. That very thought gripped his heart.

Ed had gradually started seeing more in Jill than her crusty exterior. She was soft inside, and he found her internal fortitude endearing. In fact, he admired how she not only pulled herself up to whatever she needed to do, but she also had a heart for her customers and seemed sincere when she offered her assistance.

That evening Stacy and Tracy greeted him with their chubby little arms open wide and expectant looks on their faces. "Sorry, girls. I didn't bring anything home today."

Tracy backed off, still pouting. Stacy, however, looked him squarely in the eye. "We wanted you to bring Jill home with you. Did you tell her you were making pancakes?"

"Pancakes are tomorrow night, squirt. Tonight's hamburger night."

She grinned. "Oh, then you can bring her home with you tomorrow night for pancakes. You make the bestest pancakes in the whole world."

Ed chuckled. "I'm not sure Jill even likes pancakes."

"Everyone likes pancakes," Stacy said with authority.

After dinner he read a story to the girls, then told them they could play for a few minutes before they got ready for bed. He went into the living room to pray and reflect.

His heartache over losing Marcy during their birth still hung over him, but the pain had dulled a little. Marcy had left such a wonderful part of herself behind in the girls. Although the girls were identical in looks, they had different personalities. Stacy was similar to her mother, all bubbly and lighthearted, with a touch of bossiness. Tracy was more like him—quiet and brooding with tendencies toward perfectionism and control. Both girls were very intelligent and had similar interests. And to his utter delight they got along great, sticking up for each other no matter what.

A year after Marcy's death people in the church had started introducing him to women they thought would be perfect for him. But no one could ever take Marcy's place.

"Daddy!" The shrill voice snapped him from his trance.

"Huh? Something wrong?"

"We're thirsty," Stacy said. Tracy stood beside her, nodding.

He quickly stood, took them by the hands, and led them to the kitchen, where he got them each a glass of water. "Time for bed, girls."

After they put on their pajamas, he went to their room to hear their prayers. Tracy wouldn't let go of his hand when he stood to leave.

"Can we come to your work tomorrow?" she asked.

"No, I don't think that would be a good idea."

"Please?" Stacy begged.

"No." Ed went to the door. "Let's get some sleep." He heard them whispering as he walked to his room, and he knew they'd be up to something soon.

The next morning Ed was the first person to arrive at the Junktique Shoppe. Jill came in an hour later, laden with grocery bags.

By late morning his senses were accosted by the smell of Italian sauce. He dropped what he was doing and headed into the kitchen, where she stood over a two-burner hot plate, stirring sauce in a large pot. He'd have to hand it to her for ingenuity.

"Where'd you get the burner?" he asked.

"I had it in college. It was in a box in my spare bedroom." She stirred a few more times, then put on the lid. "Hungry?"

He grinned. "I am now."

Matt came walking in a few seconds later. "Something smells awesome."

By lunchtime Jill had a couple of tables cleared and plates lined up for a nice spaghetti lunch. She seemed pleased with herself as a half-dozen workers helped themselves to seconds, and some even had third helpings.

"Where'd you learn to cook like this?" Matt asked.

"I always cooked for my dad. He liked dinner on the table every night, and since I got home from school before he came home from work, that was my job."

Ed sensed that she hadn't particularly enjoyed cooking for her dad, but he knew she felt good about this. So he remained quiet as everyone else oohed and aahed over her fabulous culinary skills. She jumped up to assist customers when they walked into the store, so the workers used that time to nudge him. One of them even said, "She's a keeper, Ed. Better latch on to her." Ed quickly changed the subject.

Once everyone had finished, Ed helped Jill clean the kitchen. "Lunch was great," he said as he dried the last of the dishes. "I was wondering. . ." He looked at her as she turned to face him, her eyes wide. He had to swallow hard to continue. "I promised the girls I'd make pancakes for supper tonight. Would you like to join us?"

She fidgeted with her hair before shaking her head. "I don't think so," she said. "Not tonight."

Ed nodded and put the leftover spaghetti sauce in the refrigerator. Once everything was done, he returned to his project in the back room.

Every once in a while he heard the bell on the front door, but for most of the afternoon the place was quiet. He was startled when he glanced up and saw Jill staring at him.

"Need something?" he asked.

"I hate asking you to do this, but I have to run over to the bank. I'll only be gone a few minutes. Would you mind—?"

"Watching your shop?" he asked, finishing her question. He wanted to kick himself the instant he did it. It used to annoy Marcy to no end.

Jill grinned. "That's what I'm talking about."

She obviously didn't mind. He let out a sigh of relief. "I'll be glad to. Is everything priced?"

A look of amusement covered her face. "Yes, and I don't mind if you want to give a 20 percent discount. I've got it built into my prices."

"That won't be—." He stopped himself. "I'll do what I can."

"Thanks." She waved as she turned to leave.

Five minutes after she left, the place became swamped with business. And then, right after he closed the register after a large, multi-item sale in the hundreds of dollars, in walked Mrs. Cooper, the nanny, with his daughters on either side of her.

"Hey, Daddy!" Stacy said as she let go of Mrs. Cooper's hand and ran toward him. He bent down and scooped her into his arms while Tracy held on to the nanny's other hand and looked around the room.

"There's a lot of stuff in here," Tracy said in awe.

Flustered, Mrs. Cooper gently shoved Tracy toward him. "I hate to do this to you, Ed, but I have an emergency at home, and no one else from the church could cover for me."

"That's fine. In fact, I'll put them to work." *And maybe Jill won't freak out.*

In a matter of seconds, Ed found himself in Jill's shop with his daughters looking around, probably wondering what they could play with first. A brief panic filled him until he made a quick decision to knock off early and resume his work the next day. And he'd leave as soon as Jill returned from the bank.

A half hour passed, and Jill still hadn't arrived. Then another half hour went by. Ed had heated up some of the spaghetti for the girls, which killed a few minutes. But he could keep them out of trouble for only so long before he needed to do something.

Finally, an hour and a half later, she breezed in. She looked as if she was on the verge of apologizing when she suddenly stopped, looked at the girls, then glanced up at him, her mouth wide open.

"Daddy, is this Jill?" Stacy asked, breaking the silence.

"Jill, meet my daughters, Stacy and Tracy." He motioned toward Jill. "And this is Jill Hargrove. Mind if they call you Jill?"

Jill slowly shook her head, but she didn't utter a word. Both girls stared right back at her without speaking. Finally Ed knew something had to give. He turned to Jill.

"The nanny had an emergency, so she dropped them off here. I hope you don't mind, but I'm knocking off early."

"You don't have to do that," Jill said. "They'll be fine here."

Ed wished she hadn't said that in front of the girls, but obviously she didn't have much experience with children. Tracy tugged on his arm. "Can we, Daddy? Please?"

"Uh. . ."

Jill gestured around the shop. "I'm sure I can find something to keep them occupied while you finish your work for the day. It's the least I can do."

By this time Stacy had found the glassware and spotted a demitasse set. "Oh, look—some teacups."

Jill's eyes widened as she scurried to their side. "Hey, I've got something even better back here." She motioned for them to follow her to the back room, and they did. Ed was right behind them.

"Cool!" both girls said in unison.

Jill had pulled out a box filled with more colorful, girl-type trinkets. "This is more stuff from that same estate sale in Roswell," she explained. "You girls can have whatever you want."

"We can take it home with us?" Stacy asked.

Ed stepped up. "I have an idea. Why don't we keep it here for emergencies—at least until I've finished fixing everything."

Jill looked up at him, hesitated a second, then nodded. "That's fine."

Ed and Jill let the girls help them carry some of the things to the area where Ed had his workshop set up. "Hey, Jill, that b'sketti was good," Stacy blurted out. "Daddy said you cooked it."

"By the way," Ed said, "I fixed them some leftovers. I hope you don't mind."

"No, of course I don't mind," Jill replied. "I have some cookies in the cupboard."

The girls snapped their attention to Ed for approval. "Later," he said quickly.

Jill made a face and whispered, "Sorry. I never know what to say around kids."

"You're doing just fine," he replied. She was doing better than fine. He could tell the girls liked her.

Ed knew it was only a matter of time before they got curious and tried to wander, so he kept a close eye on them. To his surprise they stayed occupied for a couple of hours.

❦

Jill occasionally sneaked a peek back at Ed's daughters. They looked so much alike it was confusing—until one of them opened her mouth. Then she knew who was who. The quiet one was Tracy. They were both obviously smart, but they were different in how they showed it. Stacy made noise every time she moved. She suspected Tracy could be standing right behind her and she wouldn't even know it.

When the bell on the door sounded, she assisted a couple of browsers who were just looking. They each bought something small, which was fine because Jill knew they'd be back. She was about to get some more merchandise to fill in the empty spaces when she heard a shuffling sound behind her.

"Jill?"

"Yes?" she said as she turned to face the little girl—the quiet one.

"Do you like our daddy?" The little girl stood there looking up at her with wide-eyed wonder.

Chapter 6

J ill cleared her throat. "Why, uh, yes, of course I do."

Tracy tilted her head. "Then why won't you eat pancakes with us?"

"Um, I. . ."

Ed suddenly appeared. "Tracy, honey, Jill is a busy lady. I'm sure she has other things to do."

Tracy held out her hands. "But she has to eat, doesn't she?"

Both Tracy and Ed turned to her. He shrugged with an I-give-up look on his face. Jill didn't like being put on the spot, but how did she tell that to a four-year-old?

Finally Jill sighed. "Yes, I have to eat."

"Then come have pancakes with us," Stacy said from behind.

Was this normal behavior for four-year-olds? She wasn't sure, but they acted awfully old for their age.

"How old did you say you were?" Jill asked.

"Four," Tracy replied.

"Going on five," Stacy said, correcting her. "Our birthday is in a couple months."

"And we get to start kindergarten next year," Tracy added.

Well, that explained part of it. But still. . .

"How about it, Jill?" Ed said. "I flip a mean pancake, and the girls do have a point. You have to eat. I promise it won't take long."

"Okay, I'll go," Jill replied.

Ed and the girls stayed a little while longer until Stacy started whining. "Time for a nap," Ed said as he lifted one and took the other's hand. "I left our address and directions by the register. We generally eat at six thirty, but come early if you can."

Jill nodded. What else could she do? She'd been ganged up on without a chance for defense. If it weren't for the children, she never would have agreed to go to their house.

She stayed at the shop until her posted closing time, then headed for the Mathis home in the Sandy Springs area. The neighborhood was older, but all the houses looked well maintained—especially Ed's place. Shrubs lined the front, with a row of annuals that hadn't given in to the cooler weather of autumn. She parked her car and said a short prayer that she wouldn't say something stupid as she headed up the sidewalk. She wasn't halfway to the porch when the front door swung open and both girls came bounding out of the house, nearly throwing themselves at her. She felt her heart flutter quickly.

Ed seemed as comfortable in his kitchen as he was at work. She was amazed at how orderly his home was, considering he had a couple of small children to deal with. And the pancakes were incredible!

"These are good," she said as she mopped up the blueberry syrup with the last bite.

"Want more?" Ed asked, obviously pleased with himself.

She held up both hands. "I'd love more, but I'm so stuffed I feel like I might pop."

Both girls doubled over in fits of giggles. "Don't pop, Jill!" Stacy said. "That would be gross."

Ed winked at Jill before turning to the girls. "Okay, kiddos, go play in your room for a few minutes. I want to chat with Jill before she leaves."

To her surprise they did as they were told. Jill turned to Ed. "You're doing a great job with them."

He pursed his lips and shook his head. "Thanks, but I'm afraid they might be missing some things without their mother here."

Jill had no idea what to say to that, so she carried her plate to the sink. "Let me help you clean up; then I have to go."

He took the plate and led her away from the kitchen. "I have the rest of the night to clean the kitchen. Why don't we go to the living room and talk?"

Jill was relieved Ed sat on the sofa across from the chair she'd chosen. Once they started chatting, she felt as if she'd known him all her life.

After a half hour of relaxing small talk, Jill stood. "I really need to go. Should I go say bye to the girls?"

Ed paused, a contemplative look on his face, then shook his head. "They might try to find a way to keep you here longer."

Jill laughed as she took a step toward the front door. "You have two very smart little girls."

"I'll walk you to the door before the girls come out and expect you to entertain them."

"Thanks for everything, Ed. The pancakes were wonderful. The girls are sweet, too."

All the way home she thought of how good Ed was with his girls. They were cute and sweet, but they were also a handful. And Ed was charming and fun.

That night Jill lay in bed rehashing the events of the day. She'd had more than her share of surprises. Meeting Ed had brought something into her life she'd never experienced before—a sense of community. Then she had to remind herself it was only temporary—that he'd soon be gone.

The next morning she took her time getting ready. When she arrived at the shop, she saw Ed had gotten there first and let himself in. He was waiting on a customer. She was about to take over when she heard the elderly woman's response to him. "You're such a sweet boy for showing me all those cookie jars."

"You said you collect them, so it was the least I could do." He gave Jill a wink and a wave.

The woman turned around and spotted Jill. "Is that your wife?"

Ed coughed, and Jill felt like hiding. He quickly recovered. "No, I'm just helping her out for a while until she gets everything settled. Did you want all of the cookie jars?"

The woman nodded. "Yes, dear. How can I pass up such a wonderful deal by such a charming young man?"

After she left, Jill glared at Ed. "Why didn't you wait for me?"

He looked at her sheepishly. "I'd just let myself in to do my work, and she followed me inside. I didn't want to risk having you lose business."

"What kind of deal did you give her? Twenty percent off?"

He shook his head. "No, all I told her was that they were a good value individually, but as a collection they were worth quite a bit more."

"How did you know that?"

He pointed to the book by the cash register. "She came in and looked at them first thing. While she was walking around the store, I looked them up in your book. I hope you don't mind."

"No, of course I don't mind." Ed's kindness touched her heart, but she didn't know how to tell him.

"I was starting to wonder."

Jill leaned over and glanced around him. "Where are the girls?"

"The nanny's back—at least for the time being. Her daughter's due to deliver in about a month."

He turned and went back to his work area, leaving her alone in the front of the shop. Lunchtime came and went without incident. The shop was busy all afternoon, so time passed quickly. Jill glanced up as Ed appeared shortly before she'd planned to leave.

"See ya tomorrow," he said with a wave. He hesitated before he left. Jill stared after him, wondering what would happen once he and his friends finished their work. She'd long since given up the notion of letting him go and bringing in someone else to do the work. She trusted Ed, and the more she came to know him, the more she wanted him around.

❧

Ed knew he needed to get an early start the next morning because Mrs. Cooper was starting to make sounds about her daughter needing her very soon. He asked a neighbor to come in until Mrs. Cooper arrived.

He'd fully expected to be at the shop before Jill, but to his surprise her car was parked in front when he pulled up behind her. He walked in to find her moving some of the stock from the back room.

"Do wonders ever cease?" He grinned.

She glanced up. "What are you talking about?"

"You're actually early today."

She tightened her jaw but didn't say anything. He could tell he'd annoyed her. Oh, well. He was here to do a job.

The shop phone rang, but he ignored it until Jill appeared. "It's for you," she said.

With a frown he took it. Mrs. Cooper told him she needed to drop off the girls because her son-in-law had just called and was taking her daughter to the hospital.

Jill remained standing there, staring at him. When he clicked the OFF button and handed the phone back to her, she took it but didn't budge.

"Well?" she said. "Is there a problem at home?"

"No, not a problem. Just that Mrs. Cooper is bringing the girls here, and I'm nowhere near finished."

"That's fine," Jill said. "We have that box of toys they can play with."

"But you've been around them enough to know that'll only be good for a little while."

She grinned. "Then I suggest you get movin' on whatever project you're working on now."

"Yes, ma'am."

"Smart man." Jill pulled away from her spot leaning against the doorframe. "I'll let you know when they arrive."

Ed didn't need anyone to tell him when his girls arrived. Between Mrs. Cooper's loud, husky voice and Stacy's shrill bossiness, he knew the moment they walked in the door.

"Don't you girls touch a thing," Mrs. Cooper barked. "This store has a lot of breakables."

He put down his hammer and ambled out to the front of the shop where Mrs. Cooper chatted with Jill. Stacy and Tracy had wandered over toward the stairs. He rushed over to the twins, took them by the hand, and led them away.

"But I wanna go upstairs."

"Not now. I have to finish my work; then maybe I can take you."

Stacy broke free of his grasp and ran over to Jill. "Jill, can you take me upstairs?"

Mrs. Cooper glared down at her. "Now what did I tell you on the way over here?"

Stacy planted her little fist on her hip. "Miss Hargrove's store is filled with priceless antiques. She won't like you if you break anything."

Double Blessing

Jill gasped as she turned to Mrs. Cooper. Ed understood his daughter had probably left out something. But Jill obviously didn't know that.

"I'm sure Mrs. Cooper didn't say it exactly like that," Ed said.

"I certainly didn't," Mrs. Cooper agreed. "I told her Miss Hargrove would be very unhappy if the girls broke something."

Ed noticed Jill's relief. "That's what I thought," he said. "Jill, would you mind taking one of the girls up for just a minute? I'd like to have a word with Mrs. Cooper before she leaves."

"I can take both of them," Jill said.

Ed and Mrs. Cooper simultaneously said, "No!"

Jill took a step back. "Well, in that case. . ." Jill glanced back and forth between the girls, obviously trying to decide which girl to take.

"Stacy," Ed said, "why don't you go first? I'll take Tracy up when I'm finished with Mrs. Cooper."

That satisfied Stacy. She marched right up to Jill, held out her hand, and led the way to the stairs. Jill glanced over her shoulder with another look of helplessness as she went with Stacy. Ed saw her vulnerability, and it flipped his heart once again.

After Mrs. Cooper apologized and said she had no idea when she'd be back to help with the girls, Ed realized how much denial he'd been in. He'd known for months she was planning to do this, but until now it hadn't seemed real. It was difficult to find substitute nannies for a day or two, but for an indefinite period of time? That would be next to impossible.

By the time Ed and Tracy joined Jill and his other daughter upstairs, he figured Stacy would have long since worn out her welcome. Instead he was pleasantly surprised by the sight of Jill showing Stacy some very tiny figurines in a corner beside a dollhouse. Stacy was actually behaving herself.

"Hey, you two," he said to let them know he was there. "Must be good to have both of you so interested."

Jill glanced up. "I was just showing her some fifty-year-old porcelain pieces."

Tracy tugged at him to take her closer, so he complied. When he was close, he carefully let go of Tracy's hand so she could see.

Finally, after the girls looked over everything that interested them on the second floor, Ed led them back downstairs. Jill was right behind them.

She remained in the front of the shop while he situated them beside his work area. Then he came up to thank her.

"I appreciate your understanding. Not everyone can handle my girls."

Jill tilted her head to one side. "I don't know why you're so appreciative when you're the one doing me a favor."

"Well, I—"

"Besides," she interrupted, "your girls are really sweet. I don't see a single problem with either of them."

"They have their moments," he mumbled.

"Daddy!" Tracy hollered.

That caught both his and Jill's attention. They went running back.

Tracy was standing on a chair, pointing at a cornered and frightened Tiger. "Look at the kitten!"

Somehow Tiger had slipped into the shop and stood shivering in the corner of the back room, obviously frightened by the noise. "That's Tiger," Ed said. "Be very gentle with her. She's just a kitten."

"Can we play with her?" Stacy asked as she reached down to touch the animal.

"Very carefully," Ed answered.

While the girls were busy with the kitten, Ed told Jill he had something to discuss with her. Seeing the kitten reminded him she had termites.

The exterminator had told them the place was so heavily infested with termites that there was no way around tenting it. Then, after the tent came down, some of the flooring and walls needed to be replaced.

"What?" Jill asked.

With the girls right there and Jill looking tense, he decided to wait one more day. He wanted to finish his job at hand and discuss the severity of the problem with Jill when they were both able to talk.

"Can you be here early in the morning?" Ed asked.

Jill cocked her head to one side. "Like what time?"

"How about nine?"

She thought about it then nodded. "Nine is okay. I'll be here then."

"Good," he said. "Now let me get back to my work, so I can take the girls home before they get rowdy."

Fortunately the kitten kept the girls busy long enough for him to finish what he was doing. In fact, he had to drag them away when it was time to leave. Jill waved as they left.

All night the girls chattered about how much they loved kittens. "Daddy, please can we have a kitten or puppy?" Stacy asked.

"Not now, sweetheart," he replied. "Maybe someday when you're older."

"Why not now?" Stacy said, scowling.

"I want you to be old enough to take care of an animal. You have to feed them and make sure all their needs are met."

"We can do that."

Ed sighed. "Not now, girls. Let's get supper so we can go to bed at a decent time."

The girls struggled with him for a little while, but finally they calmed down and did what he told them to do. He figured they were eager to conspire.

As soon as he had tucked them in, he grabbed his phone and punched in the number of his exterminator. "Hey, Ray, I need you to go to the Junktique Shoppe first thing in the morning. I'm ready to get an estimate for the fumigation."

Ray chuckled. "Okay, what time do you want me there?"

"She'll be there at nine, so I thought maybe you and I could meet at eight. Will that be enough time?"

"Sure thing," Ray said. "I'll see you then."

Early the next morning the neighbor, Mrs. McKnight, agreed to come over as long as the girls were asleep. She liked the girls, but two of them had been too much for her to handle the few times she'd tried to babysit them.

Ed thanked her again and took off, hoping to arrive at the shop before Jill. *Uh-oh*, he thought as he turned onto the street. He glanced at his watch and saw that it was a quarter to eight, and both Jill and Ray were parked in front of the shop.

He ran inside the shop, but neither Jill nor Ray was there. One glance out the back window, and he spotted them. He made his way through the back door as fast as he could.

Just as he thought. He saw frustration written all over her face.

"How long have you known how bad it was?" Jill asked.

Ed shuffled his feet. "Awhile."

She gave him a look of disbelief. "And when did you plan to tell me?"

"Soon."

Her cheeks puffed as she blew out a breath, pulled away from him, and started pacing in the backyard. "I don't know what to do."

"The place needs to be tented."

Ray nodded. "That's the only way. I told Ed—"

"I'm doomed," she said. "It seems like there's no end to what's wrong with this place."

Ed tried to think of a solution quickly, but he couldn't. All he could think about was how closing her doors long enough for the exterminator to fumigate the building could put her out of business. Since Ray was giving such a discounted rate, they couldn't very well rush him. He was working it in between jobs. Ed had a warehouse she could use while the place was fumigated and repaired, but he had a feeling she wouldn't go for it.

"I have a plan that'll be a hassle, but it just might work," he said.

Both Ray and Jill turned to him. He shot Ray a glance, so Ray excused himself, saying he had to look around a bit more and do some measuring.

After Ed told her about his warehouse, she shook her head. "How are we going to get all this stuff to your warehouse and back? There's no way. Besides, I can't take another handout from you."

"Do you have any other ideas?" he asked. "If you want, you can rent the space while you're there."

She frowned and set her jaw as she thought about it. Then slowly she shook her head. "I'm sunk."

"Maybe not. I can call some people from the church and—"

She held up her hands. "I don't think so. I don't know any of those people. Why would they want to help a complete stranger?"

"Because they're nice people, and they want to do what the Lord calls them to do," he said.

Jill obviously didn't know what to say. She just stood there staring off into the distance.

After a long silence Ed finally said, "Well? What do you think about me calling some of my friends?"

She kicked the ground in frustration. "Do I have a choice?" She paused, then added, "And don't forget I'll pay you rent for the time I'm there."

"Jill, you always have a choice. I'm not being bossy."

"No, I realize that. It's just that. . .everything's so overwhelming right now. I had no idea running a shop would require so much work. It's almost as bad as having a kid." The instant those words left her mouth, her eyes widened. "I didn't mean it like that." She flapped her arms by her sides, then shook her head. "I'm sorry, Ed. Your girls are wonderful. You're a great dad."

Ed felt sorry for her. She thought she'd insulted him, when in an odd sort of way she'd just given him a huge compliment. She'd let him know she was aware of the responsibility of having kids. But what she didn't seem to realize was that having a business wasn't exactly an irresponsible endeavor, either.

"You'd probably make a wonderful mother if you ever wanted kids," Ed said. "In the meantime we need to take care of this little problem."

She chuckled. "Little problem? I'm sorry, but I don't see how having termites is a *little* problem. It's pretty major to me."

"You know what my offer is, so let me know soon."

Ed backed off to let her process the news. The timing was good because Ray had come from the other side of the building. He motioned for Ed.

"Seeing's how you're trying to help this lady out and I'm not all that busy at the moment. . .if we can get moving on this by the end of the month, I can do this for half my regular fee."

Ed squinted. "Are you sure, Ray? I'm not asking for a discount."

Ray nodded. "If I can't do this for a helpless woman, what kind of man am I?"

Ed couldn't help but laugh at Ray's choice of words. "You're a good, honest, hardworking Christian man."

Ray squared his shoulders. "If I could do this for nothing I would, but I have to hire help to put up the tent and all. . . ."

"Hey, that's fine," Ed said. "I understand. Just do me a favor and don't tell

Jill how much this is gonna cost. I'm taking care of it."

Ray grinned. "You're sweet on this girl, aren't you?"

Ed gulped. He'd been avoiding his feelings for Jill, but Ray was right. He didn't have to admit it, though. "We're friends, if that's what you mean."

"Okay, whatever you say. Call me tonight, and I'll get started as soon as you give me the go-ahead."

"I have to arrange for some people to help move her stuff."

Ray gestured toward his own truck. "I can help, too."

"Thanks." Ed extended his hand, and Ray shook it then left.

"What was all that about?" Jill said from behind.

"We need to talk about when to do this," Ed said.

"Whenever you want to is fine with me."

"Good. I'll make some calls, and we'll get it taken care of right away."

"Now, is it safe for me to go back inside?" Jill asked.

Ed chuckled. "You'll be fine."

The phone in Ed's pocket vibrated. He figured it was the babysitter begging to be rescued.

He explained to Jill that he might not be back for the rest of the day. A panicked look crossed her face, but she recovered in a split second. "That's okay. Do whatever you have to do."

After he got home and relieved his neighbor of childcare responsibilities, he called the Junktique Shoppe. No one answered. Jill must have a customer, he figured.

"Come on, girls. Brush your teeth and get dressed."

"Do we hafta?" Stacy whined.

"Yep," he said. "That is, if you wanna go see Jill."

"C'mon, Tracy. Let's do what Daddy says."

Chapter 7

When they arrived at the shop, the door was locked, and Jill was nowhere to be found. "Where is she, Daddy?" Stacy asked.

"I can't imagine." He led the girls around to the back of the house, thinking she might be in the backyard. She wasn't.

"Tell you what. I have a key, so we can go inside. I have a bunch of work to finish, so you girls can play with the toys Jill set aside for you."

Stacy looked at Tracy, who sighed. He could tell they were up to something.

They'd barely gone inside and turned on the lights when a couple of elderly women came in. "We heard about this place," the taller of the two women said. "Mind if we take a look around?"

"Be my guest," he replied. "The owner isn't in at the moment, but if you need something I'll try to help you."

While they browsed, Ed settled the girls on a small braided rug in the back room with the box of colorful items between them. That ought to keep them occupied for at least an hour or two, he figured. After that he'd have to come up with something different.

About fifteen minutes later one of the women stuck her head around the corner. "We'd like to buy a few things. Can you ring us up, or do we need to come back later?"

Ed set his hammer on the floor and wiped his hands on the rag he kept by the sawhorse. "I'll do it. Give me just a minute." Once the woman went back into the shop, he bent over and instructed the girls to stay right where they were. "Don't move off this rug until I come back. Got that?"

They both nodded before they exchanged a glance. He shot them a warning look before going to the sales area to help the ladies.

The women were barely out of the door when Jill came running into the shop, out of breath. "What are you doing here?" she asked.

He lifted his eyebrow as he widened his stance and folded his arms across his chest. "The question is, where were you? You had customers."

"What did you sell them?"

He shook his head. "I can't remember everything. . . . Let's see." He shut his eyes for a moment to get a visual picture of everything on the counter as he rang it up. "A couple of parchment lamp shades, some salt and pepper shakers, and a couple of bowls from upstairs. There was other stuff, too." He tried to think of the rest of it, but there was too much. He shrugged and added, "A bunch of stuff."

By that time Jill had her cash drawer open, and she'd pulled out the checks the women wrote. "Is this what they paid?"

He nodded. "If it's not right, I'll make up the difference."

Jill gave him an odd look. "I just hope they come back. They paid a lot of money."

Ed laughed out loud. "I think those ladies will come back. In fact, they were talking about bringing their whole bridge group. I told them you were temporarily relocating, and they said it didn't matter where you were; they'd find you."

Jill slowly grinned at him. That warmed him from the inside out. He could tell she'd softened toward him, and that made him feel good.

"Now, if you don't mind, I need to get back to work. The girls have been a little too quiet, and I have a feeling my time here today is limited."

"Be my guest," she said with a dismissive wave of her hand.

❧

Ed's attitude toward her shop baffled her. He clearly didn't understand how much her "junk" meant to people; yet he seemed so eager to help. His kindness and gentle spirit had touched her deeply. He'd started to chip away at the shell she'd formed around her heart.

But something bothered her. How did he do all the things he did? Her lack of confidence only deepened when she was around people like Ed. Not only did he have his job and his girls, but he jumped in and took care of her shop while she ran home to turn off the coffeepot she'd forgotten that morning in her haste to get to the shop early. She had been right in the middle of ringing up her first customer when it had dawned on her.

She could hear Ed in the back, alternating between hammering, sawing, and chatting with his daughters. An odd, warm sensation traveled through her as she imagined what it would be like to have a nice, cozy family like that.

Matt came walking in shortly after lunch, sporting a wide grin. "My wife was pleased as punch when I told her I was bringing home dinner tonight. Whatcha cookin'?"

Panic rose in her chest as she realized she'd forgotten all about dinner. She was about to say the first thing that came to mind when Ed snuck up behind her. "How about some steaks?"

Jill spun around and saw the look of amusement on his face. "Steaks?"

"Yeah," he replied. "I bought a bunch last week. I figured I'd bring them over."

"But I thought—," Matt began before Jill turned back to face him.

Jill made a quick decision. "Never mind Ed's steaks. I'm cooking Swiss steak."

"Yum," Matt said, patting his belly.

Suddenly she thought about the girls. "Do Stacy and Tracy like Swiss steak?"

Ed shrugged. "I dunno. They've never had it."

"Maybe I should fix something else."

"No, if you want to cook Swiss steak, then do it. If they don't like it, we have plenty of peanut butter at home."

"We love Swiss steak!" screeched Stacy as she came running full steam out of the back room.

"How would you know, squirt?" Ed bent over and scooped her up in one move. He started tickling her until she nearly choked on her giggles.

"Seriously, I can cook whatever they like."

Matt made a puppy-dog face. "But I had my heart set on Swiss steak."

Ed laughed. "You just like to eat, Matt."

Matt stuffed his hands in his pockets. "True."

After Matt left, Jill asked Ed to keep an eye on the shop again for a little while. He lifted his eyebrow.

"Are you sure you trust me with your precious shop?" he asked.

Jill snickered. "I'll be back as soon as possible."

"Take your time. I want you to catch me waiting on your customers."

As soon as Jill stepped into her car, she turned the radio dial to the local Christian station. She'd heard it recently blaring from Ed's truck, and she thought about how she needed to fill her mind and heart with uplifting messages and music. She could tell Ed wanted to discuss faith because he'd touched on it several times but backed off when she'd reacted. She knew she needed to be more open, but she hated people trying to coerce her into doing something she didn't want to do. And she wasn't into attending a church where people would judge her or anything about her.

The roads were crowded with cars and service trucks, as they always were during the workweek in Atlanta. Her trip to the grocery store took a little longer than she'd planned, but she managed to get through the express line and out in record time.

She was back at the shop less than an hour later. Ed stood at the counter ringing up another customer, and the girls were busy charming the elderly woman making the purchase.

When the woman spotted Jill, she grinned. "Your little girls are so precious. I miss my grandchildren."

Jill started to correct the woman and let her know they weren't hers, but Ed interrupted. "Thank you, Mrs. Bennett. I hope you enjoy your dolls."

"Oh, I will," she said as she took the bag and made her way to the door. "And I'll be back after the move." She wiggled her fingers toward the girls, and they waved back.

"If you know her, how come she didn't know I wasn't their mother?" Jill asked.

"Oh, I didn't know her until today. I got her name off her check."

"I see," Jill said. "Let me put this stuff in the refrigerator, and I'll be right back to relieve you."

"Take your time. I'm having fun."

She snapped around to see if he was serious, but she couldn't tell. His eyes twinkled with mischief. At least by now she trusted him enough to know he wasn't doing anything to muddle up her business.

The second she opened the refrigerator door to put the food away, Stacy was by her side. "My daddy likes you," she said.

Jill felt flustered. "He's a nice man."

"Tracy and I like you, too."

Now Jill felt more comfortable since this was between her and Stacy rather than Ed. She bent over, gently cupped Stacy's chin in her hand, and looked her in the eye. "I like you and Tracy very much."

Stacy's eyebrows shot up, and a wide grin flashed on her face. "You do?"

"Yes. You and Tracy are two of the sweetest little girls I've ever met. And the smartest, too."

Suddenly Stacy's smile turned into a frown. "My daddy's sweet. Why didn't you tell me you thought my daddy was sweet and smart?"

Jill tried to dig deep to come up with an answer. She was about to say something that probably wouldn't make sense to an almost-five-year-old when Ed saved her.

"Stacy, come on—let's go," he said from the doorway. "Jill needs to get back to work." He looked Jill in the eye and added, "The pastor's wife has agreed to watch them for a couple of hours this afternoon, so I'll be back."

Jill simply nodded because she was speechless. After Ed left, she leaned against the wall and rubbed the back of her neck. She never realized how draining children could be or how they could make her smile.

Before meeting Ed and the twins, all she had to deal with was the latent anger she wasn't aware of until after her father passed away. At least that was something she could understand. Her feelings for Ed, Stacy, and Tracy were confusing. Her defensiveness toward Ed was fading quickly, and she'd begun to feel more than just a physical attraction toward him. He didn't simply talk about his faith. He lived it. The differences between Ed and her father were becoming clearer to her by the day.

She managed to get dinner cooked between customers. The two-burner hot plate was challenging, but at least she had that until she could afford a full-size range.

Ed came back after she'd put dinner in the refrigerator in individual pans ready for the guys to take home. He sniffed the air and smiled.

"Smells wonderful in here," he said. "Just like I imagine a home should smell."

Jill forced a smile. That was an odd thing for him to say. What did he mean by that?

Ed headed straight to his work area and started hammering. She knew his time was limited, so she didn't want to bother him. But later they needed to talk.

Matt stopped by and picked up his meal. "I appreciate this," he said. "But don't think you have to do it every day. In fact, I won't be by tomorrow or the next day."

"Then just let me know when you'll be back," she offered. "It's important for me to do this."

He smiled and offered a slight nod. "I understand. I'm the same way." He leaned over to look at Ed, then lowered his voice. "So's Ed, but he won't admit it."

Jill offered a conspiratorial smile. "Yes, I know. Thanks for all your help, Matt."

So far Jill had liked everyone she'd met from Ed's church. Every last one of them was open and giving, although they had completely different personalities. Rather than clashing, though, they seemed to complement each other. They had a spirit of community about them, and she'd discovered she liked the feeling of being part of it—even if she was an outsider reaping the benefits simply because Ed had put it upon himself to take care of her.

As she closed out her cash register, Ed appeared. "By the way, I've lined up a bunch of people and their trucks to move you this weekend."

Jill stifled the urge to give him another chance to back down. "Fine. I'm not sure what a move like this involves—"

"It's a lot of hard work, but it'll only take a day with all the people we'll have working."

ॐ

What Ed didn't tell her was that he'd been building shelves and getting the front part of his warehouse ready for her to move right in. He'd even taken some carpet remnants and covered the showroom floor, which would help quite a bit to prevent breakage of some of her more fragile items.

"One of these days I want to do something for every single person who helps," she said softly.

Ed fully understood. He'd always had a hard time accepting anyone's help— that is, until Marcy died. When that happened he'd gone around in a state of numbness. After he finally pulled out of it, he realized the only thing that had gotten him through it was the Lord's hand in bringing the generosity of the church people to his aid. Now it was Jill's turn to accept the same thing.

180

"Are you ready to leave yet?" she asked as she stood poised at the door, keys in hand.

"No, you go right ahead," he replied. "I'll lock up when I leave."

"Don't forget your dinner," she reminded him. "It's on the top shelf of the refrigerator."

"Trust me—I won't forget."

Out of the corner of his eye, he saw her watching him for a moment before she finally left. He stood there and stared at his handiwork as he thought about what lay ahead of them. If she had any idea of the magnitude of the problems she had, she would likely give up and disappear from his life.

He finally admitted his instant attraction and growing affection for Jill. Her warmth and kindness toward her customers showed her innate goodness. It hadn't taken him long to see through her gruff exterior. She'd been badly hurt in the past, so that was understandable. What he now saw in her was the desire to succeed in her lifelong dream while bringing joy to others. He found this even more attractive than her physical appearance. His girls clearly liked her, too, which would make it difficult when the time came to move on. He couldn't expect Jill to take on a relationship with a man and two small kids after she'd made it clear she didn't like responsibility.

The irony of the whole situation was so obvious it was painful. Jill talked about how she shirked responsibility; yet she had plenty with this shop. He'd agreed to do light handyman work while taking a break before embarking on what he knew would be a long-term project with the residential and commercial community he'd proposed. They both wound up with surprises.

When he picked up the girls, the pastor's wife, Emma Travers, offered to watch them again the next day. "I understand how hard it must be to work with them underfoot. I have to run a couple of errands, but I can take them with me."

He smiled and thanked her.

"And since you'll be here for the potluck and Bible study tomorrow night, just come straight here from the shop."

That night the girls giggled about the things they'd done at the pastor's house. "When Pastor Travers walked in, we surprised him," Stacy said.

"What did you do to surprise him?" Ed asked.

"We yelled 'boo!' " Both girls fell into giggles.

"I hope you didn't scare him too much," Ed said, pretending to be shocked.

Tracy tilted her little head forward, allowing her honey-colored curls to bob around her face. "Daddy, this is the pastor we're talking about. He's not scared of nothing."

"Anything," Stacy corrected.

"He's not scared of anything," Tracy said. "He knows he has Jesus there with him, and two little girls *can't hurt him*."

Maybe not, Ed thought, *but two little girls sure can scare Jill.*

The next morning Ed dropped the girls at the parsonage, thanked Emma profusely, and then headed back to the shop. Jill had brought in some boxes, and she'd already packed half of one row of shelves, with dozens more to go.

"This is going to take forever," she said.

"Just wait until my friends arrive. We'll have this place packed up in no time."

Jill pressed her lips together, then went back to wrapping some fragile glass. Ed wanted to step in and help, but she looked just as fragile as the collectibles.

All day he felt as if he were walking on eggshells around Jill. She was in a strange mood. Every move she made seemed tentative, almost as if she wasn't quite sure what to do next.

Shortly after lunch, she told Ed she needed to start dinner. He'd forgotten to tell her about the weekly church dinner, so he explained it to her now. "You're welcome to join us," he said.

She shook her head without a moment's hesitation. "No, thanks. I'll just go home. I'm pretty tired."

Ed instantly felt bad because he knew it seemed like an afterthought to invite her. If someone had asked him under the same circumstances, he would have turned them down, as well. He made a mental note to keep trying, but not to wait until the last minute.

A few minutes after Jill drove away, he left the Junktique Shoppe and headed for the church, making one quick stop at a bakery on the way. The girls were playing in the parsonage yard when he pulled into the church parking lot. The instant they spotted him, they took off after him, squealing in delight. Emma Travers followed right behind them, telling them to wait until he stopped the truck.

"Daddy, Daddy! Guess what! There's a stray cat at the church. Mrs. Travers says we can have her if it's okay with you."

"What?" he said as he turned his focus to the woman coming up behind the girls. "Did you say that?"

She shook her head, a smile playing on her lips. "Not exactly in those words."

Ed sighed as he lifted the bakery box from the passenger seat of the truck. "Let me think about it, girls. In the meantime let's get you settled inside. I brought brownies for the potluck."

Stacy jumped up and down beside him. "Can I have a brownie now, Daddy? Please? If I promise to eat all my supper?"

Before Ed could say a word, Tracy shook her head. "You know Daddy's not gonna let us have a brownie now. You have to eat your supper *first*."

"That's right," Ed agreed as he opened the door with one hand and ushered his daughters inside while balancing the box of brownies with the other.

He helped the girls fill their plates with the healthiest food he knew they'd eat. Then he found them a spot at one of the long tables before he went back to get his own food. Emma was at the next table, pouring a glass of tea.

"Here ya go, Ed," she said as she came around and handed it to him. "I want to apologize about the kitten. They were so excited when they saw it. Stacy said something about your new lady friend having a kitten named Tiger."

Lady friend? Where had Emma gotten that idea? "Oh, you mean the woman who owns the shop? We're just business acquaintances," he explained.

Emma's eyes sparkled. "I see."

Ed accepted the glass of tea and thanked her for taking care of the girls all day. She smiled and said it was her pleasure.

"Okay, girls," he said as he slid into position on the bench across the table from them. "Tell me all about your day."

They both started talking at the same time, which gave him a needed break from his thoughts.

During the Bible study later, Ed focused on the topic of life's challenges. He paid particular attention when the leader, Jonathan, suggested that during the biggest challenges people needed to learn endurance and dependence on the Lord. "As soon as we think we can control our lives, we've lost the battle."

Ed lowered his head and stared at the floor, thinking about it. Matt's wife sat next to him, and he could see her nudging Matt.

After the Bible study Matt approached him. "Hey, man, you okay?"

"Sure, I'm fine. I just have issues with the topic. I can't seem to get past the whole control thing."

"That's my problem, too." Matt chewed on his lip for a second before adding, "And I suspect Jill might have the same issues."

It always seemed to come back to Jill these days, since she'd been the topic of so many prayers in their group lately. "Yeah, I bet you're right."

"And speaking of Jill, I think it might be a good idea to start moving her on Friday afternoon. We can get some of the big stuff then and at least set her up in the new digs. Then the rest of us can finish up Saturday morning."

Ed nodded. "I'll run it past her."

After he socialized for a few minutes, he left the fellowship hall, fetched his girls, then headed home. They talked nonstop about one of the books their caretaker had read.

"Daddy, did you know Jesus had a brother?" Stacy asked.

"Yes, I did know that."

"But Jesus and His brother weren't twins like us," Tracy said.

Ed didn't have to say another word as the girls discussed how different it would be to have a brother or sister who wasn't a twin. After they got home, they continued their conversation through their bath time and even after he kissed them good night. After he put the girls down, he slipped into bed with his Bible.

The next morning Emma arrived on his doorstep. "I figured you could use a sitter for a few hours this morning. Why don't you run out so you can be back in time for lunch?"

"Are you sure?" he asked. "The girls aren't even up yet."

"Go on—scoot," she said, practically shoving him out the door. "I know you have work to do."

He took advantage of a free morning he hadn't expected and stopped off at the courthouse to find out how the zoning of his new project was coming along. "Looks like the paperwork is almost all done," the clerk said. "It'll only be another couple of weeks, and you're good to go."

"Perfect," Ed said. He left and headed for the shop, where Jill's car was parked by the sidewalk leading to the front door.

When he walked in, she immediately started talking about how Matt and some of the other church people were moving her out early. He'd hoped to be the one to tell her, but she didn't seem upset. In fact, she was more chipper than usual.

"Oh, and Mrs. Cooper called," she said as she grabbed a slip of paper from the desk and handed it to him. "She said her daughter is in the hospital, and she's coming back home until she delivers. She said she'll stop by this evening."

He was relieved to have his sitter back. He knew it was only temporary, but he couldn't worry about that now.

He finished replacing a wall section and reinforced one of the beams, then left to run some more errands before he had to return home. Emma told him she planned to help out with the move.

When Friday arrived, Ed was glad to have Mrs. Cooper there with the girls.

He quickly headed back to the shop where Jill waited on the porch. They walked inside together.

"Ready for the big move?" he asked.

She shrugged and looked around the shop area. "As ready as I'll ever be."

A customer walked in, took a quick look around, and said, "Are you having a going-out-of-business sale already?"

"No," Ed said. "We're just temporarily moving her to a different location so we can fix up this place."

"In that case maybe it'll be good if I do some shopping now. There won't be as much to move."

Ed laughed. Just how much could one woman buy to lighten the load enough to notice?

Chapter 8

To his surprise the woman was a professional decorator and made a substantial difference. She purchased quite a bit of glassware and some furniture that she said she'd have out of the shop as soon as her workers could get there later that afternoon.

"Some of these fabulous things will be in the finest homes in Dunwoody," she explained. "Here's my card. Let me know when you get settled. It's certainly nice to have a new source of decorative pieces."

Ed turned to Jill after she left. "A couple of more customers like her, and we won't need people from the church to help move you."

Jill was obviously delighted by her big sale. "At least I'll be able to pay my bills for another month."

The mood instantly lightened. They spent the rest of the day packing. The decorator's people came to pick up her items, and then the remainder of the merchandise was loaded onto trucks.

By mid-Saturday afternoon everything had been moved, and quite a bit had been shelved. The new space turned out to be larger, so nothing had to be put in storage.

On Saturday evening one of the guys called and ordered a dozen pizzas. Ed watched Jill chatting and laughing with the women from the church as if she'd known them all her life. He felt a flutter in his heart when she looked at him with flushed cheeks and a sparkle in her eye. He'd never seen her so happy. And she'd apparently made friends with Jennifer Schwartz, one of the women who'd helped with the move.

Mrs. Cooper had been kind enough to watch the girls all day, so he needed to go home and spend a little time with them before they went to bed. He told Jill he'd see her Monday. She gave him a funny look then nodded. "Are you okay?" he asked.

She nodded, smiling. "I couldn't be better."

ॐ

On Sunday morning Jill saw the look of utter shock on Ed's face when he spotted her in the church lobby. "Why didn't you tell me you were coming?" he asked.

"Is that a requirement?" she teased. "Do I need to tell you before I go to your church?"

"No, of course not," he said, still obviously flustered. "It's just that—." He took a look around while several people gathered to greet her. "Never mind."

Jennifer tugged on Jill's arm. "C'mon—there's a guy I'd like you to meet."

As Jennifer pulled her away, Jill saw a flash of pain on Ed's face.

It wasn't until Jennifer stopped that Jill turned to her and said, "Well? Where is this guy?"

"Um, let me see," she said as she glanced around. Then her eyes lit up. "There he is!" She pulled Jill toward a cluster of people standing around, talking and laughing. "Jill, meet my dad, the sweetest guy in town. Dad, Mom, this is Jill Hargrove. She's the one who just opened that shop I was telling you about."

It dawned on Jill that Jennifer had intentionally tried to make Ed jealous. She turned to Jennifer's parents and shook their hands. They greeted her with open arms, making Jill feel warm inside. This was how life was supposed to be.

A little while later everyone wandered into the sanctuary to find a seat. Jill sat with Jennifer and her parents. Jennifer's husband, Brian, sang, so he was in the choir loft. She had no idea where Ed was. She did her best to concentrate on what she was there for, but it was difficult knowing Ed was somewhere in the building.

She felt sort of bad because Ed had been inviting her to church practically since they met. And she'd kept turning him down, thinking that one day she'd eventually accept. After he'd left the shop the day before, Jennifer had come up to her and told her what time she was picking her up for church. She hadn't given Jill a choice, so she didn't argue.

This church was completely different than any she'd been to before. These people were truly joyful about their faith.

She thought back to some of her earlier experiences in church with her father. All she could recall were her father's harsh words and the way he had her scared of God's wrath rather than grateful for His love. If it hadn't been for some friends from college who shared the Word with her, she'd still be running from the Lord. She'd pulled out an old Bible and started reading it regularly, using Bible study guides she picked up from Christian bookstores.

During the short time she'd known Ed, he'd shown a different side of faith from her father. He was gentle and kind—like the people from school. Her heart ached as she wondered if her father even knew any better than to present the gospel in such a hurtful way. Ed was obviously a wonderful father to his children and friend to everyone else, including her. She actually had a flicker of a romantic notion toward him, but she quickly squelched it. This wasn't the time to feel romantic toward anyone—not when her business was so new.

A wonderful feeling of peace and contentment rose inside her as she sang the contemporary worship songs. Then they sang a traditional hymn she remembered from childhood. Jennifer nudged her, pointed to the next pew over, and grinned. Jill glanced over and saw Ed standing there, deeply immersed in his singing. A fresh bolt of attraction shot through her. She'd felt the attraction from the first time she saw him, but this was different. This was a feeling more intense than anything she'd ever experienced. It had more to do with who he was inside than the way he looked.

When she turned back, she saw the odd expression on Jennifer's face. Heat suddenly rose to her cheeks. There was no doubt Jennifer knew exactly what was going on.

The pastor delivered an engaging sermon that kept her spellbound the entire time. Then, when the collection plate came around, she dropped in a visitor envelope with the meager amount she'd stuffed in there. *One of these days I'll be able to give more generously.*

After church Jennifer invited her to join the large group for lunch at a nearby diner. "Who all's going?" Jill asked.

"Everyone in the singles' group," Jennifer replied. "And a few of us married folks who used to be in the singles' group." She gave Jill a nudge. "Come on—Ed'll be there."

"Um, no, thanks. I have some things I need to take care of at home."

Jennifer started to nod then stopped. She gently placed her hand on Jill's shoulder and looked her in the eye. "You should come with us. It's fun."

Again Jill's face heated up. "I know, but. . ."

"Ed's a nice man, and I think he really likes you. I understand you might be feeling a bit overwhelmed by the built-in family, but you couldn't find a nicer guy who loves the Lord more than he does."

Jill was aware of that. Deep down she knew a very large part of her attraction to Ed was his faith. Jennifer was right about her being overwhelmed by the built-in family. As much as she enjoyed Stacy and Tracy, fear of the tremendous responsibility to them was second only to the similarities between Ed and her dad.

"I'm sure," Jill said.

"Look—this is just lunch. We eat lunch and enjoy each other's company. What's the harm in that?"

Jill shrugged.

"If it's any consolation, Ed doesn't usually bring the girls. He's part of a group of parents who take turns with preschoolers so they can each have some fellowship after church."

"Oh, the girls don't bother me," Jill said too quickly. The instant she said it, she saw Jennifer's lips tweak into a smile. To cover, she added, "I've watched them a couple of times, and they're a lot of fun."

"They can be a handful, too."

"I'm sure." Jill clamped her mouth shut to keep from saying the wrong thing.

"So will you go with us?"

Jennifer was quite persuasive and obviously wouldn't let up. Jill nodded. "Yes, but just for a little while."

Brian came up to them, put his arm around his wife, then looked at Jill. "How ya feelin' after the move?" he asked.

Jill grinned. "I'll probably recover about the time I have to move back."

Rather than ride with Brian and Jennifer, Jill chose to follow them to the restaurant, a tiny café that offered a choice of three entrées and a slew of Southern-style vegetables. Country biscuits and corn bread were in baskets on every table. The restaurant had only six tables, but each of them seated eight people. She was relieved when she found an empty chair fairly close to the door. That way she could scoot out when she wanted to leave and hope she wouldn't be noticed.

She managed to avoid Ed until she decided to go home. She'd barely stood up when she saw him approach from the side. There was no way she could take off without appearing rude. She stopped, turned to him, and smiled.

"You have a very nice church," she murmured.

"Thanks." His forehead crinkled, and he looked stressed. "I needed to discuss something with you before I go pick up the girls."

"Um, sure," she said as she glanced around. Several people hastily turned away, so she knew they were watching. "Here?"

"No, let's go outside." He guided her with one hand and opened the door with the other.

As soon as they stepped out into the parking lot he stopped, and she turned toward him. "What's up?" she asked, trying to keep her voice light in spite of the fact that butterflies fluttered from her tummy to her throat.

"Mrs. Cooper warned me that she'd have to pick up and leave on a moment's notice," he said. "I still haven't found anyone to help with the girls."

Jill tilted her head. "So what are you saying?"

He shrugged and looked around, then back at her. "I just wanted you to know in case something happens."

She nodded. "Okay, I understand."

Ed looked at her with an odd expression; then he side-stepped away from her. "Well, I guess I need to go back and tell everyone bye. See ya tomorrow?"

"See you then," Jill replied as she headed for her car.

❧

Ed felt like the idiot of the year for making such a big deal out of nothing. They'd already discussed Mrs. Cooper's daughter, and Jill was well aware of what was happening. She didn't seem to have a problem with him bringing his daughters to her shop, so she certainly wouldn't say anything about them now that she was in his warehouse. They'd known each other long enough for him to realize she was a decent woman with a heart. A big heart, in fact. The way she'd softened had puzzled him at first, but when he got over the surprise, he'd let down his guard and allowed himself to be swayed by her sweetness. Yes, he'd known her long enough to see many sides of her, and with the exception of her initial skittishness he liked what he saw.

And he'd known her long enough to start feeling the pangs he thought he'd never have again. They were odd sensations, those pangs. When he looked at Jill, tenderness overcame him, and he felt immensely protective. When she looked at him or when they talked, he cared about what she thought. And when they touched—whether on purpose or accidentally—an electrical sensation shot all the way through him, straight to his heart. Her vulnerability added to his attraction.

If Jill hadn't been a Christian, he could have found the strength to continue avoiding social situations with her. She'd told him she was a believer and that she read the Bible, but he hadn't been certain she was all that committed to her faith. When he saw her in church, though, he noticed the sincerity in her eyes and how she was completely wrapped up in what the pastor was saying. He wasn't 100 percent sure, but at least it gave him some hope that her faith was real.

Then he did a mental slap to the forehead. Hope for what? A deeper-than-friends relationship? She'd made it perfectly clear she didn't want any more responsibility than she already had. And his girls needed constant attention.

He'd just have to settle for being Jill's friend. But that thought didn't appeal to him.

The girls were all giggles when he picked them up. Apparently one of the puppet ministry leaders had done an impromptu show for the kids, and they loved it. They were exhausted, too, but since it was a little past nap time Ed decided to keep them up until after dinner so they'd go to bed early.

His plan worked, except here he was at seven thirty on a Sunday night, virtually alone. He had way too much time to think, so he flipped on the TV. Nothing there but mindless sitcoms and talking-head news shows. He found his Bible and started looking for something to calm him and keep his mind off Jill.

No matter what verse he turned to, something about Jill popped into his head. It seemed she'd taken over all his waking and most of his sleeping thoughts. The woman was tiny in person, but she loomed very large when she wasn't present.

Finally, after giving in and accepting what was happening, Ed sat back and read the book of James. As long as he focused on the Word, he could find peace in almost any situation.

He had the first restful night in weeks. When he awoke to two energetic little girls jumping on his bed, he propped up on his elbows and grinned at them. "Whatcha want for breakfast?" He knew it would likely be something dripping in sticky, sweet syrup or something from a fast-food place.

"Waffles!" they both shouted.

"Then waffles it is," he said as he sat up and slowly swung his legs to the side. "Go get dressed, and I'll meet you in the kitchen in about fifteen minutes."

Stacy arrived in the kitchen wearing her shorts backward. He smiled. Tracy had her shirt buttoned in the wrong holes, making the hem lopsided. He wouldn't trade precious moments like these for anything.

The day started off great, and Ed felt as if nothing could go wrong. Mrs. Cooper arrived humming a hymn, and the girls both gave her a great big hug. Everyone was happy, the sun was shining, and Ed was raring to go. Since Jill's shop was being fumigated and he couldn't do anything there, he'd decided to use this time to run errands and finish some of the legwork for his new development. He was close to breaking ground.

But first he stopped off at the warehouse to make sure Jill was okay. She pulled into the parking lot at the same time. He took a long look at her to gauge her mood, and to his delight she was smiling.

"You were a hit with everyone at church yesterday," Ed said.

"So it's a popularity contest?" she teased.

"You know what I mean." He could tell by her smile and how her voice lilted that she was just being playful and not sarcastic.

"I'm glad I finally went," she admitted. "It's nothing like how I remember church being. Things have really changed."

Ed wondered if the only thing that had changed was her attitude, but he didn't want to dampen her spirit or insult her. So he brought up a new subject.

"So—ready to get started in the new digs?" he asked.

She offered a quick nod as she walked comfortably around the makeshift shop, turning on lights and moving a few things around. "To be honest, I thought it would take several days to get everything the way I wanted it, but it's almost as if I've been here forever."

"That's what happens when you have more than a dozen people working on it."

"Are the people in your church always this helpful?" she asked as she slipped behind the counter.

"Most of the time," he replied. "We have a nice group of believers. They take their commitment to their faith very seriously."

"Yes, I can certainly see that."

Ed studied her until he heard the bell he'd hung over the door jingling. A customer. He turned around and saw a whole group of people from the church.

"Hey, we wanted to be the first to shop in your new location," Jennifer said as she led the pack inside. "We all saw something we wanted to buy, so here we are."

Ed hung around for a few minutes until he realized he wasn't needed. Then he told Jill he had some things to do. She told him she could handle the crowd, and he agreed.

Thank You, Lord, he mouthed as he slid into his truck.

❧

Jill sensed a change in Ed. He was as sure of himself as ever, but she caught him watching her as if he wasn't sure about her.

Being honest with herself, she knew she'd undergone some monumental changes since meeting Ed. She'd learned to accept help from someone else without feeling as if she had to offer payment for every little thing. And she realized that staying away from church simply because of her own bad experience as a child was just plain ridiculous. She should have known better than to judge anyone else based on something that had happened with her father.

Jill had brought her Bible to work with her. Between waiting on customers, she read over the scripture verses the pastor had referred to in his sermon. She loved hearing him talk. He had a wonderful way of relating everything biblical to current Christian living. This was something she'd missed when she'd isolated herself from other believers.

Another customer came in, so Jill slid the Bible beneath the counter. She answered a bunch of questions; then the bell sounded at the door again. When she glanced up she was surprised to see Ed's girls trailing behind their nanny.

She grinned. "Mrs. Cooper." Jill took a step toward the woman, her hand extended, but she pulled back when it became evident the woman was frazzled.

"I have an emergency, and Ed's not answering his cell phone," the woman said. "My daughter's in labor, and she's having some complications." She gestured toward the girls. "I'm not sure—"

Jill held up her hand. "Don't worry about a thing, Mrs. Cooper. Leave the girls with me, and go do what you need to do." She looked down at the twins. "We'll be fine, won't we, girls?"

Stacy and Tracy looked at each other, then back at her, nodding. "We like Jill," Tracy said softly.

"We *love* Jill," Stacy added.

Jill felt a fullness in her chest as an emotion she'd never experienced before welled inside her.

"If you're sure. . ." Mrs. Cooper had already let go of the girls' hands and taken a step toward the door. Jill could see how worried the woman was.

"I'm positive," Jill assured her. "Now go be with your daughter. Call Ed later and let him know how everything is." She waited until Mrs. Cooper had her hand on the door. "I'll let others at the church know we need to pray for you and your daughter."

After Mrs. Cooper left, Stacy jumped up and down, clapping her hands.

"Can we be salesladies?" she asked.

Jill chuckled. "I doubt that's legal with child labor laws."

"Child what?" Stacy asked, her forehead scrunched in confusion.

"Never mind." Jill gently guided the girls to the area behind her desk. "Let's get the two of you set up back here. I think I might have some art supplies. You do like to make things, don't you?"

Both girls nodded enthusiastically, so Jill grabbed a bunch of crayons and the pack of colored computer paper she'd purchased to make signs and plopped them down at a child-sized table. She pulled up a little chair and an old milk crate. "I only have one regular chair," she apologized.

"I want that one," Stacy said, pointing to the milk crate.

Tracy pouted. "It's my turn to pick."

"Wait," Jill said, holding up her hands. "If you both want to sit on milk crates, I have more. Just give me a few seconds."

She quickly had them set up with something to do for a little while—or at least until she could think of something else. She hoped Ed wouldn't be gone long.

Unfortunately, whatever business he had took longer than the children's attention span, so Jill had to think of something else. She was going through a mental list of what she used to enjoy at that age when Stacy had a brilliant idea.

"Let's have a tea party!" she said. "You have some children's teacups over there." She pointed to the demitasse set Jill had just brought in.

Jill paused. She was pretty sure they were valuable. But what did it matter? They weren't terribly expensive, and she could wash them and sell them later. Besides, the set included twelve. If one of them broke, she'd just have one less cup to sell. No big deal.

"Fine," Jill said. "But I don't have anything to put in them."

Tracy tapped her chin with her tiny finger. Jill's heart warmed as she watched the child ponder. Suddenly Tracy's face lit up. "Daddy sometimes lets us have ginger ale for tea parties."

Stacy placed her hands on her hips, and in her bossy manner blurted out, "And where we gonna get ginger ale, Miss Smarty Pants?"

It took everything Jill had not to crack up laughing. The bell over the door jingled again. Jill glanced up, hoping Ed had come to her rescue. But it wasn't Ed. It was Jennifer from church.

"Hey, how's my favorite antique shop doing?"

Jill had an idea. "If I give you a couple of dollars, would you mind running over to that convenience store across the street and picking up a bottle of ginger ale?"

"Be glad to," Jennifer said as she ran out the door before Jill had a chance to give her the money.

While Jennifer was gone, Jill found two more milk crates for herself and Jennifer. If they were having a tea party, they might as well do it right. She carried the demitasse cups and saucers to the big sink Ed had in his workshop area, scrubbed the cups, then dried them with paper towels. Before Jennifer returned, she had four places set up at the tiny table.

Stacy and Tracy found a couple of dolls and asked if they could have tea with them. Jill didn't hesitate to say that was fine, in spite of the fact that one of the dolls was worth hundreds of dollars.

"Just be careful," Jill warned. "She's fragile."

"What's 'fragile'?" Stacy asked.

"It means you have to be very gentle with her. She breaks easily."

Stacy nodded her understanding. "We'll be very careful."

"Is my doll fragile?" Tracy asked, holding up the one she'd selected.

"Yes," Jill replied. Tracy's doll wasn't as valuable on the market, but to Tracy she probably was. "Y'all want to invite Jennifer to join us?"

Both girls immediately nodded.

Jill was glad when Jennifer finally returned, holding up a bag with ginger ale. "I got some cookies for the girls. I hope that's okay."

Jennifer's eyes lit up when Stacy told her she was invited to a real live tea party. "Ooh, it's been a long time since I've done this. Thanks! Where should I sit?"

The four of them were seated on milk crates, sipping ginger ale from demitasse cups and telling silly animal jokes when Jill heard someone clearing his throat by the door. She quickly spun around to see Ed propped against the door, his arms folded, and one leg draped over the other, a grin playing on his lips.

Jill hopped up. "Did you need something?" She glanced over her shoulder at the tea party, then back at him. "Oh, Mrs. Cooper's daughter is in labor, so I agreed to watch the twins. Would you like some ginger ale?"

"Don't let me interrupt," he replied as he pulled away from his position. He ambled a few feet toward his office area. "When you're finished, send the girls back here."

Chapter 9

Seeing his daughters having the time of their lives with Jill and Jennifer caused a swell of emotion in Ed's chest. He'd known Jennifer for years, but until now she'd never made an effort with his daughters. She always said she wasn't "into kids." Well, Jill had said essentially the same thing, and now look at them.

"Daddy, look!" Stacy said. He stopped and turned around to face her. "We have fragile dolls."

Tracy nodded. "Yeah, we have to be very careful not to break them."

Ed lifted one eyebrow and looked over toward Jill, who forced a straight face. Jennifer kept darting her glance back and forth between him and Jill.

"Would you like something to drink?" Jill repeated.

"We're having ginger ale tea, Daddy," Stacy explained.

Ed felt as if he'd walked in on a private party he hadn't been invited to, and he wasn't sure what to do. "Uh, no. I think I'll go back to my office and get some work done. Jill, when you're finished with your, uh, party, can we talk?"

Jennifer chose that moment to speak up. "If you two need to talk, I can watch the sales floor for a few minutes."

"No—," Jill said at the same time Ed spoke. "That would be great."

Jennifer cleared her throat. "Just let me know, okay?"

Ed headed to his office, but he propped the door open so he could keep an eye on his daughters. The ginger ale tea party lasted another five minutes until the girls suddenly lost interest. He jumped up and grabbed Stacy as she darted past shelves of cookware and toward some ceramic figurines.

"Okay, squirt, why don't you and your sister work on some puzzles I picked up while I was out?"

"Puzzles?" Stacy said, looking around.

"Back here." He led them to the makeshift table he'd set up a long time ago for days when he had them.

Tracy walked up to Jill and tugged on her hand. "Is it okay with you if we play with puzzles?"

"Of course it's okay. Why wouldn't it be?"

With her hands out to her sides Tracy shrugged. "I don't want you to think we don't want to play with you anymore. We like you a lot."

Ed watched as tears instantly formed in Jill's eyes. She sniffled and turned slightly so he couldn't see her expression. "I like you a lot, too, sweetie. But I have to go back to work, so it's just fine if you want to play with puzzles."

Warmth flooded Ed. He could feel himself falling for Jill, but the relationship between his daughters and Jill had caught him off guard. What shocked him the most, though, was how it affected him. He was torn between joy over Stacy and Tracy finding a female adult to look up to and concern that Jill would break their hearts. Breaking *his* heart would be bad enough, but he could handle it.

"C'mon, girls. Let's let Jill do her work. You've taken up enough of her time."

"Wait a minute," Jill said in a tone of authority he'd never heard from her before. "They haven't taken up my time. I had a tea party with them because I wanted to and not for any other reason."

"I didn't mean—"

"Contrary to what you might believe, Ed Mathis, I like your daughters. I might not have much experience with kids, but I'll play tea party with Stacy and Tracy anytime they want me to."

"Okay," he said softly, holding up his hands and taking another step away. "Sorry. I didn't mean anything by it."

Jill backed toward her showroom. He went into his office after he heard her chatting with Jennifer.

The girls were now busy with their puzzles, and Jill was safely in her space up front. This was the perfect time to do paperwork on his new development. The problem now was that he couldn't concentrate. All he could think about was Jill and how she made him feel. Her warmth and kindness when she let down her guard. Her generosity with her customers and his daughters. . .and with him when he least expected it. He felt as if he were being pulled toward her by some irresistible force he couldn't control. He kept hoping that would fade, but with each passing day she took up more and more of his waking thoughts.

His awareness of Jill's every move rendered him incapable of doing his own work. He finally gave up and started doing some physical labor. He liked to saw and hammer when he needed a physical release of any pent-up emotions.

"Daddy, are you mad at us?" Stacy asked from the table.

He stopped sawing the piece of wood and turned to face the girls. "No, of course not. Why do you think I'm mad?"

Stacy looked at Tracy, who shrugged. "Your face is red, like when you get mad at us for jumping on the bed."

Ed let out a breath and put down his saw. He crossed over to the girls and squatted beside them. "Girls, I'm not mad at anyone. It's just that I'm thinking about things you wouldn't understand."

"Are you thinking about Jill?" Tracy asked.

He started to deny that he was, but the girls could see right through him. He nodded. "Sometimes, yes."

The twins faced each other and exchanged knowing smiles. "We thought so."

"Jill needs a lot of help from us, and I'm trying to figure out what to do next."

"We can help, Daddy. We love Jill."

"Thanks, kiddos. Now get back to your puzzles, and I'll see if there's anything Jill needs before we go home."

&

When Ed appeared by the cash register, Jill jumped. "Sorry if I scared you," he said. "I just wanted to see if there was anything I could do for you before I take the girls home."

She slowly shook her head. "No, I'm fine, but thanks."

He moved toward the door. "C'mon, girls—let's get a move on." The girls dropped what they were doing and ran to his side. "See ya tomorrow, Jill." He nodded toward Jennifer. "G'night, Jen."

Both girls ran up to Jill, wrapped their arms around her waist, and gave her a squeeze. A lump of emotion filled her chest as she reached down and patted them on the back. Then just as quickly as they'd come to her, they went back to their dad, waved bye, and were out the door. *Stacy and Tracy are little whirlwinds,* she thought as she retreated to a small space behind some shelves where she could pretend to arrange stock while recovering from her emotions.

As difficult as it was for Jill to admit, even to herself, her business had taken off like a lightning bolt shortly after Ed came into her life. In fact, it was better than anything she'd ever expected. Her regular customers—many of them elderly women who bought out of nostalgia—were taken in by Ed's charm. And the people from the church were extremely supportive—even people who'd never collected antiques.

To top things off, Ed's church seemed like the kind of place she'd want to plug into for worship and friendship. But the very fact he was there all the time put a kink in that. With the attraction she felt toward him, she knew she was treading on dangerous ground. If he'd been footloose without children and she didn't have a brand-new business, she might not have felt so overwhelmed by the man. His having a built-in family gave her pause. Sure, she loved the girls, but they were a handful. She could tell they needed more than she'd ever be able to give.

"Hey, Jill, want to go out with some folks from the church? We're grabbing a burger and seeing a movie tonight." Jennifer had found her and was standing at the edge of the shelves, holding an old book filled with pictures of collectibles.

"I'm afraid not tonight," Jill replied.

"Let me buy this book; then I gotta run."

Jill fluttered her hand. "You don't have to buy it. Just borrow it and bring it back when you're finished."

Jennifer looked as if she was about to argue, but she clamped her mouth shut and nodded. "That'll be great. I won't keep it long."

"Keep it as long as you need it. I have another copy on the shelves."

Jill was glad to be alone. It had been awhile since she'd had time to gather her thoughts; the move and the church had taken her by storm.

That afternoon when Jill tallied receipts, she was surprised at how well the shop had done—and at the same time how much she'd enjoyed the day. She'd always heard about the joy of having a career she could love, and now she was seeing it truly could happen. She felt a peace she'd never had before.

Later that week, the exterminator called to say he couldn't get started because of a cat that kept darting under the tent. She'd searched for Tiger before she left, but when she couldn't find her she figured the kitten had found another home. When Jill told Ed about Tiger, he jumped into action. He and Matt went over there, and Ed finally managed to coax a very scared and hungry Tiger into his truck. Jill's heart melted at the sight of muscular Ed holding the adolescent kitten who'd grown dependent on her.

Jill found a small plastic bowl and filled it with some of the cat food Ed had remembered to pick up on his way to rescue Tiger. The kitten seemed very grateful as she settled down for a hearty meal while Ed and Jill stood back and watched. That night Jill took Tiger home with her.

"The cat set us back on timing. Looks like it'll be another couple of weeks before they can start the extermination," Ed told her the next morning. "They're having to work your job in between some that were already scheduled. And then I still need to repair the floor and walls."

As eager as Jill was to be back in her own space, she took a deep breath, slowly let it out, and said, "That's fine, as long as you don't mind me being here."

Ed stood still and looked at her, tenderness in his eyes, his jaw relaxed. Jill wanted to reach out and trace the side of his face, but she held back, hoping the urge would pass. It didn't.

"Jill," he said softly, "you may stay in the warehouse as long as it takes to—"

At that moment the bell sounded on the door, interrupting him. Jill turned around and glanced out the glass door. She noticed a large tour bus parked outside. A couple of women stood at the counter, chattering up a storm.

"May I help you?" Jill asked.

"Yes," one of the women said. "We saw the sign on the Junktique Shoppe lawn about being in a temporary location. Is this the right place?"

Confused, Jill nodded. "Yes, this is the place."

"Oh, good," the other woman said. "Let's go tell everyone."

As the two women headed out to the bus, Jill looked at Ed quizzically. He grinned. "Oh, I forgot to tell you; I had a big sign made for the yard. I didn't want you to lose any business."

Within a couple of minutes, the shop was teeming with about thirty middle-aged and elderly women, all of them loading up on knickknacks and other glassware. One woman had a basket she was filling with linens. Jill stood at the cash register, astonished at the booming business. She also knew she'd have to hustle and get more merchandise, or she'd be out of business due to not having anything to sell.

After the group left a couple of hours later, Jill stood in the center of the store and took a long look around. Ed had helped out, and he was putting a few discarded items back on the shelves.

"I have no idea what just happened," Jill said. "But it's obvious I can't keep up with it by myself."

Ed chuckled. "I bet you can probably find a few people from the church who'd love to work part-time while you go on a buying spree to replace some of this stuff."

"I'll have to look into it," she agreed.

"Better make it soon." He started back to his work area when he suddenly stopped, pivoted around to face her, and said, "Oh, by the way, the girls wanted to know if we could pick you up for church on Sunday."

She'd gone to church alone the past couple of Sundays, but the minute she stepped out of her car she'd found herself surrounded by her new friends. That was wonderful, except that Ed always seemed to be on the outside looking in. He could have made his way to her, but she noticed his hesitation. Until now.

"Tell the girls that would be nice."

Ed blinked, almost as if he wasn't sure he'd heard right. "Eight thirty okay? We can stop off and have breakfast somewhere on the way."

Jill nodded slowly. "I'd like that."

On Sunday morning Jill opened her door and was greeted by the twins, who stood there alone. "Where's your daddy?" she asked.

Stacy pointed behind them. "He's in the truck waiting. We told him we were big enough to come and get you by ourselves."

Tracy nodded. "He had to unbuckle Stacy's car seat, but I got mine undone all by myself." She tilted her head. "I'm getting big cuz I'll be five next week."

Jill had to stifle a smile as she took a step back. "Come on in while I get a sweater."

The girls giggled as they stepped into her cottage. "Do you live here all by yourself?" Tracy asked.

"Yes, I sure do," Jill replied.

"Aren't you scared?"

"No, not really."

Stacy nodded. "I know why. Jesus is always with you."

Jill beamed down at Stacy. "Yes, you're absolutely right. As long as He's by my side, I don't have to be afraid of anything."

Tracy looked down at her feet, then back up at Jill, her lips turned downward in a frown. "Sometimes I still get afraid."

Jill leaned down and cupped Tracy's face in her hands. "Honestly, I think everyone gets afraid at times. But that's normal."

"What do you get afraid of?" Stacy asked.

Being alone for the rest of my life, she thought, although there was no way she'd say that to a couple of almost-five-year-olds. "I dunno. Just silly things, like if people will keep coming to my store."

"We'll come to your store anytime you want us to," Stacy said with confidence.

Jill had to fight back tears of joy that they seemed so happy to be part of her life. "Come to my store anytime."

The three of them left the cottage and headed for Ed's truck, where he sat smiling. "Want me to sit in the back?" she asked as she opened the door. "We can put one of the girls up here with you."

Both girls shook their heads. "No!"

Ed patted the passenger seat. "I promise I won't bite."

Stacy started giggling; then Tracy chimed in. Snorting, Stacy said, "My daddy wouldn't even bite a dog if it bit him first." That made both of them laugh.

Ed glanced at his girls in the rearview mirror, then turned to wink at Jill. "They've heard me say that," he whispered. He looked back at the girls. "I wouldn't be too sure about that."

That sent the girls into another fit of giggles. The happiness level in the cab of Ed's truck was higher than Jill had experienced during her entire childhood. And she loved the way it felt to be a part of it. Ed gave her a sense of well-being and belonging. The girls were a wonderful bonus.

Ed pulled his truck into a tiny diner that specialized in breakfast and lunch. Jill had seen it before, but she'd never eaten there.

"Tracy and I like fast-food pancakes," Stacy said.

"But Daddy said you'd like this place, so we told him that was okay," Tracy added. "We want you to have fun with us."

Jill's heart melted a little bit more. "Thanks, but if you'd rather go for fast food, that's fine."

Ed turned off the ignition and cast a silly look at his girls before turning back to her. "I told them not to tell you that," he said.

"But, Daddy, we wanted her to know we're doing this special for her."

Jill unbuckled her seat belt and climbed out before helping them out of their seats in the back. Tracy had hers undone and was busy working on Stacy's until

Jill took over. "I'm happy to have such nice friends who like to do special things for me."

Once Stacy was on the ground, she looked up at Jill and, with an expression that looked more grown-up than ever, said, "You did something special for us when we had that tea party."

"I loved that tea party," Jill said quickly.

"We know that," Stacy said with confidence as she took Jill's hand. "We all liked it. Even Jennifer."

"Especially Jennifer," Jill said.

Ed cupped his hands over his mouth and whispered, "Remind me to tell you something after we drop off the girls at their classroom."

"Are you gonna tell her Jennifer used to be scared of children before?" Stacy asked.

A goofy look came over Ed's face, and Jill laughed. Ed obviously couldn't pull anything over on his girls; they were so smart.

"Jennifer is a very nice lady," Ed said. "Let's change the subject, okay?"

After breakfast they drove to the church. The parking lot was almost full. "I'll take the girls to their classroom," Ed said. "Why don't you go find a good seat?"

"Don't sit in the back," Stacy said. "Daddy hates sitting in the back."

The back was Jill's favorite place to sit in church, but after what Stacy said she didn't stop there. She found a nice spot toward the front and on the very edge of the pew. Ed joined her a few minutes later.

"What did you want to tell me that you couldn't say in front of the girls?" Jill asked.

"Stacy pretty much covered it," he whispered. "I think you might have changed things."

The choir started singing, so Jill didn't have a chance to respond. She focused on the overhead screen and sang the worship songs until it was time for the sermon. Ed's presence next to her was somewhat distracting, but she still enjoyed the message.

After church Ed stood and faced her. "Well, would you like to go to lunch?"

Jill pursed her lips. She would have loved to go to lunch, but she didn't want to overdo things with Ed.

She shook her head. "I don't think so. Not today."

"You sure?" he asked as he folded his arms and frowned.

"Positive," she replied before she had a chance to change her mind. "I have a ton of stuff to do at home. You know how things can pile up when you work all week."

"Yes," he said as he sighed. "I do know."

Jill sat and waited for him as he ran around to the other side and got in. "Where are the girls?"

"They're with some friends."

Once they were on their way, Jill started chattering about how much she enjoyed Stacy and Tracy. "They're obviously well-adjusted and super smart. I've enjoyed them quite a bit."

Ed grinned. "Thanks. I think so, too, but I figured that was just the proud father in me coming out." He paused before adding, "The girls really like you, too."

The warmth in his voice touched Jill.

When he pulled up, Jill started to jump out of the truck. But Ed reached over and gently placed his hand on her shoulder. "Jill," he said, "can we talk?"

Chapter 10

She turned to face him. "What did you want to talk about?"

He ran his thumb along the edge of the steering wheel as he sat in silence for several very long, uncomfortable seconds. Finally, when he spoke, his voice cracked. "Jill, I really like you."

"I like you, too, Ed."

"My girls are crazy about you."

Now it was Jill's turn to pause. "I, uh, well. . .I like them a lot."

The expression on Ed's face remained unreadable. She could tell his guard was up.

"You're different from what I thought when I first met you."

Jill tilted her head and looked at him. "What do you mean?"

He shrugged. "You're very responsible."

She couldn't help but laugh. "You didn't think I was responsible at first? You thought I was a flake." That last comment had slipped out, and she regretted saying it the instant she saw the mortified look on his face.

"I never said you were a flake."

Jill reached out and placed her hand on his arm. "I know. I was just kidding. Is this what you wanted to talk about?"

"I wanted you to understand why we have to be careful. When Marcy found out she had gestational diabetes, we assumed it was a complication that would disappear as soon as the twins were born. We had no idea it would be. . .fatal."

Jill's heart ached at the very thought of what Ed and the girls had been through. "I'm so sorry."

"I can't take a chance on letting the girls get hurt by someone who might break their hearts, as unintentional as it would be."

"That's understandable, but I don't plan to break their hearts. I can be their friend, can't I?"

"Their friend?"

Jill nodded. "That's what I am. Their friend." She glanced down, then decided to take a chance on letting her feelings out a little more. "Actually, I adore the girls more than I can explain. I never realized how children could make such a difference in my outlook on life."

He smiled at her tenderly. "You've made a huge difference in *our* outlook on life."

She blinked. He'd included himself. "Ed, you're a very special man."

A sheepish look came across his face, and then he turned to face her. "I'm just doing what any man would do in my shoes."

Jill swallowed hard. Ed's goodness ran so deep that he didn't realize he'd done much more than what most men would have done. He'd taken on the role of being the father and the mother to his little girls. He'd taken them to church without showing any signs of bitterness toward God. And he'd reached out to her, taken her under his wing, and made sure she didn't lose her business.

"Ready to go in?" he asked as he reached for the handle. She nodded. "Oh, one more thing. I'm having a birthday party for the girls next weekend. Can you come?"

She nodded. "Yes, of course."

He helped her out of the truck and took her by the hand. Jill felt a natural, warm glow as they walked up the sidewalk to her house.

When they reached the door, she turned to face him. She had the odd sensation they were supposed to kiss. But they didn't. Instead he stood there looking at her for several seconds before he let go of her hand, turned, said, "See ya tomorrow," then left.

When Jill was inside, she closed the door, leaned against it, and shut her eyes. She was so not prepared for this. All she'd ever wanted was to lead a quiet life alone with her own little shop to run, no one telling her what to do and not having to account for a thing. And here she was, attending a lively, energetic church and falling in love with a man with two kids. How could she deal with it? With a sigh she closed her eyes and swallowed hard before she prayed.

Lord, I've loved You for a long time, and that's all I really need. I'm sure You had the best of intentions when You brought Ed into my life, but he's not what I need right now.

Then suddenly her eyes popped open. An alarm sounded in her head. The sermon that very morning had been about trying to tell God what to do. Pastor Travers had said people needed to be still and listen. God knew what they needed without their having to say a single word.

Jill frantically moved about her house, straightening pillows on the couch, picking up tufts of cat hair from the carpet, and, when she reached the kitchen, loading her dishwasher. Then she filled the dispenser with detergent, shut the door, and hit the power button. From there she headed to her room, where she put away yesterday's clothes and made the bed.

Once she was finished she sucked in a deep breath and took a long look around. She'd just done housework. That was totally not like her. To top it off, she felt good about it. What was going on?

She spent the rest of the afternoon doing laundry and studying magazines about collectibles. Then she thought about what to get the girls for their birthday.

Throughout the next week Ed acted distant, although he was pleasant. He'd found someone to watch the girls during the day, so she didn't see them. To her surprise and dismay, she missed them. Whenever she heard a child's voice or laughter, her heart thudded until she realized it was only a customer's child and not Stacy or Tracy.

On Saturday she'd just finished helping a customer load an old wooden desk into the back of her SUV when Ed pulled into the parking lot with his daughters. She instinctively smiled when they bounded out of the truck, grins on their precious little faces, arms open wide, coming toward her at full speed. She squatted down and pulled them in for a hug as Ed stood behind them, watching.

"The girls wanted to pick you up for their birthday party," he said.

"Thank you." Jill stood, looked at each girl, and gestured toward her shop. "Come on in, girls. I have something for you."

They followed her inside to the little table in the back where Jill had put a stack of wrapped educational toys and games she'd picked up last time she went to the store. It took them about a minute to tear open the wrapping paper. "You got all that stuff for us?" Stacy asked.

Jill nodded. "Who else would I get it for? You're my favorite little birthday girls."

Tracy turned to Ed. "Daddy, is it okay if we play here for a little while?"

Ed twisted his mouth in the comical way Jill loved, glanced at his watch, then nodded. "Well, I s'pose it'll be okay. The party isn't for another couple of hours."

Jill started to go back to her sales floor when she heard Tracy call out. "Can you go to church with us again?"

Stopping in her tracks, Jill tried to make a quick decision. She couldn't think of a single reason to say no—at least, not one the children would understand. And since it was one of the girls asking, she simply nodded and said, "Sure, if it's okay with your daddy."

"It's okay with Daddy," Stacy said.

Jill glanced over her shoulder at Ed. He held her gaze for a couple of seconds then nodded. "We'll be out of town tomorrow, but I'd like for you to go with us next week."

"Okay," she said.

An hour before the party was due to start, they headed to Ed's house so he could finish setting up. Jill helped the girls slip into their party dresses. Children from the neighborhood and church came by with their parents. The party lasted an hour, but it seemed much shorter to Jill. Once the last guest left, though, both girls went to their room and fell asleep right away. Ed asked his neighbor, Mrs. McKnight, to come in and watch the girls while he took Jill back to the shop where she'd left her car.

"I had a wonderful time, Ed," Jill said.

Ed took her hands in his and pulled her closer. "Thank you for everything," he whispered. She started to pull away, but he wouldn't let go. Instead he leaned over and gave her a light kiss on the lips. Then he walked her to her car.

She had plans to go to church with Jennifer the next day. Ed had taken the girls to their grandmother's house to celebrate their birthday because she hadn't been able to attend the party.

The next week dragged by. As much as Jill loved her shop and handling the collectibles, she found herself wanting to spend more and more time with Ed and the girls. But now that he had broken ground on his property development in Ackworth, she saw little of him.

The next Sunday finally arrived. As before, Ed waited in the truck while Stacy and Tracy went to Jill's door. Only this time she'd expected them.

"Here's a surprise," she said as she handed each of them a tiny stuffed animal.

Their eyes lit up. "You got these just for us?"

Jill nodded. "Absolutely, yes."

Tracy cuddled hers close to her chest with one hand and reached for Jill's hand with the other while Stacy ran ahead of them, her arm outstretched with the stuffed kitten. "Looky, Daddy! Looky what Jill got me!"

Ed gave her a puzzled look. "You don't have to give them presents every time you see them."

"I know," she said. "It's just that I know they like kittens, and I saw these in the store, and—"

"You couldn't resist," Ed said, finishing her sentence. "Yeah, I know how that goes. Happens to me all the time."

Ed hopped out to help settle the girls in the backseat, then slid back behind the wheel.

"If you want me to quit buying them stuff, I will," Jill said softly as she got in and buckled her seat belt.

"Once in a while is nice," Ed said. "But they just had a birthday, and I think the real prize is getting to see you."

As silence fell over them, Jill pondered his last comment, which she found immensely flattering. But was he talking about the real prize for the girls or for him? She knew the girls enjoyed having her around. They'd made that obvious. But how about Ed? Did he look forward to seeing her as much as she did him?

"Whatcha thinkin'?" he asked as they turned down the street leading to the church.

She shrugged. "That I'm grateful for your church and all the nice people who go there."

❧

Ed pulled into the parking lot, found a spot, then turned to look at her. She continued to soften each time he saw her. When he'd first walked into her shop she was defensive, and he suspected she could have been combative if tested. But now he'd seen her soft side, and it was incredibly appealing. Almost everything about Jill was appealing—even her tendency to be messy, which had bugged him to no end when he first met her.

The sense of belonging washed over him as he stood next to Jill during the worship part of the service. When the pastor spoke, Ed slanted occasional glances her way and saw the intensity of her interest. Warmth flooded him as he thought about how absorbed in the Word she seemed.

After church, as soon as they fetched the girls from their Sunday school class, Stacy said, "Daddy, can we get a kids' meal?"

"I don't see why not," he replied. He turned to Jill. "Unless, of course, you have to be home at any particular time."

She shrugged. "I really don't have anything else to do today, so that sounds good. I haven't had fast food in quite a while."

"Good. Then let's go."

Jill chatted with the girls while he returned to his deep-thought mode. The cozy feeling he had was wonderful until he actually gave it some serious thought. He, Jill, and the girls seemed like family. The problem was—they weren't. Was he setting the girls up for disappointment when Jill got tired of them?

Ed ordered their kids' meals and handed them to the girls.

"Eat first," he said. "Then you can play." He turned to Jill. "Is it okay with you if we sit in the kiddy area? That way we won't have to move when they're on the equipment."

"Sure," she said, taking her tray and heading to the small dining tables in the back.

Stacy and Tracy scarfed down their food in warp speed. They were finished and had their spots on the table cleaned before Jill had time to eat half her sandwich.

Laughing, Jill said, "Now I know what to do if I want a kid to eat."

Ed nodded. "It works."

෨෨

Jill felt as though she belonged. She was more relaxed than she could ever remember being.

They spent the next hour watching the girls, chatting about church, and basically keeping the conversation light. Once in a while the girls came over to make sure Ed had seen something they'd done.

"How about some ice cream?" Ed asked.

Both girls nodded and hopped up and down. Ed took the girls to the counter and purchased a small ice cream cone for each of them; then he sat back down with Jill while the girls enjoyed their dessert before going back to play on the equipment.

About a half hour later Stacy came over to them. "Daddy, I want a cookie."

"No, honey, you've already had your dessert."

She glared at him, folded her arms, and stamped her foot. "I want a cookie."

Tracy was right behind her. "Please, Daddy, please. Can't we have a cookie?"

"No," Ed said firmly. "One dessert is plenty. You don't need that much sugar."

Then to Jill's dismay both girls started screaming and throwing a temper tantrum. She'd never seen this side of them and shrank back in her seat.

Ed tried to talk calmly to the girls, but it was obvious he wasn't getting anywhere. Finally he took both girls by the hand and held on tight. "This temper tantrum is not acceptable behavior," he said firmly. "So we're going home now."

"No!" Tracy shouted. "I wanna play some more."

Stacy managed to break free of Ed's grasp. She took off running toward the play area.

Ed turned to Jill and offered an apologetic grin. "Sorry about this. Would you mind taking over with Tracy while I go get Stacy?"

Jill gulped hard as Ed took Tracy's hand and placed it in Jill's. That terrible feeling from her own childhood hit her full force. Her father had rules that were so rigid she'd felt stifled. And here she was, participating in discipline. But she understood it now.

Tracy kept scowling while Jill held tight to her hand. What bugged Jill was that Tracy wasn't even looking at her. In fact, Jill was pretty sure Tracy hated her for being on Ed's side, and that broke her heart. If it had been up to her, she probably would have given them the cookie. What did it matter, anyway? They hadn't eaten that much ice cream. But then again she saw Ed's side, too. The instant the tantrum started, it was a matter of principle. She realized Ed couldn't let them have the upper hand when they behaved like this.

Eventually Stacy got tired and gave in to her dad. He hoisted her up in his arms and let her snuggle against his chest, still sniffling from her full-blown tantrum. Tracy turned to Jill and held out her arms. Jill wasn't sure what to do.

After glancing at Ed, who nodded, Jill reached out and lifted Tracy onto her lap. Her heart warmed a little as the girl rested her head on her shoulder. This was a nice feeling. She sighed.

Finally Ed motioned for her to follow him out the door. "Well, I s'pose it's time to head on home for nap time. Ready?"

Jill nodded. "Tracy, honey, would you mind walking? I need to carry my tray over to the trash can."

Tracy scrambled down, but she held on to Jill's hand. With her other hand Jill discarded her wrappers and stuffed her tray in the slot. Then she walked Tracy out to the truck where she helped her into the car seat.

She couldn't avoid noticing the curious glances in their direction—from the beginning of the tantrum until now. Everyone probably thought she was part of the family. Ed started the truck without saying a word, so Jill settled back in her seat to regroup.

They'd gone about a mile when Ed pointed his thumb toward the backseat. "They've zonked out already."

Jill glanced over her shoulder and saw two little curly-headed girls sound asleep in their car seats. The sight of them gave her a warm, fuzzy feeling she tried to ignore.

"Sweet, huh?" Ed asked.

"Yes," she agreed. "About as sweet as I've ever seen."

"A little different from twenty minutes ago." Ed snorted. "This is what happens when they get tired. Sorry you had to experience that."

When they reached the curb in front of her house, Ed turned toward her. "I think we need to talk."

Jill looked at him, waiting, without saying anything. She watched as he collected his thoughts.

"I bet you thought I was an ogre back at the restaurant."

She shook her head. "I didn't think you were an ogre."

"It's just that. . .I want them to understand how to behave in public."

"I agree." As difficult as it had been to witness what happened, Jill really did feel that something needed to be done.

"You do?"

"Well, yes, but. . ." She shrugged. "Well, I might have given in and let them have a cookie, but you can't very well allow temper tantrums in public like that."

Ed's expression softened as he let out a deep sigh. "I'm glad you're not upset with me." He glanced down, closed his eyes for a few seconds, then looked back up at her. "Jill, I'm feeling. . ."

She tilted her head. "You're feeling what?"

"I didn't want to fall in love again, but since I've met you, well. . ." He shrugged. "Maybe I shouldn't have brought it up."

She needed to know. "Since you've met me—what?"

He looked at her tenderly then glanced away. "I'm afraid I've let down my guard and allowed myself to care too much."

Conflicting emotions collided inside her. She cared for him, too, but she wasn't sure if the timing was right to let him know. She had no idea what to say next. "Um. . .I think I need to go now."

He blinked then nodded. "Okay, I understand. See ya tomorrow, bright and early." She quickly made her way up the walk, unlocked her door, opened it, and then turned to give Ed one last look before going inside. The instant the door closed behind her, she felt an overwhelming sense of exhaustion—and, to her dismay, loneliness. She thought about her relationship with her father and regretted not being more understanding. Had he just been overwhelmed with the responsibility of a child and not known what to do? Being with the twins was giving her a different perspective.

As independent as she'd always been, Jill knew she was missing some very important things in life. One thing was easily rectified: a church home. She wasn't positive yet, but she thought she'd probably found it. The other thing wasn't quite as simple.

She sank down in a living room chair, closed her eyes, and prayed.

Dear Lord, I know I haven't always been a faithful follower, so forgive me. Jill bumbled through the things she figured she'd done wrong in the Lord's eyes, and then she asked for forgiveness. It felt awkward, but she knew the Lord understood. She finished praying, opened her eyes, and sighed.

❦

When the girls woke up from their naps, they ran into the living room where Ed sat reading his Bible. He'd been trying to put everything into perspective since meeting Jill. He knew she loved his girls, and he suspected she cared for him, as well. But that wasn't enough. He didn't want to take risks—either with his heart or with his daughters'.

"Daddy, where's Jill?" Tracy asked.

"I'm not sure where she is right this minute, honey, but we dropped her off at her house a couple of hours ago."

"Can we go get her again?" Stacy said.

Ed chuckled. "No, I don't think that's such a good idea."

Tracy planted her fist on her hip and tilted her head. "And why not?"

"We don't need to smother her," he said.

"I don't want to smother her," Tracy said. "I just want her to come over."

"We need to let her have some breathing room, girls. Some space. Jill isn't used to having people with her all the time."

"She said she likes us," Stacy argued.

"She does. It's just that. . ." Ed wasn't sure what to say. He lifted both girls into his lap at the same time. "You two are growing so fast I won't be able to do this much longer." That thought saddened him.

"We ate all our lunch," Stacy said.

"But I'm still hungry," Tracy added. "Can we have a snack?"

Ed sighed. The girls were wonderful and one of the biggest blessings he'd ever had—even with the occasional angry outburst. But they sure did keep him running. "Sure, sweetie. Let's go see what we can find in the kitchen."

Since it was a couple of hours until dinnertime he fixed them each a piece of fruit, a few graham crackers, and a glass of milk. They sat at the table in booster seats while he pulled something from the freezer to thaw in the microwave.

"Can we call Jill and ask her to come over for dinner?" Tracy persisted.

"Not tonight," Ed said firmly.

"Okay, when?" Stacy asked.

It was obvious the girls weren't going to give up, so he thought for a moment. "I'm not sure that's such a good idea, girls. Jill is a very busy woman."

"Too busy for us?" Tracy asked.

What could Ed say to that? He finally said, "I can ask if she wants to go out to dinner with us one night this week."

"I want to eat here," Stacy said. "You're the bestest cook."

"I don't know about that," Ed said, "but I appreciate the compliment."

After their snack the girls ran to their room to play with some of the things Jill had given them. As he started preparing dinner, Ed thought about how he'd invite Jill to come over.

The next morning he arrived at the shop early, thinking he'd be there and finished with most of his paperwork before Jill arrived. But she'd already unlocked the front door.

"What brought you in at such an early hour?" he asked.

He sensed an emotional distance as she shrugged without looking him in the eye. "I have stuff to do."

"Oh," he said. He started to head back to his office when he remembered his promise to Stacy and Tracy. "The girls wanted me to ask you over for dinner one night this week. How about Wednesday?"

Jill quickly looked up, but she didn't say anything.

"If Tuesday is better, we can do it then. Or even Thursday. The girls really want you to. This was their idea."

She chewed on her bottom lip for a second, sighed, then nodded. "I guess Wednesday would be okay. Want me to bring something? Remember—I'm supposed to be cooking all those dinners for you and Matt, and I've only done it a couple of times."

"There'll be plenty of time for that," he said. He felt relief mixed with a little guilt. He knew mentioning the girls was a dirty tactic, but he really wanted her to come over. "It's just that the girls. . .well, you know."

"Okay, so tell me when you want me there."

The next two days passed by slowly. Each night the girls talked about all the things they wanted to show Jill when she came over. Ed imagined himself being invisible while Jill continued to charm his daughters. The amazing thing was, it didn't sound so bad. He even found himself smiling a time or two.

On Wednesday night Jill arrived at the door with a bottle of soda and a box of cookies. Ed made a quick decision before the girls saw her.

"Either the soda or the cookies. Not both."

"Huh?" Jill asked.

"Too much sugar for a couple of little girls to consume at this time of day."

She sighed as she reached over and set the soda down on the side of his porch. "Okay, you're the boss."

Several times that night Ed had to be firm with the girls, including when they needed to take their baths. As he left the room to go and run their bathwater, he felt Jill's studious gaze on him.

After their baths the girls ran into the living room to give Jill a big hug and kiss good night.

"Thank you for dinner, Ed," she said, standing. She leaned over and placed her hands on the girls' shoulders. "And I loved having dinner with you two."

Tracy chose that moment to look up at Jill. "Read us a bedtime story, Jill."

Chapter 11

How could Jill say no to such a sweet little cherub? She glanced at Ed who nodded, before looking back down at Tracy. "Sure, sweetie. What book do you want me to read?"

"C'mon—I'll show you all our books."

Jill let the girls pull her toward their room where she noticed the perfect neatness of the house along the way. Was there anything Ed didn't organize? She shuddered as memories of her father flashed through her mind. Then she shook off the thoughts as she remembered Ed was nothing like her father. If her father had a fraction of Ed's good qualities, like his gentle spirit and ability to listen, his other traits wouldn't have seemed so bad.

She walked into the girls' bedroom and looked around at how organized it was. Even the books were in order, according to author's last name. "We like this one," Tracy said as she pulled a thick children's Bible storybook from the shelf.

Jill chuckled nervously. "I don't have time to read that whole thing tonight."

The girls giggled. "Not the whole book, silly. Just one story."

"Oh," Jill said, smiling. "That would be just fine, then."

It took them at least ten minutes and a stern face from Ed for them to pick a story for her to read. After the story, they managed to get a glass of water each from their dad. Then they folded their little hands under their chins and took turns saying their prayers. Jill left a piece of her heart in the girls' room as she stood and walked out.

"Thanks," Ed said as they reached the front door. "That meant a lot to the girls."

Jill nodded. "It meant a lot to me, too."

"Look, Jill—there's something we need to talk about." Ed's voice cracked on his last couple of words.

"What?"

"The girls really love you, but we need to be careful not to let them get too attached to you."

Jill suddenly felt sick to her stomach. "What are you saying, Ed?"

His jaw tightened, and a serious look spread over his face. He shook his head. "The girls are starting to want more from you than just friendship."

"And what do *you* want, Ed?"

"I'm not sure it matters what I want. You know how difficult things have been for the girls."

"And for you."

He looked at her then nodded. "Yes, and for me, too. I can't deny I'm attracted to you. . . ." Her heart hammered as he paused and looked at her. "But we're so different."

She shrugged and tried to pretend she wasn't fazed. "Maybe we're not as different as you think." Now she was the one wanting more from him, but he obviously wasn't ready.

"Come on, Jill—admit that my girls can be a handful."

She sighed as she tried to find a tactful way to respond. "I know it must be hard."

They gazed into each other's eyes for several seconds before he shook his head. "We need to be careful with our relationship, or the girls will be in too deep emotionally. I don't want to destroy their spirits."

Jill looked down and swallowed deeply. "I understand."

"You're always welcome to come to church with us."

"Good night, Ed," she whispered, backing toward the door. "And thank you for everything."

He smiled. "Thanks for coming. The girls. . .and I. . .enjoyed having you."

Jill darted out the door and had to force herself to walk calmly to her car. She managed to make it home before her wobbly knees gave out on her. As she sank down into the chair, she berated herself for letting down her guard and allowing herself to fall so deeply in love with Ed. . .and his girls.

While she was getting ready for bed, she thought about the parallels between her father and Ed, as well as the differences. Everything Ed said or did had a reason, even if she didn't agree with it. And he didn't seem to mind sharing that reason with his girls. They didn't always accept it at first, but they seemed to come around without holding a grudge.

Jill knew her grudges ran deep, and this was wrong. Her father had never given her any reasons for some of his random punishment disguised as discipline, but Ed was always clear with his daughters. With her father it was always "his way or the highway"—no questions allowed.

Granted, Ed still needed to lighten up a little. And she sensed the twins needed a little less regimen in their lives by the way their eyes lit up when they saw her. Or maybe they just liked being with her. They were thrilled to explore her shop and rummage through boxes of miscellaneous stuff. It wasn't what was in the box that excited them. It was more the unknown. The mystery. The surprise. Something Ed seemed to avoid. But he was getting better. Now he needed to allow himself to let go in a relationship with her.

With a deep sigh, Jill realized she couldn't change anything. She wanted him to love her, but she couldn't force it. She also couldn't change the fact that he was a regimented neatnik and she was a loosey-goosey slob who was happy with messy hair and her things in disarray.

Lord, thank You for making things clear to me. I don't understand all of it yet, but with Your help I'm working on it.

Jill lay in bed mulling over everything. She had no doubt Ed loved his daughters with all his heart. And he clearly hadn't broken their spirits based on their unadulterated excitement over the smallest things.

The next several days felt strange. Ed stopped by the warehouse, but he didn't spend much time there. Sometimes the girls were with him, and other times they weren't.

The following Sunday Jill went to church alone and sat with Jennifer. She saw Ed briefly, but after the services were over he'd disappeared. She went home and frantically cleaned the house, and then she fell asleep exhausted.

Early the next morning she was awakened by the phone ringing. She stumbled out of bed to answer it.

"Hey, this is Jennifer. Sorry I woke you, but I wanted to catch you before you left for the day."

"That's okay," Jill mumbled. "I needed to get up anyway. What's up?"

"Ed said he's waiting for a call from Ray. He thinks you'll be moving back to your place this weekend, so I wanted to find out when you wanted to get started."

Hmm. This was the first Jill had heard of it. "Um, I'm not sure," she said. "Can I get back to you on that?"

"I was hoping you'd know, but that's okay. I'm leaving town for a few days and won't be back until late Thursday." She paused. "Tell you what. Why don't you call and leave a message on my voice mail? I would tell you to call my cell phone, but I'm not sure I'll get service where I'm going."

"Okay, I'll do that," Jill replied.

"When I get back I'll show you some pictures. Brian and I are going on a very short cruise that's long overdue. We fly out of Atlanta tomorrow. We never had a honeymoon, unless you consider a day at Six Flags and a late dinner at the Big Chicken in Marietta romantic."

Jill laughed. "It sounds good, but I know what you mean about needing to get away for a real honeymoon."

"That's why we decided on a cruise. All the temptations from home won't be there."

"A cruise sounds nice," Jill said, holding back any feelings of jealousy. "Have fun."

"Trust me," Jennifer said with a lilt in her voice, "we will. I've heard there's so much to do on those ships that we'll need a vacation when we get back."

Jill set the phone down and lowered herself into the closest chair. *A cruise*

How nice. And how absolutely wonderful Jennifer can spend the rest of her life with such a fantastic Christian man.

Jill was truly happy for her friend but sad she'd probably never find a man with whom she could share her own life.

Ed wasn't around all day. She stayed busy waiting on customers. The next day was more of the same.

The Bible study group had decided to meet on Tuesday. She was hesitant about going. But after she got home and listened to a couple of messages from her new church friends, she figured she might as well go. At least they cared enough to call. Besides, her faith was growing in importance in her life.

The first thing people asked was, "How's Ed?" or "Where is Ed?" She was as polite as she could be when she told them she had no idea. Just as politely they nodded, then changed the subject and asked how business was. She could only guess what they were thinking.

During the fellowship time before the study, she noticed people chatting in whispers until Ed arrived. They turned and looked at him, then grew quiet. He didn't seem to notice.

The Bible study was short, but Jill was glad she'd gone. It gave her something to think about until the next time the group met.

Before leaving, Jonathan, the study leader, announced they were meeting at the Peachtree Grill on Friday night. He said he'd get there early to reserve a table and wanted to know how many could come. Jill managed to glance in Ed's direction and caught him looking at her. He smiled but didn't attempt to come over and talk to her. She felt a knot forming in her stomach. She wished things were different.

Later that night, as she was getting ready for bed, the phone rang. It was Jonathan.

"Hey, Jill, you didn't put your name down for Friday night. You're going, aren't you?"

"I'm not sure. Friday and Saturday are both big days at the shop, and. . ."

When she didn't finish her sentence, Jonathan helped her out. "It won't be a late night, I promise. We're eating at seven, and we should be out of there by nine. Why don't you go? I think you'd enjoy it."

What could she say? "I'm sure I would. Okay, put me down."

"Great! See you then."

Jill wondered if Ed would be there and what she'd say if he was. But the more she thought about it, the more she realized it didn't matter. Her friendship with Ed wouldn't change. . .or at least it shouldn't.

The next morning Ed was in his office behind the shop when she arrived. He lifted his hand and waved but continued working. Jill felt disconcerted, but she went through all the motions of opening her shop.

Ed wanted more than anything to approach Jill and ask how she was doing. If he did, he knew he would be drawn into the depths of her gorgeous, warm brown eyes. Her smile brightened his day and made him want to follow her around the shop. And when he was close enough, it took every ounce of self-restraint not to reach out and tuck her hair behind her ear. None of the physical attraction would have affected him so deeply if it hadn't been for his falling in love with who she was as a person. Yes, he finally admitted to himself that he was in love with Jill—in spite of her quirky ways. Or perhaps because of them—he wasn't sure. Whatever the case, he needed to take a step back because his daughters needed stability, and he didn't want to take any chances.

The girls had been asking about Jill, and he'd managed to change the subject by being vague. He told them she was busy with her shop and that he'd bring them to see her whenever things lightened up.

He finished filling in the paperwork for the next step of his development, but he felt fidgety. He did what he usually did when he felt this way—he went out to his shop, grabbed some scrap wood, and started working with it. He decided to build the girls a dollhouse; they'd been asking for one, and this would be the perfect time to do it.

As he sawed, he thought about the phone call he'd received the night before. Jonathan wanted him to go to the dinner party on Friday night. Ed rarely went to those things, but he gave in. He thought he might get to see Jill. He knew that probably wasn't good for him, but he missed her. For the past couple of days he'd been avoiding her until he couldn't stand it anymore.

He was cutting the last of the wood to build the sides of the dollhouse when the phone in his office rang. It was Ray, the exterminator.

"Good news," Ray said. "We finished everything. The tent comes off tomorrow as planned."

"That's really good news," Ed said with a heavy heart. "Thanks. I'll tell Jill."

"I'll call her if you want me to."

"No." Ed glanced up in time to see Jill coming from behind her counter to help a customer who'd just walked in. "She's in her shop right now. After she finishes with this customer, I'll let her know."

Ed thought that was the end of the conversation, but Ray apparently thought otherwise. "I know you're not asking for advice, Ed, but I'm gonna give it to you anyway. This girl is special. You need to hang on to her."

"I don't know what you're talking about, Ray." Ed shifted his weight to the other foot.

Ray chuckled. "Oh, I think you know, buddy. She's been coming to church regularly, and from what I can tell she loves the Lord. She's a sweet woman, and you show all the signs of being smitten. That's as good a start as any of us get."

Ed swallowed hard. "Thanks for the advice, Ray. I'll think about it."

After Jill was finished with her customer, Ed approached her. "Ray just called. The extermination is finished." He tried to keep his voice on an even keel, but he knew it was shaky. The mere thought of not having an excuse to see Jill every day depressed him.

Jill glanced down then looked at him. "Good. Thanks. I'll see about moving back."

"I'll call everyone to help," Ed said. "We'll get most of it done this weekend."

Jill started to say something, but another group of customers walked in. "We can talk about it later," she said as she edged toward her customers.

Later never came. The shop stayed busy for the remainder of the day, and Ed had errands to run. Not only was Jill about to move back to her own place, he was very close to starting his new development, meaning he'd hardly have time to see her.

As always, the girls greeted him the minute he walked in the door. Emma came around the corner from the kitchen, grinning. "How's Jill?" she asked.

He shrugged. "Fine, I guess. Oh, by the way, we're moving her back into her shop this weekend. Would you mind calling a few people to let them know?"

"Can we help, Daddy?" Stacy asked.

Ed turned around to see his little girls staring up at him with hands clasped beneath their chins. His heart twitched. "Of course you can, but you have to do exactly what I tell you to do."

They jumped up and down, squealing with delight. Ed chuckled and turned to Emma.

"They'll have a good time helping," Emma said, "but I'll be there, just in case you need me to help out with them."

Emma truly was a blessing. Ever since she and George had arrived, the entire church experience was not only a great place to be fed spiritually, but it had also become a true community. Their giving nature had filtered down to the congregation, and everyone had started pitching in to serve.

"Another thing, Ed. . . ," Emma continued. "If you need someone to watch the girls Friday night, I'm available."

Ed couldn't help but smile. "You're an angel, Emma."

"No, I'm just a very good friend who cares about you. I want you to get out more and have a good time. You work hard." She moved toward the door. "What time do you want me here?"

They made arrangements; then she left. The girls were still excited, but they'd calmed down enough for dinner, which Emma had started cooking.

"This is the best b'sketti I ever had," Tracy said as she twisted her fork around a strand of noodles. "Jill would like it, too."

"I'm sure she would."

Ed needed to find another measure for both his daughters and himself. They couldn't keep thinking about everything in relation to what Jill would like.

After the girls ate, he did his regular evening routine with them, running their bathwater and reading a story once they were in their pajamas. The girls were being too well-behaved, though, which left him no doubt they were up to something.

The rest of Ed's week was extremely busy, organizing Jill's move and then finishing the paperwork on his new development. He wanted to tell Jill about it, but her shop was so crowded all the time that he didn't have much of a chance. It was certainly obvious she'd hit on something that had taken off.

He still felt out of sorts. Everything on the surface of his life looked excellent. He had two very happy, healthy daughters. He loved everything about his church, and his faith in the Lord was growing. And Jill was doing well, so he didn't have to worry about her anymore. Nevertheless, something was bothering him.

By Friday afternoon Ed was ready for a little rest. Dinner with the church group would be the perfect ending to his productive week.

Jennifer called his cell phone as he was about to leave the warehouse. "I've been trying to get in touch with Jill," she said. "Is she there?"

Ed leaned over and saw that the lights in the shop were off. "Doesn't look like it."

"She's not at home, either."

A touch of concern flickered through Ed. "Is something wrong?"

Jennifer laughed. "No, I just had a few things I needed to ask about. We've been trying to find an easier way to haul all that glass tomorrow."

Ed wandered toward the shop and took a long look around. "Seems she has everything packed in boxes—at least all the small stuff."

"Yeah, I know. I was there helping her this afternoon."

"Don't worry about the glass. We'll get it moved just fine. Oh, how was the cruise?" Ed asked, hoping to change the subject.

"It was better than I ever expected. Brian and I were talking about what a great honeymoon it would make."

Ed practically ran into the wall in front of him. "I'm sure. Look—I have some stuff to do, so I'll see you later."

"If you see Jill, tell her to give me a call. I left messages, but she doesn't always check her voice mail."

"Will do," Ed said as he clicked the END button on his phone.

Not checking voice mail was another characteristic of Jill's nature. He checked his at least three or four times a day. What if she missed something important?

Ed headed home where the girls were playing with the same old boxes of toys Jill had given them when they first met. He'd come to accept the fact that it wasn't all junk.

Emma handed him his mail as he passed her. "Mrs. Cooper called and said it'll be a few more weeks before she can come back."

Ed's insides knotted. "Oh, that's just great. In the meantime, what am I supposed to do?"

"That's what I'm here for." Emma narrowed her eyes. "You need to learn to relax, Ed, or you'll have a heart attack."

Ed rubbed the back of his neck. "Sorry I took it out on you. It's just that I've got so much going on, I don't know what to do."

"Well, first of all, prayer helps."

"Yeah," he agreed. "I do plenty of that."

"You also need to accept the blessings from the Lord." Emma paused before continuing. "He's brought a bunch of people into your life, and we're all willing to help."

"And I certainly appreciate it," Ed said with a half smile. "But I don't want to overdo it with the child care."

"We consider your girls our blessing," she said. "So stop worrying. Have you ever thought that maybe your biggest problem might be your too-high expectations rather than too much to do?"

Ed opened his mouth but decided it was better not to argue and clamped it shut. Emma studied him for another second before he started to leave.

On his way out the door, he turned to Emma. "I won't be too late. I really apprec—"

She smiled. "I know, Ed. And I love being here with the girls. Have a great time."

"Have fun, Daddy," Stacy said. "Tell Jill to come see us."

"I will," he replied. "That is, if I see her."

All the way to the restaurant he thought about how his girls had become attached to Jill. It was painfully obvious they needed a woman in their lives—and not just a babysitter. And being honest with himself, Ed realized Jill had awakened something inside him that brightened the world around him. A couple of times he'd actually entertained the thought of giving in to his attraction to Jill to see where things could go for them. But reality always kicked in when their differences jumped in the way. Marcy had been a little messy, but Jill made her look like Mrs. Clean. Even without that issue, though, he couldn't forget how devastated the girls would be if things didn't work out and Jill turned her back on them.

He parked his car and was about to open the door when he noticed a familiar figure walking toward him. He glanced up in time to see Jill, who had just spotted him, nearly trip over the curb.

Chapter 12

"Whoa there," Ed said, running up to her. "You okay?"

She nodded. "Yes, I just wasn't watching. Sorry I'm so late."

Ed glanced at his watch. "You're not late. In fact, we're both right on time."

Jill tilted her head to one side. "But I thought. . .I was supposed to be here fifteen minutes ago." She frowned then shook her head. "Never mind. Let's just go inside, okay?"

As soon as they walked in and saw the group seated at the table, with two empty chairs beside each other, Ed's suspicions were confirmed. He'd been told when to get there, and knowing he was always punctual, everyone else had arrived early. Based on what Jill said, they must have wanted her there waiting for him—or they figured she'd be late.

Rather than make a fuss, Ed accepted that it was a setup with Jill. She looked as uncomfortable as he was.

The entire two hours were spent being on show for the rest of the people in the group. Everyone obviously wanted him and Jill to get together. He wanted it, too, and he had missed her so much he was finally willing to take a risk.

As soon as she finished her dinner, Jill grabbed her purse. "Sorry, but I have to run. I have an early morning tomorrow with the move and all."

It was dark outside by then. Ed stood. "I'll walk you to your car."

"You don't have to," Jill said quickly.

"He's being a gentleman," Jennifer whispered.

Jill looked at her friend then at Ed. "Okay," she told him.

Jill's discomfort ripped at Ed's heart. Once they reached her car, he made sure she was safely inside. She rolled down her window. "Thanks, Ed. I'll see you tomorrow, okay?"

"You know I wasn't in on this setup, don't you?" he said.

She paused then nodded. "Yes, of course."

He couldn't think of a way to mention how he felt, so he said, "Drive safely. I'll see you bright and early along with the rest of those clowns." He took a step back. "Stacy and Tracy are coming, but Emma will take them home if they start acting up."

Jill smiled. His heart did a double-loopy thing.

"G'night," she whispered. He waved then turned and walked away.

Double Blessing

He must have been brushing me off, Jill thought. He made such an issue of not being in on the setup. Deep down she'd hoped he'd set it up himself. She loved everything about him—including his incredible sense of responsibility. Through Ed she'd learned that discipline was a good thing if done right. Not only did she love his girls, but she was also in love with everything about Ed—from his desire to fix her life to the Christian kindness he showed everyone in his path. Jill had never met a man with such integrity.

She tossed and turned all night, mulling over his reaction to what the group had tried to do. Even though it was meddlesome, she thought it was sweet that they cared enough to go to that much trouble.

When morning finally arrived, Jill dressed in jeans and her favorite T-shirt from the bank. She took a couple of sips of coffee before heading out. It was unseasonably warm, but in north Georgia that wasn't unusual. It could be snowing one day and short-sleeve weather the next.

The parking lot at the warehouse was already filled with pickup trucks and SUVs. Ed had let them in, but no one had started loading yet. The second she arrived, a couple of the men approached her.

"We'd like to take the big stuff over first while y'all pack the smaller boxes," one of them said.

Jennifer's husband, Brian, pointed toward a white truck with the tailgate down. "How about the desk first?"

"Sure," Jill replied. "Whatever you think is best."

Three hours later Jill was back in her own shop with the desk in place. She'd shown them which boxes needed to go first; then Ed suggested she go to the shop to supervise unloading. By the end of the day everything was at the shop, and all the big pieces were in place. Ed's daughters had helped unpack a couple of boxes, but they lost interest and begged to go home. Before they left with Emma, they ran up to Jill for a hug.

She noticed Ed watching, but he quickly turned away when their gazes met. The rest of the afternoon went by in a flash.

"This is simply amazing," Jill said as she took a long look around.

"Yeah, we have a good group," Brian said. "If you need anything else, just give us a holler."

After a few minutes the place had cleared out, with the exception of Ed and Jill. "Want me to stick around a little longer?" he asked.

"No, thanks. I have everything under control," she replied. *Except my heart, but that's not open for discussion.*

"Then I need to get home to the girls. I'll see you in church tomorrow."

After he left, Jill blew out a deep breath. The emotional roller coaster she'd been on since she'd met Ed had left her exhausted even more than the physical move. Now maybe she'd have some time to think and figure out how to manage her personal life. With the shop in place and plenty of regular customers, she felt more confident she'd be able to make a living.

After putting the last of the glass knickknacks on the shelves, Jill locked the door and sat in an old wooden rocker for some quiet time. She bowed her head in prayer and focused on all she had to be thankful for. Closure with Ed was on her mind, but she didn't know where to begin with that prayer.

She went to church the next morning, but she saw the gleam in some eyes as people looked back and forth between her and Ed. So she scooted out of there as quickly as she could without being rude.

Over the next couple of weeks, Ed stopped in when he could to finish his work. He updated her on the progress of his development and how busy it was keeping him. After he had completed the last of the projects, Jill asked about the girls.

"Emma's been watching them," he said. "Mrs. Cooper's coming back next week, so things should be pretty much back to the way they were."

"Oh," Jill said. "That's nice." She couldn't even force a smile.

Ed had taken a step back, but he stopped. "What are you thinking, Jill?"

She shrugged. "I don't know. I miss seeing them. I sort of got attached, you know?"

He chuckled. "Yeah, I know what you're saying. I'm kind of attached to them myself."

She managed to grin. "Why don't you bring them by sometime so I can see them?"

His face lit up. "They'd like that," he said. "But I know you're busy."

She watched as Ed drew closer. "I'm never too busy for your daughters, Ed. I really enjoy being around them."

He looked down at his feet. "Well, I guess I'd better run," he finally said. "See ya."

Suddenly she knew she couldn't let him go that easily. "Wait, Ed."

He turned to face her, one eyebrow lifted. "Do you need something?"

She nodded slowly. "We need to talk."

"Talk?"

He sure wasn't making this easy for her. "Yes. About us. I, uh. . ."

Ed paused then closed the gap between them. "What's on your mind?"

Jill swallowed. She knew exactly what she wanted to say, but it was risky. Until now she'd been willing to take risks, but this was different. This wasn't just about money or a business. This dealt with her heart.

He reached for both of her hands and squeezed them. "It must be important for you to hold back like this. Are you afraid of something?"

She nodded. "Yes, very."

"You don't have to be. This is me. Ed. I'm your friend, remember?"

Finally she sucked in a breath. "That's part of the problem."

He blinked. "Huh?"

"Before I met you, I thought I knew exactly what I wanted; then you came along with your girls. You were there to help, and that confused me because I didn't understand why you were so eager to help someone who obviously couldn't pay you. Now I do."

He smiled. "You've come a long way, Jill, but then so have I. I think we understand each other better now."

"I'm not so sure. After watching you in action, fixing my shop and being a father—a wonderful father—I see things differently now. Faith in Christ is personal, but it's also a way of life."

Now his smile spread across his face, and his eyes even crinkled. "I see a few things differently now, too. You're a wonderful, kindhearted, responsible woman who's been badly hurt. Let's give our thoughts and feelings some time to simmer; then perhaps we can talk more later."

Before she'd gotten to know Ed, that kind of talk would have made her crazy, but his slower, methodical process made sense to her now. She was willing to wait until they were both ready to talk more.

He pulled her close, tilted her face up, and kissed her on the tip of her nose. Then he let go of her and slowly backed away. "I'll check on you every now and then. Call if you need me."

After he left, Jill immersed herself in organizing things in the shop. She felt a combination of emotions—from elation to concern. When she felt worry tugging at her heart, she went to the Lord in prayer.

The next week was busier than ever for Jill. Now that she had more capital to work with from early sales and she knew what her clientele wanted, she was able to carry a higher quality of antiques. Ed had stopped by periodically and made comments about the changes. The fact that he noticed warmed her heart even more.

"I know this seems like a random thought, but would you like to join the girls and me for dinner on Friday night?" Ed asked one afternoon when he'd stopped by on his way to the courthouse to take care of business on his development.

Jill wanted more than anything to be with him and the girls, but her feelings for Ed had intensified even more now that she only saw him on Sundays and once in a while when he had time to stop by the shop. "I don't know," she said. She didn't want to be a random thought.

"The girls wanted me to ask you," he said. "What should I tell them?"

This put a different light on things. She didn't like disappointing Stacy and Tracy. "The girls put you up to this?"

He nodded. "They miss you."

"*They* miss me?"

He paused, grinned, and added, "I miss you, too. Please say yes."

How could she turn down such an offer? "Okay, I'll be glad to go."

"Since you close at six we can pick you up at six thirty at your house, if that's okay with you."

She nodded. "That'll be just fine."

The rest of the week Jill kept hoping Ed would stop by again, but he didn't.

On Friday, before going to the shop, Jill put out some clothes to change into after work. Then she headed for the shop, hoping for a busy day so it would go by quickly. Her wish came true. She had a steady stream of customers throughout the day.

She couldn't seem to get out of there fast enough. As soon as she could, she flipped the sign to CLOSED, then dashed to her car. Ed was always on time, so she drove home, ran inside, and changed. A glance at the clock in her living room let her know she'd barely made it with one minute to spare. She sat on the edge of the sofa to kill the minute she had, but six thirty came and went, and still no Ed. Her nerves almost got the best of her when he was ten minutes late. She'd just stood to call his cell phone when the doorbell rang. It was Tracy.

"Daddy and Stacy are in the car waiting," she said. "They made me come get you cuz I'm the one who made us late. Stacy unbuckled me as soon as Daddy stopped the car. All Daddy had to do was open the door for me."

Jill smiled at the worry lines etched on the little girl's face. "That's okay, honey. I'm usually the one who's late, so it's no big deal."

"I know that. Daddy told me you're always late, and that's why we never take you with us."

Suddenly Jill felt as if she'd hit a brick wall. "Your daddy told you that?"

Tracy nodded. "But that's okay. Stacy and I still love you. And we think Daddy does, too, because he's so happy you're going out to eat with us."

Now Jill had no idea what to think as she walked out to Ed's truck with Tracy. Stacy's little face was pressed against the window.

"Sorry we're late," Ed said as he climbed out and helped her and Tracy into the truck.

Jill offered a half smile. "Don't worry about it."

Throughout the meal Jill chatted with the girls about everything that was going on in their lives. Stacy told her about Sunday school, and Tracy told her about the dollhouse her daddy had made for the dolls she'd given them. Jill avoided looking at Ed. Out of the corner of her eye she saw him watching her, a pained expression on his face.

After dinner the girls wanted to play in the arcade next door. Ed asked Jill if that was okay, and she nodded.

"Is something bothering you, Jill?" Ed asked the minute they were alone.

She had to ask him. "Yes," she finally said. "Did you tell Tracy you didn't want to take me with you anywhere because I'm always late?"

Ed's eyes widened. "No, but I guess I can imagine where she got the idea. One time when they asked if we could take you to church I said no, that we would be late if we came to pick you up, especially if you didn't know we were coming."

Jill let out her breath and smiled then. She was glad she had asked.

They were there for a half hour when Stacy started whining and stamping her feet. When Ed reprimanded her, Jill looked away.

Finally, after Ed had told Stacy not to do something and she did it anyway, he took both girls by the hand and said it was time to leave. Stacy continued whining and talking back, but Ed stayed firm. It was evident to Jill that the girls were tired.

Ed helped Stacy into the truck while Jill buckled Tracy into her car seat. By the time they arrived at Jill's house, both girls were sound asleep.

He reached out and took her hand. "Thanks for going out with us. I'm sorry about the girls' behavior."

"I totally understand."

He tilted his head and looked at her before a grin spread across his face. "Yes, I think you really do understand."

"Thanks for the great evening, Ed. Tell the girls I enjoyed being with them, and I hope to see them again soon."

Jill sat and studied him for a moment before he reached out and touched her cheek. "I'll call you, okay?"

She nodded before she let herself out and headed up the sidewalk to her house. She'd had fun until the temper tantrum, but even that didn't take away from the pleasure of being with Ed and the girls.

Saturday was busy at the shop, which kept her from thinking about Ed too much. But Sunday was different. Each time she was near Ed, she felt flustered and giddy, which made her uncomfortable around their friends.

Jennifer stopped by the shop the next morning. "Okay, girl, what's going on between you and Ed?"

Jill hadn't come out and said anything about her feelings to anyone, and she preferred not to now. But she didn't want to brush Jennifer off.

"I understand what you all are trying to do," she said, "but there are some things Ed and I need to work out."

"Like what?"

"Well, for one, we're really different."

"So?" Jennifer said. "Brian and I are different, but that's what makes our relationship so interesting."

"Yeah, but he didn't have kids when you met him."

Jennifer frowned. "But I thought you loved Ed's girls."

"I do, but. . ." Jill tried to find the right words but finally lifted her hands in surrender. "Oh, never mind. It's useless to try to explain."

Jennifer gazed at her a moment then nodded. "I think I have a pretty good idea of what's going on. It's obvious to the rest of us that you and Ed are crazy about each other, and it seems like a no-brainer to us. But you both have conflicting issues."

"Yeah," Jill said with a snicker. "That's an understatement."

"What neither of you seems to realize is that you don't have to agree on everything. If people only got together with other people who agreed with them, no one would ever get married."

"Some of our differences are pretty major," Jill replied.

Jennifer sighed then glanced at her watch. "I have to run now. I'm sorry." She smiled. "Just think about what I said, okay?"

"Sure. But don't get your hopes up."

For the rest of the day Jill thought about Jennifer's comments. They weighed so heavily on her that she couldn't focus on business. Her distraction must have shown because one of her regular customers, Mrs. Brighton, asked her if she was having "man problems," as she put it.

"I was always out of sorts when Henry and I had an argument," she said. Then she offered a sly grin and wiggled her eyebrows. "But things always got better, and we more than made up for whatever we were arguing about. That man was the best kisser in the whole world."

Jill smiled at the older woman. "That's sweet."

Mrs. Brighton blushed. "Don't let petty differences ruin your day. Life's too short for that. Might as well start kissing and making up right away, sweetie. That's the whole point of the argument, anyway."

Everyone seemed concerned about her. Even Matt stopped by to ask if she was okay.

"I'm fine, but I'd be better if you'd let me finish cooking all those meals to pay you back."

"It's better to spread it out," he said, chuckling. "Unless you want to get it over with."

"No, that's okay. We can do it over time. I just don't want you to think I've forgotten about it."

The next morning when she arrived at the shop, Ed was sitting on the front porch waiting for her, holding a paper bag. "I brought bagels," he said. "Raisin bagels with extra cream cheese, the way you like them."

"Thanks," Jill said as she unlocked the door to the shop. "Come on in."

He followed her inside and helped her turn on the lights. Finally, once everything was ready for opening, Ed walked up to Jill and took her hand. "I've been wondering if maybe we could start over."

"Start over?"

He nodded. "Yeah, like maybe go out on a date and get to know each other all over again."

"Has everyone been talking to you, too?"

Ed tilted his head back and laughed. "Of course they have. And I'm okay with that. How about you?"

She shrugged. "People have said stuff." She turned and headed toward the counter where Ed had left the bagels.

"Well? How do you feel about it?" he asked.

"About what?"

"Maybe we could get together and see how things go." He glanced down then looked up at her, waiting for her answer.

Her heart thudded. "That would be nice."

"Let's go somewhere Saturday evening. I promised the girls I'd take them out for tacos on Friday, but I'm free Saturday."

"Saturday's fine," Jill replied.

"Okay, I'll pick you up at seven. Gotta run. I have a ton of work to do on the new development tomorrow."

"How's the project coming?"

He shrugged. "I've had more glitches than I'm used to, but I think we're on track now."

After he left, Jill thought about her date with Ed. It was weird how he'd just stopped by like that. She had no delusions that anything would be different, but she couldn't flat out turn him down when he'd met her with her favorite bagels—with extra cream cheese, at that.

She had a banner sales week, so by the time Saturday night arrived she was exhausted but in a wonderful mood. Ed commented on her good mood when he picked her up.

"Want to go to a movie?" he asked.

"That's fine. Is there something you'd like to see?"

He shook his head. "No, I can't think of anything. I don't even know why I suggested it. It's hard to talk in a movie. We should probably do something different."

"How about bowling?"

Ed chuckled. "Do you like to bowl?"

She smiled back at him. "I don't know. I've never done it, but I'm willing to give it a try. I guess it's about time I tried something new." This was a major turning point for her, and she wanted him to know it, too.

With a smile he took her by the hand and led her to his truck. "After you catch on to the technique, I have a feeling you'll be an excellent bowler."

At first Jill rolled a few gutter balls at the bowling alley, but she couldn't remember ever having so much fun. She felt giddy and lighthearted for the first time since she was a little girl.

"See?" he said as they pulled out of the parking lot. "You caught on fast."

"That's because you're a good teacher."

"So are you," he said softly.

Her eyes widened. "Huh? I've never taught you anything," she said, then added, "Have I?"

He pulled into the parking lot of a convenience store, then turned to her. "Since I've known you, you've taught me to lighten up. You've shown me how to be spontaneous. You've brought beauty and joy into my life, Jill."

Tears stung the backs of Jill's eyes as she took in everything he was saying. "Thank you," she whispered.

"No." He leaned over and dropped a soft kiss on her lips. "Thank you."

Without another word he pulled out of the parking lot and drove her home. He walked her to her door and then stood and gazed at her. Jill reached up and touched her palm to his cheek. "Good night, Ed," she said softly.

Then he did the unexpected. He took her hand in his and drew her to him. Next thing she knew, his lips were gently on hers. She felt as if her heart were turning somersaults as he kissed her good night.

He released her and quickly stepped away. "Good night, Jill," he said.

Her lips still tingled from his kiss as she got ready for bed. The next morning she almost decided not to go to church. How could she face Ed after last night? That kiss meant much more to her than it could possibly have meant to him.

Then she came to her senses. She needed to go to church. That was what kept her grounded all week. So she reined in her feelings and went, but she stayed in the back and avoided contact with any of her friends. When church was over, she pretended not to see Jennifer waving to her. Instead she darted out the side door and hurried to her car before anyone could say something.

Monday morning was slower than usual. When she heard the bell on the door jingle right before noon, she looked up, expecting a customer. It was Ed and the twins. Tracy and Stacy ran to her and flung their little arms around her. She hugged them before looking up at Ed.

"They wanted to see you," he said as he strode toward her like a soldier on a mission.

Something in the way Ed was looking at her made her feel woozy inside. She couldn't pull her gaze away from his.

"Girls," he said firmly, "take your puzzles and go play in the back room while I talk to Jill for a minute."

The girls exchanged a glance then did as they were told. Once he and Jill were alone, Ed studied her for several seconds before he finally spoke. "We need to talk about this before it gets any worse."

"Talk about what?"

"You know," he replied. "Our feelings."

Jill's heart pounded. "What about our feelings?"

"I love you, and I think you love me."

Suddenly Ed's cell phone rang. "Excuse me a second, okay?"

Ed took the call while Jill went to the back room and asked the girls how they were doing. With excitement they talked over each other, telling her about everything in their lives—from their new toys to Mrs. Cooper's new grandbaby.

When Ed got off the phone, he was grimacing. "Sandra Chimensky's little girl locked herself in the bathroom, and they can't get the door open. Sandra called a locksmith, but she can't afford the fee. She knows I have the tools to take the door off the hinge. Would you mind watching the girls while I run over there and let her out?"

"Go ahead," Jill said. "We'll be fine."

Ed was gone only a few minutes when the shop became crowded. Jill took the girls back to the table and pulled out some things for them to play with. "I'll be right out there if you need me," she said.

She waited on a couple of customers before she realized how quiet it was in the back of the shop. An uneasy feeling crept over Jill as she headed back to find out what they were doing. The instant she rounded the corner, a strong sulfur smell overwhelmed her. She paused. To her surprise both girls were striking matches against a matchbox.

"No!" she hollered, running to them. "Stop! Now!"

At once Stacy looked up, her eyes wide open. When she saw Jill, her chin began to quiver. Tracy took a step back in fear.

"What do you think you're doing?" Jill cried. She'd never yelled at anyone, but these were extreme circumstances. By the time she yanked the matches from their hands and grabbed both of the girls' arms, Tracy was crying and calling for her daddy. Stacy was pouting, but she didn't cry.

"Sit down, both of you," Jill demanded, pointing her finger toward the chairs. An unfamiliar fear washed over her as she imagined the result if she hadn't caught them before it was too late. The building was old and had a wood frame. It would have gone up in flames so fast she didn't want to think what might have happened to the girls.

"Do you know how dangerous it is to play with matches?" she said firmly.

"We weren't playing with matches," Stacy said.

"Don't lie, Stacy," Jill said. "I saw you."

"She's not lying. We were trying to light these candles we found. You were busy. We didn't want to bother you," Tracy said.

"Those are for adults, not children." Jill shook her finger at both girls. "You are not allowed to touch a match again until you're grown. Do you understand?"

They both nodded.

"I know your daddy well enough to know he'd never allow you to light matches."

Stacy suddenly leaned forward and looked past her. "Daddy, Jill's yelling at us!"

Jill whirled around and saw Ed standing in the doorway, taking it all in. "How long have you been standing there?" she asked.

"Long enough to know what's going on. I got the Chimensky door open quickly and came right back." He walked over and bent over toward the girls. "Were you listening to Jill just now?"

Stacy sniffled and nodded. "She's being mean to us."

Ed rolled his eyes. "You know better than that. I've told you girls never to play with matches. Jill cares about you, and she's letting you know."

"B—but she yelled."

"I know." Ed turned to Jill and gave her the thumbs-up sign. "And I would have yelled, too, if I'd caught you lighting matches."

Tracy had stopped crying, but Stacy was sobbing now. Jill watched as Ed squatted between them with his arms around their shoulders.

"You realize this means you can't go to that movie party on Friday night, don't you?"

"But, Daddy," Stacy whimpered, "that's not fair."

Ed glanced up at Jill. When she nodded and turned to Stacy, he said, "You owe Jill an apology for misbehaving in her shop."

In the past Jill would have told him that wasn't necessary, but things were different now. She understood his need to discipline his daughters, and she knew humility was part of the training.

"Girls, I want you to know the only reason I yelled at you was because I love you," Jill said. "If anything ever happened to either of you. . ." She shuddered. "I don't even want to think about that."

Tracy stood up and came over to her. "We love you, too."

To Jill's surprise Stacy came, too, and the three hugged each other. Stacy sniffled as she mumbled, "We're sorry we were bad. We won't ever do that again."

❧

Ed's heart melted as he watched this tender moment between Jill and his daughters. He could see her as part of his family. She'd appreciated his parenting methods, and he understood her softness with the girls. Not only was he deeply in love with her, but he knew she'd be a positive influence on the girls. He needed to take the girls home now, though.

"C'mon, girls. Let's give Jill a break so she can work." He looked at Jill. "I'll talk to you later, okay?" Jill nodded. He took them out to the truck and put them in their car seats.

"Daddy," Stacy said once they were on their way home, "I don't want Jill to be mad at us."

"She was upset because you were doing something really bad, something that could have hurt you," Ed said. "Jill loves you."

"Are you sure she loves us?" Tracy asked.

"I don't think she'd say anything she doesn't mean."

He looked at the girls in his rearview mirror in time to catch them exchanging a glance.

"Daddy, do you love Jill?"

"Why are you asking?"

"Since we love Jill, and she loves us back, we were thinking—." He saw Tracy hold her fingers up to her lips. Stacy stopped midsentence.

"What's going on?" he asked.

The girls giggled. "Can Jill be our mommy?"

Ed chuckled. Just what he'd thought. "Why don't we let her recover from the match incident first; then we can talk about that."

Fifteen minutes later they approached him again. "Do you think she's recovered yet?"

"Maybe."

"Can she marry us?"

Ed sighed. He couldn't keep his feelings to himself any longer. He'd already decided he wanted to marry her, but he also wanted to have a romantic proposal—alone with Jill. He didn't want to deny his daughters the pleasure they'd obviously get from his decision, though.

He looked into each expectant face and smiled. "I plan to ask her very soon."

Both girls turned to each other and squealed with delight. The girls were remarkably well behaved for the rest of the day. That night, they even got ready for bed and turned in early.

The next morning Ed was awakened by two little girls jumping on his bed. He rolled over and squinted.

"Get up, Daddy."

"What time is it?"

Stacy held out her hands and shrugged. "The big hand is on the twelve, and the little hand is on the seven."

"Let me sleep a few more minutes."

"But we have to go to work."

"Huh?"

"We want to go to work with you at Jill's shop."

"I've finished my work at Jill's shop."

"Daddy," Stacy said firmly, "we want to see Jill. So get up and let's go."

He wasn't in the mood to argue, so he swung his legs over the side of the bed. Besides, the thought of seeing Jill sounded pretty good. "Okay, but I have to shower and get dressed first."

By the time he was dressed, both girls had their clothes on and were at the kitchen table eating cereal. Mrs. Cooper had put plastic bowls within their reach and small, pint-sized cartons of milk on the lower refrigerator shelf so they could be more self-sufficient. "We fixed you some, so sit down and eat," Stacy said, pointing to a bowl with soggy corn flakes floating around.

Fifteen minutes later they were on their way to the shop. "She might not be in yet," Ed said. "It's still early."

"She'll be there," Stacy said, pointing her finger. "See? There's her car. We called her and said it was a 'mergency."

"You what?" He'd just pulled up in front of the shop and stopped the truck. Before either girl answered they were out of their car seats and trying to get out of the door. He laughed at how they'd teamed up and unbuckled each other's seat belts. He started to hold back and not let the girls out, but at this point he knew it was useless. The second he opened the door, they were out of the truck and halfway up the sidewalk.

Jill opened the front door of the shop, and the girls ran right up to her. Ed was on their heels.

"Jill," Stacy said, "we wanna ask you something real important." She turned to Ed. "Daddy, c'mere."

Ed did as he was told. "Now what?"

"Will you be our mommy?" Tracy blurted.

"Huh?" Jill said.

Tracy rolled her eyes. "That's not how you do it, Stacy." She turned to Jill. "Will you marry our daddy?"

Jill looked as if she might fall over backward. Ed rushed to her side. "You okay, Jill?"

"I, uh," she stammered, "I don't know what to say."

The corners of his lips curled as he gave her a teasing look. "Just answer their question."

Jill's eyes widened in disbelief.

Ed reached down, cupped her face in his hands, and whispered, "Please say yes."

Epilogue

B rush my hair, Jill," Stacy said. "I want to be pretty like you."

"You look beautiful," Jill said as she ran the brush through Stacy's curls. "How's my veil?"

She leaned toward the girls, who inspected it and nodded. "You're the prettiest bride in the whole wide world," Tracy told her.

Jill's eyes misted as she hugged her soon-to-be daughters. "And you two are the prettiest flower girls in the whole wide world."

The organ began to play. Jill stood and gently guided the twins out the door. "It's time to go down the aisle, girls."

Stacy nudged in front of Tracy. "I wanna go first."

"No, I want to go first."

"Girls," Jill said, her voice low and firm. They giggled. "You can walk together, side by side, okay?"

After the girls were halfway down the aisle, Jill had an overwhelming surge of maternal feelings. She wished her father could have been there to witness this wonderful moment. She glanced over at Jennifer, who'd taken her position right behind the twins and was about to walk toward the front of the church.

Matt extended his elbow, and she took it. "Thanks for walking me down the aisle, Matt."

"Trust me—it's an honor to bring my best buddy the woman he loves."

She giggled. As the music changed, her heart pounded with excitement and anticipation of the full life she had ahead of her.

The doors opened wide, allowing everyone in the church to see her as she made her entrance. She took her first step toward Ed, the man she loved with all her heart. "Oohs" and "aahs" echoed throughout the church.

Then suddenly the girls piped up. "Here comes our new mommy!"

If the Dress Fits

Dedication

This book is dedicated to Kim Llewellyn, Tara Spicer, and Kathy Carmichael—friends who have stuck with me through everything.

I'm also thankful to my fabulous agent, Tamela Hancock Murray, for her energy and enthusiasm.

Chapter 1

Tears stung the back of Cindi Clark's eyes as she reached out and gently stroked the satin bodice of the bridal gown she'd lovingly put on the mannequin. She'd dreamed of working in a bridal shop for as long as she could remember, and here she was, the owner, and less than a year before she turned thirty.

She should be happy, but her parents had announced they were splitting up. If they couldn't stay together, how could she, in good conscience, keep perpetuating the myth of happily-ever-after? With a heavy heart, she'd contacted a commercial Realtor from her old neighborhood to list the shop, and now her place was for sale.

"Sometimes I wish I could buy the place," Elizabeth said.

Cindi turned around to face her longtime best friend and only full-time employee. "Yeah, me, too."

"But without you here, it wouldn't make sense. Besides, I really want kids."

Cindi chuckled. "I used to want them, too."

Elizabeth dropped the tiara back into the box she'd been unpacking, crossed the showroom, and gently placed her hand on Cindi's arm. "I know your parents' split is hard on you, but you shouldn't become jaded over it."

With a nod, Cindi forced a smile. "Yeah, I know. I just don't want to participate in something that's probably going to end in heartache eventually. I mean, look at the number of brides who come in a year later and say it didn't work." She turned back to the gown and sighed. "Too bad marriage goes downhill right after the wedding."

"That's not always true, ya know." Elizabeth stared at the dress Cindi was putting on the mannequin. "I think this is my favorite dress in the shop."

"They're all your favorite," Cindi teased. "You're like I was a few years ago—filled with all kinds of romantic notions of a fairy-tale marriage to match the wedding."

Elizabeth shrugged as she turned and headed back to her unpacking. "Personally, I don't see anything wrong with that. So what if I'm a romantic at heart? I have a good marriage."

"You're unusual. That's not the reality for most people."

Before Elizabeth had a chance to argue, Cindi pulled her key ring out of her pocket, went to the door, and unlocked it. Cindi was relieved they had an early appointment for a fitting. She was growing weary of Elizabeth trying to talk her out of selling.

Her appointment showed up right on time with her mother right on her heels. Angelina Dillard was a soft-spoken girl, the polar opposite of her clearly excitable mother.

"Would you like some orange juice?" Cindi asked.

Angelina nodded, but her mother adamantly shook her head no. "Orange juice has calories, and I don't want my daughter bloated for the fitting."

Her daughter scowled.

"Maybe afterward, then." Cindi took a step back and gestured around the showroom. "Why don't the two of you peruse the racks and find some different styles to try? We can alter any of these dresses for a perfect fit."

Mrs. Dillard scanned the room then zeroed in on one of the front racks. "I want to see my daughter in this dress," Mrs. Dillard demanded. She turned to look over the rest of the assortment then pointed toward the circular rack by the back wall. "And that one over there."

Cindi turned to Angelina with a questioning gaze. "Is there anything else you'd like to try?"

Angelina barely had her mouth open when her mother grabbed another dress off the rack. "Let's see how this one looks."

"Mom, I really don't like the full skirts," Angelina said softly. "I'd rather—"

Mrs. Dillard flipped her hand at the wrist. "How would you know what you like when you haven't even put one of these on? I think you'll look like a princess in a full skirt."

Cindi glanced at Elizabeth and winked before turning back to Angelina. "Why don't you try on several different styles before you decide?"

Elizabeth had already pulled a few off the rack and headed back to the fitting room. They'd seen this same scenario many times—the overbearing mother dragging the weary future bride through the store. And rather than pick sides, Cindi and Elizabeth managed to remain neutral as they tried to make peace during one of the most stressful times in the bride's life.

As Cindi listened to Angelina's desires and thoughts about the dresses, she directed Elizabeth to bring in more gowns, each one getting closer to what the bride wanted. They'd learned early that instantly jumping from one side to the other wasn't the best way to handle this touchy situation.

The skirts grew less full and more formfitting with each try-on, and the long sleeves gradually shrank to three-quarter sleeves, short sleeves, then sleeveless until Angelina finally had what she obviously wanted to begin with. As Cindi zipped the shiny white satin dress with the floral lace overlay on the bodice, both Angelina and her mother beamed.

"See?" Mrs. Dillard said. "I told you I'd find the perfect gown. This is absolutely lovely on you." She took a step back and studied her daughter in silence.

Cindi met Angelina's gaze then quickly glanced down to keep from smiling. Angelina turned back to face herself in the three-way mirror. "This is the one I want."

Her mother's reticence quickly evaporated. She sprang back into action, grabbing a hunk of material at the waist. "This dress is way too big for my daughter. It needs to be taken in here. . . ." She pointed to the hem. "And there. It's way too long. Is there any way you can hem it without ruining the train?"

Elizabeth popped into the room sporting a pincushion on her wrist. "Absolutely. We do it all the time."

"It has to be perfect," Mrs. Dillard screeched. "We've invited everyone from the country club, and they'll notice everything."

Cindi felt that awful, familiar constriction in her chest. "Angelina will be a beautiful bride." She nearly choked on the words, but she meant it.

Mrs. Dillard beamed. She reached out and smoothed her daughter's hair. "She sure will. By the time we get her hair done and all my heirloom diamonds on her, she'll make all my friends jealous."

Angelina looked annoyed. She'd obviously had this conversation with her mother before.

"Even now, with her hair down and no jewelry, she's beautiful," Elizabeth said.

Before Cindi had a chance to agree, Mrs. Dillard started flapping her jaw again, going on and on about the guest list, yapping about how all the girls would swoon and wish they were the bride—all the wrong reasons for this wedding. Cindi had heard it all before. The last bride who'd tied the knot cried at the first fitting and said she'd changed her mind about the wedding and wanted to elope. Elizabeth had managed to soothe her nerves.

"Would you like some orange juice now?" Cindi offered. "We also have some muffins if you're hungry."

Angelina smiled and nodded. "I'm starving."

Mrs. Dillard frowned. "Are they low-fat?"

"I believe we have some low-fat in the freezer," Elizabeth said. "I can thaw them in the microwave."

"Never mind," Mrs. Dillard said. "We don't have that kind of time."

Angelina frowned and stared at her shoes.

Cindi recognized the look of dejection. "It'll only take a minute." She turned to Elizabeth. "Why don't you pour the orange juice while I get a couple of muffins ready?"

They scurried to action, leaving no room for argument. Even from the back room, they could hear Mrs. Dillard talking about watching every single bite because

Angelina needed to stay slim and trim—at least until after the wedding.

"Don't let it get to you," Elizabeth whispered as they arranged the tray of orange juice and muffins.

"We just need to make sure Angelina gets the gown she wants," Cindi agreed. "The rest of it is out of our hands." She squeezed her eyes shut and said a silent prayer for the patience to continue working with Mrs. Dillard.

When she opened her eyes again, Elizabeth had already carried the tray to the showroom where Angelina and her mother sat on the love seat in the corner. Cindi joined them and gave her talk about how they wouldn't have to worry about a thing related to the dress because Cindi's Bridal Boutique had the experience with all the details ironed out.

The phone rang, so Cindi excused herself, leaving Elizabeth to finish the first session with the Dillard women. It was her Realtor.

"I have a potential buyer for the shop," Fran Bailey said.

Cindi's heart thudded with an odd mix of anticipation and unexpected sadness. "Good." That's all that would come out.

"He wants to see the shop tomorrow afternoon, if that's convenient."

Cindi opened her appointment book before she realized what Fran had said. "He? As in a man?"

"Yes, he's a very successful businessman who likes the thought of owning a bridal shop."

How odd. In all the scenarios Cindi had envisioned, a male buyer hadn't even crossed her mind. "Well, I guess that would be okay."

Fran chuckled. "I know his mother, and she's a very nice lady. Besides, we can't very well turn down potential male buyers."

"Oh, I understand. I'm booked until noon, but after that I'm free until two tomorrow afternoon."

"Excellent!" Fran said. "I'll bring him by at one. He's already seen the shop from the outside, and he wants to come in and take a look around inside."

"I'll stay out of the way," Cindi offered.

"Um, he asked that you stick around."

"I thought you said—"

Fran interrupted. "I know when you listed I said it's best for you to make yourself scarce in the beginning stages, but occasionally buyers make specific requests. I told him it might be better to wait until he's closer to a decision, but he insisted."

Cindi paused for a moment and tried to imagine why someone would insist she be there. "I'll do whatever you feel I should," she finally told Fran, "if you think that would help sell this place."

༄

Jeremy took another spin around the block and slowed down as he got close to

Cindi's Bridal Boutique. He was amazed at how much of herself she'd put into the window display. If someone had shown him pictures of a dozen bridal shops and said one of them was Cindi Clark's, he would have picked this one without a second's hesitation.

He came to a near stop and stared at the window, half hoping he'd see Cindi and half hoping he wouldn't. Ever since she went away to college, he'd wondered about her. The breakup had ripped him up inside, and he wished he'd handled things differently. He should have been completely up front with her rather than acting like the tough guy. But he was a kid back then. What did he know?

The car behind him honked, so after a quick glance in the rearview mirror, he accelerated. He needed to head back to his parents' condo in Roswell.

He pulled into the condo parking lot right after his mother, who'd just closed and locked her car door. She smiled as she turned to him. "Productive day?" she asked.

Jeremy shrugged as he loosened his tie. "I've narrowed down a few places to look at."

"It would be nice for you to find a business here in the Atlanta area so we can see more of you."

He gently put his arm around the woman who'd sacrificed so much for him and his brother. "I know. After I nail down a business, I'll look for a house."

"You can buy the condo at the other end of our building," she quickly offered.

With a chuckle, he shook his head. "As tempting as that is, I'm afraid I need to be a little farther away so you won't feel like you have to cook for me every night."

"I really don't mind," she argued.

"I know you don't, and that's very sweet." He leaned over and kissed her cheek. "But I'll be fine. Speaking of dinner, how about I take you and Dad out tomorrow after work?"

"Think we might have something to celebrate?" she asked as she slowed her pace.

"Maybe."

&

Cindi had arrived early to make sure the showroom was perfect for the Realtor. "I totally don't get why I have to meet this guy."

"I'm sure he just wants to ask some questions about the profitability," Elizabeth said.

"Probably, but I'm thinking he'll take one look at the place and leave when he realizes we're strictly a bridal shop." She rolled her eyes. "After all, what would a man want a place like this for?"

"Maybe it's for his wife or something."

"I didn't think about that. Whatever the case, I want to make sure nothing's out of place."

Elizabeth tilted her head back and laughed. "Nothing's ever out of place here. You're the most meticulous person I know."

Cindi took a rag out from behind the counter, squirted some furniture polish on it, and took one more swipe at the wooden shelves by the desk. "That'll have to do." She went to the back and tossed the rag into the hamper to take home later.

When she came back out to the front, Elizabeth was standing at the front of the store chatting with Fran and her client, who looked amazingly like. . .

"Jeremy?" she squeaked.

The man glanced at Fran, who cast a curious look first at Cindi then at Jeremy. Then he took a tentative step toward her. Cindi felt numb from the tip of her toes to the top of her head—she couldn't budge, she was so shocked. She felt she'd just taken a giant step back in time—and her tall, dark, and handsome boyfriend had just entered the room. His brow-hooded brown eyes had a few crinkles around them, but she would have recognized him anywhere.

After a couple of seconds, she cleared her throat and looked at Fran. "Is this your. . .client?"

Fran nodded. "I understand you two knew each other a long time ago."

"We were high school friends," Jeremy quickly said.

"Um, Jeremy," Elizabeth blurted, "it's nice to see you after all these years."

Jeremy offered a grin. "Nice to see you, too, Elizabeth. Things going well for you?"

Cindi turned to Elizabeth, who clamped her mouth shut and shrugged as she took a small step back. Elizabeth was obviously just as surprised as she was.

"So this is what you've been doing since college, huh?" Jeremy asked, breaking the short silence.

"Yes." The lump in Cindi's throat was so big she was afraid to try to say more.

"Nice," he replied with a nod as he walked around, looking everything over, making Cindi feel she was being scrutinized. "Very nice."

"Why are you here, Jeremy?" Cindi asked.

His attention quickly returned to her. "I like buying thriving homegrown businesses and taking them to the next level."

Fran's smile widened. "And he's been quite successful at it."

"So I've heard," Cindi said. "You don't live here, so how can you run a bridal shop?"

"I'll just hire someone to work it for me." He reached out and touched one of the gowns before pulling back to face her. "At least for a while. I'm thinking about moving back to Atlanta."

Cindi's shock had finally worn off, replaced by annoyance. "This isn't exactly the kind of business someone can hire unskilled workers to run."

Fran quickly dropped her smile. "Perhaps it wasn't such a good idea for the two of you to be here together so early in the process. Why don't we come back later, Jeremy?"

"No, that's okay. I'll just take a quick look around, and maybe Cindi can show me her books."

As tempted as she was to tell him her place was no longer for sale, Cindi just nodded. His appearance at her store had taken her completely by surprise—she was afraid she'd slip up and say or do the wrong thing.

She and Elizabeth stuck close together the rest of the time Jeremy was in the shop. A customer came in, so she didn't have a chance to show him her books. As soon as he and Fran left, Elizabeth turned to her, eyes wide, forehead crinkled, and slowly shook her head.

"I never saw that one coming. That totally surprised me."

Cindi snorted. "You and me both."

"What are you gonna do?"

"What can I do? Never in a million years would I have expected to see Jeremy Hayden thinking about buying my store."

"You can take it off the market."

"I know, but I don't think I'll do that."

"What if Jeremy makes an offer?" Elizabeth asked.

"I guess I'll have to deal with it if it happens—but it probably won't. A commitment-phobe like Jeremy isn't likely to actually buy a bridal shop."

Elizabeth nodded. "Yeah, you're right. I'll never forget. . ."

When she didn't finish her sentence, Cindi offered a half smile. "You can say it. He jilted me right before high school graduation. I won't forget it, either, but I got over it a long time ago." At least she thought she had—until now. "I went away to college, and he went into the army. Besides, I don't think he was a Christian, so it wouldn't have worked out between us anyway."

"It's just weird how it all happened. One day he seemed to be so into you, and the day after you told him about your scholarship and acceptance to the University of Georgia, he suddenly acted so cold."

"Yeah, that was weird, but at least it showed me that side of him. Good thing I found out early, huh?"

"I guess." Elizabeth shrugged. "It was so sudden, though. I kept thinking there was more to it than that."

"Maybe," Cindi said. "But I remember what the pastor said when he caught me in the hallway crying. He reminded me that not only did Jeremy not seem to be a believer, but he heard Jeremy had a history of breaking girls' hearts and I needed to count my blessings."

Their two o'clock appointment came in, so they spent the rest of their afternoon scurrying around, appeasing nervous brides and demanding mothers-of-the-brides. Cindi sometimes considered her job more of a counseling position than that of a bridal gown salesperson.

Elizabeth had to leave an hour early, so Cindi had the rest of the afternoon to herself. She had one more customer who wasn't due for a half hour, so she decided to rework the showroom window. She'd barely gotten the mannequin turned around when she saw the car slowing down in front of the shop. When she focused on the driver, she realized who it was. Jeremy. Her heart pounded hard and her mouth went dry, but she forced herself to turn away.

⁓

After all these times of driving by, he'd grown confident he wouldn't see Cindi—or more precisely that she wouldn't see him. But she had. He could tell when she recognized him because she jerked into quick action and moved out of direct view. She'd changed a little, but for the better. Her blond hair that once hung to her waist was now stylishly below her shoulders with long layers. Rather than contacts, she wore glasses that gave her more of an intellectual look yet didn't cover up her big blue eyes that sparked with emotion. He was happy to see she hadn't starved herself to get skinny like so many women her age did. She still had a pretty, round face and a smile that would light up any room.

He slammed his hand on the steering wheel. For the first time since becoming a businessman, he was unsure of himself. All his other business acquisitions had been effortless and calculated. This one, however, was nothing but an emotional roller-coaster ride. He'd heard the rumor that Cindi Clark owned a boutique of some sort. Then as soon as he spotted Cindi's Bridal Boutique in Fran's listing book, he remembered his old high school flame's dreams, and the name *CINDI* on the sign jumped out at him. Just by chance it was hers, he asked. Fran had given him a questioning look but nodded.

That was the last time he'd circle the block. It was time to leave her alone until he had more of a chance to think of what to do next. He looked at his watch and saw it was almost time for his dad to get home from work. He'd promised to take them out to dinner. He pulled out his cell phone and called his mom.

"We understand if you're too busy," she said.

Jeremy laughed. "I'm never too busy to take my favorite people out. I'll be there in half an hour. Think you can be ready then?"

"I'm ready, and I'm sure your father will be very quickly. All he'll want to do is change clothes and wash his hands."

"The timing will be good, then," Jeremy said.

"Where are you taking us?"

He laughed. "It's a surprise."

"You know we don't care where you take us. We're easy to please."

"I know, Mom, but I want to treat you and Dad to something wonderful."

"Just don't go getting any ideas of taking us someplace too fancy."

After he hung up, he paused and considered where he'd planned to take his parents. Atlanta Fish Market in Buckhead was one of the finest restaurants in the area, and he doubted his folks had ever been there. What if they didn't like it? Maybe it would make them uncomfortable.

Oh well. If he pulled into the parking lot and they insisted on going someplace else, he'd call from his cell phone and cancel their reservations. But he wanted to at least try to give them something they weren't likely to do for themselves. With money scarce during his childhood, his mother pinched pennies at the grocery store. They rarely went out for dinner. They sacrificed even more when they moved him and his brother to their first house right before he started high school. And they waited until both boys were gone before selling the house and buying the condo.

A few minutes after he arrived at their place, his dad came walking out of the bedroom all dressed up in his best navy suit and tie. "You don't think I'd want my son to outshine his old dad, do you?"

"I'll never outshine my dad," Jeremy said.

His mom squeezed between them and hooked her arms in theirs. "I'm the luckiest girl in the world to be with the two most handsome men in Atlanta."

Jeremy's dad wanted to drive, but Jeremy was more insistent. Since his own car was a two-seater, they took his dad's car. "You two sit in the backseat, and I'll play chauffer."

As soon as he pulled up to the Atlanta Fish Market, his mother let out a sound he'd never heard her make, causing him to glance in the rearview mirror. "You okay back there?"

Her eyes round and wide, she nodded. "Can you afford this place?"

Jeremy's heart sank. He had a feeling she'd make him turn around and go someplace else—like Old Hickory House where the food was good but not nearly as pricey and much more down-home.

"Mom, I wouldn't take you here if I couldn't afford it." He paused before adding, "It is okay with you, isn't it?"

She nodded then broke into giggles. "Imagine me eating at a place like this. Son, you're so good to us."

❧

The next morning Cindi arrived at the shop early to look over her books. Fran had called late the previous day and said she was bringing Jeremy back. Cindi had mixed feelings. On the one hand, she didn't want to sell her business to an absentee owner, but on the other hand, she wanted to show him she was doing well.

Before opening her computer spreadsheet, she said a silent prayer for the ability to know what to do and the emotional stability to get through this. She'd been surprised to see Jeremy, but even more shocked at how she felt after all these years. The attraction was still there, but there was something else. The way he looked at her showed something she couldn't quite put her finger on. It was almost as though he was as nervous about seeing her as she was about seeing him.

She looked everything over and made sure all the fields were filled in. Between her and Elizabeth, the books had been painstakingly maintained. They were a good team. Too bad she'd lost faith in her business.

All the numbers balanced, and everything looked great. She closed the software program and walked around the shop once more to make sure it was sparkling. Even if she didn't sell it to Jeremy, she had pride in her work.

The phone rang. It was Elizabeth calling to let her know she'd been asking around about Jeremy and had learned that not only was he a successful businessman as they already knew, but he bought and sold businesses to turn a quick profit. "He's a business flipper."

"Thanks, Elizabeth," Cindi said, "but I already knew that." Jeremy had become somewhat of a celebrity among a bunch of the guys they graduated with because he'd made something of himself—at least in their eyes.

"Don't let him do that to something you've worked so hard for. I'd hate to watch all your blood, sweat, and tears go down the drain just because he sees a golden opportunity."

Cindi assured her she'd think before acting on this deal. After she got off the phone, she leaned against the counter and closed her eyes.

Her mind flashed back to the pain of Jeremy's breakup. It had taken years to get past the pain—until now.

The flash of sunlight on the door as it opened caught her attention. She spun around and saw Jeremy. Alone.

Fran was nowhere in sight.

Chapter 2

"Fran's meeting me here," Jeremy said before Cindi had a chance to ask. "I was hoping you and I could talk first."

"There's really not much to talk about."

He stepped closer—so close, in fact, Cindi was certain he could hear her heartbeat. He stopped about three feet away. She slowly let out the breath she was holding.

"I'm impressed with what you've done," he said softly.

Her mind raced with all sorts of comebacks, but she didn't want to risk letting him know how hurt she'd been, so she didn't let any of them out. "I've worked hard for all of it."

"I can see that. Looks to me like you haven't missed a single detail. What I don't understand is why you'd get this far and want to sell."

She shrugged and turned away. "I don't know. Maybe I'm ready to move on."

"That's not like you, Cindi."

Suddenly she felt a burst of adrenaline mixed with anger. "No, it isn't, is it?" She spun around to face him. "I'm the steady type. The kind of girl who stays with things unless there's a very good reason to quit."

He tightened his jaw and looked down. She instantly regretted showing her frustration, but it was too late now.

"I'm probably going to make an offer," he said.

"Fine. " Cindi saw Fran approaching the shop, so she turned to face the door.

"Oh, good," Fran said as she made her entrance. "You're here. I was afraid you'd sleep in after last night." She offered Jeremy a conspiratorial wink.

Last night? And what was with that wink? Maybe he'd had a date he'd told Fran about. An annoying, unexpected pang of jealousy shot through Cindi. She looked away to prevent either of them from noticing.

"Thanks for recommending Atlanta Fish Market," he said.

A date to one of the best restaurants in the entire Atlanta area. Whoever she is must be special. Cindi bit her bottom lip.

"I was afraid my mom would balk," he continued. "She's always hated spending too much money."

"Yes, I know," Fran said with a smile. "She and I have gone bargain hunting together many times. Did your dad like the seafood?"

Peachtree Dreams

A double date with his parents. Sounds serious. Maybe he is buying this bridal shop for the woman in his life.

"He loved it. In fact, he said if he'd known how good it was, he would have taken Mom there before. I was surprised I was able to get reservations on such short notice."

Fran nodded. "It's not too hard to squeeze in a table for three at the last minute."

Table for three? So he went there with his parents and no date? To her dismay, a flood of relief nearly overcame her.

Jeremy turned to Cindi. "I've been staying with my parents while I look for real estate, and I wanted to do something nice for them."

"Dinner at the Atlanta Fish Market is *very* nice," she agreed.

"Maybe I can take you there next time?" he asked.

"Um. . .I don't think so."

A stricken look crossed his face. "Oh, I'm sorry. I didn't even ask if there was someone. . . . I should have known."

Cindi started to say there was no one in her life, but she refrained. She hadn't dated anyone more than a couple of times since high school, but he didn't have to know he'd left her so raw that she didn't trust herself in a relationship.

"Speaking of parents," he said with a smile, "how are yours? I'll never forget those Friday nights with your family playing Monopoly and watching Nickelodeon."

"Um, my parents. . ." She didn't feel like discussing their split, so she figured she might as well just be general. "They're fine."

"Still doing the Friday night thing?"

Cindi slowly shook her head. "Not since Chad and I moved out."

He smiled and nodded. "Makes sense. I guess they must be doing their own thing these days. Well, good for them." He turned to Fran. "I was just about to ask Cindi if I can take a look at her records. Ready to get started?"

Cindi turned toward the tiny office in the back, then heard someone come in. She turned around in time to see a harried woman nearly dragging a younger woman who looked as though she'd rather be anywhere but there.

"I need a gown in a size six," the woman demanded. "Whaddya got in stock?"

"What time is your appointment?" Cindi asked.

The woman waved her hand as if she couldn't be bothered. "I don't have an appointment. No time for that. I caught my daughter in the nick of time—she was about to elope, but I caught her—and we need a gown real quick."

"We normally. . ." Cindi sucked in a breath while she decided what to do. This wasn't the first time someone needed a wedding gown on the spur of the moment, but she never had a potential buyer of the shop standing there waiting for her to finish her business before.

Jeremy nodded toward the customers, a smirk of amusement on his face. "Go ahead and take care of business. I'll wait."

Cindi licked her lips, smoothed her hands over her slacks, and tried to regain her composure. "We keep a few samples in stock. Do you have a particular style in mind?"

"Something decent," the middle-aged woman said as her daughter sulked by the door. "I don't want anything showing, if you know what I mean."

Cindi leaned over to get a handle on what the bride wanted. "Do you prefer a full gown or something more fitted?"

The younger woman just shrugged and turned completely around. Her mother, on the other hand, knew exactly what she wanted. "Long sleeves, full gown, lots of lace, long train, the whole nine yards."

"Mama," the girl said. "Please stop. Eric and I just want a quiet little wedding in a park."

"That's nonsense, Melissa. You're the only daughter I've got, and I'm not about to let you go off and get married by some justice of the peace in a filthy park somewhere."

Cindi's heart went out to the young woman, but she couldn't get involved. She stood there and waited before doing anything.

The older woman spun back around. "You heard me. I need to get the dress today."

"Our alterations person isn't in yet, but she can get right on it once she's here," Cindi explained.

"No time for that. We have to find something that fits off the rack."

To Cindi's surprise, Melissa finally gave in and tried on everything her mother picked out. However, she clearly felt miserable in all the dresses.

Exasperated, the mother left the fitting room saying they weren't leaving until they found the perfect dress. Once she was gone, Cindi turned to the bride.

"Did you have something in mind?" she asked.

Melissa sighed. "I really didn't want a traditional wedding dress. They're too fussy for me."

"Maybe I can help you out. We carry a collection that has simple lines." She paused and gave Melissa a chance to think.

"Since it doesn't look like I have any choice in this, I guess it wouldn't hurt to try one on."

Her mother breezed back into the fitting room with the most ornate dress in the shop slung over her arm. She shoved it at Melissa. "Here, try this."

Cindi offered the bride a sympathetic smile. "Why don't you work on getting into that while I go find a dress in our most exquisite line that's the latest rage with celebrity brides this year."

"Latest rage? Celebrity brides?" Melissa's mother asked. "What's that?"

"I'll bring one in for you to look at," Cindi replied. "In the meantime, since you went to the trouble of getting that one, why don't you help her into it?"

She gently closed the door behind her. "I'm really sorry, Fran, but Elizabeth isn't here yet and. . ."

"Don't worry about it. Jeremy said he doesn't mind waiting."

Cindi glanced around. "Where is he?"

"I sent him on an errand so you wouldn't feel so rushed. I'm enjoying just looking around at all the gorgeous gowns. Take your time."

Cindi relaxed a little since Jeremy wasn't in the showroom pacing. She went to the area where she kept samples that were for sale and pulled out one of the dresses with the cleanest lines. It was a brushed satin with a sweetheart neckline and three-quarter sleeves. It had a short train and a small amount of lace overlay on the bodice—just enough to make the mother happy.

When she opened the door to the fitting room, she saw the anguished look on Melissa's face. She had to admit the dress totally overwhelmed the petite young woman.

"Now that's what I call a wedding dress," her mother said. "Isn't she the most gorgeous bride you've ever seen?"

"She is very pretty, but I'm not sure. . ." Cindi's voice trailed off as both Melissa and her mother watched her expectantly. She changed her mind mid-sentence, but she couldn't think of anything else to say.

"What's that?" her mother finally said after a few seconds of silence, pointing to the dress in Cindi's arms.

"Oh, it's one of the hottest dresses on the market. Celebrity brides are going crazy over this one."

Melissa's mother clasped her hands together as Cindi made a production of hanging it on the hook. She'd been in this business long enough to know a large part of selling a style was the unveiling.

Once she had it on the hook and arranged, she sucked in a breath, said a very short prayer, then turned around to see the reaction. At first there was none. Then a wide grin spread across the mother-of-the-bride's face.

"Yes, I've seen that one in the supermarket magazines. It's perfect."

Melissa's lips turned up into a grin. Cindi could tell she liked this one.

A few minutes later Melissa stood in front of the three-way mirror while her mother and Cindi admired her. "I like it," she finally said.

"We'll take it." Her mother turned her around and started unzipping the back.

"It won't take long to alter it so she can have a perfect fit," Cindi said. "When do you need it?"

"There's no time. The wedding's this afternoon in the small chapel behind the big church."

"This afternoon?" Cindi said, her voice cracking. She wasn't kidding, there wasn't any time.

"Yes, and it's a good thing I caught her heading out the door with her suitcase, or I never would've been able to witness my only daughter tying the knot. To think she didn't want me there or even bother to tell me. . ." Tears sprang to her eyes.

"Mama," Melissa said, "it's not that I didn't want you there. I just didn't want a big wedding with a lacy dress and a wedding cake taller than me."

"Well, consider yourself a fortunate girl that Kroger had a cancellation on a wedding cake and they were able to make the changes I wanted."

Cindi managed to get the dress ready and the two women out the door a half hour later. After they were gone, Fran turned to her and laughed.

"They're quite a pair, aren't they?"

"That's an understatement."

Fran shrugged. "There's something about a Southern mother-of-the-bride. It's not so much the bride's wedding as it is hers."

She'd pretty much summed it up. Jeremy had come back into the shop and was standing at the door until Melissa and her mother left. He joined Cindi and Fran.

"Very interesting," he said. "Does this sort of thing happen very often?"

"I can't say it's the first time," Cindi replied, "but it's not a regular occurrence."

He leaned back and laughed. "That's a relief."

Cindi lifted one eyebrow. "Situations like that have to be handled very carefully."

"Obviously," he said. "I guess that's something you can train whomever I get to manage the store to do."

"I guess." She pulled up the spreadsheet with all her sales figures and inventory numbers, then printed them. "Here ya go. It's all there."

❦

Jeremy's hand brushed hers as she handed him the papers. He wanted more than that. He wanted to hold her hand, to pull her close, to take a deeper whiff of her floral scent. He wanted to brush her hair from her face and study the features he'd only seen in his mind for the past several years.

When he'd first decided to check out her business, he'd half hoped some of the chemistry between them would have faded, but it was there—stronger than ever. He wondered if she felt it, too. It didn't appear so, based on the way she turned her back on him every chance she could get—including now.

"Sure you don't mind if I take these?" he asked, hoping she'd turn around and look at him again.

She tossed her hair over her shoulder but didn't face him head-on. "I have nothing to hide. If you like what you see, we can talk about it. If not, then that's fine, too."

For someone who had her business up for sale, she sure didn't seem to want it sold that badly. Or perhaps it was a ploy to make him want it more. Whatever the case, she wasn't desperate. And he liked that.

"Anything else you need?" Fran asked. "I have another appointment at noon, so if you don't mind, I'll just scoot on out of here."

"No, I'm fine," he said as he thumped the papers. "Looks like I have what I need."

Elizabeth came in and got right to work. Jeremy was impressed with how Cindi and Elizabeth worked so well together. They both had the quiet confidence of people who enjoyed what they did and knew what they were doing. It made him wonder what else was going on to make Cindi put the shop on the market.

Since he had the rest of the day to himself, he decided to drive around and check out the changes to the place he'd called home all his life until he'd joined the army almost ten years ago. He drove through Sandy Springs, crossed the Chattahoochee River, and headed out on Johnson Ferry Road. New developments had sprung up, and the place was obviously thriving. It was a little too busy for his taste, but it still felt like home.

He drove all around Marietta and found his old house. It was much smaller and closer to the main road than he remembered. Many of the shops in downtown Marietta had changed, but it still had the flavor of old mixed with new.

By the time he headed back to his parents' condo, he was emotionally exhausted. Seeing things that brought back so many memories had worn him out. He looked forward to looking over Cindi's business figures and assessing the exact amount of success she'd had. She was obviously doing well, and now he'd know just how well.

"Have a good day, son?" his father asked during dinner.

"Pretty good. I think I've found a business to purchase."

"Oh yeah?" His dad put down his fork and leaned forward with interest. "What kind of business?"

There was no way to hedge, so he just came out with it. "A bridal shop."

His parents exchanged a look; then his father turned back to him. "Isn't that sort of a girlie business?"

Coming to his rescue, his mother said, "Not necessarily. Men get married, too."

"But a bridal shop sells wedding dresses for girls, right?"

"Well, yes," Jeremy replied, "but that really doesn't matter. I'm just in it for the business." He quickly looked down at his plate, trying to figure out a way to change the subject. He didn't want his parents to keep digging for information.

They'd always liked Cindi, and they didn't understand the breakup.

"I don't get it. Isn't there a more manly business you can buy—like a hardware store or something?"

&⁊

"I don't want someone to buy this place just to be an absentee owner," Cindi said. "I think I'll talk to Fran and tell her I can't sell to Jeremy since he doesn't even live here."

"I heard them talking, and he wasn't just looking to buy a business," Elizabeth said. "She's also trying to help him find a house."

"I don't care. I just can't see him running this place."

Elizabeth looked down then back up at her. "I understand what you're saying, but what I don't understand is why you care. I thought you were sick of the illusion of a happily-ever-after."

"I am."

"Then what's your problem? Why do you care who runs this shop if there's no happily-ever-after?"

Cindi sighed. "I don't know. It's just that I spend so much time coddling my customers and trying to make their wedding day special. Even if it doesn't last, don't you think brides at least deserve something special?"

Elizabeth clicked her tongue and shook her head. "I think you're confused."

"Maybe I am. My parents seemed perfectly happy all my life. I don't understand what happened. If they can't stick together, then who can?"

"It has nothing to do with your shop, Cindi. Maybe they were miserable all this time, but they stuck it out for you and your brother."

"Maybe so. I asked Mom how she could reconcile it with God. She hasn't even been to church since Dad left, ya know."

"That's very sad. How about your dad? I haven't heard you talk about him since he left."

Cindi lifted her head and snickered. "That's because I've only heard from him once since he left. He called me that one time, said he'd be in touch, then *poof*! He vanished."

"It's been what—two months? Give him time."

"I'm his daughter. You'd think he'd at least answer his cell phone when I called."

"What happened is awful, but I think you're taking it wrong. Maybe there's something you don't know about."

"Let's change the subject, okay?" Cindi said. "This is too upsetting."

"Whatever you want. Just remember I'm here, and I'm praying for you."

"Thanks," Cindi said with a forced smile. "We have an appointment in a half hour. Better put on our game faces."

The appointment was one of the few where the bride and her mother actually agreed. "We want to keep it simple," the daughter said. "I want something nice and understated."

Her mother nodded. "And there's a budget we have to watch very closely."

"No problem." Cindi was more than happy to accommodate people who were realistic and didn't have their heads in the clouds. She appreciated how up front these people were, so she worked hard to help them get the best they could afford.

"I have a sample dress that's on sale," Cindi said. "Elizabeth can alter it so it'll look custom-made."

"That would be wonderful," the mother-of-the-bride said with a smile.

The bride walked around the showroom and looked at not only bridal gowns but mother-of-the-bride dresses. "Do you have something on sale for my mother?"

Cindi studied the girl's mother then nodded. "I have several dresses I think she'd like. Do you prefer long or short?"

The bride liked the second dress she tried on, and her mother was excited she could afford to choose among three dresses. They left with smiles on their faces and a spring in their step.

After all the rejected dresses were put away, Elizabeth sighed. "Now that's how it's supposed to be."

"I agree. If the groom is as agreeable and nice as the bride's mother says he is, I have a feeling this will be a rare, wonderful union."

Cindi felt Elizabeth's scrutiny. Finally, Elizabeth cleared her throat. "Just think. If we weren't here and someone else was, they might not have been as happy. Someone else might have taken advantage of them and tried to sell them something they didn't want."

"Yes, I realize that."

"I wish you'd change your mind about selling, Cindi. You're the ideal person for this work. Ever since I can remember, you've wanted to work with brides."

Cindi shrugged. "That's all changed."

"So you're saying you didn't enjoy helping those people a few minutes ago?" Elizabeth tilted her head and studied her boss and friend.

"I didn't say that."

"Like I said, I think you're just very confused." As soon as she spoke her mind, Elizabeth took the pinned dresses to the back room to start on alterations.

A few minutes before closing time, the phone rang. It was Fran.

"I just heard from Jeremy," she said, her voice shrill with excitement. "He's ready to make an offer. When is a good time for me to present it? How about tomorrow?"

Cindi felt her heart drop. She dreaded this part but knew she had to face it. "Tomorrow's fine. I get here at nine, and we open at ten."

"How about if I get there right after you? It won't take long."

"Okay, I'll see you then." Cindi dropped the phone back in the cradle and stared at the wall.

"What happened?" Elizabeth asked as she came around the corner.

"Fran's coming by first thing in the morning with an offer from Jeremy."

Elizabeth stood in silence for several seconds before speaking. "Do you plan to tell her then that you're not selling to Jeremy?"

Cindi backed away from her spot. "I'm not sure yet." She reached for her handbag and moved toward the door. "I need to leave now. Do you mind locking up?"

"Of course not. Do you want me here when Fran presents the offer?"

"No, but thanks. See you at ten tomorrow."

Streetlights twinkled in the dark as Cindi drove home. The shop stayed open late several nights each week to take care of working clients. She was tired, but she knew she wouldn't be able to rest much, knowing she was an inch away from selling the shop she'd dreamed about most of her life.

Between prayers for guidance, Cindi allowed herself to flash back to the times when she and Jeremy were together. It was high school, and they were kids. He'd moved from an apartment on the other side of Atlanta. He was so sweet and loving, she actually thought they might have a more lasting relationship than most high school romances. She'd heard rumors that he wasn't so wonderful from people who had friends from his old school. Apparently he'd started breaking girls' hearts back in middle school. He had a reputation for buying cheap trinkets and selling them for a hefty profit. Since she'd never seen that side of him, she assumed they were mistaken—and perhaps a little jealous.

He never had an interest in going to college, but that didn't matter to her. She was able to go because of her scholarship, but she'd entertained the thought that after college she'd come home to Jeremy and they'd be just as happy as they were in high school.

Now she had an offer on the shop—from the only guy she'd ever loved. She couldn't miss the irony of it all.

The next morning she got to the shop fifteen minutes before Fran showed up. "Hey there!" Fran said in a voice that was a tad too cheerful.

"Let's sit at the table," Cindi said, pointing to the consulting table.

Fran laid out some paperwork and turned a copy of the contract around to face Cindi. She went over each point and presented the offer. "Would you like to think about it?" she asked. "You have a couple of days."

Slowly, Cindi stood and shook her head. "No, I'm afraid I can't accept this offer."

Fran's smile quickly faded. "Why not?"

"I want my full asking price."

"Your asking price is a little steep, you have to admit," Fran said. "I assumed it was just a starting point so you'd have some room for negotiation."

Cindi cleared her throat and looked Fran in the eye. "It's not just the price. Jeremy and I have a past, and I really don't want to sell my shop to him."

Fran reached out and patted Cindi's hand. "I figured there was more to it than I realized. I can tell Jeremy is quite fond of you."

Cindi shrugged. "He's the one who dumped me."

"Perhaps there is more to it than meets the eye."

"I still don't want to sell to someone who doesn't understand a bride's needs during such an emotional time."

Fran offered a warm smile. "Jeremy has been very successful in business, so I think he'll figure it out."

"He was always an entrepreneur," Cindi said. "When I met him, he bought and sold concert T-shirts at school. He told me he started out in elementary school buying packs of gum and selling it on the playground, one stick at a time." She paused before adding, "And I heard he sold other stuff, too."

Fran let out a soft chuckle. "I'm not surprised. Jeremy is an intelligent man with a nose for what'll succeed."

"I'm not taking this offer," Cindi said firmly as she stood to end the conversation. "Sorry to waste your time."

"Oh, that's okay," Fran said as she gathered the papers. "It's all part of my job. This sort of thing happens all the time." She jabbered so quickly, Cindi could tell she was nervous. "I'll let Jeremy know, and I'm sure he'll come back with a counter to your counter." She paused. "You might want to let some of the past go, Cindi. . . . That is, if you really want to sell your shop."

Later that day, Fran called and said Jeremy had a counteroffer.

"What is it?" Cindi asked.

"Normally I don't do this over the phone, but I think you'll be pleased. He's offering your full price."

"Is he willing to run the shop?" Cindi asked.

"I talked to him about that and let him know how important that is to you. He said he'll run it, but not from there. He's talking about hiring someone to manage it on-site."

"I'm sorry, but I want the owner to actively manage my shop."

Fran started coughing but recovered quickly. "Don't you feel that's a little unreasonable?"

"No, not in this business. I've spent the last several years of my life making sure all the brides have gotten royal treatment. Their marriages might not last, but their weddings are important to them."

"You drive a hard bargain, Cindi."

"Maybe so, but I'm sticking to it."

Fran sighed. "Okay, I'll let him know."

Elizabeth was standing a few feet away and could obviously hear Cindi's part of the conversation, but she didn't say a word. Cindi was grateful her friend understood her enough to know when something wasn't open for discussion.

The next morning, about five minutes after she got to the shop, she watched Jeremy walk up to the door, try to open it, and knock when he realized it was locked. She let him in. He didn't offer a greeting or make small talk. Instead, he got right to the point.

"Cindi, I'd like to talk to you about your terms."

Chapter 3

W hy are you turning down my perfectly good offers?" he persisted.

Cindi hadn't expected him to be so abrupt, so she took a step back. "I. . .uh. . ."

"You don't want to sell to me, do you?"

"It's not that," she said. "It's just that. . .well, I wanted someone to come in and be more hands-on."

"What makes you think I won't do that?" He widened his stance and folded his arms.

"Are you saying you've changed your mind?" she challenged.

He dropped the front. "Okay, so I'll be the first to admit I don't know a thing about running a bridal shop. That's why I'll hire someone to run it for me until I figure it out."

"That's not good enough. It needs to be run by someone who truly cares about making these women's most important day the best it can be."

She squirmed as he narrowed his gaze and studied her for several very long seconds. "Seriously, Cindi, why would it even matter? You clearly don't want to do this anymore, and I'm a willing buyer. Why don't you just sign on the line, and this shop will be my problem to deal with?"

"This shop is not a problem," she said more indignantly than she'd intended.

He shook his head. "This makes no sense to me."

"And that's precisely why I shouldn't sell it to you."

He lifted his hands in frustration and backed toward the door. "Whatever. I sure hope you get whatever it is you're looking for out of this deal. I thought it would be a win-win situation for both of us—a lucrative business for me and a way out for you to do whatever it is you wanted to do with your life."

His words stung much worse than she wanted him to know. She had to remain strong, though, as long as he stood in front of her.

"I'm sure you'll find other successful businesses that can make you the profit without having to be there," she said. "It's just not gonna be this one."

Jeremy was at the door already. He turned back to her before he left. "I'd like to discuss this further, but now isn't the right time for either of us. Just do me a favor and let me know before you sell to anyone else, okay?"

"Bye, Jeremy," Cindi said as she turned her back to him. She stood and waited until she was fairly certain he was gone. When the sounds of Atlanta traffic were muted by the closed door, she paused for a moment before turning around to face her shop.

ᏄᎬ

Jeremy had no idea what had just happened. He'd been blindsided by her abrupt negativism toward him. Surely she'd gotten over their breakup from high school.

But had *he*?

His feelings toward her were as complicated as the business deal he couldn't seem to snag. He'd been turned down by many sellers, and it had never bothered him before. He just moved on and found something else.

Why was buying Cindi's Bridal Boutique so important to him?

Jeremy knew the answer without having to do much thinking. He wanted something of Cindi's simply to have a part of her. Giving her up so she could pursue her academic dreams had been difficult enough. The only reason he let her go was to give her the freedom she needed, but he couldn't tell her that.

He met Fran at the real estate office. She drove him around to different houses and condos, but none of them seemed right. Finally, she pulled over and turned to face him.

"What, exactly, do you want, Jeremy?".

Alarms went off in his head as he remembered wondering the exact same thing of Cindi. He sucked in a deep breath and blew it out in a long sigh.

Fran continued, "I have a feeling you know what you want, but you're trying to deny yourself. If you'll just say it out loud, maybe I can help you find it. I can see that you and Cindi have some unresolved issues. Care to talk about it?"

He snickered and shook his head. "Afraid it's not that easy. Tell you what. I'm really not in the mood to be looking at real estate today. Take me back to my car, and I'll call you when I won't be wasting your time."

"You're not wasting my time. This is my job. But I do want to help you find a nice place to live and a fabulous business that you can enjoy. Why don't we look at some other businesses? There are plenty in the book."

"Sounds good," he replied, "just not today."

He stopped off at the florist and picked up some flowers for his mother. Then he headed to a bookstore, where he found a simple question-and-answer book on the Bible so he could gently witness to his father. They'd been exceptionally good to him, and all he'd given them in return was one night out at a nice restaurant. It was the least he could do for the people who had loved him unconditionally all his life. Besides, he needed something to get his mind off Cindi Clark.

The instant he walked into the house, his dad greeted him. "How'd it go today, son?"

Jeremy took off his suit coat and draped it over the back of a living room

259

chair. "Not so good. I haven't found the right business yet."

"Maybe you and your mother should think about opening a restaurant," his dad suggested. "With your business sense and her cooking talent, it would be a huge success."

Jeremy already had restaurants he was trying to sell. They were profitable, but they required too many hours. He wanted to pull everything in and settle down, but he didn't need to tell his parents that—not now, anyway. They'd worry something else might be wrong.

"Jeremy, would you mind giving me a hand in the kitchen?" his mother asked.

He was relieved to end the conversation with his father. He didn't want to have to explain anything about Cindi's bridal shop.

"How did your day go?" his mother asked once they sat down to eat.

Jeremy started to answer, but his dad stepped in. "He hasn't found his golden egg yet."

"Give him time." His mother grinned at him. "Our boy took his army talent and turned it into a gold mine."

"I was just a clerk in the army, Mom. All that did was give me time to think and help me grow up a little."

"It obviously did something good for you, son." His dad folded his napkin and placed it on the table. "You certainly didn't learn anything about business from us."

His mother immediately started clearing the table. "Why don't you two go watch the news while I clean up?"

Jeremy jumped up and took the plate from her. "I'll take care of that. Sit down."

She firmly held her ground. "We can clean the kitchen together." She slanted her gaze toward Jeremy's dad, who made a face but began to pitch in.

It took the three of them five minutes to carry everything into the kitchen and load the dishwasher. Afterward Jeremy said he was tired and needed to go to his room.

"Thanks for the flowers, sweetie," his mom said as she stood on her tiptoes and kissed him on the cheek. "You've always been good to me."

His dad followed him to his room. "Anything you want to talk about?"

Jeremy pondered the question for a few seconds then nodded. "Sure, Dad, come on in."

Once inside his room, he motioned for his dad to have a seat at his old desk while he sat on the edge of the bed. He pulled the package from the bookstore out of his bag and opened it. "You know, Dad, there's something I've always wondered about."

"What's that?" his dad asked as he glanced at the book Jeremy held.

"Why didn't you and Mom take us to church?"

His father hung his head and stared at the floor before looking back up at him. "We worked so hard just to put food on the table and keep you and your brother in clothes. Sundays were our only days off, and we needed the rest."

"I understand." And he did. "You know I've been going to church for several years now."

With a chuckle, his dad nodded. "That's another thing that puzzles me. You're a successful businessman who's gone and gotten religious."

Jeremy opened his mouth to explain the difference between his faith in God through Jesus and his father's perception of it being religious, but he needed to take this discussion slowly. He closed the book and handed it to his dad. "I picked this up for you at a Christian bookstore. It might explain some things better than I can."

A knock on the door brought Jeremy to his feet. "Mind if I come in?" his mother asked.

"Sure, come on in. I was just about to tell Dad about today."

Jeremy started explaining that he thought the bridal business seemed extremely lucrative. "But the owner is digging her heels in because she doesn't think I can run it successfully."

His mom tilted her head to one side. "What's the name of the bridal shop?"

"Cindi's Bridal Boutique."

"Oh, now I understand." His mother nodded and smiled. "Cindi Clark owns that place."

After Jeremy explained more, his father gave him a perplexed look. "I still don't understand, son. What would you do with a bridal boutique?"

"It's a business, Dad."

"I'm sure it is to you," his mother interjected. "But it's really much more than that. I see Cindi's point. You don't know the first thing about what a bride wants or needs on her special day."

Jeremy groaned. "What's up with you women?"

His mother pointed her finger and shook it at him. "That kind of attitude is the very reason she's not selling it to you."

With a surrendering sigh, Jeremy slumped. "I'm sorry, Mom. I guess I just don't understand what the problem is. She wants to sell her shop, and I want to buy it. I've never seen this kind of resistance without a reason in business before. I've even offered her asking price, which is much higher than what it's worth."

"Have you stopped to think maybe it's not just a business to her? I remember Cindi. She's a very sweet girl. Maybe a little too romantic for her own good, but that's probably why she's so successful as a bridal shop owner. Did she say why she wants to sell?"

"She said she's ready to move on."

"That's not a good reason." His mother folded her hands and looked pensively at them. "There has to be something else. Want me to find out?"

"No!" Jeremy and his father both said at the same time.

"Why not? It would be simple. I could just go into her shop and strike up a conversation with her."

"Mom, please don't. I wish I hadn't told you anything about it."

She stood up, a pained expression on her face. "Don't worry, I won't go near her if you don't want me to. But if you're serious about her. . .I mean about buying her shop, you should come right out and ask her why she's selling. And don't take her first answer, either."

"You don't understand," he said.

"I'm your mother. I understand much more than you think I do. Don't think I wasn't aware of how hard it was to let her go."

"Mom—"

She held up both hands to shush him. "I'm just saying that maybe the two of you need to sit down and have a heart-to-heart talk. Clear the air. Maybe then you'll find out what's going on with her."

Jeremy thought about what his mother had said, and she was right. This was the first time he'd ever had a hard time being rejected. It was obvious it wasn't because he wanted to be in the bridal business so badly—even to him.

He wanted to be near Cindi.

❧

The next morning Elizabeth was at the shop waiting for Cindi. "What're you doing here so early?" Cindi asked.

"I thought I'd unpack some of the accessory samples that came in yesterday."

"I have to finish entering the deposits, so I'll be at the computer until our first appointment."

"Cindi," Elizabeth said, then paused.

"Did you need something?"

"If you feel like talking, I'm all ears."

Cindi chuckled. "Thanks, but I really don't feel like talking. Sorry if I'm acting like a grouch."

"You're not a grouch, but I can tell you're bothered."

"It's just the shop. I wish someone would make a decent offer. Someone who cares as much as I do."

"I'm afraid that won't happen," Elizabeth said. "This shop is your baby. The only reason it's so successful is because of the time and energy you've put into it."

"With your help, of course," Cindi added.

"Yeah, well. . ."

Suddenly an idea dawned on Cindi. "Hey, it's really not a bad idea if you want to buy the shop. I can work out terms. I know you want to have children someday, but if you're in charge, you can bring the kids here."

"No thanks. I like working here, but I don't want what goes with owning a business. And Mike wouldn't want me to be away from home all those hours. You have to admit it can be pretty consuming."

"Good point."

"Besides," Elizabeth added, "without you here, it won't be as much fun."

Cindi glanced at the wall clock. "We have an appointment at eleven, so I need to get this work done."

"Who's the appointment?"

"Gail from church." Cindi pushed the power button on the monitor. "She wants to try on some bridal gowns and get color swatches for bridesmaid dresses."

"I'll get them ready," Elizabeth said as she disappeared around the corner.

At 10:55 the front door opened. Cindi grinned as she looked up, fully expecting to see Gail breezing in. But it wasn't Gail. It was Jeremy.

He marched right up to where she stood, stopped, and looked at her. She frowned. "Did you forget something?"

"We need to talk, Cindi."

"Not now. I have an appointment in just a few minutes."

He didn't move an inch. "When will you be available?"

Cindi pushed away from the computer and came around from behind the desk. Jeremy followed her to the storage room, where she turned to face him. "Please, Jeremy, don't keep doing this. I don't want to sell my shop to you or any other absentee owner."

"What if I agree to work here—full-time?" he asked. "Will you sell it to me then?"

She laughed. "As if I actually believe you'd do something like that."

"Are you assuming things?"

"No." She knew she was scowling as she folded her arms, but she couldn't help it.

"Cindi!" Elizabeth called. "Gail's here."

"I'll be right there!" Cindi called back.

"Why don't I observe while you work with your customers?" he offered.

"Right."

"Seriously, Cindi. I'm very interested in what goes on here."

She turned at an angle as she thought about it. Five minutes with a future bride, and he'd run out of there screaming for mercy. "Fine. You're welcome to observe for a couple of days. But that still doesn't guarantee I'll sell the shop to you."

"Understood."

"When do you want to observe?"

He shrugged, palms up. "How about today?"

Cindi thought for a moment then nodded. "Remember Gail Rhodes, the music teacher?"

"Of course!" he replied. "I always liked Ms. Rhodes."

"She's out there waiting."

"Cool." Jeremy didn't wait for Cindi. He just turned around and headed out to the showroom.

The instant Gail spotted him, her face lit up with a huge smile. "Jeremy! What are you doing here?" Her smile was replaced by a puzzled expression as she looked at Cindi. "Are you two. . .well. . ."

"No, I'm just here to observe the business," Jeremy replied.

"I heard you were a business tycoon."

He chuckled. "I don't know about tycoon. I prefer to be called an entrepreneur."

"At any rate, welcome home." She turned back to Cindi. "Ready to make me a gorgeous, blushing bride?"

"The gorgeous part is easy because you already are, but I don't know about blushing," Cindi said.

"Yeah, it takes quite a bit to make me blush," Gail admitted. "I think I've seen everything."

"So who's the fortunate fella?" Jeremy asked.

"You probably don't know him. Isaac McClaury."

"Oh, I remember Coach McClaury. He was the coach of our biggest rival and the reason we lost our last game of the season. His team went on to win the league championship."

"Yep, that's him," Gail said. "He's still coaching."

"Well, congratulations," Jeremy said. "So when's the big day?"

Cindi cleared her throat. "I hate to interrupt, but we have a fitting to do, remember?"

Jeremy took a step back. "Sorry, I got carried away. I'll see you at church tomorrow."

"When did you start going to church?" The instant the words came out, Cindi regretted the way she said it. "Sorry, I didn't mean that the way it sounded."

"I understand," Jeremy said. "Look, why don't you do the fitting, and we can talk about it later?"

Gail walked around the showroom picking out dresses, and Cindi made a few suggestions. Jeremy started to help, but he quickly backed away when Cindi glared at him. Elizabeth went into the fitting room to help Gail into the dresses while Cindi gathered some accessories to complement them.

"There's quite a bit more to this than I realized," Jeremy said as Cindi brushed past him.

"Well, yeah."

"You're extremely good at what you do, and you seem to enjoy it."

Cindi didn't respond; instead, she focused on gathering things for Gail. He was right. She loved what she did. But she couldn't help but remember the statistics on marriage. More than half of them would end in divorce, whether they bought dresses from her shop or not.

She got to the door of the fitting room, her arms full of tiaras, veils, undergarments, and a pair of shoes. Before opening the door, she turned to Jeremy. "Look, why don't we talk later?"

"When?"

"How about after work?"

He nodded and waved as he walked toward the door. "See you then."

As soon as he was gone, she knocked gently on the fitting room door. When Elizabeth opened it, she saw Gail standing on the platform, looking like a princess.

"You're absolutely gorgeous!" she said. "Here, try this tiara and veil. Are you wearing shoes?"

Gail lifted the front of the dress and stuck out her old brown clog. The three of them laughed.

"Now that's a wedding shoe original," Elizabeth said.

"I brought some great shoes for that dress." Cindi pulled the white satin pumps from the stack she'd placed on the floor. "All you have to do is step into them."

Once Gail had everything in place, she turned and got views from all sides. "Does anyone ever get the first dress they try?" she asked. "Because I absolutely love this one."

"Lots of girls do, but not until they try on other stuff," Cindi said. "I want to see you in more than one style."

Gail laughed. "You just want to confuse me. You know how I hate shopping."

"I know, but this is different. It's your wedding." She nearly choked on the words, and she didn't miss the knowing glance exchanged between Elizabeth and Gail.

"Okay, you're the expert." Gail sighed as she slipped out of the shoes and turned so Elizabeth could unzip the dress. "How about that one?" She pointed to a beaded, fitted gown they'd just received from a new designer. "I can't imagine liking anything more than this one, but I'll try on a few more."

Six dresses later, Gail pointed to the first dress. "I still like that one best. I'll bring the bridesmaids in for their fittings as soon as I decide on the color."

"Take your time," Cindi said. "It only takes a week to order the dresses, then another two weeks for alterations."

Gail took turns hugging Cindi and Elizabeth after she changed back into her regular clothes. "Thanks, both of y'all, for taking all this time with me. I'm much more relaxed now that I've found the perfect dress."

After she left, Elizabeth nodded. "We make a good team, don't we?"

A lump formed in Cindi's throat as she nodded. "The best."

The remainder of the day was busy with first appointments, final fittings, and paperwork. About five minutes before closing, Jeremy showed up. "Ready to talk?"

She nodded. "I'll be right with you. Let me close out of the computer."

"I'll stick around and lock up," Elizabeth said.

"Where do you want to go?" Jeremy asked.

"Let's just go for a walk."

"Sounds good."

Cindi was grateful Jeremy didn't jump right into negotiations for the shop. She needed to unwind before explaining anything.

"You look nice," Jeremy said as he looked her up and down. "You were always the prettiest girl I knew."

Cindi rolled her eyes. "That's not going to work, Jeremy. I've known you a long time."

He snickered. "It's true. You really are beautiful, but I understand."

They chatted for a few minutes. Jeremy started squirming, so Cindi assumed he was eager to discuss the business.

"Okay, let's get this over with," she said. "I think you need to let this opportunity go, because I'm not selling to you."

"Whoa. You sure are blunt."

"No, just honest."

"And you think I'm not?"

"I didn't say that." Cindi felt her stomach churning. "Look, Jeremy, I don't know why you came back or why you're so bent on buying my shop, but I don't want a confrontation."

"You still haven't given me a convincing reason you want to sell Cindi's Bridal Boutique."

"I didn't know I needed to convince you of anything."

"Touché."

"Sorry," she said. "I guess I'm a little touchy right now."

"You have every right to be. There's something I should probably tell you— something I was too immature to admit when we were kids."

"What's that?"

Cindi watched Jeremy's expression change as he gathered his thoughts. "Back when we were together, I was happier than I've ever been. I loved you, Cindi, but I wasn't man enough to handle it."

"You don't have to do this." Cindi's voice cracked, so she cleared her throat.

"But I want to." She felt an odd sensation as he reached for her hand. "When you got that scholarship, I didn't want to stand in your way. I let you go so you could follow your dreams."

His admission sent a shock wave through her. She opened her mouth to speak, but nothing came out.

"A lot of time has passed since then. I just figured, well. . .I thought we'd be able to work this out somehow."

By the time they arrived back at the shop, Cindi had recovered enough to respond. "Look, Jeremy, I understand what you're doing, but I really don't think a bridal shop is what you want."

"Are you sure about that, or is it more a case of something you can't face?"

"Is that what you think?"

Jeremy closed his eyes for a couple of seconds before turning back to her with a softness in his expression she'd never seen before. "I'm thinking there are some things you're dealing with that you don't want to face."

"It's not about you, Jeremy." It annoyed her to no end that he'd gotten so close to the truth, but she wasn't ready to tell him about her parents.

Jeremy reached out and took her hand, gently stroking the back of it. She felt the chemistry between them again, but she couldn't deal with it. She stiffened, so he let go.

"If you need to talk, I'm all ears," he said softly as she stepped away.

If he only knew how close he'd come to her raw nerve.

Chapter 4

Jeremy went to his car and stared after her, wondering what to do next. At this very moment he knew exactly what he wanted, and it wasn't her shop. It was Cindi.

Breaking up with her had been one of the most difficult things he'd ever done, but at the time he'd felt it was best for her. He couldn't help but wonder how different things would have been if he'd let their relationship take its course.

He'd always known she went to church a lot with her family, and he often wondered about it. She'd invited him, and he'd gone a few times. But he felt so out of place among people who understood the Bible that he found excuses to not return.

It wasn't until later, when one of his commanding officers in the army had witnessed to him and accepted the fact that Jeremy knew very little about the Bible, that he'd overcome his self-consciousness. Major Sharpe started by sharing short verses with explanations. When Jeremy had questions, the officer patiently answered all the ones he could and then admitted he didn't have all the answers. The chaplain was open and eager to share the gospel.

Hungry for the Word, Jeremy spent many hours studying his Bible and reading commentaries Major Sharpe and the chaplain recommended. After he got out of the army, he found a church close to where he lived. When he traveled, he chose whatever church was closest to his hotel, which gave him an interesting perspective on different ways to worship. Regardless of whether the services were contemporary or traditional, his favorite part of almost all services was the sermon, during which he never failed to pick up another rich morsel of God's greatness.

Jeremy had called one of his old high school buddies to find out where Cindi went to church these days. It didn't take his friend long to get back with him. She seemed surprised to hear he'd be there, and he couldn't blame her.

He went to his parents' house and put the breakfast dishes into the dishwasher before heading to his room. As much as the Atlanta area had changed, some things remained the same. Looking around at the posters on the walls, he realized his parents had moved everything from his old room to the condo. Knowing how sentimental his mother was, he figured she did it so he'd feel as though he'd never left. He removed his tie, loosened the top button on his shirt, and took off his shoes before lying on top of the comforter. It had been a long day.

When a knock came, he instantly sat up. "Mom?"

She opened the door a couple of inches. "You okay, Jeremy?"

"Sure," he replied as he stood, rolled up his shirtsleeves, and slid his feet into some loafers. "Need help setting the table?"

"No thanks, honey. Dinner is already on the table. You looked so tired, I didn't want to disturb you."

As he sat down with his parents to eat, he bowed his head and thanked the Lord for the meal. When he glanced up, he noticed his father looking at him curiously. Right when he started to witness, his mother asked him to pass the basket of biscuits; then his dad started talking about his day at work. He made a mental note to seize the next opportunity to talk about his faith as soon as he had an opening.

That night after dinner, his mother asked what his plans were for the weekend. "You've been so busy all week, I'd like to see you take it easy," she said.

"I plan to go to church." He paused as he watched for a reaction. "Wanna go with me?"

She crinkled her forehead and let out a nervous laugh. "Me in church? It's been so long, I'm not sure God would know who I am."

Jeremy chewed on his bottom lip as he searched for the right words. His mother studied him expectantly, so he reached out and touched her cheek. "Trust me, God knows who you are. He loves you."

She shook her head and looked away. "I don't know, Jeremy. It's been almost thirty years since I've stepped foot inside a church."

His heart ached at her admission, but he tried not to show how he felt. "Mom, I don't want to force you to do anything you're not comfortable with, but I'd love for you to go with me."

"I'll stick out like a sore thumb."

"No, you won't," he assured her. "I've been going to church ever since my last year in the army, and I've seen new people come in many times. It would make me happy to have you and Dad with me."

"I don't know about your father. You know how stubborn he can be."

Jeremy laughed. "I'm the most stubborn person I know, and I went."

Finally, she offered a slight smile. "Okay, you ask him."

"Then you'll go with me?"

She paused then nodded. "Yes, if your father agrees to go, but I have to go shopping for something nice to wear."

Jeremy's heart sang. He hadn't expected his mother to agree so quickly. Now all he had to do was talk to his father.

After she left, he approached his father, who'd settled into his recliner with the remote control in his hand. "Dad, can we talk for a minute?"

"Sure, son." He put the TV on mute then turned to Jeremy. "Whatcha got on your mind?"

"I'm going to church on Sunday, and I'd like for you and Mom to go with me."

"I've never been much of a churchgoer," his dad said.

"I wasn't, either, but now I am."

"Yeah, but that's different. You're much younger than me. It's easier for you to adapt." He turned back to stare at the silent TV.

Jeremy didn't want to jump on any argument, so he let a little bit of time elapse before making his case. "It wasn't easy the first time I went. In fact, I was scared to death that either I'd be rejected by God or someone from the church would point their finger at me and let everyone know I didn't belong there."

His dad pursed his lips then turned to face him. "I'd feel like a foreigner in church. I wouldn't know what to do or how to act."

Rather than argue that no one had to act, Jeremy chose to take a different approach. "I'll be there. If you need to know something, I'll tell you."

He saw how difficult it was for his dad to talk about church, but that was okay. Sometimes things were better if they weren't easy.

"Can I let you know tomorrow? I need to think about it."

"Sure." Jeremy stood and took a few steps before turning back to face his dad, who still had the TV on mute. "By the way, Mom said she'll go if you do."

Jeremy knew that would get him, even if not immediately. He smiled, offered a clipped nod, and turned toward the guest room. "I think I'll head to my room now. I'd like to study some business figures and then read my Bible."

As soon as Jeremy got to his room, he closed the door and leaned against it. His love for Christ had become his driving force, which was the reason he wanted to unload some of his businesses and settle near his parents. With so many things pulling him in so many different directions, he felt the distractions weren't healthy for him spiritually. He needed the calm serenity of home—a place where he could hoist an anchor and feel the love of friends from church and be near family.

He understood his parents' reluctance to go with him, but he wasn't going to give up on his call to share his faith. When he'd first thought about it, he imagined his father being more resistant than he was. He was surprised he hadn't gotten a resounding *no*.

The Lord had gently nudged Jeremy back to Marietta. Shortly after he'd decided it was time to settle down, he'd spoken to his mother, who assumed he meant he was coming home. He didn't have the heart to tell her he hadn't decided exactly where he wanted to settle, and since the Atlanta area had been his home for the first nineteen years of his life, he figured why not go back? And here he was.

If the Dress Fits

Sunday morning Cindi stood in front of her full-length mirror and turned to the side. She'd put a couple of pounds on lately, so the skirt didn't hang right. With a sigh of frustration, she changed into a dress that hid her midriff bulges. She was still petite, but she wouldn't be for long if she wasn't careful. How did Elizabeth get away with not putting on an ounce after eating nonstop cake, ice cream, brownies, and anything else she wanted, while one fattening meal was all it took for Cindi's silhouette to change completely? She'd had this problem all her life. Her mother once told her it was genetic—that she was supposed to have a little extra meat on her bones.

After she finally found an outfit that didn't make her look as though she'd been stuffing herself with marshmallows, she left for church. Elizabeth always saved her a seat near the front on the right-hand side.

She arrived just a few minutes before the service was due to start, so she quickly parked her car, hopped out, and ran up the church steps. She was focused on getting to her seat. When she heard her name, she turned to see who was calling her.

There was Jeremy, standing between two people. She would have recognized his mother, but his dad was shorter and thinner than she remembered.

"Why, Cindi Clark, you sure have grown into quite a young woman," Mrs. Hayden said. "Isn't she lovely, Jeremy?"

Jeremy grinned at her. "Yes, very lovely."

"Thank you. It's nice to see y'all." Cindi was at a loss for words, but she didn't want to be rude.

Mr. Hayden looked uncomfortable in his dark suit and tie. "Nice to see you, too," he said as he shifted from one foot to the other.

Cindi glanced around as people filed past her. "Why don't you come on in and find a good seat? I'm supposed to meet Elizabeth in our regular place. We always sit together since her husband is in the choir. Maybe there are a few extra seats nearby."

"Oh, go on, then," Mrs. Hayden said as she waved her away. "We'll be fine."

Jeremy nodded. "Thanks anyway. See you tomorrow."

"Um. . .okay." Cindi turned and scurried into the church toward Elizabeth, who had turned completely around to watch.

"Was that Jeremy I saw you talking to?" Elizabeth asked as soon as Cindi plopped down on the seat next to her.

"Yep."

"Who are the people with him?"

"His parents."

"Did you expect to see them here?" Elizabeth asked.

"Jeremy wasn't that much of a surprise, but I've come to expect the unexpected with him. However, I never thought I'd see his parents in a church. They never went when he was growing up."

Elizabeth smiled at her. "The Lord is amazing, isn't He?"

Throughout the service, Cindi couldn't get her mind off the fact that Jeremy was somewhere in the building. At first she marveled at the miracle of his parents being there. Then she wondered why he'd chosen this particular church to bring them to. She even thought perhaps he was using church for business purposes. By the time the service was over, anger had swelled inside her at the notion that he might be using church to get her to sell him the bridal shop.

As soon as the last worship song was sung, Elizabeth stood and turned around. "I see them."

"Who?" Cindi asked.

"Jeremy and his folks. They're over by the exit."

❧

Jeremy glanced at his parents, who remained seated next to him. They didn't seem so uncomfortable now.

"Well, son, would you like to go out for lunch?" his dad asked as people filed past them.

His mother laughed. "Just like you to always be thinking about your next meal."

"Isn't that what you're supposed to do? Leave church and pack the restaurants?" Jeremy laughed at his dad's deadpan tone.

"Why don't we head over to the Old Hickory House?" Jeremy said as he stood and gestured for his parents to do the same. "I'm in the mood for some biscuits and country ham."

He glanced over his shoulder in time to see Elizabeth looking directly at him. When their gazes met, she flashed a wide smile and waved. He waved back then turned to leave.

As he ushered his folks out the door, he thought about how Cindi had acted toward him. He decided to work harder at getting to know her again.

He helped his parents into his dad's car then went around and got behind the wheel. "My treat."

His dad nodded. "Sounds good."

Old Hickory House was crowded, but the host seated them within half an hour. Once the waitress took their order, his mother turned to him. "Church was very nice."

Jeremy looked at his dad. "Did you enjoy it, too?"

His dad lifted a hand to his mouth and coughed. "It was okay."

That was as good as he expected. "Since I'm moving back to the Atlanta area, I need to find a church home. I figured we'd start there and go to different places each Sunday."

"Why look at other churches when that one is just fine?" his dad asked.

That caught Jeremy by surprise. "So you actually liked it?"

"Like I said, it was okay. . .for church."

Jeremy couldn't resist probing deeper. "What, exactly, do you mean by that?"

"The sermon was interesting, and the music sounded good."

His mother tapped her finger on the side of her chin. "Did you know Cindi would be there?"

Leave it to her to be so direct. He wasn't about to lie.

"Yes."

She narrowed her eyes and studied him. "I still think there's something between you two—besides you trying to buy her shop. I saw how the two of you looked at each other."

Jeremy looked down at the table as he hesitated, then figured he might as well level with his parents. "There's some unfinished business between us."

"I thought so," his mom said. "It's been a long time, so don't get your hopes up."

"Trust me. I've dealt with disappointment many times. I can handle it."

Their food arrived, so their conversation turned to how much he'd missed the Old Hickory House biscuits. His mother kept giving him a look that let him know she was concerned about him. He wasn't sure if hinting at his feelings toward Cindi had been a good idea, but it was too late to worry about that now.

They were almost finished with their meal when his mother looked him squarely in the eye. "Jeremy, rather than let her think all you care about is her business, why don't you just level with her? I think it would be easier to start your own business from scratch—something more suitable for a young man than a bridal shop—than to chase after hers if what you really want is her."

He started to tell her that was exactly what he planned to do, but he didn't. "You're right as usual," he said with a smile. "That's what I'll do."

"Sure you will," she retorted. "I've known you all your life, and you've never given up if there's something you really want."

The next morning he awoke with a new plan. He'd stop off and visit Cindi to let her know his new business plans. While he was at it, he might just see what he could do to rekindle their relationship. The more he thought about the prospect of being with Cindi again, the more determined he was.

His mother grabbed him before he got out the door. "I have something I almost forgot about. I remembered after church, but by the time we got home, it slipped my mind again."

"What's that?"

"Go look in the shoe box on the table."

After a quick peek inside, he smiled. His mother had just given him an opening with Cindi. "Thanks, Mom. Mind if I take it?"

"Go ahead. It's yours. I was just holding on to it for safekeeping."

When he pulled up in front of the bridal shop a few minutes before it was due to open, he saw someone was already inside with the lights on. He paused, said a prayer, then got out to see if Cindi would give him the time of day.

He watched Cindi through the glass door as he approached. As soon as she heard someone enter, she glanced up with a bright smile. When she realized it was him, her expression instantly changed.

Chapter 5

The first flutter of excitement at seeing Jeremy faded to annoyance. What was he doing here so early? Did he think being here would change anything?

"Good morning," he said as he thrust a shoe box toward her. "My mother found this in my old room. Thought you might like to see it."

Cindi glanced at the box. "What is it?"

He put it on the counter. "See for yourself. Go ahead and open it."

She cautiously lifted the lid and glanced in the box. Inside was a nice neat stack of pictures that had been carefully layered between tissue. The top picture was a duplicate of one she had stuck away in an old photo album and avoided for years.

"You kept all these?" she asked as she lifted the one that was a duplicate of hers. "We really went all out for prom, didn't we?"

He laughed. "I remember how nervous I was. My mother helped me pick out your corsage, and my dad had to help me with my tie because my hands were shaking so much."

Cindi thumbed through the stack before putting the lid back on top. "I'm surprised you still have these."

He tilted his head. "Why?"

"I never thought you were the sentimental type."

Jeremy stood there in silence for a few seconds while Cindi watched. Finally, he shook his head.

"To be honest, I'd forgotten about them. These were at my parents' house. My mom gave them to me this morning."

"Oh, so you weren't holding on to them. Your mother was." Unexpected disappointment flooded her. "That's sweet of her."

"Yes, very sweet." He remained standing there, watching. . .waiting.

"Thanks for the nostalgic moment, Jeremy, but I have work to do."

"I'm not stopping you."

"Look, Jeremy, I think I know what you're doing, but it's not going to work. I don't know how many times I have to tell you I'm not selling my business to anyone who doesn't care about brides."

He tilted his head forward and set his jaw, holding her gaze for a couple of seconds before she averted her attention to the piece of paper on the counter.

She was almost certain he could hear her heart pounding, so she reached over and turned on some music.

She felt her cheeks grow hot as he continued standing there staring at her. Had he sensed her pounding heart and her yearning for the same feeling she'd had as a hopeful teenage girl?

As abruptly as he'd arrived, he backed toward the door. Her muscles gradually relaxed when he was across the room.

"I'm not giving up, Cindi—but I'm not talking about business now."

She tilted her head with a puzzled expression. "Then what are you talking about?"

"We used to be good together, and I still think there's a chance for us."

Had she just heard him correctly? "You're kidding, right?"

"Nope. I'm as serious as I've ever been." He took a step backward. "I don't give up easily, so you might as well get used to seeing me around."

As soon as he was gone, Cindi's knees weakened, so she lowered herself into the chair by the counter. She bowed her head in prayer for the strength to withstand anything Jeremy said or did. He'd gotten to her years ago, and he was getting to her now.

"Hey, girl, are you okay?"

Cindi jumped. "How did you get in here without me hearing you come in?"

Elizabeth shrugged. "I dunno. I thought you were asleep." She leaned over and looked Cindi in the eye. "You look like you don't feel well."

"I'm okay, just a little rattled."

"Jeremy?" Elizabeth went around behind the counter and pulled out her appointment book.

Rather than deny the obvious, Cindi just nodded. "He's been here already this morning. The man simply won't give up."

Elizabeth's glance darted toward the box Jeremy had left on the counter. "What's this?"

"Go ahead. Open it and see for yourself."

Elizabeth lifted the lid and looked inside. "Whoa."

"His mother kept those all these years, so he thought I needed to see them."

"As if you didn't already have your own pictures." She'd pulled out the whole stack and started studying each one.

"Hey, I'm in this one."

Cindi joined Elizabeth behind the counter. "Let's see."

They spent the next several minutes going through the pictures and recalling the events. "It's amazing how something like this can make the memories so clear—it's almost like it happened yesterday," Elizabeth said. "Look. This one was taken at the Varsity after we won the last football game of the season."

"Yes, I remember," Cindi replied softly. In fact, she even remembered what she ordered that night, but she wasn't about to share that. The whole evening was vivid in her mind because that was the night Jeremy had told her he loved her.

Elizabeth belted out a hearty chuckle. "Look at this one. Remember when we all piled into that new guy's car and headed out for Macon? We'd gotten halfway there when you suddenly remembered you had to be home early."

How could Cindi have forgotten? She was embarrassed she had an early curfew that night, so she didn't say anything right away. But when she did, Jeremy didn't hesitate to make sure she got home on time. He'd been such a gentleman before he suddenly. . .

"Are you okay?" Elizabeth asked.

Tears stung the back of Cindi's eyes as she nodded. "I'm fine. I just need to concentrate on business right now."

Elizabeth put the pictures back into the box, lifted it from the counter, and stuck it in a cubbyhole. "I understand." She flipped open the appointment book. "Let's see. . .we have one appointment this morning for a final fitting, then three brand-new brides coming in back-to-back."

The phone rang, signaling their busy day had begun. Cindi welcomed the pace, but with each new bride she helped, she wondered how the marriage would work out. Would the bride still be happy a year later? Would her husband continue to be as attentive as he was during the dating period and the honeymoon? The statistics were downright heartbreaking.

Cindi had mixed feelings at closing time. She was exhausted, but without the steady stream of customers to assist and vendors to contact, she had to face her own thoughts.

She'd just locked the shop door when Jeremy pulled up in front of her and lowered his window. "It's a nice night. Want to go for a drive?" he asked.

A lump formed in her throat. She slowly shook her head. "I really need to go home, Jeremy."

"And do what?" he asked.

She wanted to tell him it was none of his business—that her time was her own and she needed that time away from him. All he did was muddy her thoughts. But she couldn't. Her will wasn't strong enough to resist talking to the man who had her emotions swirling among her confused thoughts.

"I really don't have specific plans." She shrugged. "But I had a busy day, and I'm tired."

"Then hop in and you can tell me all about it."

She squinted and stared at him for a few seconds. Was he serious, or was he being sarcastic?

There didn't appear to be any mischief in his expression. In fact, he looked hopeful.

He continued watching her as she mulled over the thought of being with him. Her initial reaction was *no way*. But seeing the pictures had brought out something in her that she hadn't felt in years—since she'd last been with him—and she sort of enjoyed the feeling.

Finally, she nodded. "Okay, but I can't stay out late."

"Want me to follow you home and leave from there, or do you want me to take you back to your car here?"

She shook her head as she tried to organize her thoughts. It was time to be direct. "Why don't you just follow me home? My place isn't too far away."

He smiled. "I know."

&⌇

It didn't take long to get to her place. She pulled into the driveway, and he was right behind her. As soon as she got in his car, he turned to her. "We really need to talk about what happened. I was such an idiot for how I handled myself when we were kids."

He watched her expression change from surprise to resignation. "That's just it, Jeremy. We were kids. It was just a high school crush."

"Oh, I think there was more to it than that," he replied. "And I believe, deep down, you agree with me."

"I don't think it'll work, Jeremy," Cindi said as she tried to look everywhere but at him. "It's been a long time."

"Can we at least give it a shot?"

When she glanced at him, he felt a surge of emotion he had to fight to keep down.

"I don't know. I'm so busy, and my life is exactly how I like it."

That raised another question. "Then why are you selling your shop?"

Cindi closed her eyes momentarily then opened them. She looked him in the eye and said, "I don't believe in what I do anymore."

"You what?" That was an answer he hadn't expected.

"Ever since my parents split up, I realized all I'm doing is trying to peddle a fairy-tale life that doesn't exist."

"Your parents split?" He couldn't imagine how he'd feel if that happened to him. "They always seemed fine to me."

She snorted. "They seemed fine to everyone, including me, which is why it was such a shock. When I first started my business, I imagined all marriages being as wonderful as my parents'. When brides came to me looking for a dress, I spent time helping them pick out the perfect gown to wear as they walked toward their life partner. After I was open a year, one of the brides came in to tell me she was getting a divorce. That shocked me. And I felt bad that I'd been part of an illusion. But at least then I had my parents' marriage to hold up as a model."

"People get divorced, Cindi. It had nothing to do with you."

"I know."

As he watched her wince, he felt an overwhelming grief at how her dream had shattered.

"But it still hurt. Then I found out about other bridal customers whose marriages hadn't worked out."

"Okay, so some of your brides divorce, and your parents have split. That's going to happen. Granted, it's an awful thing, but you can't control what happens to other people after you do your job."

"You're right," she agreed, "but I can stop playing the game of happily-ever-after when it's nothing but an illusion."

Oh, she's really hurting. He wanted to reach out and comfort her—to touch her cheek and feel the softness of her skin.

She offered a forced smile. "So that's why I'm selling my business."

"Let me get this straight," he said as he carefully chose his words. "You don't believe in marriage anymore, so you're selling your very profitable bridal shop."

"Right."

"Then why does it matter what the new owner does with it—whether the person is hands-on or an absentee owner?"

"I know this probably doesn't make sense, but I still care."

"It does make sense," he replied. "I've known you for a very long time, Cindi Clark. You care about everything. Sometimes too much for your own good." He paused to smile, and he was delighted that she grinned right back at him. "You're a sweet, honest, caring woman who doesn't want any part of less than the best."

She glanced down then shyly looked back at him. "Thanks."

"I mean every word of it, too."

"Good. Now are we going for a drive, or did you just want to sit here?"

He snickered. "I was so caught up in the conversation, I forgot." He put the car in reverse. "So what do you plan to do after you sell your business?"

"I have no idea." She blinked a couple of times before grinning. "Okay, now it's my turn. Why did you come back to Marietta?"

"Good question." He took a moment to decide whether or not to let her know the real reason versus the shorter version he reserved for when he didn't feel like talking. He chose the latter. "I've been feeling sort of nostalgic for my family, and my parents aren't getting any younger."

"Your parents look pretty good to me."

"Yes, they do, don't they?" he agreed. "That's not all. I felt like I needed to make amends with you after the way I botched the best relationship I ever had."

"Jeremy." Her voice held a warning tone.

He pulled off the road into a parking lot and put the car in park before turning to face her. "You do understand the reason I broke up with you that night, don't you?"

She closed her eyes and folded her arms. With a heavy heart, he unfastened his seat belt, scooted closer to her, and gently put his arm around her. At first she stiffened, but she gradually relaxed. However, she didn't lean into him the way she did back in high school.

He reached over and turned her chin so she was facing him. "I never stopped loving you, Cindi. I figured since I wasn't going to college, I needed to let you go so you could fulfill your dreams."

She frowned. "So you're saying you did it for me?"

He nodded.

She pulled away. "I don't buy that, Jeremy."

She might as well have sprayed him with water then tossed a load of bricks at him. He took a deep breath and slowly let it out. He'd hurt her more than he realized. He needed to give her a little space and let things happen more naturally.

"Hey, let's lighten up a bit," he said. "Why don't you fill me in on what everyone is doing?"

She looked at him with suspicion, but she took the question and ran with it. He enjoyed watching her as she told him about several of their old high school friends, letting him know who was doing what and where they were. He wanted to know more about her family, but after her revelation about her parents, he wasn't about to go there—at least not now.

Finally, she pointed to the road. "I really need to get home now, Jeremy. I have a long day tomorrow, and I haven't eaten yet."

"We can grab something if you want."

She offered him a smile. "Thanks, but I'll just get something at home."

"I'd like to get together again. This was fun."

She didn't respond directly to his comment. She waited until they got to her driveway. "Thanks for explaining things."

Being with Cindi brought back memories and gave him a different perspective of who he was. His business dealings since he'd left town had been cold and calculating. Now he had to do things differently. He had to be softer. Gentler. In a way, even coddle her. But he couldn't be the least bit condescending. He didn't want her to think he was interested in anything but her.

❧

The rest of the evening Cindi's thoughts vacillated between how Jeremy made her feel and whether selling her business was such a good idea. When she'd listed it with Fran, she figured some stranger—some woman she didn't know—would come in and fall in love with running a bridal shop. Cindi thought she'd teach the basics of running this sort of nurturing business to a person who'd never done it before. At first when she turned Jeremy down, she thought she was protecting her business from someone who didn't care about it. However, now that he'd backed off, she knew she was protecting her heart.

This was insane! She could have dreamed all day of how things would go, and this scenario never would have crossed her mind. Being with him had opened the floodgate of memories that brought her back to a time in her life when she was innocent and naive.

Being naive at this point in her life wasn't an option. However, she'd maintained her innocence to keep from giving in to the ways of the world. After losing Jeremy years ago, Cindi had held out hope that one day she'd meet a great guy who loved the Lord as much as she did. Until then, she'd keep running her shop and being there for young women who'd found their Prince Charming.

Even after announcing they were separating, her mother had tried to talk her into keeping her shop. "This is what you've wanted all your life. Don't give up on your dream," her mother had said.

But how could she hang on to a dream that involved something that didn't exist? Everlasting love. Unconditional love. The type of love the Lord wanted for His followers. It was the idea the Lord had designed but the world had scorned.

Her parents had always gone to church and brought her and her brother to church, yet they'd still decided to go their separate ways. No amount of explaining would justify how that could happen.

"What do you plan to do once the shop sells?" her mother had asked.

Cindi had no idea. Her business degree had given her the basic knowledge she needed for the shop, but it was too general to give her any specific idea for later. For the first time in her life, she was acting out of character and doing something on impulse. She knew she needed a plan, but since all she'd ever wanted was to be in the bridal business, nothing had come to mind.

During the next several days, business was steady, but nothing major happened. Every day they had new brides-to-be coming in with stars in their eyes, and it took everything Cindi had not to squelch their enthusiasm.

"Where's Jeremy?" Elizabeth asked when they hadn't seen him in a week.

Cindi shrugged. "I guess he finally got the hint."

※

Jeremy had been called to Savannah, where he closed on a couple of restaurants and a tour business near downtown. He'd been trying to sell all of them, but the market had been soft until recently, so he was glad to be done with them. Even though he had someone running the places, there was always the risk of having to go back.

Now that he had them off his mind, he could concentrate on what he really wanted—Cindi. Because of Cindi's reluctance to sell to him, he had to figure out a different excuse to come around.

He left behind what had been his favorite businesses when he'd decided to return to Atlanta. As much as he loved being a part of people experiencing the dolphin cruise and a carriage ride through the old part of town followed by a good old-fashioned Southern meal, he was ready to settle into a new life—one that involved being immersed in church and his family. He wished Cindi was part of that equation, but unless something major happened, he didn't see that in his near future.

After he finished his business in Savannah, he let out a sigh of relief. When he reached the parking lot of his parents' condo, he sat in his car and stared at the dashboard. He knew there would be questions he wasn't in the mood to answer as soon as he went inside. His bank account was padded with the proceeds of the businesses, so at least he could go looking for a place of his own now. He loved his folks, but he needed his own space.

To his surprise, his mother greeted him with nothing more than a hug and a kiss on the cheek. "I cooked spaghetti for supper, and I put the leftovers in the refrigerator if you want to heat them up in the microwave."

His dad had already gone to bed, so he thanked his mother and fixed himself a quick dinner before going to the guest room. Once there he made a list of things to do the next day, which included a brief stopover at Cindi's shop.

He got there before she did the next morning and was waiting for her by the front door.

"What're you doing here so early?" she asked.

"You didn't think I'd give up, did you?"

After she rolled her eyes, Cindi unlocked the door and stepped inside. Jeremy followed right behind her.

She glanced over her shoulder. "Would you mind flipping the light switch by the door?"

He reached over and did as he was told. She still hadn't commented on the flowers in his hand, but he'd seen her glance at them.

After she had everything set up and turned on, she walked over to him. "I've been thinking about our talk the other night. Maybe it's not such a good idea for you to keep coming around."

"Cindi," he said softly, taking a step toward her. "I'd really like us to get to know each other better. As adults. I want you to see me in a different light."

"You know how I feel, Jeremy."

"No, I really don't. All I know is that ever since I've come to Christ, my whole perspective has changed. I feel I've been led here, and I'm not about to turn back now."

"But—" She paused and widened her eyes. "Stop it right now, Jeremy. Whatever you're up to isn't right for me."

He'd mentioned his new faith in Christ, but how could she tell if he was being honest with her? All she knew for certain was that he'd stop at nothing to get what he wanted. He'd started out wanting her business and finally seemed to give up on that, so he must not have wanted it all that badly. Either that or he had a new tactic that involved a bluff. After the pain he'd caused so many years ago, how could she trust that he wasn't pursuing her business through her heart?

Chapter 6

She had to turn away quickly or she feared she might buckle under the temptation to get emotional about Jeremy. Old feelings flooded her.

"Like I told you, we have some unfinished business," he added.

She squared her shoulders and looked him directly in the eyes. "The only business I have is this one, and I need to get back to work."

Jeremy glanced down at the floor and sighed. He looked sad, but she wasn't sure if it was sincere or part of an act. Whatever the case, she needed him to leave.

"Okay, I'll go now. But you need to understand I don't give up easily." He took a step toward the door, pivoted to face her, and added, "On anything."

Elizabeth came in as he walked out the door. She lifted an eyebrow. "Looks like a man on a mission."

"Yes, I'm afraid so," Cindi agreed. "He says he's not going to give up."

"Just remember how he broke your heart back in high school. I'm not saying he hasn't changed, but be careful, okay? I've always thought Jeremy was charming, but I don't want to see you get hurt again."

Cindi pulled out the two appointment books and handed Elizabeth's to her. "Yes, of course." She flipped hers open. "I have back-to-back appointments until about three. You have a final fitting at ten; then I need your help. My eleven o'clock is the entire wedding party."

"Is this the Myers group?"

"That's the one," Cindi said with a snicker. "I told Lynda she needed to give me a final count on the number of bridesmaids, but she keeps adding them."

"How many is she up to now?"

Cindi pulled out the Myers file and glanced at her notes. "Last I checked, eleven."

Elizabeth shrugged. "She might as well make it a dozen."

"Yeah, why not? It's good for business, right?"

Elizabeth glanced up from her appointment book and studied Cindi. "You sound cynical."

"I can't help it with all the broken hearts and shattered dreams in the world today. Weddings aren't what they used to be. I know I sound like a broken record, but I remember thinking it was a wonderful celebration with family and friends witnessing the union of two people before God—promising to love and respect each other until the end."

"That's still what it's supposed to be," Elizabeth reminded her. "Are you okay? I can handle everything if you need to go home."

Cindi shook her head. "No, I'm fine. I guess I just needed to vent. Let's set up for the first appointment. The bride said she wants something simple. It's a church wedding, and she only has two bridesmaids. Her father is deceased, and her mother is walking her down the aisle."

The discussion quickly turned to what they'd show the bride and her mother. Cindi was relieved they'd moved on from talking about Jeremy, who'd taken over most of her thoughts when she wasn't at work.

The first appointment didn't take long. As soon as the bride tried on her third dress, she made her decision. "I've never been much of a shopper," she said. "This is what I want, so there's no point in trying on more." She picked the dresses for her two bridesmaids then left.

"She must not be from the South," Elizabeth quipped.

Cindi laughed. Leave it to Elizabeth to crack a joke like that. "Actually, she's from Macon."

"I bet her parents are from up North."

The next appointment took almost three hours, causing Cindi and Elizabeth to skip lunch. They had to take turns working with a conflicting appointment to keep from backing up the rest of their schedule.

By late afternoon, they were exhausted. "One more bridal party this afternoon; then we can coast," Elizabeth commented.

The next day, they both arrived at the shop at the same time. Elizabeth had to work on alterations, while Cindi needed to prepare for the day's appointments. They both looked over their schedules and worked up a plan to handle all their tasks.

Then Jeremy walked in. Elizabeth took that opportunity to go to the sewing room. "If you need me, I'll be in there," she said.

"So," Jeremy said when they were alone, "is there any way I can convince you to go out with me tonight?"

He obviously meant what he said when he told her he wouldn't take no for an answer. "You really don't give up, do you?"

"Not often," he admitted.

"Tell you what," Cindi finally said. "Maybe later. I'm busy today."

He lifted his hand in a wave and moved toward the door. "At least you didn't say no this time. See you soon."

As soon as he left the shop, Cindi headed straight for the sewing room. "I can't believe the nerve," she growled.

"Um, what did you expect? He's obviously a man in love."

Cindi narrowed her eyes. "Whose side are you on, anyway?"

"I don't have to give up my romantic outlook just because you've become cynical."

"True." Cindi moved a few things around on the counter for something to do with her hands. "Just don't get those romantic notions about Jeremy and me."

"Sometimes I think he's changed, but I agree. You were hurt too badly to go there again. No point in taking any chances."

"We've both seen him at church. I think he's changed," Cindi admitted, "at least a little."

"Don't get me wrong," Elizabeth continued as she closed the gap between them. "I like Jeremy. Deep down, I think he's basically a good guy. It's just that there's an edge to him that we'll never understand."

"That's probably why he's been so good in business."

"Don't forget you have one of the most successful bridal shops in the Southeast. You're good in business, too."

"I'm sure some people would argue that point."

"You can't control what other people think, Cindi. This shop means a lot to you, no matter what you say. Even now. Look at you." Elizabeth gestured toward her. "The very thought of someone coming in here and doing anything to hurt what you've built has you in a total tizzy." She paused then asked, "Have you figured out what you'll do once you sell?"

Cindi didn't want to think that far into the future, so she avoided answering the question directly. "So you think I'm making a mistake?"

Elizabeth tilted her head and offered a pitying look. "I don't want to tell you what to do."

"I'm not saying I want you to tell me what to do. All I'm asking—"

A walk-in customer arrived, cutting their conversation short. The rest of the day was busy, so they didn't have another chance to talk.

After work Cindi went to her car and found a note stuck to the window. She didn't have to look at it to know whom it was from; his handwriting hadn't changed since high school.

Cindi, give me a call after you get home. Here's my cell phone number:
555-3738.

Love, Jeremy

She started to crumple it up but changed her mind. She folded it instead and dropped it into her purse. She'd decide later if she should call. After dinner.

Cindi made a stop at Publix for some quick and easy food from the deli, then headed home. Her stomach growled and her head ached. It had been a very long day.

As soon as she got inside, she kicked off her shoes and headed straight for the kitchen, where she dropped the grocery bags and her purse. Most of the time she turned on the TV to watch the news while she ate, but not tonight. She had some serious thinking to do.

She prepared a plate, carried it to the table, sat down, and said her blessing. The food tasted good, but after a couple of bites her stomach ached from anxiety.

Elizabeth had challenged her decision and given her quite a bit to think about. And now Jeremy wanted her to call. She felt torn. There were so many angles she hadn't thought of when she'd abruptly put her shop on the market. With each new event, she realized her issues were deeper than she'd originally thought.

As an adult child of newly separated parents, Cindi still had a hard time getting over feeling betrayed. How long had they been thinking about splitting? Was there anything she could have done to keep them together? Her brother had long since been gone, and when she'd contacted him with the news, he hadn't even offered to come home. His techie job was demanding and he was up for a promotion, so he couldn't come home to help her talk some sense into their parents. That bugged her, but she couldn't control him. So she'd set out to talk to them on her own. Her father avoided her, and her mother didn't understand her reasoning—that they were supposed to stay together through the good and the bad. Besides, from her vantage point, how bad was their life, really? Her mother claimed her father never listened to her, and when she called her father, he said her mother didn't support him. Weren't those both typical problems they could talk through?

The most upsetting aspect was they'd gone to church all her life, and now they rarely went. Her mother said they'd attended church for the children, and her dad said he was too busy. This confused her. Their reasoning sounded silly and selfish—the total opposite of how they'd been during her childhood.

What really baffled her was how lightly they seemed to take the split. Her mother told her it had nothing to do with her. They'd both moved on with their lives, and they said they couldn't understand why she refused to do the same.

Her throat constricted, and a knot formed in her stomach as she thought about it. Her parents were no different from anyone else, it seemed.

When she couldn't eat another bite, she scraped the contents of her plate into the trash and stuck the plate in the dishwasher. Then she opened her purse and pulled out Jeremy's note. If she called him, she might have to answer questions. However, if she didn't call him, he might stop by unannounced and ask questions anyway.

She finally sucked in a breath, grabbed the phone, punched in his number, and exhaled. Maybe he wouldn't be able to talk. She could only hope. . . .

"Jeremy?" she said as soon as he answered.

"I was afraid you wouldn't call."

"What did you need?" she asked.

"I don't want to discuss it on the phone. When can we get together?"

"I don't know, Jeremy."

"Sorry if I'm annoying you, but I need to explain some things, and I won't give up until we have another chance to talk."

Cindi decided it was time to give in. "I'll look at my schedule and let you know, okay?"

"Sounds good," he said. "I'll see you soon, okay? My mom wants me to help her with something, so I need to run."

"Okay, fine."

She needed to go to bed early because they were booked full the next day. However, it took what seemed like hours to fall asleep. She was glad when daylight finally came so she could get busy and not have her head filled with so many thoughts of Jeremy.

Their first appointment arrived right on time, with Jeremy right behind them. The young bride and her mother were deep in discussion as they entered. Jeremy stepped off to the side so they could assist their customers.

"I've changed my mind," the bride said. "I hope you haven't started altering my dress yet." She'd chosen one of the samples on sale, and it needed to be taken in a few inches at the waist.

Elizabeth shook her head. "I was going to do yours next, so you're okay."

Cindi pulled out the checkbook. "I'll write you a check for your refund. Good thing you're backing out now rather than after the wedding."

The bride's mother laughed. "Oh, that's not what she meant. She's still getting married, but she decided to go with the other dress."

Cindi felt the heat rise to her cheeks. "I'm so sorry I assumed—"

The woman laughed again and waved her hand. "I certainly understand. Don't worry about it." She turned toward her daughter. "Do you remember which dress you liked? I sure hope they still have it."

"We do," Elizabeth interjected. "In fact, it's right here." She crossed the room and lifted a dress from one of the racks. "Why don't I set you up in the second fitting room so I can pin it?"

The bride and her mother went into the room, and Elizabeth followed right behind them with her pincushion. Cindi stayed behind the counter, still embarrassed by her faux pas.

As soon as they were out of earshot, Jeremy joined her at the counter. "It was an honest mistake," he said. "Don't worry so much about it."

"I'm not worried," she snapped.

He grinned and winked. "*Sure* you're not."

Elizabeth ducked her head out of the room. "They want another opinion,

Cindi. Would you mind taking a look?"

"Sure." Cindi darted into the room to help out, leaving Jeremy behind in the showroom. As soon as she saw the dress on the young woman, she gave a thumbs-up. "Gorgeous! I agree this one is much better."

Elizabeth circled the stand. "It doesn't need much alteration, either. In fact, she could actually get away with only one small tuck."

The mother-of-the-bride had wandered over by the door and was looking out into the showroom. She stepped back in, looked directly at Cindi, and said, "Do you think your husband would mind giving us a man's opinion?"

Cindi shot her a curious look. "Husband?".

"Yes, that young man you were talking to when we arrived. He is your husband, isn't he?"

"Uh, no, he's not my husband."

The woman shook her head and smiled apologetically. "I'm terribly sorry. I was just telling my daughter what a cute couple you were."

Cindi was rendered speechless, and she glanced over in time to catch Elizabeth silently snickering. Her voice caught in her throat, and she couldn't speak.

"He might not be your husband, but he seems like a nice young man. Does he work here with you?"

In unison, Elizabeth and Cindi said, "No!"

"Do you think he'd mind telling us what he thinks of my daughter's dress?"

Elizabeth told Cindi to stay right where she was while she went to ask Jeremy. Cindi was thankful for the reprieve. Facing him immediately after the woman's innocent but clearly misguided comment would have been next to impossible.

Chapter 7

The dress is beautiful," Jeremy announced. "I'm sure the groom will consider himself a very fortunate man."

The mother-of-the-bride's chest swelled with pride. "I think so, too, but of course I would."

"Seriously, she looks great. I think you made an excellent decision." He glanced at Cindi, but to her surprise, he didn't look the slightest bit uncomfortable. "But I didn't see the other dress on her, so I don't have anything to compare this one to."

The woman's eyebrows shot up. "Would you like to see the other one on her so you can compare them?"

"Mo–om," the bride moaned. "I'm sure he has better things to do with his time than stand around a bridal shop with a bunch of strangers."

"Oh, I don't mind," he said. "In fact, I'd love to see the other dress." He turned to Cindi. "That is, if you have the time."

What could Cindi say now? He'd put her on the spot in front of a valued customer. "We're okay on time. Our next appointment isn't for another twenty minutes."

As Cindi ushered him away from the fitting room, the bride's mother said, "Just keep in mind the other dress will need many more alterations."

Once the fitting room door closed, he looked at Cindi with contrition. "Sorry if this is inconveniencing you."

"Oh, don't be ridiculous, Jeremy. This is what I do all day. It's not an inconvenience."

"Whoa. Looks like I might have pushed a hot button."

Before she had a chance to defend her reaction, the fitting room door opened and out stepped the bride. Jeremy tilted his head to one side and studied her for a few seconds; then he moved around to get a view from a different angle. "It looks very pretty, but I agree with you all. The other one is perfect. It accents all your best features, while this one calls too much attention from your face."

The bride's mother beamed. "You have a great eye. Have you thought about going into the bridal business?"

Cindi was instantly stunned speechless. Elizabeth started coughing. Jeremy chuckled. "Yes, I've thought about it."

"Oh, you ought to do it. You'd be very good. Not many men would be as comfortable as you in a roomful of women voicing their honest opinion."

Jeremy thanked her then took a step back. "Great chatting with you ladies, but I need to run." He headed for the door then stopped, turned, and faced Cindi. "I'll call you later."

The bride's mother didn't waste a moment before turning to Cindi. "Who is that man?"

"His name is Jeremy Hayden, and he's a businessman who is trying to establish himself here in Atlanta," Cindi replied, trying hard not to let on how she felt deep down.

"I'll definitely be watching for him. If he has a business I can use, I'll be one of his best customers."

After the bride and her mother left, Elizabeth turned to Cindi. "If he winds up owning a bridal shop, I sure hope she has more than one daughter."

Cindi laughed. "Yeah, me, too."

Elizabeth suddenly grew serious. "So has he completely backed off trying to buy this place?"

"Looks that way."

"That was a fast change of heart."

"Yeah, it was, wasn't it?"

Elizabeth shrugged. "I never saw him in action until today. He has finesse."

"It's all a ruse to get what he wants," Cindi reminded her. "Remember? He's always been good at going after the prize then losing interest."

❧

Jeremy left the shop with an odd feeling in the pit of his stomach. Giving his opinion to that bride actually made him feel good—much better than when he worked in the candy store he'd first purchased years ago on a whim. He'd been looking for something to do with his life after the army. He got what he thought would be a temporary job working behind the counter—until something better came along. Then when the owner got in some financial trouble and said he'd have to either sell the shop or close it, Jeremy impulsively made a lowball offer. To his surprise, it was accepted. Once he owned the place, he made a few changes, hired people who knew how to sell, and offered samples. Those few things brought great rewards. He bought the video store next door when the owner had to leave the country.

When Jeremy grew tired of the candy store, he offered a special seller-financing deal to his employees, who jumped at the chance to own their own business. He carried the business skills he'd learned there to the video store and his next business after that and made it a point to learn everything he could to be successful.

His parents had been surprised at his business acumen and called it instinct. However, Jeremy knew better. He worked hard, learned from his mistakes, and treated people fairly—from the employees and vendors to the customers.

He now had a better understanding of the allure of running a bridal shop besides the business aspect. What would Cindi say if he told her he'd reconsidered and wanted to run it himself? Would she believe him?

He'd have to talk to her later, when she wasn't staring back at him with a look of distrust. Elizabeth, on the other hand, had actually smiled at him—a major feat as far as he was concerned. He'd sensed a lack of connection when he'd first come back, most likely due to Elizabeth's deep devotion to her lifelong best friend. Ever since he could remember, those two had practically been joined at the hip. One could almost always finish the other's sentences. There were times in high school when he'd felt a little jealous of what they had.

Sure, he'd had friends, but the relationships were mostly built around sports. He played basketball, so he and his teammates picked up games off-season on weekends. But when it was over, they either headed out for food or went their separate ways. There was never anyone he could talk to about anything meaningful.

When Cindi had brought him to church, he felt like a misfit, so he found ways to avoid it. At the time, he figured his parents managed to get by without it, so what was the point? However, now he knew that without Christ, life didn't hold much meaning beyond the here and now, and where was the joy in that? Once something in this world was gone, it was over. With the Christian perspective he now had, he realized how valuable life was and what he had to look forward to in eternity.

When he first became a believer, he thought once he got out of the army he might give up all his worldly possessions and go into the ministry. However, the base chaplain explained that not all believers are called to do that.

"The Lord wants us to go out and spread the gospel through everyday life. Being in the service or taking on the role of a successful businessman gives you quite a few opportunities to be in places I'm not likely to be."

So he'd prayed about it and made the decision to finish out his army stint and focus on opportunities to share the Word. He loved the Lord now, and he understood what Cindi had believed since childhood.

When he got home that night, his parents told him they wanted to go back to the same church. He was ecstatic and let them know how much that meant to him.

After his mother left the room, his dad asked him to sit down. "I think this is the very thing we've needed for a long time, but I'm still worried I'll look stupid because a man my age should know more about the Bible."

Jeremy jumped up. "Stay right here, Dad! I've got another great book that'll help."

He went to his room, dug into his nightstand drawer, and pulled out a book he'd been given when he first started attending church. It explained a little more than the basics of Christianity, and that bit of knowledge armed him with confidence. What better person to give it to than his dad?

"What's this all about, son?" His dad turned the book over and studied the back flap.

"A friend in Savannah gave it to me, and it helped me with the very thing you're worried about."

His dad's eyes lit up. "Oh, okay. It has answers to some of my questions. Mind if I borrow it for a few days so your mother and I can look through it?"

"Keep it, Dad. After you and Mom read it, you can pass it on to someone else who needs it."

Jeremy felt closer to his father than he'd ever been in his life. Amazing what coming to the Lord had done for him.

On Sunday Jeremy and his parents got to church early so they could find a good seat. His mother said she didn't like sitting in the back, so they moved closer toward the middle. He tried to avoid any confrontation with Cindi, because he didn't want her to think he was there for anything besides worship.

His mother belted out the worship songs, while his dad was more reserved. That was okay, though, because he was there worshipping his Savior. Jeremy felt as if he might burst with joy.

After church he and his parents made it all the way out to the parking lot when he heard someone call his name. He turned around and spotted Elizabeth running toward them.

"Why didn't you tell us you were coming?" she asked.

"I didn't think I needed to," he replied. "Besides, I don't want to annoy Cindi any more than I already have."

He saw the corners of Elizabeth's lips start to curl into a smile, but she caught herself. "Well, I just wanted to welcome you."

"Thank you, Elizabeth," Jeremy said.

His mother stepped forward. "Why don't you, your husband, and Cindi stop over for dinner later?"

"Um. . ." Elizabeth nervously glanced over her shoulder. "I don't think so. Not today."

"Mom," Jeremy said softly.

"Okay, okay, I'm sorry I embarrassed you. I shouldn't do that to you."

"You didn't embarrass me," he said.

Elizabeth took a step back. "I really need to run."

Jeremy held up a finger to get her to wait and turned to his mom. "Why don't you two go ahead and get in the car? I want to talk to Elizabeth for a moment, okay?"

His mother looked nervously back and forth between Jeremy and Elizabeth. "You won't be long, will you?"

"No, of course not." After his parents were safely out of listening range, he turned back to Elizabeth. "I wanted to let you know I'd never do anything to hurt Cindi or her shop. All I wanted—"

"You don't have to explain anything to me. It's between you and Cindi."

He could tell she still didn't completely trust him. All she'd wanted to do was show good manners and welcome him and his parents. He pursed his lips then smiled. "I understand."

Elizabeth started walking away but quickly turned. "By the way, Cindi loves vanilla mocha drinks from that coffee shop down the street."

He chuckled. "Thanks for the tip."

Once he and his parents got in the car, his mother turned to him. "What was that all about?"

"Nothing. Just chitchat about business."

"I hope you're not still trying to buy that bridal shop from Cindi."

"Mom, please leave my business dealings to me. It's not open for discussion."

She lifted her hands in surrender. "Whatever you say, Jeremy. Who am I to understand what's going on between you and that girl? You've never let love get in the way of what you wanted before, so why should I expect it to start now?"

That comment bothered Jeremy more than he wanted to admit. He thought about it the rest of the afternoon, and it woke him up in the middle of the night. Maybe his mother was right. Perhaps he should take a step back and look at his life from a different angle. He lay there staring at the ceiling for a few minutes before he decided to stop worrying so much.

He shut his eyes and prayed for direction, only now he prayed specifically for what to do with Cindi. By now, he knew he loved her even more than he had as a high school kid. He finally fell asleep, only to be awakened by his alarm clock.

He thought about what his mother had said all the way to the shop, and he knew she was probably right. He stopped off at the coffee shop for a couple of vanilla mocha drinks then headed to Cindi's Bridal Boutique.

Elizabeth grinned when she saw him come through the door. "How nice of you!" she said a little too loudly, letting him know she wanted Cindi to hear. "Cindi!" she hollered. "Jeremy brought us something wonderful!"

Cindi came from the back looking puzzled. When she spotted the coffee shop logo cups, she gave him a quizzical look.

"A little birdie told me you liked vanilla mocha."

She lifted one eyebrow and shot a glance in Elizabeth's direction. "I wonder who that little birdie is." A softer look covered her face when she turned back to him. "I saw you in church with your parents yesterday. I think it's nice you're bringing your family to worship."

Jeremy sensed Cindi's shell was starting to crack. He knew once that happened, he had the ability to totally knock it away by really pouring on the charm. But that was his old self. Although he never meant any harm, he didn't want to do anything that remotely hinted of underhandedness. He wanted her to trust him without any of the smoke and mirrors he once relied on to get what he wanted from people.

❧

Cindi's first reaction when she'd seen Jeremy in church had been that he was more persistent than anyone she'd ever known, and she'd put up her defense for when he approached her. However, he hadn't bothered to come up to her or use the church in any way. In fact, he seemed to be hiding from her. Elizabeth talked to her and said that in spite of her earlier concerns, she now felt Jeremy had sincerely become a Christian.

She'd thought about it all Sunday afternoon and lay in bed thinking about it half the night. She prayed about her own judgment, and when she woke up, she felt a heavy weight lift. In fact, she actually looked forward to the next time she saw Jeremy.

The vanilla mocha drink was a bonus.

"Thanks for the coffee," she said as she reached for it. "I really need it this morning."

"I wish I liked coffee," he admitted. "It smells good, but I still don't like the taste."

"Just enjoy the aroma." She lifted the lid and moved the coffee cup in the front of him. "Wanna try a little?"

He leaned over and inhaled. "It doesn't smell as strong as hot coffee, but I have to admit, I'd be tempted to taste it if I didn't know what it was like."

"I remember how much you used to enjoy milk shakes and malts."

"Still do," he said as he patted his belly. "But I can't indulge as much as I used to."

Elizabeth backed away from them. "I have to finish a hem, so I'll leave the two of you alone."

Cindi felt a little awkward chatting with Jeremy like this, but it wasn't too bad. He did seem very nice, and after Elizabeth had that talk with her, she sensed Jeremy was relaxing and not being so pushy.

"So did your folks enjoy church?"

He nodded. "Yes, very much so. In fact, my dad has been asking quite a few questions. I gave him a book someone gave me when I first came to Christ."

"You really are a Christian now, aren't you?"

"Yes," he said with a nod. "I really am."

Joy filled her heart. "That's the best news ever."

❧

He stood and watched her for a moment until a customer entered. That gave him an excuse to edge toward the door. After he said good-bye, he overheard her asking questions about the needs of the bride-to-be, and he was impressed with her subtle salesmanship. Cindi handled each customer as if she was the most important person in Cindi's life. It was obvious she truly loved what she did, and it was the perfect work for her. He went straight to the real estate office and asked for Fran.

While he waited, he flipped through some of the residential booklets and spotted a couple of houses that appealed to him. Fran came out ten minutes later.

"Hi, Jeremy. What can I help you with?" she said as she clasped her hands together. "I have an appointment in about an hour, but if you'd like to come back to my office, I can spare a few minutes."

He followed her through the maze of offices until they reached her tiny office with the window overlooking Peachtree Street. He sat down in the chair across from her desk.

"I'd like to start looking at other businesses," he said right off the bat.

"Are you still interested in the bridal shop?"

He paused then said, "Not at the moment. I need to see how things work out between the owner and me."

She leaned forward and leveled him with a concerned look. "I don't normally recommend potential buyers spend so much time talking to the sellers, but when I realized the two of you knew each other from a long time ago, I didn't say anything."

Jeremy nodded. "I'm beginning to think it might have been a huge mistake for me to keep going over there. She might be getting the wrong idea about my intentions. It's hard for me to forget how I used to be, but I know now that I need to leave my old, immature self behind. I don't think I really want to buy the shop anymore. All I want is to buy a good business, boost the earnings, then sell it for a big profit."

He saw Fran's glance dart to something behind him, so he quickly turned around. There stood Elizabeth looking down at him with a scowl on her face, and he fidgeted, wondering if he'd done something wrong.

Chapter 8

"Elizabeth," he said with a smile. "What are you doing here?"

She didn't smile back. "I just came to talk to my friend who works here. She said you were with Fran, so I wanted to stop by to say hi." Her eyes had narrowed, and she was still scowling.

"Are you okay?" he asked, hoping she'd let him know what was going on.

Instead, she shook her head. "I almost believed you."

Fran looked back and forth between Jeremy and Elizabeth, then stood. "I'll leave the two of you alone so you can talk."

Elizabeth shook her head. "That's not necessary. I've heard all I need to hear."

Jeremy stood up to leave. Something strange was happening here, and he didn't want to make it worse.

As she made her way to the door, Elizabeth turned to him. "Don't bother following me. I don't have anything else to say to you."

❧

Cindi had just taken out the last of the shipment and hung it to be steamed. When she heard the door, she turned and saw Elizabeth moving toward her with a mission.

"I was right about Jeremy Hayden."

"What?" Cindi said, confused. "What happened?"

Elizabeth was clearly out of breath. She stood there, her chest heaving as she tried to compose herself. Finally, she let out a deep breath and said, "Be careful!"

"You're not making a bit of sense, Elizabeth. Tell me what's going on."

Cindi guided Elizabeth toward the love seat and encouraged her to explain what had happened. Then she listened as Elizabeth told her about the encounter with Jeremy at Fran's office.

"You were right," she said. "He was still planning to buy and sell your shop."

"You've been saying that all along, so why are you so upset now?"

"He so much as admitted to Fran that you were getting the wrong idea about his intentions and all he wanted to do was turn a profit after boosting the earnings. He's playing games with you just to make a buck."

A sense of dread washed over Cindi. She'd just started letting down her guard with Jeremy.

Elizabeth looked up and shook her head. "He's super slick."

"Okay, so what now?" Cindi asked.

"Since he has a history of being too charming for a nice girl like you, I suggest you avoid him at all costs. He isn't any different now from when he dumped—" She stopped midsentence.

Cindi lifted her eyebrows. "That's virtually impossible."

"I'll tell him to get lost if you want me to," Elizabeth offered.

"No," Cindi said. "I don't want to react to anything he does. That'll make him think I'm weak. I can still talk to him."

"I don't want to see you get hurt again," Elizabeth said softly.

"I realize that," Cindi replied as she turned to her friend and smiled. "I'll be careful, but I don't want to turn my back on him, now that he's at least going to church."

Elizabeth paused then nodded. "You're right. Just remember you can count on me to run interference if needed."

Cindi belted out a laugh. "I've never doubted you'd do that for me. Now let's get back to work. We have a crazy day ahead of us, and it looks like it might be that way for the remainder of the week."

Their next appointment involved a family—bride, mother-of-the-bride, aunt on her mother's side, very young aunt on the groom's side, her sister, the groom's sister, and a couple of very wiggly, giggly flower girls from both sides of the family. In spite of the extra time they required, this was one of Cindi's favorite scenarios. She loved the dynamics of the blended families, and she found the children delightful.

"Mommy, I want this dress!" one of the little girls shouted across the store. "Can I have this dress? It looks like a princess dress."

The other girl looked at it before turning to Cindi. "I'm a flower girl, and so is she." The sassiness in her voice was funny, but Cindi could tell this one was a handful.

"How fun!" Cindi said. She looked up at the bride-to-be. "I'll get Elizabeth to work with the flower girls, and then I'll help you all. Did you want them in long white dresses?"

The bride glanced at her mother, who nodded. "I'm pretty open."

Elizabeth grinned at the little girls. "Let's go try on a bunch of princess dresses, and we'll see what looks best, okay?"

"Oh, goody! We get to play dress up!"

Cindi asked the bride all the pertinent questions, such as what style wedding dress she wanted and what colors she wanted her bridesmaids to wear. Cindi sensed the bride was overwhelmed by all the choices, so she leaned toward the woman. "You don't have to make a decision today," she whispered.

The bride smiled at her and nodded. "Thanks."

All the pressure had been lifted, so the bride and her entourage finally enjoyed trying on dresses. The women chattered while the little girls squealed and giggled.

Cindi had to rescue a couple of the mannequins from the children, but she didn't mind. They were excited, and they brought such joy and fun energy to the room. She'd always enjoyed being around children.

"Here are some wedding gown brochures." Cindi handed them to the bride. When she saw that the other women looked left out, she handed them some brochures from the designer the bride seemed to prefer.

The groom's aunt looked startled for a split second, then straightened up. "Oh, thanks," she said as she took it.

Cindi gave the bride her card and told her to call back by the end of the day to schedule the second appointment. As the bridal party left, Cindi glanced at Elizabeth, who made a face and pointed to the corner of the room.

She looked in the direction Elizabeth pointed and saw Jeremy standing there, arms folded, looking amused. How long had he been watching?

Once the women were gone, he slowly ambled to the counter. "You did an amazing job once again, Cindi. I continue to be impressed."

"Give me a break," Elizabeth said.

Jeremy and Cindi both snapped around to face her. Cindi realized her friend was feeling protective of her, but she needed to hold back the sarcasm.

"Excuse me for a minute, Jeremy," Cindi said as she took Elizabeth by the arm and ushered her into the fitting room. Once she had her friend alone, she turned to her. "Let me handle him, okay?"

"It annoys me that he thinks he can wear you down," Elizabeth argued.

Cindi loved that about Elizabeth, but she could take care of herself. "I know, but remember he can't wear me down unless I let him." She looked around the room at some of the mess left behind by the last group. "Why don't you take care of reboxing those shoes, and I'll join you to get this place straightened up after I get rid of Jeremy."

"Be strong," Elizabeth said as Cindi left the room.

"What was that all about?" Jeremy asked.

Cindi crossed her arms and looked him in the eye. This was no time for mincing words. "She's trying to protect me."

"From what?"

"You."

The expression on his face went from confused to understanding. "I thought she'd finally warmed up to me, but she hasn't, has she?"

"Not at all."

"That's not good." He looked around the room while Cindi continued staring at him. He looked very uncomfortable. Almost a minute later, he finally settled his gaze on her. "Why don't we—the two of us—get together and talk?"

"We can talk now," Cindi said as she glanced at her watch. "I don't have another appointment for a while."

The phone rang, so she excused herself to answer it since Elizabeth was still in the fitting room. She answered some questions then turned back to Jeremy.

He tilted his head forward. "I think we need to go somewhere else without the distractions. How about tonight after work. Got plans for tonight?"

"Uh. . ." She didn't have plans, and she didn't want to lie, but the very thought of going somewhere alone with him worried her. His mere presence sent her senses into a spin.

"Or another night this week. I don't want to put you on the spot. I just want to let you know what's going on with me and what I've decided. And I think there are a few other things we need to discuss."

Cindi took a step back and thought it over while he silently waited. It was unnerving having him standing there so close scrutinizing her every move. If going somewhere to talk meant removing the distraction of him always popping in like this, she figured she needed to agree.

"Okay, tonight will be just fine. Want to meet somewhere?"

A smile played on his lips. "How about Chastain Park?"

Suddenly she felt herself go numb. Chastain Park was where they used to go when they were teenagers. And it was where he first kissed her.

"How about someplace else?" she asked.

He narrowed his gaze. "What's wrong with Chastain Park?"

"Nothing." She didn't want to let on how she'd clung to certain memories, so she fidgeted behind the counter, pretending to look for something. "We can meet at Chastain Park if it's so important to you."

"How about we meet at the playground by the pavilion?"

She swallowed deeply. That was the exact spot where he first kissed her. Without looking him in the eye, she said, "Okay, we can meet there, but not for long."

"I understand. You're a busy woman."

She couldn't tell if he was serious or if he was being sarcastic. "I really need to get back to work, Jeremy. Elizabeth is closing up tonight, so I can leave around five thirty."

"See you at six, then," he said. "Oh, and don't make plans for dinner. There's a wonderful place I'd like to take you."

Before she had a chance to tell him she wasn't available for dinner, he left. Elizabeth came out of the fitting room.

"Well?" she asked.

❧

Jeremy was fully aware he had one shot at showing Cindi his integrity after the way Elizabeth had acted. Something new had happened, and he aimed to find out what it was. Also, it was time to let Cindi know what happened many years ago, but he wasn't sure if she wanted to hear it.

He pulled out his phone and punched in his mother's work number. She answered immediately.

"Mom, do you mind if I bring a guest home for dinner?"

"Of course I don't mind. I'm cooking stew in the Crock-Pot, though. It's nothing special."

"I think that's pretty special. I'll stop somewhere and get bread and dessert. Anything else you need?"

"No." There were a few seconds of silence before she asked, "Is it Cindi?"

"Yes."

"That's good. I like her."

"Yes, I know."

"Maybe one of these days you'll feel like you can trust me enough to let me in on the details of what happened between you two."

He didn't feel like explaining anything, so he mumbled a few words then told her he had to run. After he flipped his phone shut, he went back to Fran's office. She wasn't in, so he left a message that he'd be in touch the next day.

Jeremy went to his parents' condo and ran the vacuum. His mother worked hard all day, and he didn't want her to feel as if she had to do additional work when she got home. As things changed, he wanted to adapt and make the lives of his loved ones easier. He hadn't always been that way, and he felt the need to make up for those times.

After the place was clean, he ran out for bread, dessert, and drinks. Then he got ready for his date. . . . *No, better not think about it that way.* For his *meeting* with Cindi.

❧

Cindi's nerves were on edge when she arrived at Chastain Park. She parked her car and headed straight to their meeting spot. Not much appeared to have changed since she'd last been here. Chastain Park was huge, and she'd been to a couple of concerts at the amphitheater, but this was the first time she'd been back to this spot. *Their* spot.

She was a few minutes early, so she hoped she'd get there first. However, once she got closer, she saw Jeremy standing there waiting—a flower in his hand. Her heart fluttered.

Chapter 9

I remembered how much you like white roses," he said as he extended the flower.

She hesitated before reaching out to take it. "Thank you," she said softly.

"How was work since I last saw you? Did you have a calm afternoon?"

Cindi chuckled. "It's all relative. It was calmer than what you saw, but there were a few tense moments when a bride changed her mind about a dress after it was altered."

"That's not good."

"We've had this sort of thing happen before, and you're right—it's not a good thing. Once a dress has been altered, most vendors won't let us send it back, so we're stuck."

His forehead crinkled. "So you're stuck with the dress?"

"Not this time, fortunately. She told us what she wanted different, and we managed to reconfigure the dress to her liking."

"It's good you can do that," he said.

Again, Cindi laughed. "It's good Elizabeth can do that. Not a day goes by that I'm not thankful for her fabulous seamstress skills. She can make almost any alteration and customize dresses so brides feel they're having gowns made especially for them."

Cindi wondered when they'd cut the small talk and get to whatever he wanted to discuss with her. Her feelings were mixed. In a way, she wanted to get whatever it was over with, but she didn't feel like confronting anything distasteful.

She looked up at him in time to see a familiar gaze—identical to the one they'd shared right before he told her he loved her.

"It's a nice evening, isn't it?" He reached out and touched her cheek with the back of his hand.

"Yes, it's a very nice evening," she said as she looked at the ground. Each time she looked at him in this setting, old memories flashed through her mind.

❧

Jeremy felt Cindi might be warming up to him, but as quickly as she looked up at him, she seemed nervous. "What are you thinking, Cindi?"

Without missing a beat, she asked, "Why did you want me to meet you here?"

"There are some things I needed to explain."

Cindi took a step back and folded her arms. "Okay, so start explaining."

He saw the distrust on her face. "Do you remember what I told you the first time we were here?"

She wanted to deny she remembered anything, but she couldn't. With a slight nod, she sniffled.

"I meant it then, and I mean it now."

"How can you say that, Jeremy, after what you did to me later?"

He tightened his jaw. This was one of the most difficult things he'd ever done in his life—but still not as hard as letting her go.

"When I told you I didn't love you anymore, I was lying. I just wanted you to be free to pursue your dreams."

"So you said. That's ridiculous."

"Is it?" he asked as he lowered his head and held her gaze.

"It makes no sense. We were supposedly in love. Everything was going just fine."

"For you, maybe. You had colleges begging you to attend."

She snickered. "Not really begging me. I just got accepted to a few that I applied to."

"That's what I'm talking about," he said. "I had nothing. No college. No hopes for the future. No dreams."

"Everyone has hopes and dreams."

"Trust me when I tell you this, Cindi. I had no idea what I'd do the day after graduation, let alone for the rest of my life. I figured if I didn't let you go, I'd be holding you back from a prosperous life."

"You've been at least as prosperous as I have," she replied.

"Maybe. But I didn't know it would turn out this way back then."

She shrugged. "Okay, so now what?"

"I'm not sure. But I'd like to find out if we can bring back something we once had."

She tilted her head and looked at him before her lips turned up at the corners into a smile. "Let me think about it, okay?"

"Fair enough," he agreed. "Want to go for a walk?"

She lifted one shoulder then let it drop as she offered a slight grin. "Sure, why not?"

They meandered around a small area of the park and talked about anything that came to mind. She was a great conversationalist, something he remembered about her from high school. In fact, it was one of the many things he'd loved about her.

"So tell me more about how you came to faith," she said.

He told her all about his commanding officer's gentle witness and how he'd been willing to answer even the most basic of questions. She nodded and interjected a few comments, which let him know she was really listening. He could tell when she softened toward him because she looked at him with more trust than he'd seen since they were teenagers.

"That's a really nice story," she said after he told her about his Christian journey. "How about your parents? When did they start going to church?"

"Just recently. In fact, your church is the first one they've gone to since I can remember."

"You're kidding." She looked sincerely surprised. "They seem comfortable."

"Yeah, I noticed that, too." He stopped walking and reached out to turn her toward him. "Cindi. . ."

A brief look of fear came over her face as she took a step back, so he didn't finish his sentence. He'd been about to tell her he was comfortable, too—both in church and when he was with her. But based on the look she gave him, now wasn't the time.

Instead, he chose a different topic. "Are you hungry?"

A quick giggle escaped her lips. "Hungry?" She visibly relaxed, and her fearful look faded. "You've always thought about food."

"Yeah, well, maybe so, but food's important. I'd like to take you someplace special."

"I don't know," she said. "I really don't feel like eating out tonight."

"This is sort of like not eating out."

"You're talking in riddles, Jeremy. Where do you want to take me?"

"My folks'."

"Um, I don't think that's such a good idea." She shifted her weight from one foot to the other as she appeared to grow uncomfortable again.

"I thought you liked my parents. My mom adores you."

Cindi smiled as she looked back at him. "I think your parents are very nice people. What I don't understand, though, is why you want to take me to their place."

He shrugged. "I thought it would be a nice thing for all of us."

"What have your parents been up to—besides going to church?"

Jeremy could hear the caring tone of her voice. Cindi had never looked down on him or his family, while other kids in school had made him feel bad because he wasn't as well off as most of them. Cindi treated him and his parents as if she didn't see any difference at all.

"They're doing a lot better, now that they're both working. They sold our old house and bought a nice condo a few years ago."

Cindi offered a sincere smile. "That's great. Your parents are good people."

"Then come have dinner with us. I called my mom and told her I was inviting you, and she was delighted."

"I *could* get mad about that," Cindi said with a throaty chuckle, "but I choose to be flattered instead." She paused for a moment before adding, "Okay, I'll go. But I want to bring something."

"You don't have to. I got bread and dessert to go with the meal she's been cooking in the Crock-Pot all day."

"I'm not going empty-handed."

"Fine. We can stop at the grocery store on the way. Why don't you leave your car here, and I can bring you back?"

She bought a basket of fruit to leave with them. "I remember your mother always put an apple in your lunch every day."

He laughed. "Yeah, she believed that old saying about an apple a day and the doctor."

"I believe that, too." Then she grew quiet as he took the last turn onto his parents' street.

Instinctively, he reached over and placed his hand on hers. She looked at him in surprise, but she didn't pull her hand out of his. It felt so right, he didn't ever want to move. Finally, he reluctantly withdrew his hand to maneuver his car into the driveway.

"Ready?" he asked.

She offered a quick nod then opened the door and got out. He ran around and escorted her to the open front door where his mother stood waiting.

"Hi, Mrs. Hayden," Cindi said. "It's really nice to see you again."

His mother opened her arms and pulled Cindi in for a long embrace. "You've become quite a beautiful young woman. I'm glad my son got in touch with you so I could see for myself."

"I brought this for you." Cindi handed his mother the fruit basket.

Jeremy ushered them all inside as his mother protested that she wasn't expecting a gift, but Cindi told her she was happy to bring it. Warmth flooded him from his head to his toes as he realized how much it meant to him to have his two favorite women together.

"So this is the girl you should have married."

All heads turned toward the booming voice at the foot of the stairs. "Now, James, you shouldn't embarrass them. Cindi's our guest for dinner."

"I know," he continued, "it's just that—"

"Dad." Jeremy was angry with his father, but he forced himself to keep his voice low and his temper cool. He didn't want to make Cindi squirm any more than she was now.

His father darted a glance over at Cindi then looked back at him. "Sorry, son, I guess that was uncalled for." He looked back at Cindi. "I like your church. The people seem pretty nice, and that preacher is a mighty interesting fella, even if he is young enough to be my son."

"Yes," Cindi said as she visibly relaxed. Jeremy was relieved she could recover so quickly. "He's good at holding our interest without losing the message we all need to hear."

"I think we just might keep going back." He rubbed his neck. "What's for dinner, Donna? I had a rough day, and I'm starving."

꩜

Cindi remembered how kind, spontaneous, and full of life Jeremy's parents were, and they hadn't changed a bit. Every occasion in their home was centered around food, something she could tell hadn't changed. No wonder Jeremy was always thinking about his next meal. His mother had always been very gracious and sweet, while his father was loud but deep down was a softy. They weren't as well off as most of the people in the area, but they had heart.

And they were still together, unlike her own parents.

After dinner, Cindi joined Jeremy's mother in the kitchen. "Go sit out there with the guys," the older woman said.

"What guys?" Jeremy asked as he rolled up his sleeves. "You mean Dad?" He took the stack of plates from his mother. "Why don't both of you go in there while I take care of the kitchen?"

"But it's a mess," his mother argued.

He looked around. "It's not that bad. Now shoo."

With a giggle, Mrs. Hayden took Cindi by the hand and led her to the living room where Mr. Hayden sat staring at the TV with the remote control in his lap. Without even glancing up, he bellowed, "Tell me all about college."

Cindi felt awkward and didn't know what to say, so she was grateful when Mrs. Hayden piped up, "She's been out of college for a long time, James." She glanced at Cindi. "What has it been—something like five years now?"

"Almost seven," Cindi corrected her.

Mrs. Hayden grinned as she turned back to her husband. "She's a businesswoman now."

"Okay," he said, shaking his head and giving them a silly look. "So tell me about business. I'm tired of talking about stuff that doesn't matter, but the wife gets mad when I don't behave at the table."

Cindi opened her mouth to answer, but again, Mrs. Hayden spoke for her. "She owns a bridal shop. You know that, James. I bet business is always good at that kind of place. Girls are always getting married."

"So what would you know about a bridal shop?" he asked Cindi. "You ever get married?"

"Um. . .no, sir," Cindi replied. Now she was more uncomfortable than ever. "I sort of learned the business as I went. I worked for a couple of years in retail after college and learned a little about working with customers. I lived with my parents, then got a roommate after college to save money." She didn't tell him about the humongous bank loans her parents cosigned for. She was thankful she'd been able to pay them off quickly.

"Well, I guess that's okay. So what all do you do at your bridal shop?"

Mrs. Hayden winked at her before turning to her husband. "She sells bridal gowns and bridesmaid dresses, silly."

"I think that's great. How much is a bridal gown, anyway?"

Cindi knew he was just making conversation, but the questions were starting to sound rude. She gave Mrs. Hayden a look for help. To her relief, the woman came to her rescue.

"That's not something you need to know, James. It's part of the bridal mystique."

He made a grumbling noise. "That just means they're way too expensive. Otherwise, you'd tell me. If brides had a lick of sense, they'd rent their dresses just like the guys do their tuxes."

Cindi could have told him there actually were bridal gown rental shops, but she didn't want to get into all the reasons she wouldn't recommend them. Instead, she focused her attention on Mrs. Hayden.

"Dinner was delicious. I didn't know what to expect when Jeremy told me he wanted to take me someplace special."

Tears instantly formed in Mrs. Hayden's eyes. "He said that? What a sweet thing to say."

Jeremy appeared at the door wiping his hands on a dish towel. "Let me know when you're ready to go, and I'll take you back to your car."

Cindi stood. "Since we all have to work tomorrow, I'd better head out now. It was very nice seeing both of y'all again. Stop by the shop sometime."

Mrs. Hayden's eyes lit up, and she nodded. "I'd love to!"

Mr. Hayden grumbled, but then he stood and took her hand. "You're a good girl, Cindi. I'm glad you came over tonight."

On the way back to the park, Jeremy slipped a CD in the car stereo, and the strains of contemporary Christian music filled the air. Neither of them said anything until they were almost at the Chastain Park parking lot. Cindi was the first to talk.

"Thanks for bringing me to your parents' house. It was really nice."

"They love you, ya know. My mother was upset when we. . ." He cleared his throat then shrugged. "Anyway, maybe the two of you can chat after church sometime."

"I'd like that." After he stopped beside her car, she opened the door, got out, leaned over, and said, "If you want to come by the shop and see me sometime, well, maybe. . ."

His face lit up. "You can count on it."

That night she thought about everything that had happened and all Jeremy had said. Could it be possible she was wrong about him? What he'd done made sense in a childish sort of way—and since they were both children when it happened, she could understand. Jeremy seemed sincere in his faith, so that obviously put a different light on things. However, would she ever be able to forgive him for leaving her so brokenhearted?

The next morning when she got to the shop, Elizabeth was in the sewing room deeply immersed in alterations. She glanced up and waved. "How was last night?"

Cindi saw she wasn't smiling. "It was fun. I met Jeremy, and he took me to dinner at his parents' house."

"Oh my. He's pulling out all the stops, isn't he?"

"I've always liked his parents—especially his mom."

"So," Elizabeth said as she lowered the foot behind the sewing machine needle and flipped off the light switch, "what lines did he feed you to try to get you to sell him the shop?"

"No lines. We didn't talk about him buying the shop."

"I'm sure he's just waiting for the right time."

"Maybe, maybe not."

"Please, please don't fall for his charm again. You were so hurt before, and I'd hate for it to happen again."

Cindi nodded. "I appreciate your concern more than you know. I just see things differently now, so I'm fine. Even if he's got a hidden agenda, I can handle it."

There was nothing Elizabeth could say to that. She hung up the dress she'd been working on and joined Cindi at the desk. By the time the first appointment walked in, they were a cohesive team.

Jeremy showed up at noon. "Want some lunch?" he asked. He'd obviously inherited his mother's penchant for feeding people.

"Not today," Cindi replied. "I brought a sandwich I'll have to eat on the run. Are you trying to make me fat?"

"You look great, Cindi."

She felt her cheeks heat up. "Thank you."

"Maybe tomorrow?"

"Maybe." The phone rang, so she answered it.

He chatted with Elizabeth while she talked to the caller. Elizabeth still didn't believe him, and Cindi appreciated the fact that she was making an effort for her sake. After Cindi hung up, he said good-bye then left.

"I can say one thing for him," Elizabeth said once he was gone. "He's persistent."

"Which is probably why he's been so successful in business."

Jeremy stopped by a few more times that week. Cindi eventually gave in and went out with him. Elizabeth finally quit commenting, which was almost as bad as the interrogation. Cindi knew her friend still didn't trust him, but she was holding everything inside.

On Thursday morning Jeremy didn't show up. "This seems strange," Elizabeth said. "We never know when he's coming, so it's like we're always expecting him."

"I've found if I don't expect anything, I'm never disappointed," Cindi replied.

By the end of the day, Cindi was exhausted. Fran arrived just as they were about to leave. "Oh, good," she said. "You're still here. I just got a call from someone who's interested in taking a look at the shop."

Cindi's heart fell. "That's good." She was too tired to hide her remorse.

Fran frowned. "You do still want to sell, don't you?"

"Yes, of course. It's just been a long day, and I'm tired."

"If it's okay with you, then, I'll bring them by tomorrow around noon."

"Them?" Cindi paused.

"Yes, the prospects are a couple of newlyweds who think this will be the perfect way to work together."

Elizabeth laughed. "Fancy that. A married couple who want to be together."

Cindi didn't miss the sarcasm. "Noon is fine."

"See you then," Fran said as she curiously glanced back and forth between Cindi and Elizabeth.

Once she was gone, Cindi stood and stared at the door of her shop. Elizabeth reached out and gently touched her shoulder.

"Having second thoughts about selling?"

"Sort of." Cindi stuck the key in the lock, turned it, and spun around to face Elizabeth. "But I'm sure that's normal. Now let's go home and get some rest. We have to impress some prospective buyers tomorrow."

The next morning, Cindi got to the shop before Elizabeth arrived. She changed a couple of the mannequins and rearranged the accessories case to give it a fresher look. Then she stepped back and admired her work. She'd miss many things about the business once she sold it, and this was one of them. It truly made her happy to help bring out a woman's pure beauty on her wedding day. Times like this made her stop and think—maybe she shouldn't sell. She still loved running her shop.

When the door opened, she expected it to be Elizabeth, but it wasn't. It was her mother.

"Mom, hi! What are you doing here?"

Her mother looked around and then turned to her. "The place looks really nice, Cindi. I just stopped by to see if you had plans for later. We need to talk." She gulped and added, "It's very important."

Cindi checked the appointment book to make sure she could leave early before replying, "I think Elizabeth will probably be able to stay until closing, and our last scheduled appointment is at three. I think I can be out of here by four."

Her mother's lips twitched as she nodded. "That'll be great. Have you spoken to your father lately?"

Slowly shaking her head, Cindi replied, "Not in several weeks. Why?"

"I'll tell you later."

Elizabeth walked in and gave Cindi's mother a hug. "Come by and see us more often, Reba," Elizabeth said.

"I just might do that. And if you're ever looking for someone to work part-time, I'm interested."

"What?" Cindi said.

"Look, Cindi, I've got to run. I'll see you this afternoon. I'll run by your place. . .four thirty?"

"Sounds good," Cindi said.

Once she was gone, Elizabeth tilted her head. "What was that all about?"

"I have no idea. I'll find out at four thirty if you can hang out here and close the shop."

"Yes, of course." Elizabeth opened the door to the sewing room then turned to face Cindi. "Looks like it'll be an eventful day for you."

"Certainly seems that way."

"Maybe this couple will be exactly what this shop needs," Elizabeth said with slow deliberation.

An odd sensation of internal free-falling came over Cindi. She turned away so Elizabeth wouldn't see her expression.

Chapter 10

Jeremy hesitated before heading toward Cindi's shop. She'd encouraged him to stop by to see her, something he'd been doing all along. However, he sensed a turning point in their relationship, and he wasn't sure if it was too soon.

And then there was Elizabeth. Cindi had warmed toward him, but it was painfully obvious Elizabeth didn't like him. He couldn't blame her, though—if someone had hurt one of his friends, he would have been just as protective. Perhaps a complete breakup hadn't been the right move, but he was just a kid, and that was all he knew to do at the time. He decided he'd given her enough time to work through things and it was time to talk to her about whatever issues she still had with him.

For nights he'd stared at the ceiling, unable to sleep, wondering what he'd been thinking. He couldn't erase Cindi from his mind—from the happy moments with her glowing smile to the look of despair when he'd told her he wanted his class ring back. It had taken every ounce of self-restraint to hold himself back when she refused to look at him again.

The army had been good for him. Not only did it provide him with a modest living, but he learned how to be a man. Fortunately for him, his commanding officer saw his need for Christ, which proved nothing was impossible for the Lord.

His candy store job was obviously not a career position, but the Lord had allowed him to be at the right place when the opportunity to make something of himself had come open. After buying it, he learned how to run a business the hard way. When he was twenty-six, he was listed as one of the youngest businessmen to watch in the state of Georgia. And now at twenty-nine, he was ready to settle down and stop trying to prove himself.

He was good at what he did and he enjoyed it, but traveling all over Georgia was wearing on him. It was time to go home to Atlanta and settle down. He'd now sold all of his businesses, with the exception of a men's shop in Savannah and a tire store in Macon.

An overwhelming urge to see Cindi again gave him the strength to head to her boutique. He'd have to be patient with Elizabeth and prove he'd changed.

As he pulled up in front of the bridal boutique, he saw Elizabeth by the window looking out. She looked his way then disappeared. His heart hammered as he thought about how he still felt toward Cindi.

"Hey, Elizabeth," he said as he entered the store.

"Hi." She forced a smile then went back to her paperwork.

"Is Cindi here yet?"

She lifted an eyebrow. "Not yet. Is there anything I can help you with?"

At least she was talking to him, but she didn't bother trying to hide her feelings. He decided to try to make small talk for a few minutes—partly to get a feel for how to win over the best friend of the woman he loved, but mostly to kill time until Cindi arrived. "How long have you been working with Cindi?"

She sighed. "Practically all my life."

"You make a great team."

"So we've been told."

Okay, so this wasn't going well at all. He racked his brain to try to think of another subject. "By the way," he began, "I've been thinking about that day in Fran's office."

Elizabeth turned to him, snorted, and shook her head. "Yeah, I think about that day myself."

"I'm not sure what happened—"

He was cut off when he heard a door close from the back of the store; then Cindi appeared. "Hey, you two." She glanced over at Elizabeth. "Any calls from the Hansen-Showers bridal party?"

"Not yet." Elizabeth's voice was still clipped.

Cindi gave her a puzzled look then turned to Jeremy with a smile. "We used to have a wedding season, but things are changing. There's almost an equal balance of weddings year-round these days."

Jeremy could take a hint. She was busy, but she didn't want to tell him to get lost. "I just wanted to stop by on my way to Fran's. She's supposed to line up some other businesses for me to look at."

He couldn't help but notice her quick gasp and odd expression. She recovered quickly and smiled. "I hope all goes well. I really need to get to work, though. See you later?"

"Sure." He lifted a hand in a wave and left the shop. The silence that fell behind him made him wonder what the women were thinking.

❧

"He must want this shop pretty badly to keep coming by like this," Elizabeth said as they stood in front of the open refrigerator staring at all the food.

Cindi sighed. "I'm not so sure I want to sell now, but if I do, I'm thinking he might be okay."

"How about that other couple Fran's supposed to bring by at noon?"

"I don't know them. I know Jeremy."

"I thought y'all decided to move on," Elizabeth argued. "He agreed to look for something else, and you're not selling to someone who won't be here to run it. How can you do that?"

With a shrug, Cindi replied, "No one else has made an offer. Besides, Jeremy just might have changed."

"Don't tell him that yet, okay?" Elizabeth pleaded. "I don't want to take any chances."

Cindi thought about how she had Elizabeth to think about as well as herself, so she shook her head no. "You're right. I'm not really in that big of a hurry anymore. I'll give it a little more time. Who knows? I might just keep it a little longer."

Fran brought the young prospects by the shop at the precise moment a difficult bride went on a tirade about none of the dresses fitting. The expression on the wife's face was priceless. Cindi wasn't surprised when the couple politely said they'd talk about it and have Fran get back with her.

"Looks like no sale," Elizabeth whispered.

"And that's probably a good thing," Cindi agreed. "If something that minor turns her off, she has no business owning a bridal shop."

"So true."

The next couple of hours were much calmer. Then a few minutes after three o'clock, Christina, one of the brides who'd gotten married a couple of months earlier, came in with her wedding photo proofs. "I wanted you to see how pretty all the girls looked," she said, "and Jonathan loved my gown. He said it was the prettiest wedding dress he'd ever seen."

"He would have said that no matter what you wore," Cindi said as she studied the pictures. "But you do look beautiful."

"Thanks to you two, I didn't have to worry about any of the dresses," Christina said. "I've heard some horror stories from my friends who got their dresses elsewhere."

"So how's your marriage?"

Christina sighed as a dreamy expression crossed her face. "The best."

After Christina left, Cindi saw Elizabeth staring at her. "Okay, I know what you're thinking. This is more proof that I need to keep the shop."

"You said it—I didn't," Elizabeth said. Her expression changed and became contemplative. "I wonder what's up with your mother."

Cindi grimaced. "I wish I knew. I'm worried about her."

"I've been praying for your parents. . .and you. I know how difficult this must be."

"Yeah, when your parents spring that kind of news on you, it's pretty jolting."

"Why don't you go on home now? I can take care of the shop from now on."

Cindi grabbed her keys and purse and headed home, where she immediately put on a fresh pot of coffee. By the time her mother arrived, the coffee was done.

"Who gave you the rose?" her mother asked as she leaned over and sniffed the single bloom in the vase in the middle of the kitchen table.

"Jeremy."

Her mom froze, eyes wide. Finally, she raised her eyebrows and said, "Jeremy? As in Jeremy Hayden?"

"The one and only."

"I heard he was in town. When did you see him?"

Cindi touched a finger on one hand and said, "Yesterday"; then she touched the next finger. "And the day before yesterday, and the day before that."

"So what's going on between you two?" Her mother poured herself a cup of coffee then sat down at the kitchen table. "I heard he was looking to buy a business and a house."

"For such a big city, word sure does travel fast," Cindi said.

"Well, it helps to know the Realtor's sister."

"I'll tell you all about it, but not until you let me know what's going on with you."

Her mother inhaled and then slowly blew out her breath. She shut her eyes for a couple of seconds the way she always did when she needed to gather her thoughts. "Your father and I have agreed to go to counseling. We're taking things slowly, but we'd like to try working on our problems."

Cindi's mood lifted instantly. "Really? That's wonderful news. When did you decide to do that?"

"A couple of weeks ago he stopped by to pick up a few things. I'd just baked a casserole, and since he hadn't eaten supper yet, I. . .well, I asked him to join me. You know how much I hate to eat alone."

"Yes," Cindi said as she leaned toward her mother. "So he ate dinner with you?"

Her mother nodded and smiled. "We had the best time, too. I'd forgotten what a great conversationalist he is."

Cindi shook her head. "What do you think happened?"

"I'm not sure, but the counselor I called said it was fairly common for couples to split up once the children are gone."

"And Daddy agreed to go to counseling?" Amazing.

"Yes, that's the best part. He said he'd been thinking about working things out, but he didn't know how to bring it up, and he was glad I took the first step." She fidgeted for a few seconds then looked at Cindi. "You know how your father's pride is."

"Yes, I remember that."

"I'm feeling pretty good about things. I hope you're happy."

Cindi let out a sigh of joy. "You couldn't have brought better news that would have made me any happier."

"Please pray for us, honey. I never stopped loving your father, and I want this to work out."

"Trust me, Mom, I'll pray night and day. I want it to work out as much as you do."

"Now tell me what's going on with your shop."

Cindi explained how she felt and why she was still selling. The whole time she talked, her mother never interjected a word until Cindi finally said, "What are you thinking?"

"I think you're making a huge mistake. You've always dreamed of running a bridal shop, and you're living your dream. How many other people can say that?"

"You of all people should understand why I don't want to perpetuate a myth—a fantasy that marriage is so wonderful."

"To be honest with you," her mother said softly, "it's as wonderful as a couple makes it. If two people keep their focus on the Lord and their family, they can work through almost anything. Being married to your father was almost like living my own fairy tale until one day everything seemed out of place."

"I still don't understand why you split up."

"Ya know, I'm not sure, either, but maybe we needed a little time apart to realize how good we had it together. The Lord let us separate, but don't forget we didn't divorce."

After her mother left, Cindi cleared the dishes and thought about how quickly things could change. She was relieved her parents seemed to be heading in the right direction.

The next day Cindi told Elizabeth about her parents' efforts to reconcile. "I feel so much better now," she admitted.

"Do you feel good enough to keep this place?"

"Maybe."

The conversation ended quickly when a bride came in frazzled and in tears because another bridal shop had messed up her order. "I have to have something by the week after next. Is that even possible?"

Cindi and Elizabeth exchanged a glance before they turned to her, nodding. "Yes, as long as you keep an open mind," Elizabeth said. "We can take one of our sample dresses and customize it for you."

By the time she left, the bride was shedding a different kind of tears—those of joy over the fact that she liked the dress Elizabeth was customizing even more than the one she'd originally found. "I'll tell all my friends about this place," she said. "You two are the very best!"

"That does it," Cindi said. "I think I'll withdraw my listing. I can't imagine letting someone suffer like that poor girl obviously was."

"Attagirl." Elizabeth grinned and nodded. "Back in the saddle and stronger than ever."

The rest of the day went smoothly. Cindi was so happy about her decision, she felt as if she were walking on clouds. Elizabeth kept looking at her and giving her the thumbs-up gesture.

On Sunday Cindi arrived at church early and watched for Jeremy. When she didn't see him by the time the first song began, she focused all her attention on the service. During private prayer time, she thanked the Lord again for her parents' reconciliation and asked for guidance with Jeremy. Her attraction had only grown stronger, yet she wasn't sure what to do.

After the closing benediction, Cindi turned toward the exit. That was when she spotted Jeremy, his mother, his dad, and. . .his brother, Jacob? She hadn't seen Jacob since high school when he'd come home to visit his parents. Jacob was several years older than them. He'd gotten married and moved away, so they didn't see him often.

Fortunately, Jeremy spotted her, so he waited until she could reach them. Jacob leaned over to hug her. "I heard you were doing great," he said. Then he whispered, "You've got my baby brother doing all kinds of things I never thought he'd do."

Cindi thought that was a curious comment. "Like what?"

"Like considering getting into the wedding business."

"Oh." He obviously hadn't told anyone his change of plans. And she hadn't yet gotten around to telling Fran she wanted to withdraw her listing. "I'm not so sure that's what he really wants."

Jacob offered a conspiratorial grin. "I'm positive that's not what he really wants."

Cindi quickly grew very uncomfortable, and she wanted to change the direction of the conversation. "So how are things with you and your wife?"

He cleared his throat and shook his head. "I'm divorced. I've moved back home until I figure out what to do next."

She felt awful. "I'm so sorry—I had no idea."

"I know. Don't worry about it. Just don't make a stupid mistake like I did and think love conquers all."

Jeremy slipped between them and took over the conversation. "We're going to lunch. Want to join us?"

"No, that's okay," she said. "I have other plans. Let's talk later."

The rest of the afternoon, Cindi did a few things she didn't have time to do during the week. Once everything was finished, she went to visit her mother. Her father had just left.

"I was hoping to catch the two of you together," Cindi said. "Why isn't he staying here?"

"We're taking it very slowly," her mother replied. "I think he'll be moving back by the end of the month, though. The counselor has really helped. If you ever decide to get married, I'd highly suggest getting Christian counseling beforehand. That way you can nip problems in the bud before they start."

"Good thinking," Cindi agreed. "From what I've heard, most pastors do premarital counseling these days before they'll perform the ceremony."

"I wish they'd done that back when your father and I got married. We had so many unrealistic expectations that caused problems later on, it's a wonder we stuck it out as long as we did. We still have a couple more counseling sessions, because there are still some issues we haven't resolved."

Cindi heard that, but she chose to assume everything would be just fine. Both of her parents had taken the steps they needed to keep their marriage together, so what could go wrong?

The following week Cindi was faced with all sorts of problems, starting Monday. One of the weddings she'd put quite a bit of time into had been canceled. The groom got cold feet and said he changed his mind, so the bride and her entire wedding party wanted to cancel their orders.

Then the next day one of the brides she'd worked with a couple of years earlier walked in wanting another wedding gown—only this time she wanted tea length because she didn't think it was appropriate to wear a long white gown for a second wedding. Cindi and Elizabeth listened to her go on and on about how different this marriage would be because they were signing prenuptial agreements and they were each keeping their own residence in case things didn't work out.

After she left, Elizabeth shook her head. "How sad for her. She still doesn't know what marriage is all about."

It seemed as though each day brought even more bad news. Within two weeks, Cindi was once again doubting the business she'd once loved. Her emotions were still on edge and very tender.

"Don't let it get you down," Elizabeth said. "Look at your parents. They're working things out."

"Maybe so, but they're still not living together. Apparently my dad isn't sure reconciling is in their best interest. I think he likes seeing my mom but remaining on his own."

"That's silly," Elizabeth said. "What does their counselor say?"

"I wish I knew. Mom's starting to get depressed about it. I think she's even worse off now than she was before they started trying to get back together."

That night her mother called crying. "This is so hard, Cindi. I can't go on like this. I hate living in a state of limbo, not knowing if we'll ever figure out where we went wrong."

Nothing Cindi said could pull her mother out of her depression. The hope she'd had just a few weeks ago went up in a puff of smoke.

The next morning, Cindi stormed into the shop, dropped her purse into the file cabinet, and slammed it shut. "That's it. I'm selling this place. I was right before. A good marriage is just an image."

"Come on, Cindi," Elizabeth begged. "You can't really mean it. At least give it another year or two."

"Nope. I'm getting out while I'm still young enough to find something else, and I don't want to waste another day." She paused to take a breath before adding, "I'm calling Fran to let her know Jeremy can have it—that is, if he's still interested. I might have blown my only chance to get out. At least now I'm convinced Jeremy is on the up-and-up. If he says he'll personally run the shop, then that's what I believe he'll do."

Chapter 11

Jeremy pulled the cell phone out of his pocket, saw it was Fran, and answered it. Fran didn't even bother identifying herself. Instead, she blurted, "Cindi's changed her mind, and she wants to sell you her shop."

"She what?"

"I think you heard right. She said she'll sell the shop to you, and the sooner the better."

"Wait a minute—let me get this straight. Just a couple of weeks ago, she wanted to keep it."

"Yes," Fran said, "I know. So if you still want the shop, you need to act quickly before she changes her mind again."

Cindi was an intelligent woman, so something had obviously happened. He told Fran he'd get back to her by the end of the day after he had some time to think about it.

Immediately after he flipped the phone shut, he started to call Cindi. But before he pushed the SEND button, he changed his mind. He needed to think before reacting. This situation called for something he could count on. He lowered his head and closed his eyes in prayer.

Lord, give me guidance in what to do about this Cindi thing. Granted, her shop is exactly the type of business I'm looking for, but You know I don't want to take advantage of a weak time in her life. If she's meant to keep the place, show her. Make it clear to her. If You want me to have it, then make that clear, as well.

When he opened his eyes, he knew he needed to be patient and pay attention to the answer. The times he'd gone about his business without regard to what he knew the Lord wanted him to do, things had gone awry.

He had business to tie up in Macon, and he wouldn't be back in Atlanta until late in the evening. The manager of his tire store had turned in his resignation the day before, so he was interviewing new candidates. Fortunately, the two very capable assistant managers could run the place without him, and only one of them wanted the lead position. Jeremy planned to promote him and give the other one a raise for doing such a good job of supporting the business. However, he still had a position to fill, and the candidate pool wasn't as deep as it had been the last time he'd needed someone.

At the end of the day, he hadn't found anyone who seemed capable of filling the very big shoes of the assistant manager he was promoting, but he needed to get back to Atlanta. His employees assured him they'd be fine without him, and he had confidence in them.

He left the tire store in Macon at four thirty hoping to get to his parents' place by dinnertime. Normally the drive back to Atlanta took less than two hours, but traffic was slow. He pulled into the driveway after dark and knew his parents would have finished eating by now. Knowing his mother, though, she'd have a plate filled with leftovers ready for him to microwave.

He was right. The instant he walked into the condo, his mother let him know she was worried. "You should have called," she said.

Back when he was a younger man, her fussing annoyed him. Now, however, her concern touched him deeply. "Yes, I know, and I should have. Sorry. I'll do better next time."

She smiled at him. "You're a good boy, Jeremy. I'm proud of who you've become."

After dinner he went up to his room and placed a call to Cindi's house phone. When she didn't answer, he tried her cell phone. Still no answer.

§‰

When Cindi heard the house phone ring, she sank lower into the tub of bubbles. Whoever it was could leave a message, and she'd get back to them when she was finished with her much-needed, relaxing bubble bath. Then her cell phone rang immediately afterward. Maybe it was an emergency.

Knowing she couldn't get to it in time, she slowly rose from the tub, dried off, and wrapped her robe around her. She picked up her cell phone and checked the caller ID. It was Jeremy. She punched in the voice mail number and listened. He said she needed to call him back as soon as she got the message. What could he possibly want that was important enough to call her now?

She toyed with the thought of waiting until the next day to return his call. But what if it really was important?

She got into her pajamas then called his number. He picked up before the end of the first ring.

"Why are you selling the shop?" he asked. "I thought you decided to keep it."

"Is that why you called, Jeremy?"

"Yes. I'm worried about you."

"Do you want it or not?" she asked, trying to ignore how his voice made her feel inside.

"Before I answer that, we need to talk. I'm not about to take something away from you that you need to keep."

Cindi sighed. "Look, Jeremy, it's not up to you to decide what I need to keep. I just had a change of heart, and I've decided my first instinct to sell was what I should have stuck with."

"What happened?"

She didn't want to tell him the details. "I prayed for guidance, and let's just say I got it."

"So you had a setback, huh?"

"More than a setback." Cindi felt herself growing impatient. "Look, Jeremy, I don't want to have to explain every single decision I make. Do you want the shop or not?"

He paused long enough to rattle her. "I'm not sure now. I've been praying, too, and it's not clear to me yet."

Cindi couldn't respond to that immediately. If they were both praying for guidance and they were getting different answers, what did that mean?

Finally, she knew she had to say something. "Then I'll just put it back on the market and let things fall into place."

"With prayer."

"That goes without saying."

She heard him sigh. "If you truly want to sell, I'd like to take you up on your offer and buy it. I'll get with Fran and resubmit my offer."

Cindi felt sick to her stomach. She mumbled a few words then told him she needed to go.

After she got off the phone, Cindi's emotions swirled. She went from being confused to angry to remorseful. Although she was now fairly certain she wanted to sell, doubts still tugged at the back of her mind and heart.

❧

Even though Jeremy doubted Cindi really wanted to sell, all he could think about now was Cindi selling her shop to the wrong person. She'd been worried about him coming in and working the bottom line at the expense of her precious store's integrity. What he did was nothing compared to what he'd seen out there in the business world.

He'd watched successful businesses get milked and then squeezed for the last dime of profit before the profiteer boarded the doors and sent employees scurrying to the unemployment line. Jeremy had never done that—not even once. In fact, in some cases he'd built businesses then sold them to the employees with a generous payback plan. It sickened him to watch others get taken advantage of.

He needed to figure out what had happened to change Cindi's mind and send her back to the Realtor. Her passion for life—the same passion that had attracted him to her in the first place—was the exact same thing that put the spark in what she did with her clients.

Cindi had always been a Christian. Now her love for the Lord gave her a quiet confidence that came through in everything she did—except in one area: her confusion about what to do with her boutique. He had to find out what was going on to make her change her mind so quickly.

In the meantime he called Fran, who advised him not to submit an offer he didn't want to go through with. "She's a very motivated seller now," Fran said. "I have to admit, I'll be glad when she makes up her mind. The other folks in my office are advising me to pull out of the listing, but I'm afraid she'd be taken advantage of by someone else if I did that."

As difficult as it was, Jeremy knew he couldn't pursue this until he got to the heart of the matter. "Let's just hold off for a few days. Hopefully she won't get any more offers until she has time to decide what she really wants to do."

Fran paused then said, "You're quite a man, Jeremy. The Lord has blessed you, and you've honored your faith."

ॐ

When Fran called Cindi and told her Jeremy was holding back his offer, she wasn't surprised, but she was very annoyed. As soon as she got off the phone, she told Elizabeth what had happened.

Elizabeth shook her head. "I wonder what Jeremy's game is. If he really wanted this place, you practically just handed it to him."

"I don't know. He seems to think I'm supposed to keep this place."

"That's one area where I agree with him," Elizabeth said. "But I'm not so sure we have the same motives."

"Does that really matter?"

"Yes, it absolutely does," Elizabeth stated firmly. "And you know it, too. If he's backing out because he truly feels you're supposed to keep this shop, that's one thing. However, if he's trying to pull away from the sale to get you to lower your price, then he's nothing but a...a...." She cleared her throat.

"Don't say it," Cindi said. "I know what you're thinking."

"Well, I suspect his motives aren't as pure and holy as he'd like you to believe. Going to church doesn't make him a good guy."

"True, but after he explained things, I don't think he was ever a bad guy."

Elizabeth lifted her hands in a gesture of exasperation. "How can you be so nice after what he did to you? I remember you cried for days."

Cindi nodded. "Yeah, the breakup hurt me pretty badly."

"And if I remember correctly, he didn't exactly let you down easy. What he said was harsh." Elizabeth tilted her head forward and looked at Cindi from beneath hooded eyes. "What he did then is similar to now, only then it was his love he pulled back. Now it's the offer to buy this place."

Looking down at the floor, Cindi mentally rehashed the scene that had played over and over in her mind for months. Back in high school, Jeremy had told her he loved her every time they were together, and then one day, out of the blue, he said he didn't love her anymore and he wanted his ring back. She begged him to tell her what she'd done, but he never came out and gave her any specifics. He just said they weren't meant to be together. She asked if he'd found another girl, and he shrugged, saying there were lots of other girls. His comment made her sick to her stomach, so she'd run away. Even his explanation about giving her up so she could have the freedom to pursue her dream and go to college seemed lame now.

With a deep sigh, Cindi nodded. "You're right, it was harsh. But we were kids then."

"You know that old saying about a leopard's spots."

Cindi nodded. "There's some merit to that, unless a person has truly accepted Christ. In that case, the saying doesn't count."

"But why take chances with something as important to you as this shop? Maybe Jeremy has changed, and he's a wonderful Christian guy with the best of intentions. But then again, maybe he's the same old person who takes advantage of other people. An opportunist." She paused before adding, "How would you feel if you sold it to him and then a year later he closed the doors after draining all the profit?"

She'd feel as though someone had twisted a knife inside her. "You've thought about this a lot, haven't you?"

Elizabeth nodded. "Yes, I'm afraid so. It not only affects you; it matters to me."

"I'm sure you can find another job."

"Of course I can, but it won't be the same. However, it's not the job I'm talking about. It's more that I'll have to watch you suffer."

The more Cindi listened to Elizabeth, the more convicted she was to wait just a little while—at least until she had a clearer idea of what she needed to do, or Jeremy decided to move on to something else.

"It does seem a little strange that he spent so much time trying to woo me. I assumed he was still interested in the business—especially after what you heard in Fran's office. But immediately after I offer to let him buy it, he reminds me that he's changed his mind," Cindi admitted.

"Yeah, it doesn't sound right to me."

"I don't understand what he'll gain from this, and I don't want to think he's playing games, but still. . ." She lifted one shoulder then let it drop. "I have to admit, I'm a little confused. He just needs to be straight up about what he wants."

"That's right. You have too much self-respect for that, and you're too smart to let him keep pulling stunts to get what he wants."

A bride and her mother came in, so they turned all their attention to their customers. They were almost finished when the phone rang. Elizabeth answered it, so Cindi scheduled the next appointment for the bridesmaids to come in for their fittings. Elizabeth didn't rejoin them, which aroused Cindi's curiosity.

After the customers left, Cindi went directly to where Elizabeth stood. "Who called?"

Elizabeth looked at her and shook her head. "Jeremy. He said he needed to talk to you, and I told him to quit bothering you. This is taking up way too much of your time and energy."

"Yeah, but—"

"Don't go soft on him," Elizabeth warned. "He knows how to get what he wants, and if he's playing the game we think he's playing, we need to let him know we're not falling into it."

"Exactly what did he say?" Cindi asked.

"He asked if you were in. That's when I told him to back off."

"That's all he said?"

"Yup. I wasn't about to give him a chance—"

Elizabeth was interrupted by the door opening, and they both looked up.

"Jeremy," Cindi said softly.

He wasn't looking at her. Instead, his gaze fixed on Elizabeth. "Why did you hang up on me?" he asked.

Cindi snapped around to see Elizabeth's reaction. Elizabeth shrugged as she played with the rubber band in her hands. "We don't have time for games," she mumbled.

Jeremy turned to Cindi. "Do you think I'm playing games?"

His direct question caught Cindi off guard. In fact, this whole situation made her want to run and hide. But she had to face him and admit her thoughts, or this kind of encounter would never end.

"I don't know what to think," Cindi replied. She could see Elizabeth glaring at her from the corner of her eye, but she ignored it. "I thought you'd want to buy the place if I agreed to it. It doesn't seem right."

Jeremy rested an elbow on the counter and turned to Elizabeth, who'd remained in the same position, scowling, since he arrived. "So tell me what you think I'm up to."

Elizabeth took a step toward them. "In sales it's called the takeaway close. People want what they can't have."

Cindi turned to Jeremy, who looked perplexed. "Have you ever heard of that?"

He nodded. "I'm familiar with the takeaway close, but I can assure you that's not what I was doing."

"Then what were you doing?" Elizabeth asked, fist planted firmly on her hip.

Cindi turned to her. "Thanks, Elizabeth, but I can handle this."

Elizabeth backed away and held up her hands in surrender. "Okay, okay, I'll be in the sewing room if you need me."

After she left, Jeremy turned back to Cindi. "She really cares about you. It's nice to have a friend who's willing to stick up for you like that."

"Yes, I know."

"But I'm afraid she has it all wrong. Cindi, I know I've been a jerk in the past, but I've completely changed. I'd never want to hurt you in any way, which is why I'm backing off." When he paused, Cindi thought he looked like a tortured man. "I've prayed about the right thing to do, and I think it's obvious you're exactly where you should be with this shop. I need to go find something else to buy."

"Go buy whatever you want," Cindi said. "Just don't try to tell me what I should or shouldn't do."

Jeremy closed his eyes for a few seconds. Cindi wondered if he was praying; he certainly looked as though he was.

When he opened his eyes, they focused directly on her. "I would never tell you what you should do. What I'm saying is, I don't want to get involved in something that would ever hurt you or upset you in any way. . .again. I thought you understood that."

Cindi's mouth went dry. She felt that old aching sensation in her chest—the one that had faded since he'd broken her heart.

"Ever since I put my faith in the Lord, my business practices have changed." He paused and cleared his throat. "Everything about me has changed. I pray for guidance when I first wake up. I end my days in prayer, and I fill in every moment possible with prayer. The Lord has been good to me, even when I was hardheaded."

There was no mistaking the conviction in Jeremy's voice as he spoke of his faith. She'd been wrong to jump to conclusions. Her pain shifted to an emotion she'd never felt before. It was a connection to the man standing before her, but it was much deeper than the attraction that was there years ago.

"I've grown in many ways because of my faith," he continued. "Emotionally, mentally, and even physically. I never want to forget my blessings, and I honor all He's given me." As he took a step closer, Cindi's heart hammered in her chest. "And I want with all my heart for you to believe me. I care about you more than I ever did."

Chapter 12

After Jeremy left, Elizabeth appeared in the showroom. "So what all did he say to get you to sell him your shop?"

Cindi moved toward the door and looked out to avoid squaring off with Elizabeth. "He didn't even try."

"Ooh, he's smooth."

"He really doesn't want to buy it now," Cindi said as she turned around and faced Elizabeth.

"And you believe him?"

Cindi nodded. "Yes, I do."

Elizabeth looked frustrated, but she quickly recovered. "Then why don't you tell me what happened, and we can try to figure it out."

"No, I really don't want to try to figure anything out—at least not what concerns Jeremy. I just want to know what I should do about this place."

"You know how I feel," Elizabeth said. "This bridal shop is the perfect fit for you."

"It goes much deeper than that," Cindi said. "But I don't want to discuss it anymore. Let's get back to work."

As the day wore on, Cindi's mind kept drifting back to her conversation with Jeremy. His last sentence kept playing through her mind until she knew she had to find out exactly what he meant by that. She'd never completely gotten over the breakup, but until now she'd figured she'd just have to live with him in her past. But he said he cared about her more than ever.

About an hour before closing time, Elizabeth approached her at the desk. "You've been distracted all day, and after your conversation with Jeremy, I can understand. Why don't you go on home? I can close up."

Cindi nodded. "I think I will. Thanks." She gathered her belongings and headed home.

Being alone only escalated her thoughts, so finally she decided she needed to call and ask Jeremy exactly what he meant. If he was sincere about his faith, he wouldn't mind. And if he wasn't sincere, what did she care about what he thought?

She called his cell phone, but he didn't answer. Maybe he was at his parents' house. After a brief hesitation, she looked up their number and called.

"He's in Savannah." It wasn't Jeremy or his dad. "Who's this?"

"Cindi Clark," she replied. "Is this Jacob?"

His voice instantly softened. "Hey, Cindi. Yeah, this is Jacob."

"Um. . .do you know when Jeremy will be back?"

"He had some business to take care of in Savannah, and it might take awhile. Is this an emergency?"

"No, it's not an emergency, but would you mind letting him know I called?"

"I'll be glad to," Jacob said. "Jeremy hasn't stopped talking about you since I've been here."

"Um. . ." She had no idea how to respond.

"I'll have Jeremy call you when I hear from him."

"Thanks."

"It was nice talking to you, Cindi."

After she hung up, Cindi found herself reading between the lines and wondering what all had been said about her.

❧

The cell phone went off in Jeremy's pocket, so he pulled it out to see who it was. The call was from his parents' house, so he excused himself and answered it.

"Hey, bro. You might want to wrap things up quickly and head on back."

Jeremy took another step back from the counter of the men's clothing store where he'd been talking to Brad, the manager, about buying the place. "Why? What happened? Are Mom and Dad okay?"

"They're fine. I just heard from your woman."

"My woman? Which one?" Jeremy was used to his brother, so he played along.

"Seriously, dude, I'm talking about Cindi. She just called here."

"What did she say?"

"She wanted to know when you'd be back. I asked her if it was an emergency, and she said it wasn't, so don't worry. I just think you need to know she wants to talk to you."

"Okay, I'll call her. Thanks for letting me know."

"One more thing. . ."

"What's that?"

"Don't let her get away again. And you know what I'm talkin' about."

Jeremy didn't even try to pretend. "Yes, I do know. Thanks."

He told the manager of the store he'd be back soon before stepping outside. Tourists passed him as they headed toward the shopping district on River Street a block away. He'd seen the unrealized potential of this menswear store a couple of years earlier, so he'd walked in, made an offer, and owned the business a month later. With a strong Web presence and referrals from the Chamber of Commerce and River Street Association, he'd tripled the profits. And now it was time to sell so he could focus on his move back to Atlanta.

He opened his flip phone, found Cindi's number, and pressed SEND. She answered immediately.

"You didn't have to call me right back," she said. "I told Jacob it wasn't an emergency."

"Did you need something?"

There was a long pause before she finally said, "Yeah, I wanted to know what was going on with you. Even after you said you didn't want to buy my place, I thought you were just changing your game." She cleared her throat before adding, "And that part about caring for me more now than before. . . well, never mind."

He was a little surprised she came right out and said that. "I meant it."

"It doesn't matter. What we had as kids was just a high school crush anyway."

"Not for me," he said quickly. Should he have admitted that? Maybe not, but it was done now, and he didn't regret it. "I was hoping you'd feel. . .well, you know."

"I'm not sure of anything anymore."

"I. . ." What was the right thing to say now? He glanced around at the people strolling past him and decided it would be best to take up this conversation again in person. "Tell you what, Cindi. I'd like to talk some more so we can get this thing resolved. Why don't we get together and lay everything on the table when I get back?"

"Okay, that's fine with me."

After they hung up, Jeremy sucked in a deep breath and slowly let it out before going back inside to finish his discussion with the manager. He loved Savannah, but he loved being home in the Atlanta area even more. However, now that he was here, he planned to enjoy a few of his favorite things.

Jeremy was hungry as usual, so he decided to stop off at one of his favorite eating places—a well-known former boardinghouse that had turned into a country-style restaurant—where he could get his fill of some of the finest Southern cooking he'd ever tasted. One of the servers, Bonnie, told him he looked anxious.

"I'm not anxious. Just eager to get home."

She offered a wide grin. "Must be a pretty girl."

No point in arguing. "Absolutely. What else could it be?"

"You'd better let her know how you feel, 'cause from what I've seen, if a girl can make you want to run back to see her, there's other fellas wantin' to do the same thing."

"Thanks, Bonnie. I'll try to remember that."

"After she says yes, bring her back here so I can see what got my favorite customer so in a flutter."

"Says yes?"

She planted her fist on her hip and shook her head. "Some men can be so dense. Don't let her get away. Get to know her real good, find out what's in her heart. See if she loves Jesus, and if you still feel this way, you'd better walk that girl down the aisle."

He nearly choked on his corn bread. "Got any more sweet tea?"

"Sure thing." Bonnie walked away from the table laughing.

He paid his tab and left, feeling a mixture of confusion and anticipation. His conversation with Bonnie had made him think.

As he drove past rows of Victorian houses and antique stores, Jeremy thought about what a fabulous honeymoon destination Savannah would be. He passed one of the historic squares where a couple sat on a bench laughing and snuggling. A warm feeling traveled from his head to his toes, and he knew he wanted more out of life than what he currently had.

Lord, if it's Your will, give me the strength to share my feelings with Cindi. And give me even more strength to deal with her response.

The drive home seemed to take forever, but he finally arrived in his parents' driveway at dinnertime. When he walked inside, his mother said dinner was being served in a few minutes.

"Thanks, Mom, but I'm going to see if Cindi wants to go out."

She grinned. "I would tell you to invite her over, but I think the two of you need to be alone."

Am I that obvious? He guessed so.

Cindi was still at the shop when he called, and she said she still had quite a bit to do. "Elizabeth just had pizza delivered so we can finish up here. Why don't we talk later? Can you come to my place around eight?"

At least she wasn't pushing him away. "I'll be there at eight on the dot."

He told his mother, so she handed him a plate. "Set yourself a place, and we'll eat together as a family—just like old times."

When they sat down, Jeremy was happy his father bowed his head, then looked up and told everyone else to do the same. His brother winked and bowed his head. Their father finished the very short blessing, thanking the Lord for the meal. This gave Jeremy hope for even more great things to come.

At exactly seven forty-five, he left for Cindi's place. She opened the door before he had a chance to knock.

"So what did you want to talk about?" she asked.

No point in beating around the bush. "Us."

She blinked, and her face turned red. "Okay, come on in and have a seat."

He followed her into the living room that had been tastefully decorated with what he remembered were her favorite colors: peach and green. She had a couple of live plants flanking a small entertainment center across from a tan sectional sofa with peach and green pillows in various patterns and prints. "Your place looks really nice, Cindi."

"Thanks." She sat down and looked around the room. He could tell she was nervous.

"I don't want to play games anymore, Cindi," he began, "so I might as well get straight to the point. I fell in love with you back in high school, and the feeling never went away. I couldn't hold you back in good conscience. There were so many things you wanted that I couldn't give you at the time."

"But I didn't want anything," she said softly, "except you."

"We've been down that road before. You know I was a confused, broken kid with no idea what was in my future."

"I never cared about money," she said. "I thought you knew that about me."

He could hear the pain in her voice. "I didn't want to hurt you, Cindi, but it was the only way I knew to make going away to college easy for you."

She didn't say a word. Instead, she looked away, shaking her head.

"But things have changed now, and I have quite a bit more to offer—namely, my faith. I just hope it isn't too late."

She slowly turned to face him. "I'm not sure, Jeremy. I was hurt very badly, and it'll take a long time for me to learn to completely trust you again." She fidgeted with the edge of the cushion. "I have to admit, I still have feelings, and I believe you when you say you have faith in God. It's just that, well, I don't want to put myself in a vulnerable position."

"I understand that. All I ask is that you give me time. I'll do whatever it takes. I've even sold all my out-of-town businesses so I can focus all my energy on establishing myself here in Atlanta."

"Let me think about this, okay?" she said.

He stood and walked toward the door. "Thanks, Cindi." She walked toward him, so he instinctively reached for her hand.

She paused then took his hand in hers. He squeezed, and she offered a small grin, which gave him a flicker of hope.

All the way to his parents' house, he thought about ways to win her over. He knew she wouldn't be impressed by fancy restaurants, but he wanted to take her to the finest places. She'd come out and said she wasn't motivated by money, but he wanted to buy her the world. The guys at the tire store had pooled their resources and offered to buy him out. He was glad to help them get started. And now he was in the final stages of selling the men's clothing store. All he had to do was go back for the closing, and then he could turn all his attention toward what was really important.

As difficult as it was, he decided to stay away from her shop for a few days and give her time to think. On Thursday night he got a call from Brad in Savannah. "I finished all the paperwork, and I've been approved. The bank said we can sign off on the paperwork tomorrow morning. We can handle it by mail and I'll be the owner by the end of next week, or if you can be here tomorrow, we can be done with it."

"I'll be there first thing in the morning," Jeremy said. There was no reason to put it off.

❧

Friday morning after she got to the shop, Cindi decided to call Jeremy and see if he could come over that night. She'd thought about what she wanted, and it was clear after not seeing him since their heart-to-heart talk that she wanted the same thing he said he wanted. She tried his cell phone first, but he didn't answer, so she called his parents' house.

Again, Jacob answered the phone. "Seems like every time you call, my brother's in Savannah at his store."

His store? Had he lied when he told her he'd sold all his businesses?

"Want me to give him a message?" Jacob asked.

"N–no, that's okay."

After she hung up, she saw Elizabeth watching her from across the room. She tried to busy herself with some papers, but she knew she couldn't fool her best friend.

"Okay, what gives?" Elizabeth asked. "What did Jeremy do this time?"

Cindi fought the tears as she shrugged. "He's back in Savannah at *his shop.*"

Elizabeth lifted one eyebrow. "His shop, huh? Well, that pretty much lets you know how much you can trust him, doesn't it?"

The tears suddenly took control and streamed down Cindi's cheeks. She couldn't stop them. Elizabeth wasted no time in coming over to her and pulling her into an embrace.

"How could I have been so wrong to trust him?" Cindi asked. "Why did he tell me he'd sold everything when he still had a place in Savannah?"

"Who knows why Jeremy Hayden does anything?" Elizabeth said.

"He said he wanted to settle down in Atlanta, and that was just a few days ago."

"Something still doesn't seem right."

The phone rang. When Elizabeth hesitated, Cindi nodded for her to answer it.

Based on Elizabeth's side of the conversation, she gathered there had been a mix-up of some dress measurements, which would require some last-minute scrambling on their part. After Elizabeth got off the phone, both of them sprang into action.

Her tears dried as she managed to deal with the distraction. As much of a hassle as it was, she was glad it happened. This disaster turned out to be a blessing to keep her busy.

However, the rest of the day only grew worse. Another of her former customers stopped by to say hi and to let her know the marriage didn't even last a year. Her mother later called and said her father was so wrapped up in his job that he'd missed a counseling session. By closing time, Cindi wanted to crawl into a hole and never come out.

"Wanna go see a movie?" Elizabeth asked. "There's a new action flick playing, and I figure it'll get your mind off everything else."

"No, that's okay."

"I don't want you to be alone when you're this upset. Want me to come over to your place for a little while?"

"I appreciate your concern, but this is one time I probably need to be alone. I have to sort out some of my thoughts."

"Are you sure?"

Cindi nodded. "Positive. I'll be fine."

She headed home and dropped her purse in the kitchen. Then she grabbed her Bible and sat on the couch in the living room, where she flipped to some places she'd marked over the past several weeks during church. A quiet peace came over her as she realized she'd been neglecting this very important part of her life and trying to make things go the way she thought they should.

When her phone rang, she got up to answer it. When she saw it was Jeremy, she backed away. Now wasn't a good time to talk to him—not when she was still reeling over his lies.

After more than an hour of reading her Bible, she bowed her head in prayer. She asked for guidance in her decision about not only Jeremy but also her shop. It was time to stop worrying about selling the business and focus more on her walk with the Lord.

Chapter 13

You totally won't believe this," Elizabeth said as she stormed out of the fitting room where a bride was being fitted. "They sent the wrong size."

Cindi tilted her head to one side. "Can't you fix it?"

Elizabeth's eyes widened, and she held out her hands, palms up. "Not this time. The dress is, like, two sizes too small."

Cindi groaned. "This is the same vendor we've been having all the problems with. Well, I guess this will be the last time we use them."

"In the meantime, we have to get this girl a dress."

"Okay, tell her I'll be right there. Let me make a quick phone call."

As soon as Elizabeth went back into the fitting room, Cindi called all the vendors she knew would work with her. Armed with half a dozen brochures and a few more samples, she knocked on the fitting room door. The bride, Marisa, was sitting hunched over on a chair, a blanket wrapped around her, looking stunned and on the verge of tears.

It was time to pull out all the stops. "I have some dresses you'll like even more," Cindi said. "This one retails for about 20 percent more than the other one sells for, and I'll let you have it for the same price."

Marisa looked at the dress. "Will you be able to get it for me in time for the wedding?"

"Absolutely," Cindi said. "In case you don't like that one, I have others. I'll see to it that you have the wedding dress of your dreams."

She tried on all the dresses Cindi brought into the room, and she chose one that she liked even more than her original one. It was quite a bit more expensive, but Cindi wasn't about to let that be a deal breaker. "Like I told you, I'm not charging a dime more. They can overnight it, and you can be fitted tomorrow." Cindi saw the look of panic in her eyes. "Or if you don't mind taking a sample, I'll let you have this dress with an extra 10 percent discount."

"You'll do that?" Marisa said with a smile.

Cindi and Elizabeth exchanged a glance and nodded. "It's my job to help make your wedding day be one of the best days of your life."

As soon as Marisa left, Cindi called the vendor, thanked the woman for her willingness to work with them, then told her she'd sold the sample to the bride. Afterward she flopped onto the love seat by the front desk. "That was a nightmare."

Elizabeth sat down across from her. "Ya know, I sort of enjoyed being part of fixing the problem. Not everyone in our position would have helped her like we did."

Cindi thought about it, nodded, and smiled. "Yeah, you're right. It feels really good to be a problem solver in the eleventh hour."

Elizabeth held up one hand. "High five?"

Cindi slapped her friend's hand. "Okay, now it's time to get back to work. We have another appointment in an hour, and you need to start the alterations on that dress. I'll straighten up the fitting room."

"What do you plan to do with the dress she ordered?" Elizabeth asked as they stood up. "The one that didn't fit."

Cindi shrugged. "I guess I'll send it back."

"It's a gorgeous dress."

"I agree. Too bad it was the wrong size."

Elizabeth stood there as though she wanted to say something, but she didn't say a word. Cindi wasn't sure what her friend was thinking, so she decided to break the silence.

"Why don't you try it on?"

Elizabeth's eyes lit up. "Great idea!" She glanced up at the clock. "We still have awhile before our next appointment. Mind if I do it now?"

Cindi gestured toward the fitting room. "Be my guest."

"I'll need you to zip it for me."

"Just holler when you're ready."

A few minutes later when Cindi didn't hear a peep out of the fitting room, she edged a little closer. She heard the swishing sound of a dress.

"Is it on yet?"

"It doesn't fit," Elizabeth called back. "I'm too bony for a dress like this."

"Bummer. I was looking forward to seeing it on you. It's one of the prettiest dresses I've ever seen."

"Then why don't you try it on?" Elizabeth said.

"No way."

"And why not?" Elizabeth said. "Afraid?"

"No, I'm not afraid," Cindi said as she tried to laugh it off. "I just don't see any point in trying on a dress I'll never wear."

"So what? It's pretty. What's the harm in trying it on?"

Elizabeth stood at the door of the fitting room straightening her top. She pointed to the dress she'd hung on the rack behind her.

"I think it'll look great on you. The bodice is fitted, but the skirt has a graceful flare, just like what you always said you liked."

Cindi looked at the dress on the hanger. It was truly one of the prettiest dresses she'd ever seen, with simple but elegant lines, the high scoop neck just low enough to wear a necklace without being self-conscious, a cascade of pearl beading down the front, and off-shoulder sleeves.

With a shrug, Cindi turned away. "I just don't think I need to get in the habit of trying on the merchandise."

"We used to do it all the time," Elizabeth reminded her.

"That was a long time ago. I don't want to do that anymore."

"Chicken." Elizabeth added a few clucking sounds for effect.

Cindi clicked her tongue and edged past Elizabeth. "Oh, all right, I'll try it on. I'll call you when it's time to zip me up."

After Elizabeth left the fitting room and closed the door, Cindi stood and stared at the dress. It really was a gorgeous gown. Finally, she inhaled deeply, blew out her breath, and undressed. As she stepped into the wedding gown, an odd sensation washed over her. It was a combination of anticipation and dread, because at the rate things were going, this would be the only way she'd try on a dress.

She stood in front of the mirror and stared at the dress for a couple of minutes before she heard Elizabeth outside the door. "Are you ready?"

"Almost."

"What's taking you so long?"

"Okay, you can come in now," Cindi finally said.

Elizabeth's eyes widened as she stepped inside the room. "You look absolutely stunning. This dress was made for you."

Cindi couldn't say anything for several seconds. Rarely did a dress fit perfectly. Sometimes all a bride needed was a simple tuck or a hem, but a fit like this had only happened a couple of times in all the years she'd owned this place.

If she ever got married, this was the dress she'd have to have. There wasn't even a close second.

As Cindi looked away from the mirror and toward her friend, she knew what Elizabeth was thinking. "Unzip me."

Elizabeth did as she was told. Neither of them said a word until the dress was hung back up and they were out on the sales floor.

"Are you okay?" Elizabeth asked softly.

Cindi nodded as a lump formed in her throat. She coughed then turned the page of the appointment book and pointed to the next entry. "I have a feeling this one will be difficult. The bride's bringing her mother and the groom's mother."

Elizabeth groaned. "I'm not in the mood for a bridal meltdown."

With a chuckle, Cindi nodded. "I know what you mean, but tending to bridal meltdowns is one of the things we do best."

The threesome was difficult and required all their tact and energy, but between the two of them, they managed without breaking stride. The bride,

Ginger, let them know what she wanted from the beginning, so they slanted their presentation in her direction.

When it appeared the mother-of-the-bride and mother-of-the-groom were growing restless, Elizabeth looked at Cindi, who nodded. It was time for them to spring into action.

"Hey, moms," Elizabeth said in her most enthusiastic voice. "I think we have some great gowns that'll look fabulous on both of you." She pulled one off the rack and held it up. "This comes in almost all the color selections, and it's flattering on most women."

The mothers turned all their attention to Elizabeth while Cindi got information from the bride on what she was looking for in a dress. While Elizabeth helped the mothers, she found Ginger a strapless gown with a sleek A-line and very little embellishment—just like she'd wanted.

"I have a necklace and earrings from my grandmother, so this will be perfect."

"Oh, I agree," Cindi said. "Let's get you set up in fitting room one. I can find a couple more, just in case you don't like the way this one fits. Just don't think you have to make your final decision today."

"I don't want to waste your time," Ginger said.

"You won't be wasting my time. I'd much rather have you come back in a more relaxed mood and get a dress that'll make you happy." Cindi smiled at her. "And perhaps you'll only want to bring your mom next time."

Ginger giggled. "Sounds good to me."

After the mothers settled on their gowns, Ginger was ready for them to see her. Even the groom's mother agreed the dress she chose was stunning.

"My son will be so happy when he sees you walking down the aisle." The woman's eyes glistened with tears, and Ginger's mother reached out and rubbed her back.

The scene was so touching that Cindi had to look away. She saw Elizabeth starting to tear up.

Cindi nodded. "When you put on that dress, it was obvious that was the one." She'd seen brides' eyes light up as they stepped into the dress they loved more than all the rest. "It didn't take long at all to find it, either."

They scheduled future appointments for the bride and her mother to come back for her first fitting, and then for the groom's mother to come in with the bride's mother for their gowns. Ginger said she wanted to wait until the moms had their dresses picked out before she brought the bridesmaids.

After they left, Cindi gave Elizabeth a thumbs-up. "Good job."

"As always," Elizabeth agreed.

Cindi looked toward the fitting room where the dress she'd tried on still hung on the hook. Each time she looked at it, she felt an unfamiliar tug at her heart.

"Go try it on again," Elizabeth urged. "You have plenty of time." She smiled at Cindi. "I can tell you really want to."

There was no point in arguing, because Cindi knew she was transparent. "Okay, but just once more."

"But first, let me get a necklace and veil to go with it," Elizabeth said.

Elizabeth helped her into the gown and wouldn't let her turn toward the mirrors until she had the jewelry and veil in place. She held Cindi's hands as she looked her up and down.

"You look even more amazing, girl. No one else can ever wear this dress and do it justice like you do."

"Okay, so I need to turn around and see for myself. That is, if you'll let me have my hands back."

Elizabeth let go of her hands and motioned toward the mirror. "Go ahead."

When Cindi saw her reflection, she let out an involuntary gasp.

Chapter 14

Amazing," Elizabeth said. "And stunning."

Cindi was breathless at first, but then reality hit hard. "Stunning for someone who'll never wear the thing." She stepped away from the mirror and backed up to Elizabeth. "Unzip me, please."

After she was out of the gown and back in her work clothes, Cindi shook her head. "Don't let me do that again."

"Do what?" Elizabeth challenged. "See yourself as a blushing bride when you think it's not possible? That's really silly, you know."

"First of all, getting married isn't a guarantee of happiness."

"True." Elizabeth tilted her head and folded her arms without blinking. "So?"

"Secondly, I don't even know a guy I'd want to marry, so it's a moot point."

"Whose fault is that? There are plenty of guys at church who'd love to go out with you."

"Says who?" Cindi said.

"Come on, Cindi. Blake and Andrew have both asked you out."

"Okay, so let's say I'm not interested in them. They're nice and all, but. . ." She shrugged. "As long as I keep this business, I'm not likely to meet many bachelors."

Elizabeth lifted one shoulder and let it drop in a half shrug. "You're selling the place, and you'll eventually have to find a job, so you can look for a place with a nice selection of men."

"Christian men," Cindi reminded her.

"That's fine. Christian men are all over the place. I'm sure you can find someone."

Cindi felt her shoulders sag. "But I can't get past the fact my parents are separated. If they can't make a marriage work, who can?"

"There are plenty of people who make marriage work," Elizabeth said. "Remember a few weeks ago when we celebrated the Siebels' golden anniversary after church? And how about some of the mothers of our brides who have been married a long time?"

"Most of them are divorced and either still single or married to second or third husbands."

"And me," Elizabeth reminded her. "I'm happily married."

Cindi smiled at her. "You're unique."

Elizabeth gently reached out and placed her hand on Cindi's shoulder. "Look, hon, why don't you calm down and not think about this whole divorce thing so much? I know you're heartbroken about your parents' split, but maybe they'll work things out. All you can do is pray for them that they'll find a solution to whatever problem we don't understand."

Cindi finally nodded. "Okay, you're right. I've become such a worrier about my parents, and I know the Lord doesn't want that."

"So go home and get some rest. I'll close up here."

All the way home Cindi thought about Elizabeth's words, and she knew she was right. She really did need to stop worrying about something she couldn't control. As soon as she pulled into her driveway, she bowed her head and asked for peace and the ability to see the blessings rather than the problems.

As she changed into casual clothes, she caught glimpses of herself in the dresser mirror. The memory of how she'd looked in the wedding gown flashed through her mind, and she found herself thinking about how she'd once had hope for finding Mr. Right and floating down the aisle in a gorgeous dress. The only guy she'd ever loved was Jeremy, but he obviously didn't feel the same way. She'd found the dress, but Mr. Right hadn't hung in there for her.

She dumped some salad from a bag into a bowl and topped it with some leftover chicken. This was the extent of her culinary energy at the moment, so she was doing well having a salad.

After she finished most of her salad, she got up and rinsed her bowl. Then the doorbell rang.

She hollered, "Be right there," as she stuck the bowl in the dishwasher and dried her hands on the kitchen towel.

Expecting either Elizabeth or her mother, she was surprised to see Jeremy standing there holding a small bouquet of flowers. "I stopped off at the grocery store on the way here. All the florists were closed."

She shivered with a momentary flash of joy as she stepped aside and let him in. "You didn't have to bring flowers."

"You don't like them?"

"Of course I like them." She took them from him and motioned for him to follow her to the kitchen. She mentally told herself to be aloof and distant or she'd risk showing her feelings. If he'd been honest with her about selling his business in Savannah, she wouldn't have felt this way.

"Have I told you how impressed I am that you've managed to be so successful in business and buy your own place?"

"Thanks." Cindi looked away to keep from letting Jeremy see her cheeks as they heated.

"I'm curious about something. How long have you been in this house?"

"A couple of years. I tried living with my parents after college, but it was hard since I'd been away for four years. Then I shared an apartment with Elizabeth for three years while I saved for a down payment." *Don't look him in the eye,* she reminded herself.

"You're way ahead of me," he said as he leaned against the counter and watched her arrange the flowers in a small vase. "I have a car and a nice portfolio of businesses I've bought and sold, but that's about it."

"This isn't a competition, Jeremy. Why did you come here?"

"My brother said you called. I tried to call you back, but you never answered."

Cindi shrugged. "I figured there wasn't anything to talk about since you were so busy with *your business* in Savannah." As soon as the words left her mouth, she knew she sounded sarcastic.

He tilted his head and looked at her with a confused expression. "What's wrong, Cindi? What did I do to make you so angry?"

She hadn't wanted to get into a deep discussion with him, but now that he'd come right out and asked, she figured she might as well tell him to clear the air. "I don't like being lied to."

"Who lied?" he asked. "I don't get it."

"You really don't know, do you?"

"You're right," he replied. "I really don't know."

"I thought you said you'd sold your businesses, but when I called, Jacob said you were at your store in Savannah."

He frowned then pursed his lips. "Okay, so you got me on a technicality. I still officially owned the store until I went to sign the papers turning it over to the manager who bought me out."

"So you don't have any more businesses in Savannah?"

"Nope. I don't own a single business at the moment, and I have to admit it's a little disconcerting. This is the first time since I purchased the candy store that I haven't been a business owner."

Cindi felt a strange sensation in her chest—a combination of relief and embarrassment. "I'm really sorry, Jeremy. I shouldn't have assumed anything."

He reached his hand toward her. "Friends?"

Slowly and as calmly as she could, she accepted his gesture. As their hands touched, she felt the intensity of the moment. She tried to pull away, but he wouldn't let go. So she led him to the living room, where they sat on the sofa but remained silent. Cindi liked being here with him, but she wondered what he was thinking. He stared at her then closed his eyes for a few seconds before looking at her again.

❧

Jeremy couldn't take his eyes off the girl he'd loved for many years. As they sat in silence, he rehashed what he'd learned during the past several hours.

He'd kept the deepest of his feelings to himself, but there wasn't a reason to continue doing that. Before coming to her house, he'd stopped by her shop. Elizabeth asked what he wanted, and her tone made it obvious she wasn't happy with him.

That was when he decided to let her know his feelings toward Cindi. As he talked, her manner grew less combative and more open. Finally, when he finished by saying he'd always pictured himself married to Cindi, she actually smiled.

"What is going on, Elizabeth?" he asked.

"There are some things you need to know." Elizabeth went on to explain how devastated Cindi was when he broke up with her. Then she told him how Cindi's parents' separation had affected her.

"I was surprised when Cindi told me they were separated. They always seemed like the perfect family," he said.

"There's no such thing as a perfect family. Her father was very busy with work, and her mother poured everything she had into her children. Once the children were gone, her mother felt lonely and suffered from a serious case of empty-nest syndrome. Unfortunately, her father still hasn't figured out he's got something to do with it. We're praying both of them will open their eyes and see the big picture."

"Wow," Jeremy said. "No wonder Cindi's become so disillusioned. I'm glad you told me. Why can't people be more open and honest with each other? That sure would solve a lot of problems."

She grinned. "Looks like you and Cindi have reached a point where you need to talk—and I mean *really* talk. You've been working so hard at being a businessman, and she's been busy trying to guard her heart."

As he thought about it, he realized she was right. "I guess it's time to rectify this situation."

"Just do yourself a favor and don't expect too much too fast, okay?" she said. "Now, do you need directions to her place?"

"Nope. I know exactly where she lives."

With a wide smile, she nodded. "I thought you might."

Now here he was sitting on her sofa, still immersed in silence. He was waiting for the right moment to propose.

"So what will you do now?" Cindi asked.

"I don't know," he said. "Before you ask me anything else, I have a question for you." *This is as good a time as any,* he figured as he mentally prepared himself to get down on one knee. He shifted slightly before she yanked on his hand.

"My answer is yes," she said, stunning him into silent immobility.

"Huh?"

"Yes, I'll sell my shop to you. I quit believing in the fairy tale, so it's no big deal to me anymore. And based on how you've gone to all this trouble, I think you'll do a good job with it, even if you do hire someone else to run it for you." She paused for a moment then added, "In fact, if you want me to, I can stick around and manage it until we get someone trained."

"Um, okay. . ." He wasn't sure what to say or do next. She'd just thwarted his first attempt at a marriage proposal. "I have another question for you," he said.

She leaned toward him. "What?"

"Did you really love me?"

All color drained from her face as she slowly nodded. "Yes, I did."

"How do you feel about me now?"

She quickly averted her gaze. "I don't know," she replied. Then she surprised him and looked him squarely in the eyes. "How about you? Did you really love me?"

"Yes," he replied, "very much. And I still do."

She blinked, turned red, then snickered. "You have an odd way of showing it, Jeremy."

"I made some mistakes when I was younger because I didn't have the slightest idea what to do. I've already told you I wanted to do the right thing and send you off to college without feeling like you had a ball and chain holding you back."

She shook her head. "Yes, you've said that, but like I told you, I never would have felt that way."

Tilting his head to one side, he studied her. There was something he wanted. . .no, needed to know. "If I hadn't been such a foolish kid and let you go, do you think we would have. . .well, you know."

Shaking her head, she said, "Would have what?"

"Do you think we might have ever gotten married?"

She looked stunned then quickly recovered. "I'm not sure. I really meant it when I told you I loved you."

He felt a warmth travel from his heart to the rest of his body. But he couldn't dwell on what would have been. "Oh well, that's history. We need to move forward and try not to make the same mistakes."

"That's right," she agreed. "We have a whole future ahead of us, first with the sale of this business and then who knows what."

"Would you consider seeing where a relationship between us could go?" He cleared his throat and added, "I mean, if I do things right this time, will you consider. . .uh, going out with me and. . ."

She nodded. "Yes, Jeremy. I will. Just don't expect too much from me. I've been through a lot already, and I want to be cautious."

As he watched for any signs of remorse, he realized this was the happiest he'd seen her since he'd been back. Joy radiated from every pore.

"But nothing serious too fast," she added.

His insides fell, but he did his best to maintain his composure. "I'll take what I can get, just to be around you."

"So what do we do next?" she asked. "About the business, I mean."

He looked down so he could gather his thoughts and act like an intelligent businessman. "First of all, I need to get with Fran and sign the papers. There's the matter of negotiation, but I'll just pay your asking price, so that shouldn't be an issue. Since you said you'd run the shop until I know what I'm doing, I'll have an agreement drawn up."

"Sounds good." Her forehead crinkled for a split second, but she quickly recovered as she hopped up off the sofa and looked down at him. "I think we've just verbally agreed to a business deal."

As much as he wanted more from her than a business deal, that other stuff would have to wait. He wanted her to be a customer of her own shop, and he wanted her to stick around and run the place as long as they owned it, but that was something he'd tell her later. In the meantime, he'd have to settle for her willingness to sell him her shop, which was at least a move in the right direction.

Chapter 15

"Are you sure you want to go through with this?" Elizabeth asked the next morning after Cindi told her about her agreement with Jeremy.

"Positive." She felt a tiny tug at her heart, but she knew deep down this was the right thing. "But I'll still work here, and I'm sure he'll want you here, too."

"But when you leave, it won't be the same."

"Let's just take that as it comes," Cindi said. "I'm tired of worrying about things."

The next few days were busy with bridal appointments and real estate meetings with Fran. Cindi wanted things to go as smoothly as possible, and apparently, so did Jeremy. There was virtually no negotiation, with the exception of her agreement to run the shop. Cindi wanted a limited time on the agreement. Jeremy insisted on making it open-ended until he was sure he knew all the ins and outs of the business.

"I don't think he'll budge on this issue," Fran said. "But he can't keep you here against your will if you've shown you've acted in good faith."

Cindi finally agreed and signed the paperwork. The day after, she practically skipped into her shop. Elizabeth laughed. "You look like you've lost the weight of the world that's been sitting on your shoulders for months."

"That's exactly how I feel," Cindi replied.

"Oh, before I forget, your mother called right before you arrived. She wants you to call her back."

"I'll call later," Cindi said. "After—"

"She says it's urgent. Go call her now before our first appointment arrives."

"Okay," Cindi said as she lifted the phone and carried it to one of the fitting rooms.

She punched in her mother's number, and her dad answered. "Dad, what's going on? Is Mom there?"

"Yes, but I wanted to be the first to tell you we're getting back together. For good. I've moved back home."

"You have?" Cindi squealed. She forced herself to calm down. "That's wonderful news. What happened?"

"When your mother came by my office and told me what I did was inexcusable, I had no idea what she was talking about. I'd forgotten an appointment with the counselor, but I figured she could take care of that without me like she's always done before. Then I saw a side of your mother I'd never seen. She meant business this time." Cindi heard a little scuffling on the other side of the phone before her dad said, "Here, your mother wants to talk to you."

"Hey, Cindi, your father finally came to his senses."

"I'm super happy about this," Cindi said. "Want me to come over after work tonight?"

"Not tonight, sweetie. Your father's taking some time off from work, and we're heading out on a cruise first thing in the morning. He got us a good deal because some people canceled and they needed to fill that cabin."

"Let me know when you get back, okay?" Cindi said. "Tell Dad this is wonderful news, and y'all made my day."

"Will do. Love you, sweetie."

After she hung up, Cindi couldn't stop smiling. She walked out to the counter to put the phone back on the hook and caught Elizabeth staring at her.

"Why the silly grin?" Elizabeth asked.

"My mom and dad are back together, and it sounds like it might stick this time."

Elizabeth jumped up and down, clapping like a little girl. "Way cool! That's the best news I've heard all day."

"It's only nine thirty in the morning," Cindi said, "and all is right in my world."

"I hope this sets the stage for a magnificent day." Elizabeth nodded toward the door. "Get ready for another round of excitement. Here comes the Pinkney-Armistead bridal party."

A few hours later, at noon, Jeremy walked in. "Wanna go for a walk in the park?"

Cindi snickered. "It's the middle of a workday."

Elizabeth nudged her. "Go ahead for a little while. We don't have another appointment until two. I can handle walk-ins."

"Why do I feel like I've been set up?" Cindi asked as she grabbed her purse from behind the counter.

Jeremy grinned at her. "Maybe because you have. I called Elizabeth and asked if you had any time available this week, and she said you weren't too busy today."

"That rascal. I'll have to talk to her."

To Cindi's surprise, Jeremy had a picnic basket packed. They went to a small park near the shop. "I didn't want to keep you away too long."

"This is really nice," Cindi said as she helped him spread the red-and-white-checkered cloth on the ground beneath an oak tree.

As they nibbled on sandwiches, Cindi felt herself relax. Jeremy talked about some of the houses he'd been looking at with Fran. "I'm just a little confused about what I'm looking for," he admitted.

"When you see the right house, you'll know it," Cindi said.

"Kind of like when a bride finds the right dress?" He looked her in the eye. Slowly, she nodded. "Sort of like that, yes."

Jeremy put down his sandwich and reached for Cindi's hand. As he gently held it between both of his hands, he licked his lips then said, "You already know I've never stopped loving you, Cindi. And I just want to keep saying it over and over until you believe me."

Her heart hammered as she tried to think of a way to avoid admitting her feelings. But with him looking at her like that and the feelings washing through her, she knew she couldn't continue to run from him. Finally, she inhaled deeply, blinked, and smiled. "In spite of trying hard not to, I love you, too."

His smile brightened the day even more. Next thing she knew, she was in his arms, and his lips were softly on hers. "You couldn't have made me any happier than you just did," he whispered.

When they got back to the shop, Jeremy walked her to the door. "Thanks for the picnic," she said.

"It was all my pleasure," he replied. Cindi stood on the sidewalk and watched him walk to his car with a spring in his step before she turned around and went inside the shop.

"Well, you look like you've been up to something special," Elizabeth said. "What happened?"

Cindi briefly contemplated not saying anything and relishing her experience privately. But after all she'd been through with her best friend, she couldn't deny her the pleasure of this major turning point.

"Jeremy and I are in love," Cindi said with a sigh.

Elizabeth snickered. "I could've told you that. So what else is new?"

The next several days went by in a whirlwind of activity—both in the shop and after work. Jeremy was pulling out all the stops, not letting an opportunity go by without letting Cindi know how he felt. She loved every minute of it, too.

On the morning before they were supposed to transfer ownership of the business, Cindi arrived early to look over the books one more time. Elizabeth was already there, putting some finishing touches on a gown she was personalizing for a bride. After their first appointment left, they went to the front of the showroom, where they heard commotion from outside.

Elizabeth frowned. "What's going on?"

A couple of men had set up some ladders and were now dropping some canvas on the sidewalk. "I have no idea. Let me go check." She went to the door and opened it just enough so they could hear her. "What's going on? What are y'all doing?"

"New owner just ordered a transitional sign until the new one he ordered can be made. He wanted us to come the day after tomorrow, but we had a cancellation today. We thought we'd go ahead and do it now." He stopped. "That is, if it's okay with you."

"I don't mind."

Cindi turned and told Elizabeth, who nodded. "Just tell them they need to move over when customers come in."

The guys said they were used to working around customers and they'd be happy to get out of the way. After she went back to the counter, Cindi didn't feel so carefree.

"What's the matter?" Elizabeth asked. "Seller's remorse?"

Cindi shrugged. "I have to admit I feel a little strange. I knew he was changing the name since I won't be the owner anymore. But this makes everything seem so final."

"Trust me, you'll be okay. It'll take some getting used to." She glanced over toward the men. "Do you think we should answer the phone with the new name?"

"Not until after the sale is final," Cindi said. "We're supposed to close on it tomorrow, but those guys weren't supposed to be here until the day after, so it's not really Jeremy's fault."

"Never said it was," Elizabeth said softly. "You're overthinking things again."

"Yeah, you're right. It's just that so much has happened lately, I'm not sure whether I'm coming or going."

"Do you regret selling this place?" Elizabeth asked. "I mean, now that your folks have gotten back together, maybe you see things differently."

Deep down, she did sort of regret it, but it was too late now. "I can't allow myself to regret anything," Cindi admitted. "I just need to focus on what's ahead."

"Good attitude."

They had a couple of morning appointments. Then they had several walk-ins that afternoon, but they didn't have another set appointment until late afternoon. The guys hanging the sign finished midafternoon. Finally, after the last appointment left, Elizabeth gathered her belongings to leave. Her eyes darted, and she seemed a little nervous as she moved toward the door.

"Are you okay?" Cindi asked.

"Uh, sure, I'm fine. Just eager to get out of here."

"What's going on?" Cindi stared hard at her friend, who'd finally made it to the door.

"Nothing. See you in the morning," she said as she carefully opened the door and quickly stepped onto the sidewalk.

Cindi watched her friend walk toward her car then turn around. Suddenly Elizabeth's eyebrows shot up, and she started laughing as she pointed to the sign. She spotted Cindi and motioned for her to come outside.

Her behavior is bizarre, Cindi thought as she went to see what Elizabeth was pointing to. When she turned around, she saw the sign. There in big, bold letters was a sign above the door that read CINDI AND JEREMY'S BRIDAL BOUTIQUE.

"Wha—?" She looked at Elizabeth, who was still laughing.

"Don't ask me," Elizabeth finally said when she calmed down. "Ask him." She pointed to the door where Jeremy stood.

Cindi glared at Elizabeth. "I'll discuss this with you later." Then she marched right up to the shop and went inside. "What is going on?" she demanded. "Why does the sign say CINDI AND JEREMY'S BOUTIQUE?"

"Correction," he said. "It's CINDI AND JEREMY'S *BRIDAL* BOUTIQUE."

"Okay, whatever. Why does it say that?"

He shrugged. "It's the transitional sign until—"

"I know. The workers already told me, 'until the permanent sign is made.' But what's going on with this?" She went outside again and looked at it, then walked back in.

"I figured since you were staying on for a while and—"

"How did you get in here? I didn't see you walk in."

Jeremy hung his head. "Elizabeth let me in the back door. Don't be upset with her. I talked her into it."

"What is going on, Jeremy? I—"

He closed the gap between them and got down on one knee, which silenced her. When he pulled out a little black box and opened it, her breath caught in her throat.

"Well?" he asked. "Will you marry me?"

Cindi started to sway as she felt light-headed. Then she caught sight of the bridal gown behind him—the one she'd tried on and loved. "Stay right where you are," she ordered. "And whatever you do, don't turn around."

"Huh?" He started to turn.

She reached down, turned his face toward her, and repeated, "Don't turn around. I'll be right back."

"Um. . .okay."

She quickly ran toward the dress, grabbed it off the hook, and carried it into the stock room. When she came back out, she got into position in front of Jeremy. "Now where were we?"

"What was that all about?" he asked.

"I had to hide the dress. You're not supposed to see it until the wedding day when I walk down the aisle."

A wide grin spread across his face. "Oh, okay."

"That doesn't let you off the hook, though," she said. "Back to what you were saying."

Still smiling, he took her hand, kissed the back of it, and said, "Cindi Clark, will you make me the happiest man in the world and be my wife?"

"Of course I will!"

Epilogue

I still can't get over how perfect this dress is," Elizabeth said. "You could have tried wedding gowns on all day and not found one that looked as good as this one."

Cindi looked at her reflection in the three-way mirror and nodded. "I know. It's like a fairy tale. Sort of a twist on Cinderella."

Elizabeth went to the other mirror and refreshed her makeup, leaving Cindi alone. Her parents stood off to the side having their own private moment, which was a wonder in itself.

The usher came and got her mother. Cindi could tell her dad was nervous by the way he played with his tie. This was a day she'd never forget—one of miracles and a joy she never dreamed she'd realize.

When the music changed, Elizabeth jumped. "There's my cue. See ya at the altar." She got to the door, paused, and said, "After all this, I hope you never doubt Jeremy's love for you."

"Trust me, I won't," Cindi replied.

Elizabeth gave their familiar thumbs-up gesture; then she was off and marching down the aisle. Cindi couldn't help but laugh, because this was a one-eighty for Elizabeth, who'd been the most protective person of all.

Cindi's dad turned to her and extended his arm. "Ready, sweetheart?"

She nodded and took his arm. As she took her first steps, she sent up a prayer of thanks to the Lord for softening her heart and bringing her true love back. Then she locked gazes with Jeremy, whose smile warmed her heart and reassured her that she was about to embark on the journey of a lifetime—with the Lord's blessing.

A Letter to Our Readers

Dear Readers:

In order that we might better contribute to your reading enjoyment, we would appreciate your taking a few minutes to respond to the following questions. When completed, please return to the following: Fiction Editor, Barbour Publishing, Inc., P.O. Box 719, Uhrichsville, OH 44683.

1. Did you enjoy reading *Peachtree Dreams* by Debby Mayne?
   ❑ Very much—I would like to see more books like this.
   ❑ Moderately—I would have enjoyed it more if _____

   _____

   _____

2. What influenced your decision to purchase this book?
   (Check those that apply.)
   ❑ Cover   ❑ Back cover copy   ❑ Title   ❑ Price
   ❑ Friends   ❑ Publicity   ❑ Other

3. Which story was your favorite?
   ❑ *Love's Image*   ❑ *If the Dress Fits*
   ❑ *Double Blessing*

4. Please check your age range:
   ❑ Under 18   ❑ 18–24   ❑ 25–34
   ❑ 35–45   ❑ 46–55   ❑ Over 55

5. How many hours per week do you read? _____

Name _____

Occupation _____

Address _____

City _____ State _____ Zip _____

E-mail _____

HEARTSONG
PRESENTS

If you love Christian romance...

$10.⁹⁹

You'll love Heartsong Presents' inspiring and faith-filled romances by today's very best Christian authors. . .Wanda E. Brunstetter, Mary Connealy, Susan Page Davis, Cathy Marie Hake, and Joyce Livingston, to mention a few!

When you join Heartsong Presents, you'll enjoy four brand-new, mass market, 176-page books—two contemporary and two historical—that will build you up in your faith when you discover God's role in every relationship you read about!

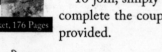

Mass Market, 176 Pages

Imagine. . .four new romances every four weeks—with men and women like you who long to meet the one God has chosen as the love of their lives—all for the low price of $10.99 postpaid.

To join, simply visit www.heartsongpresents.com or complete the coupon below and mail it to the address provided.